Rhoda Fleming by George Meredith

George Meredith, OM, was born in Portsmouth, England on February 12th, 1828, a son and grandson of naval outfitters. His mother died when he was only five.

As a fourteen year old teenager he was sent to a Moravian School in Neuwied, Germany, staying there for two years.

After reading law he was articled as a solicitor, but quickly abandoned that career path for journalism and poetry. He collaborated with Edward Gryffydh Peacock, son of Thomas Love Peacock in publishing a privately circulated literary magazine, the Monthly Observer.

At age twenty-one he married Mary Ellen Nicolls, Edward Peacock's beautiful widowed sister, and mother of a child, on August 8th, 1849. Mary Ellen was twenty-eight. The marriage produced one child; Arthur (1853–1890).

Meredith collected his early writings, all previously published in periodicals, in an 1851 volume, Poems.

In 1856 he posed as the model for The Death of Chatterton, a well-known picture by the English Pre-Raphaelite painter Henry Wallis, which romantised the teenage Chatterton's demise.

Although Meredith received some publicity for this his wife received rather more attention from Wallis because of it. Mary Ellen ran off with Wallis in 1858, shortly before giving birth to a child that all assumed to be Wallis. Tragically she died three years later.

From that dreadful experience emerged a collection of sonnets entitled Modern Love in 1862 together with much of his first major novel; The Ordeal of Richard Feverel.

Meredith married Marie Vulliamy on September 20th, 1864 and they settled in Surrey. Together they had two children; William (born in 1865) and Mariette (born in 1874).

He continued writing novels and poetry, often inspired by nature. He had a keen understanding of comedy and his Essay on Comedy (1877) remains a reference work in the history of comic theory.

In The Egoist, published in 1879, he applies some of his theories of comedy in one of his most thoughtful and enduring novels.

During most of his career, he had difficulty crossing over from critical acclamation to popular success. It was only in 1885 that his first genuine commercial success appeared; Diana of the Crossways.

An artist's life throughout the ages, when not subsidised by a patron, is often difficult. Meredith found it no different. With an unreliable income stream he sought to bolster that with a job as a publisher's reader.

The company that gave him this lifeline was Chapman & Hall (an eminent publishing house who could include Charles Dickens, William Makepeace Thackeray, Elizabeth Barrett Browning and Anthony Trollope on their roster). His advice to the company was very well received and made him influential in the world of letters.

To this influence he was able to add a circle of friends that included William and Dante Gabriel Rossetti, Algernon Charles Swinburne, Cotter Morison, Leslie Stephen, Robert Louis Stevenson, George Gissing and J. M. Barrie.

In 1868 Meredith was introduced to Thomas Hardy. Hardy had submitted his first novel, The Poor Man and the Lady. Meredith felt the book was too bitter a satire on the rich and told Hardy to put it aside as it was likely it would be savaged by reviewers and destroy his nascent career. Meredith had received the same reaction with The Ordeal of Richard Feverel. Although it had brought him success it was judged so shocking that Mudie's circulating library cancelled an order of 300 copies.

But these years, creatively, were very prolific and successful for Meredith. Novels and poems flowed from his pen including everything from The Adventures of Harry Richmond to Diana of the Crossways and many poetry volumes include The Lark Ascending (which later inspired the Vaughan Williams music)

In 1886, tragedy struck the Meredith household when his second wife, Marie Vulliamy, died of cancer.

Whilst his personal life was producing horrendous scars he was receiving many accolades. Oscar Wilde was a fan. In The Decay of Lying, (originally published in the January 1889 issue of The Nineteenth Century) he says of Meredith "Ah, Meredith! Who can define him? His style is chaos illumined by flashes of lightning".

In 1891 Meredith was even the subject of homage when Sir Arthur Conan Doyle in his Sherlock Holmes short story The Boscombe Valley Mystery, (published in the popular Strand magazine) when Sherlock Holmes turns to Watson during case discussions and says "And now let us talk about George Meredith, if you please, and we shall leave all minor matters until tomorrow."

Before his death, Meredith was honoured from many quarters: he succeeded Lord Tennyson as president of the Society of Authors; in 1905 he was appointed to the Order of Merit by King Edward VII.

George Meredith, aged 81, died at his home in Box Hill, Surrey on May 18th, 1909. He is buried in the cemetery at Dorking, Surrey.

Index of Contents

BOOK I

CHAPTER I

THE KENTISH FAMILY

Remains of our good yeomanry blood will be found in Kent, developing stiff, solid, unobtrusive men, and very personable women. The distinction survives there between Kentish women and women of Kent, as a true South-eastern dame will let you know, if it is her fortune to belong to that favoured portion of the county where the great battle was fought, in which the gentler sex performed manful work, but on what luckless heads we hear not; and when garrulous tradition is discreet, the severe historic Muse declines to hazard a guess. Saxon, one would presume, since it is thought something to have broken them.

My plain story is of two Kentish damsels, and runs from a home of flowers into regions where flowers are few and sickly, on to where the flowers which breathe sweet breath have been proved in mortal fire.

Mrs. Fleming, of Queen Anne's Farm, was the wife of a yeoman-farmer of the county. Both were of sound Kentish extraction, albeit varieties of the breed. The farm had its name from a tradition, common to many other farmhouses within a circuit of the metropolis, that the ante-Hanoverian lady had used the place in her day as a nursery-hospital for the royal little ones. It was a square three-storied building of red brick, much beaten and stained by the weather, with an ivied side, up which the ivy grew stoutly, topping the roof in triumphant lumps. The house could hardly be termed picturesque. Its aspect had struck many eyes as being very much that of a red-coat sentinel grenadier, battered with service, and standing firmly enough, though not at ease. Surrounding it was a high wall, built partly of flint and partly of brick, and ringed all over with grey lichen and brown spots of bearded moss, that bore witness to the touch of many winds and rains. Tufts of pale grass, and gilliflowers, and travelling stone-crop, hung from the wall, and driblets of ivy ran broadening to the outer ground. The royal Arms were said to have surmounted the great iron gateway; but they had vanished, either with the family, or at the indications of an approaching rust. Rust defiled its bars; but, when you looked through them, the splendour of an unrivalled garden gave vivid signs of youth, and of the taste of an orderly, laborious, and cunning hand.

The garden was under Mrs. Fleming's charge. The joy of her love for it was written on its lustrous beds, as poets write. She had the poetic passion for flowers. Perhaps her taste may now seem questionable. She cherished the old-fashioned delight in tulips; the house was reached on a gravel-path between rows of tulips, rich with one natural blush, or freaked by art. She liked a bulk of colour; and when the dahlia dawned upon our gardens, she gave her heart to dahlias. By good desert, the fervent woman gained a prize at a flower-show for one of her dahlias, and `Dahlia' was the name uttered at the christening of her eldest daughter, at which all Wrexby parish laughed as long as the joke could last. There was laughter also when Mrs. Fleming's second daughter received the name of 'Rhoda;' but it did not endure for so long a space, as it was known that she had taken more to the solitary and reflective reading of her Bible, and to thoughts upon flowers eternal. Country people are not inclined to tolerate the display of a passion for anything. They find it as intrusive and exasperating as is, in the midst of larger congregations, what we call genius. For some years, Mrs. Fleming's proceedings were simply a theme for gossips, and her vanity was openly pardoned, until that delusively prosperous appearance which her labour lent to the house, was worn through by the enforced confession of there being poverty in the household. The ragged elbow was then projected in the face of Wrexby in a manner to preclude it from a sober appreciation of the fairness of the face.

Critically, moreover, her admission of great poppy-heads into her garden was objected to. She would squander her care on poppies, and she had been heard to say that, while she lived, her children should be fully fed. The encouragement of flaunting weeds in a decent garden was indicative of a moral twist that the expressed resolution to supply her table with plentiful nourishment, no matter whence it came, or how provided, sufficiently confirmed. The reason with which she was stated to have fortified her stern resolve was of the irritating order, right in the abstract, and utterly unprincipled in the application. She said, `Good bread, and good beef, and enough of both, make good blood; and my children shall be stout.' This is such a thing as maybe announced by foreign princesses and rulers over serfs; but English Wrexby, in cogitative mood, demanded an equivalent for its beef and divers economies consumed by the hungry children of the authoritative woman. Practically it was obedient, for it had got the habit of supplying her. Though payment was long in arrear, the arrears were not treated as lost ones by Mrs. Fleming, who, without knowing it, possessed one main secret for mastering the custodians of credit. She had a considerate remembrance and regard for the most distant of her debts, so that she seemed to be only always a little late, and exceptionally wrongheaded in theory. Wrexby, therefore, acquiesced in helping to build up her children to stoutness, and but for the blindness of all people, save artists, poets, novelists, to the grandeur of their own creations, the inhabitants of this Kentish village might have had an enjoyable pride in the beauty and robust grace of the young girls,—fair-haired, black-haired girls, a kindred contrast, like fire and smoke, to look upon. In stature, in bearing, and in expression, they were, if I may adopt the eloquent modern manner of eulogy, strikingly above their class. They carried erect shoulders, like creatures not ashamed of showing a merely animal pride, which is never quite apart from the pride of developed beauty. They were as upright as Oriental girls, whose heads are nobly poised from carrying the pitcher to the well. Dark Rhoda might have passed for Rachel, and Dahlia called her Rachel. They tossed one another their mutual compliments, drawn from the chief book of their reading. Queen of Sheba was Dahlia's title. No master of callisthenics could have set them up better than their mother's receipt for making good blood, combined with a certain harmony of their systems, had done; nor could a schoolmistress have taught them correcter speaking. The characteristic of girls having a disposition to rise, is to be cravingly mimetic; and they remembered, and crooned over, till by degrees they adopted the phrases and manner of speech of highly grammatical people, such as the rector and his lady, and of people in story-books, especially of the courtly French fairy-books, wherein the princes talk in periods as sweetly rounded as are their silken calves; nothing less than angelically, so as to be a model to ordinary men.

The idea of love upon the lips of ordinary men, provoked Dahlia's irony; and the youths of Wrexby and Fenhurst had no chance against her secret Prince Florizels. Them she endowed with no pastoral qualities; on the contrary, she conceived that such pure young gentlemen were only to be seen, and perhaps met, in the great and mystic City of London. Naturally, the girls dreamed of London. To educate themselves, they copied out whole pages of a book called the `Field of Mars,' which was next to the family Bible in size among the volumes of the farmer's small library. The deeds of the heroes of this book, and the talk of the fairy princes, were assimilated in their minds; and as they looked around them upon millers', farmers', maltsters', and tradesmen's sons, the thought of what manner of youth would propose to marry them became a precocious tribulation. Rhoda, at the age of fifteen, was distracted by it, owing to her sister's habit of masking her own dismal internal forebodings on the subject, under the guise of a settled anxiety concerning her sad chance.

In dress, the wife of the rector of Wrexby was their model. There came once to Squire Blancove's unoccupied pew a dazzling vision of a fair lady. They heard that she was a cousin of his third wife, and a widow, Mrs. Lovell by name. They looked at her all through the service, and the lady certainly looked at them in return; nor could they, with any distinctness, imagine why, but the look dwelt long in their hearts, and often afterward, when Dahlia, upon taking her seat in church, shut her eyes, according to custom, she strove to conjure up the image of herself, as she had appeared to the beautiful woman in the dress of grey-shot silk, with violet mantle and green bonnet, rose-trimmed; and the picture she conceived was the one she knew herself by, for many ensuing years.

Mrs. Fleming fought her battle with a heart worthy of her countrywomen, and with as much success as the burden of a despondent husband would allow to her. William John Fleming was simply a poor farmer, for whom the wheels of the world went too fast:—a big man, appearing too difficult to kill, though deeply smitten. His cheeks bloomed in spite of lines and stains, and his large, quietly dilated, brown ox-eyes, that never gave out a meaning, seldom showed as if they had taken one from what they saw. Until his wife was lost to him, he believed that he had a mighty grievance against her; but as he was not wordy, and was by nature kind, it was her comfort to die and not to know it. This grievance was rooted in the idea that she was ruinously extravagant. The sight of the plentiful table was sore to him; the hungry mouths, though he grudged to his offspring nothing that he could pay for, were an afflicting prospect. "Plump 'em up, and make 'em dainty," he advanced in contravention of his wife's talk of bread and beef.

But he did not complain. If it came to an argument, the farmer sidled into a secure corner of prophecy, and bade his wife to see what would come of having dainty children. He could not deny that bread and beef made blood, and were cheaper than the port-wine which doctors were in the habit of ordering for this and that delicate person in the neighbourhood; so he was compelled to have recourse to secret discontent. The attention, the time, and the trifles of money shed upon the flower garden, were hardships easier to bear. He liked flowers, and he liked to hear the praise of his wife's horticultural skill. The garden was a distinguishing thing to the farm, and when on a Sunday he walked home from church among full June roses, he felt the odour of them to be so like his imagined sensations of prosperity, that the deception was worth its cost. Yet the garden in its bloom revived a cruel blow. His wife had once wounded his vanity. The massed vanity of a silent man, when it does take a wound, desires a giant's vengeance; but as one can scarcely seek to enjoy that monstrous gratification when one's wife is the offender, the farmer escaped from his dilemma by going apart in a turnip-field, and swearing, with his fist outstretched, never to forget it. His wife had asked him, seeing that the garden flourished and the farm decayed, to yield the labour of the farm to the garden; in fact, to turn nurseryman under his wife's direction. The woman could not see that her garden drained the farm already, distracted the farm, and most evidently impoverished him. She could not understand, that in permitting her, while he sweated fruitlessly, to give herself up to the occupation of a lady, he had followed the promptings of his native kindness, and certainly not of his native wisdom. That she should deem herself `best man' of the two, and suggest his stamping his name to such an opinion before the world, was an outrage.

Mrs. Fleming was failing in health. On that plea, with the solemnity suited to the autumn of her allotted days, she persuaded her husband to advertise for an assistant, who would pay a small sum of money to learn sound farming, and hear arguments in favour of the Corn Laws. To please her, he threw seven shillings away upon an advertisement, and laughed when the advertisement was answered, remarking that he doubted much whether good would come of dealings with strangers. A young man, calling himself Robert Armstrong, underwent a presentation to the family. He paid the stipulated sum, and was soon enrolled as one of them. He was of a guardsman's height and a cricketer's suppleness, a drinker of water, and apparently the victim of a dislike of his species; for he spoke of the great night-lighted city with a horror that did not seem to be an estimable point in him, as judged by a pair of damsels for whom the mysterious metropolis flew with fiery fringes through dark space, in their dreams.

In other respects, the stranger was well thought of, as being handsome and sedate. He talked fondly of one friend that he had, an officer in the army, which was considered pardonably vain. He did not reach to the ideal of his sex which had been formed by the sisters; but Mrs. Fleming, trusting to her divination of his sex's character, whispered a mother's word about him to her husband a little while before her death.

It was her prayer to heaven that she might save a doctor's bill. She died, without lingering illness, in her own beloved month of June; the roses of her tending at the open window, and a soft breath floating up to her from the garden. On the foregoing May-day, she had sat on the green that fronted the iron gateway, when Dahlia and Rhoda dressed the children of the village in garlands, and crowned the fairest little one queen of May: a sight that revived in Mrs. Fleming's recollection the time of her own eldest and fairest taking homage, shy in her white smock and light thick curls. The gathering was large, and the day was of the old nature of May, before tyrannous Eastwinds had captured it and spoiled its consecration. The mill-stream of the neighbouring mill ran blue among the broad green pastures; the air smelt of cream-bowls and wheaten loaves; the firs on the beacon-ridge, far southward, over Fenhurst and Helm villages, were transported nearer to see the show, and stood like friends anxious to renew acquaintance. Dahlia and Rhoda taught the children to perceive how they resembled bent old beggar-men. The two stone-pines in the miller's grounds were likened by them to Adam and Eve turning away from the blaze of Paradise; and the saying of one receptive child, that they had nothing but hair on, made the illustration undying both to Dahlia and Rhoda.

The magic of the weather brought numerous butterflies afield, and one fiddler, to whose tuning the little women danced; others closer upon womanhood would have danced likewise, if the sisters had taken partners; but Dahlia was restrained by the sudden consciousness that she was under the immediate observation of two manifestly London gentlemen, and she declined to be led forth by Robert Armstrong. The intruders were youths of good countenance, known to be the son and the nephew of Squire Blancove of Wrexby Hall. They remained for some time watching the scene, and destroyed Dahlia's single-mindedness. Like many days of gaiety, the Gods consenting, this one had its human shadow. There appeared on the borders of the festivity a young woman, the daughter of a Wrexby cottager, who had left her home and but lately returned to it, with a spotted name. No one addressed her, and she stood humbly apart. Dahlia, seeing that every one moved away from her, whispering with satisfied noddings, wished to draw her in among the groups. She mentioned the name of Mary Burt to her father, supposing that so kind a man would not fail to sanction her going up to the neglected young woman. To her surprise, her father became violently enraged, and uttered a stern prohibition, speaking a word that stained her cheeks. Rhoda was by her side, and she wilfully, without asking leave, went straight over to Mary, and stood with her under the shadow of the Adam and Eve, until the farmer sent a messenger to say that he was about to enter the house. Her punishment for the act of sinfulness was a week of severe silence; and the farmer would have kept her to it longer, but for her mother's ominously growing weakness. The sisters were strangely overclouded by this incident. They could not fathom the meaning of their father's unkindness, coarseness, and indignation. Why, and why? they asked one another, blankly. The Scriptures were harsh in one part, but was the teaching to continue so after the Atonement? By degrees they came to reflect, and not in a mild spirit, that the kindest of men can be cruel, and will forget their Christianity toward offending and repentant women.

CHAPTER II

QUEEN ANNE'S FARM

Mrs. Fleming had a brother in London, who had run away from his Kentish home when a small boy, and found refuge at a Bank. The position of Anthony Hackbut in that celebrated establishment, and the degree of influence exercised by him there, were things unknown; but he had stuck to the Bank for a great number of years, and he had once confessed to his sister that he was not a beggar. Upon these joint facts the farmer speculated, deducing from them that a man in a London Bank, holding money of his own, must have learnt the ways of turning it over—farming golden ground, as it were; consequently, that amount must now have increased to a very considerable sum. You ask, What amount? But one who sits brooding upon a pair of facts for years, with the imperturbable gravity of creation upon chaos, will be as successful in evoking the concrete from the abstract. The farmer saw round figures among the possessions of the family, and he assisted mentally in this money-turning of Anthony's, counted his gains for him, disposed his risks, and eyed the pile of visionary gold with an interest so remote, that he was almost correct in calling it disinterested. The brothers-in-law had a mutual plea of expense that kept them separate. When Anthony refused, on petition, to advance one hundred pounds to the farmer, there was ill blood to divide them. Queen Anne's Farm missed the flourishing point by one hundred pounds exactly. With that addition to its exchequer, it would have made head against its old enemy, Taxation, and started rejuvenescent. But the Radicals were in power to legislate and crush agriculture, and "I've got a miser for my brother-in-law," said the farmer. Alas! the hundred pounds to back him, he could have sowed what he pleased, and when it pleased him, partially defying the capricious clouds and their treasures, and playing tunefully upon his land, his own land. Instead of which, and while too keenly aware that the one hundred would have made excesses in any direction tributary to his pocket, the poor man groaned at continuous falls of moisture, and when rain was prayed for in church, he had to be down on his knees, praying heartily with the rest of the congregation. It was done, and bitter reproaches were cast upon Anthony for the enforced necessity to do it.

On the occasion of his sister's death, Anthony informed his bereaved brother-in-law that he could not come down to follow the hearse as a mourner. "My place is one of great trust;" he said, "and I cannot be spared." He offered, however, voluntarily to pay half the expenses of the funeral, stating the limit of the cost. It is unfair to sound any man's springs of action critically while he is being tried by a sorrow; and the farmer's angry rejection of Anthony's offer of aid must pass. He remarked in his letter of reply, that his wife's funeral should cost no less than he chose to expend on it. He breathed indignant fumes against "interferences." He desired Anthony to know that he also was "not a beggar," and that he would not be treated as one. The letter showed a solid yeoman's fist. Farmer Fleming told his chums, and the shopkeeper of Wrexby, with whom he came into converse, that he would honour his dead wife up to his last penny. Some month or so afterward it was generally conjectured that he had kept his word.

Anthony's rejoinder was characterized by a marked humility. He expressed contrition for the farmer's misunderstanding of his motives. His fathomless conscience had plainly been reached. He wrote again, without waiting for an answer, speaking of the Funds indeed, but only to pronounce them worldly things, and hoping that they all might meet in heaven, where brotherly love, as well as money, was ready made, and not always in the next street. A hint occurred that it would be a gratification to him to be invited down, whether he could come or no; for holidays were expensive, and journeys by rail had to be thought over before they were undertaken; and when you are away from your post, you never knew who maybe supplanting you. He did not promise that he could come, but frankly stated his susceptibility to the friendliness of an invitation. The feeling indulged by Farmer Fleming in refusing to notice Anthony's advance toward a reconciliation, was, on the whole, not creditable to him. Spite is more often fattened than propitiated by penitence. He may have thought besides (policy not being always a vacant space in revengeful acts) that Anthony was capable of something stronger and warmer, now that his humanity had been aroused. The speculation is commonly perilous; but Farmer Fleming had the desperation of a man who has run slightly into debt, and has heard the first din of dunning, which to the unaccustomed imagination is fearful as bankruptcy (shorn of the horror of the word). And, moreover, it was so wonderful to find Anthony displaying humanity at all, that anything might be expected of him. "Let's see what he will do," thought the farmer in an interval of his wrath; and the wrath is very new which has none of these cool intervals. The passions, do but watch them, are all more or less intermittent.

As it chanced, he acted sagaciously, for Anthony at last wrote to say that his home in London was cheerless, and that he intended to move into fresh and airier lodgings, where the presence of a discreet young housekeeper, who might wish to see London, and make acquaintance with the world, would be agreeable to him. His project was that one of his nieces should fill this office, and he requested his brother-in-law to reflect on it, and to think of him as of a friend of the family, now and in the time to come. Anthony spoke of the seductions of London quite unctuously. Who could imagine this to be the letter of an old crabbed miser? "Tell her," he said, "there's fruit at stalls at every street-corner all the year through—oysters and whelks, if she likes—winkles, lots of pictures in shops—a sight of muslin and silks, and rides on omnibuses—bands of all sorts, and now and then we can take a walk to see the military on horseback, if she's for soldiers." Indeed, he joked quite comically in speaking of the famous horse-guards—warriors who sit on their horses to be looked at, and do not mind it, because they are trained so thoroughly. "Horse-guards blue, and horse-guards red," he wrote—"the blue only want boiling." There is reason to suppose that his disrespectful joke was not original in him, but it displayed his character in a fresh light. Of course, if either of the girls was to go, Dahlia was the person. The farmer commenced his usual process of sitting upon the idea. That it would be policy to attach one of the family to this chirping old miser, he thought incontestable. On the other hand, he had a dread of London, and Dahlia was surpassingly fair. He put the case to Robert, in remembrance of what his wife had spoken, hoping that Robert would amorously stop his painful efforts to think fast enough for the occasion. Robert, however, had nothing to say, and seemed willing to let Dahlia depart. The only opponents to the plan were Mrs. Sumfit, a kindly, humble relative of the farmer's, widowed out of Sussex, very loving and fat; the cook to the household, whose waist was dimly indicated by her apron-string; and, to aid her outcries, the silently-protesting Master Gammon, an old man with the cast of eye of an antediluvian lizard, the slowest old man of his time—a sort of foreman of the farm before Robert had come to take matters in hand, and thrust both him and his master into the background. Master Gammon remarked emphatically, once and for all, that "he never had much opinion of London." As he had never visited London, his opinion was considered the less weighty, but, as he advanced no further speech, the sins and backslidings of the metropolis were strongly brought to mind by his condemnatory utterance. Policy and Dahlia's entreaties at last prevailed with the farmer, and so the fair girl went up to the great city.

After months of a division that was like the division of her living veins, and when the comfort of letters was getting cold, Rhoda, having previously pledged herself to secrecy, though she could not guess why it was commanded, received a miniature portrait of Dahlia, so beautiful that her envy of London for holding her sister away from her, melted in gratitude. She had permission to keep the portrait a week; it was impossible to forbear from showing it to Mrs. Sumfit, who peeped in awe, and that emotion subsiding, shed tears abundantly. Why it was to be kept secret, they failed to inquire; the mystery was possibly not without its delights to them. Tears were shed again when the portrait had to be packed up and despatched. Rhoda lived on abashed by the adorable new refinement of Dahlia's features, and her heart yearned to her uncle for so caring to decorate the lovely face.

One day Rhoda was at her bed-room window, on the point of descending to encounter the daily dumpling, which was the principal and the unvarying item of the midday meal of the house, when she beheld a stranger trying to turn the handle of the iron gate. Her heart thumped. She divined correctly that it was her uncle. Dahlia had now been absent for very many months, and Rhoda's growing fretfulness sprang the conviction in her mind that something closer than letters must soon be coming. She ran downstairs, and along the gravel-path. He was a little man, square-built, and looking as if he had worn to toughness; with an evident Sunday suit on: black, and black gloves, though the day was only antecedent to Sunday.

"Let me help you, sir," she said, and her hands came in contact with his, and were squeezed.

"How is my sister?" She had no longer any fear in asking.

"Now, you let me through, first," he replied, imitating an arbitrary juvenile. "You're as tight locked in as if you was in dread of all the thieves of London. You ain't afraid o' me, miss? I'm not the party generally outside of a fortification; I ain't, I can assure you. I'm a defence party, and a reg'lar lion when I've got the law backing me."

He spoke in a queer, wheezy voice, like a cracked flute, combined with the effect of an ill-resined fiddle-bow.

"You are in the garden of Queen Anne's Farm," said Rhoda.

"And you're my pretty little niece, are you? 'the darkie lass,' as your father says. 'Little,' says I; why, you needn't be ashamed to stand beside a grenadier. Trust the country for growing fine gals."

"You are my uncle, then?" said Rhoda. "Tell me how my sister is. Is she well? Is she quite happy?"

"Dahly?" returned old Anthony, slowly.

"Yes, yes; my sister!" Rhoda looked at him with distressful eagerness.

"Now, don't you be uneasy about your sister Dahly." Old Anthony, as he spoke, fixed his small brown eyes on the girl, and seemed immediately to have departed far away in speculation. A question recalled him.

"Is her health good?"

"Ay; stomach's good, head's good, lungs, brain, what not, all good. She's a bit giddy, that's all."

"In her head?"

"Ay; and on her pins. Never you mind. You look a steady one, my dear. I shall take to you, I think."

"But my sister—" Rhoda was saying, when the farmer came out, and sent a greeting from the threshold,—

"Brother Tony!"

"Here he is, brother William John."

"Surely, and so he is, at last." The farmer walked up to him with his hand out.

"And it ain't too late, I hope. Eh?"

"It's never too late—to mend," said the farmer.

"Eh? not my manners, eh?" Anthony struggled to keep up the ball; and in this way they got over the confusion of the meeting after many years and some differences.

"Made acquaintance with Rhoda, I see," said the farmer, as they turned to go in.

"The 'darkie lass' you write of. She's like a coal nigh a candle. She looks, as you'd say, 't' other side of her sister.' Yes, we've had a talk."

"Just in time for dinner, brother Tony. We ain't got much to offer, but what there is, is at your service. Step aside with me."

The farmer got Anthony out of hearing a moment, questioned, and was answered: after which he looked less anxious, but a trifle perplexed, and nodded his head as Anthony occasionally lifted his, to enforce certain points in some halting explanation. You would have said that a debtor was humbly putting his case in his creditor's ear, and could only now and then summon courage to meet the censorious eyes. They went in to Mrs. Sumfit's shout that the dumplings were out of the pot: old Anthony bowed upon the announcement of his name, and all took seats. But it was not the same sort of dinner-hour as that which the inhabitants of the house were accustomed to; there was conversation.

The farmer asked Anthony by what conveyance he had come. Anthony shyly, but not without evident self-approbation, related how, having come by the train, he got into conversation with the driver of a fly at a station, who advised him of a cart that would be passing near Wrexby. For threepennyworth of beer, he had got a friendly introduction to the carman, who took him within two miles of the farm for one shilling, a distance of fifteen miles. That was pretty good!

"Home pork, brother Tony," said the farmer, approvingly.

"And home-made bread, too, brother William John," said Anthony, becoming brisk.

"Ay, and the beer, such as it is." The farmer drank and sighed.

Anthony tried the beer, remarking, "That's good beer; it don't cost much."

"It ain't adulterated. By what I read of your London beer, this stuff's not so bad, if you bear in mind it's pure. Pure's my motto. 'Pure, though poor!'"

"Up there, you pay for rank poison," said Anthony. "So, what do I do? I drink water and thank 'em, that's wise."

"Saves stomach and purse." The farmer put a little stress on 'purse.'

"Yes, I calculate I save threepence a day in beer alone," said Anthony.

"Three times seven's twenty-one, ain't it?"

Mr. Fleming said this, and let out his elbow in a small perplexity, as Anthony took him up: "And fifty-two times twenty-one?"

"Well, that's, that's—how much is that, Mas' Gammon?" the farmer asked in a bellow.

Master Gammon was laboriously and steadily engaged in tightening himself with dumpling. He relaxed his exertions sufficiently to take this new burden on his brain, and immediately cast it off.

"Ah never thinks when I feeds—Ah was al'ays a bad hand at 'counts. Gi'es it up."

"Why, you're like a horse that never was rode! Try again, old man," said the farmer.

"If I drags a cart," Master Gammon replied, "that ain't no reason why I should leap a gate."

The farmer felt that he was worsted as regarded the illustration, and with a bit of the boy's fear of the pedagogue, he fought Anthony off by still pressing the arithmetical problem upon Master Gammon; until the old man, goaded to exasperation, rolled out thunderingly,—

"If I works fer ye, that ain't no reason why I should think fer ye," which caused him to be left in peace.

"Eh, Robert?" the farmer transferred the question; "Come! what is it?"

Robert begged a minute's delay, while Anthony watched him with hawk eyes.

"I tell you what it is—it's pounds," said Robert.

This tickled Anthony, who let him escape, crying: "Capital! Pounds it is in your pocket, sir, and you hit that neatly, I will say. Let it be five. You out with your five at interest, compound interest; soon comes another five; treat it the same: in ten years—eh? and then you get into figures; you swim in figures!"

"I should think you did!" said the farmer, winking slyly.

Anthony caught the smile, hesitated and looked shrewd, and then covered his confusion by holding his plate to Mrs. Sumfit for a help. The manifest evasion and mute declaration that dumpling said "mum" on that head, gave the farmer a quiet glow.

"When you are ready to tell me all about my darlin', sir," Mrs. Sumfit suggested, coaxingly.

"After dinner, mother—after dinner," said the farmer.

"And we're waitin', are we, till them dumplings is finished?" she exclaimed, piteously, with a glance at Master Gammon's plate.

"After dinner we'll have a talk, mother."

Mrs. Sumfit feared from this delay that there was queer news to be told of Dahlia's temper; but she longed for the narrative no whit the less, and again cast a sad eye on the leisurely proceedings of Master Gammon. The veteran was still calmly tightening. His fork was on end, with a vast mouthful impaled on the prongs. Master Gammon, a thoughtful eater, was always last at the meal, and a latent, deep-lying irritation at Mrs. Sumfit for her fidgetiness, day after day, toward the finish of the dish, added a relish to his engulfing of the monstrous morsel. He looked at her steadily, like an ox of the fields, and consumed it, and then holding his plate out, in a remorseless way, said, "You make 'em so good, marm."

Mrs. Sumfit, fretted as she was, was not impervious to the sound sense of the remark, as well as to the compliment.

"I don't want to hurry you, Mas' Gammon," she said; "Lord knows, I like to see you and everybody eat his full and be thankful; but, all about my Dahly waitin',—I feel pricked wi' a pin all over, I do; and there's my blessed in London," she answered, "and we knowin' nothin' of her, and one close by to tell me! I never did feel what slow things dumplin's was, afore now!"

The kettle simmered gently on the hob. Every other knife and fork was silent; so was every tongue. Master Gammon ate and the kettle hummed. Twice Mrs. Sumfit sounded a despairing, "Oh, deary me!" but it was useless. No human power had ever yet driven Master Gammon to a demonstration of haste or to any acceleration of the pace he had chosen for himself. At last, she was not to be restrained from crying out, almost tearfully,—

"When do you think you'll have done, Mas' Gammon?"

Thus pointedly addressed, Master Gammon laid down his knife and fork. He half raised his ponderous, curtaining eyelids, and replied,—

"When I feels my buttons, marm."

After which he deliberately fell to work again.

Mrs. Sumfit dropped back in her chair as from a blow.

But even dumplings, though they resist so doggedly for a space, do ultimately submit to the majestic march of Time, and move. Master Gammon cleared his plate. There stood in the dish still half a dumpling. The farmer and Rhoda, deeming that there had been a show of inhospitality, pressed him to make away with this forlorn remainder.

The vindictive old man, who was as tight as dumpling and buttons could make him, refused it in a drooping tone, and went forth, looking at none. Mrs. Sumfit turned to all parties, and begged them to say what more, to please Master Gammon, she could have done? When Anthony was ready to speak of her Dahlia, she obtruded this question in utter dolefulness. Robert was kindly asked by the farmer to take a pipe among them. Rhoda put a chair for him, but he thanked them both, and said he could not neglect some work to be done in the fields. She thought that he feared pain from hearing Dahlia's name, and followed him with her eyes commiseratingly.

"Does that young fellow attend to business?" said Anthony.

The farmer praised Robert as a rare hand, but one affected with bees in his nightcap,—who had ideas of his own about farming, and was obstinate with them; "pays you due respect, but's got a notion as how his way of thinking's better 'n his seniors. It's the style now with all young folks. Makes a butt of old Mas' Gammon; laughs at the old man. It ain't respectful t' age, I say. Gammon don't understand nothing about new feeds for sheep, and dam nonsense about growing such things as melons, fiddle-faddle, for 'em. Robert's a beginner. What he knows, I taught the young fellow. Then, my question is, where's his ideas come from, if they're contrary to mine? If they're contrary to mine, they're contrary to my teaching. Well, then, what are they worth? He can't see that. He's a good one at work—I'll say so much for him."

Old Anthony gave Rhoda a pat on the shoulder.

CHAPTER III

SUGGESTS THE MIGHT OF THE MONEY DEMON

"Pipes in the middle of the day's regular revelry," ejaculated Anthony, whose way of holding the curved pipe-stem displayed a mind bent on reckless enjoyment, and said as much as a label issuing from his mouth, like a figure in a comic woodcut of the old style:—"that's," he pursued, "that's if you haven't got to look up at the clock every two minutes, as if the devil was after you. But, sitting here, you know, the afternoon's a long evening; nobody's your master. You can on wi' your slippers, up wi' your legs, talk, or go for'ard, counting, twicing, and three-timesing; by George! I should take to drinking beer if I had my afternoons to myself in the city, just for the sake of sitting and doing sums in a tap-room; if it's a big tap-room, with pew sort o' places, and dark red curtains, a fire, and a smell of sawdust; ale, and tobacco, and a boy going by outside whistling a tune of the day. Somebody comes in. 'Ah, there's an idle old chap,' he says to himself, (meaning me), and where, I should like to ask him, 'd his head be if he sat there dividing two hundred and fifty thousand by forty-five and a half!"

The farmer nodded encouragingly. He thought it not improbable that a short operation with these numbers would give the sum in Anthony's possession, the exact calculation of his secret hoard, and he set to work to stamp them on his brain, which rendered him absent in manner, while Mrs. Sumfit mixed liquor with hot water, and pushed at his knee, doubling in her enduring lips, and lengthening her eyes to aim a side-glance of reprehension at Anthony's wandering loquacity.

Rhoda could bear it no more.

"Now let me hear of my sister, uncle," she said.

"I'll tell you what," Anthony responded, "she hasn't got such a pretty sort of a sweet blackbirdy voice as you've got."

The girl blushed scarlet.

"Oh, she can mount them colours, too," said Anthony.

His way of speaking of Dahlia indicated that he and she had enough of one another; but of the peculiar object of his extraordinary visit not even the farmer had received a hint. Mrs. Sumfit ventured to think aloud that his grog was not stiff enough, but he took a gulp under her eyes, and smacked his lips after it in a most convincing manner.

"Ah! that stuff wouldn't do for me in London, half-holiday or no half-holiday," said Anthony.

"Why not?" the farmer asked.

"I should be speculating—deep—couldn't hold myself in: Mexicans, Peroovians, Venzeshoolians, Spaniards, at 'em I should go. I see bonds in all sorts of colours, Spaniards in black and white, Peruvians—orange, Mexicans—red as the British army. Well, it's just my whim. If I like red, I go at red. I ain't a bit of reason. What's more, I never speculate."

"Why, that's safest, brother Tony," said the farmer.

"And safe's my game—always was, always will be! Do you think"—Anthony sucked his grog to the sugar-dregs, till the spoon settled on his nose—"do you think I should hold the position I do hold, be trusted as I am trusted? Ah! you don't know much about that. Should I have money placed in my hands, do you think—and it's thousands at a time, gold, and notes, and cheques—if I was a risky chap? I'm known to be thoroughly respectable. Five and forty years I've been in Boyne's Bank, and thank ye, ma'am, grog don't do no harm down here. And I will take another glass. 'When the heart of a man!'—but I'm no singer."

Mrs. Sumfit simpered, "Hem; it's the heart of a woman, too: and she have one, and it's dying to hear of her darlin' blessed in town, and of who cuts her hair, and where she gets her gownds, and whose pills—"

The farmer interrupted her irritably.

"Divide a couple o' hundred thousand and more by forty-five and a half," he said. "Do wait, mother; all in good time. Forty-five and a-half, brother Tony; that was your sum—ah!—you mentioned it some time back—half of what? Is that half a fraction, as they call it? I haven't forgot fractions, and logareems, and practice, and so on to algebrae, where it always seems to me to blow hard, for, whizz goes my head in a jiffy, as soon as I've mounted the ladder to look into that country. How 'bout that forty-five and a half, brother Tony, if you don't mind condescending to explain?"

"Forty-five and a half?" muttered Anthony, mystified.

"Oh, never mind, you know, if you don't like to say, brother Tony." The farmer touched him up with his pipe-stem.

"Five and a half," Anthony speculated. "That's a fraction you got hold of, brother William John,—I remember the parson calling out those names at your wedding: 'I, William John, take thee, Susan;' yes, that's a fraction, but what's the good of it?"

"What I mean is, it ain't forty-five and half of forty-five. Half of one, eh? That's identical with a fraction. One—a stroke—and two under it."

"You've got it correct," Anthony assented.

"How many thousand divide it by?"

"Divide what by, brother William John? I'm beat."

"Ah! out comes the keys: lockup everything; it's time!" the farmer laughed, rather proud of his brother-in-law's perfect wakefulness after two stiff tumblers. He saw that Anthony was determined with all due friendly feeling to let no one know the sum in his possession.

"If it's four o'clock, it is time to lock up," said Anthony, "and bang to go the doors, and there's the money for thieves to dream of—they can't get a-nigh it, let them dream as they like. What's the hour, ma'am?"

"Not three, it ain't," returned Mrs. Sumfit; "and do be good creatures, and begin about my Dahly, and where she got that Bumptious gownd, and the bonnet with blue flowers lyin' by on the table: now, do!"

Rhoda coughed.

"And she wears lavender gloves like a lady," Mrs. Sumfit was continuing.

Rhoda stamped on her foot.

"Oh! cruel!" the comfortable old woman snapped in pain, as she applied her hand to the inconsolable fat foot, and nursed it. "What's roused ye, you tiger girl? I shan't be able to get about, I shan't, and then who's to cook for ye all? For you're as ignorant as a raw kitchen wench, and knows nothing."

"Come, Dody, you're careless," the farmer spoke chidingly through Mrs. Sumfit's lamentations.

"She stops uncle Anthony when he's just ready, father," said Rhoda.

"Do you want to know?" Anthony set his small eyes on her: "do you want to know, my dear?" He paused, fingering his glass, and went on: "I, Susan, take thee, William John, and you've come of it. Says I to myself, when I hung sheepish by your mother and by your father, my dear, says I to myself, I ain't a marrying man: and if these two, says I, if any progeny comes to 'em—to bless them, some people'd say, but I know what life is, and what young ones are—if—where was I? Liquor makes you talk, brother William John, but where's your ideas? Gone, like hard cash! What I meant was, I felt I might some day come for'ard and help the issue of your wife's weddin', and wasn't such a shady object among you, after all. My pipe's out."

Rhoda stood up, and filled the pipe, and lit it in silence. She divined that the old man must be allowed to run on in his own way, and for a long time he rambled, gave a picture of the wedding, and of a robbery of Boyne's Bank: the firm of Boyne, Burt, Hamble, and Company. At last, he touched on Dahlia.

"What she wants, I can't make out," he said; "and what that good lady there, or somebody, made mention of—how she manages to dress as she do! I can understand a little goin' a great way, if you're clever in any way; but I'm at my tea"—Anthony laid his hand out as to exhibit a picture. "I ain't a complaining man, and be young, if you can, I say, and walk about and look at shops; but, I'm at my tea: I come home rather tired there's the tea-things, sure enough, and tea's made, and, maybe, there's a shrimp or two; she attends to your creature comforts. When everything's locked up and tight and right, I'm gay, and ask for a bit of society: well, I'm at my tea: I hear her foot thumping up and down her bedroom overhead: I know the meaning of that: I'd rather hear nothing: down she runs: I'm at my tea, and in she bursts."—Here followed a dramatic account of Dahlia's manner of provocation, which was closed by the extinction of his pipe.

The farmer, while his mind still hung about thousands of pounds and a certain incomprehensible division of them to produce a distinct intelligible total, and set before him the sum of Anthony's riches, could see that his elder daughter was behaving flightily and neglecting the true interests of the family, and he was chagrined. But Anthony, before he entered the house, had assured him that Dahlia was well, and that nothing was wrong with her. So he looked at Mrs. Sumfit, who now took upon herself to plead for Dahlia: a young thing, and such a handsome creature! and we were all young some time or other; and would heaven have mercy on us, if we were hard upon the young, do you think? The motto of a truly religious man said, try 'em again. And, maybe, people had been a little hard upon Dahlia, and the girl was apt to take offence. In conclusion, she appealed to Rhoda to speak up for her sister. Rhoda sat in quiet reserve.

She was sure her sister must be justified in all she did but the picture of the old man coming from his work every night to take his tea quite alone made her sad. She found herself unable to speak, and as she did not, Mrs. Sumfit had an acute twinge from her recently trodden foot, and called her some bitter names; which was not an unusual case, for the kind old woman could be querulous, and belonged to the list of those whose hearts are as scales, so that they love not one person devotedly without a corresponding spirit of opposition to another. Rhoda merely smiled.

By-and-by, the women left the two men alone.

Anthony turned and struck the farmer's knee.

"You've got a jewel in that gal, brother William John."

"Eh! she's a good enough lass. Not much of a manager, brother Tony. Too much of a thinker, I reckon. She's got a temper of her own too. I'm a bit hurt, brother Tony, about that other girl. She must leave London, if she don't alter. It's flightiness; that's all. You mustn't think ill of poor Dahly. She was always the pretty one, and when they know it, they act up to it: she was her mother's favourite."

"Ah! poor Susan! an upright woman before the Lord."

"She was," said the farmer, bowing his head.

"And a good wife," Anthony interjected.

"None better—never a better; and I wish she was living to look after her girls."

"I came through the churchyard, hard by," said Anthony; "and I read that writing on her tombstone. It went like a choke in my throat. The first person I saw next was her child, this young gal you call Rhoda; and, thinks I to myself, you might ask me, I'd do anything for ye—that I could, of course."

The farmer's eye had lit up, but became overshadowed by the characteristic reservation.

"Nobody'd ask you to do more than you could," he remarked, rather coldly.

"It'll never be much," sighed Anthony.

"Well, the world's nothing, if you come to look at it close," the farmer adopted a similar tone.

"What's money!" said Anthony.

The farmer immediately resumed his this-worldliness:

"Well, it's fine to go about asking us poor devils to answer ye that," he said, and chuckled, conceiving that he had nailed Anthony down to a partial confession of his ownership of some worldly goods.

"What do you call having money?" observed the latter, clearly in the trap. "Fifty thousand?"

"Whew!" went the farmer, as at a big draught of powerful stuff.

"Ten thousand?"

Mr. Fleming took this second gulp almost contemptuously, but still kindly.

"Come," quoth Anthony, "ten thousand's not so mean, you know. You're a gentleman on ten thousand. So, on five. I'll tell ye, many a gentleman'd be glad to own it. Lor' bless you! But, you know nothing of the world, brother William John. Some of 'em haven't one—ain't so rich as you!"

"Or you, brother Tony?" The farmer made a grasp at his will-o'-the-wisp.

"Oh! me!" Anthony sniggered. "I'm a scraper of odds and ends. I pick up things in the gutter. Mind you, those Jews ain't such fools, though a curse is on 'em, to wander forth. They know the meaning of the multiplication table. They can turn fractions into whole numbers. No; I'm not to be compared to gentlemen. My property's my respectability. I said that at the beginning, and I say it now. But, I'll tell you what, brother William John, it's an emotion when you've got bags of thousands of pounds in your arms."

Ordinarily, the farmer was a sensible man, as straight on the level of dull intelligence as other men; but so credulous was he in regard to the riches possessed by his wife's brother, that a very little tempted him to childish exaggeration of the probable amount. Now that Anthony himself furnished the incitement, he was quite lifted from the earth. He had, besides, taken more of the strong mixture than he was ever accustomed to take in the middle of the day; and as it seemed to him that Anthony was really about to be seduced into a particular statement of the extent of the property which formed his respectability (as Anthony had chosen to put it), he got up a little game in his head by guessing how much the amount might positively be, so that he could subsequently compare his shrewd reckoning with the avowed fact. He tamed his wild ideas as much as possible; thought over what his wife used to say of Anthony's saving ways from boyhood, thought of the dark hints of the Funds, of many bold strokes for money made by sagacious persons; of Anthony's close style of living, and of the lives of celebrated misers; this done, he resolved to make a sure guess, and therefore aimed below the mark.

Money, when the imagination deals with it thus, has no substantial relation to mortal affairs. It is a tricksy thing, distending and contracting as it dances in the mind, like sunlight on the ceiling cast from a morning tea-cup, if a forced simile will aid the conception. The farmer struck on thirty thousand and some odd hundred pounds—outlying debts, or so, excluded—as what Anthony's will, in all likelihood, would be sworn under: say, thirty thousand, or, safer, say, twenty thousand. Bequeathed—how? To him and to his children. But to the children in reversion after his decease? Or how? In any case, they might make capital marriages; and the farm estate should go to whichever of the two young husbands he liked the best. Farmer Fleming asked not for any life of ease and splendour, though thirty thousand pounds was a fortune; or even twenty thousand. Noblemen have stooped to marry heiresses owning no more than that! The idea of their having done so actually shot across him, and his heart sent up a warm spring of tenderness toward the patient, good, grubbing old fellow, sitting beside him, who had lived and died to enrich and elevate the family. At the same time, he could not refrain from thinking that Anthony, broad-shouldered as he was, though bent, sound on his legs, and well-coloured for a Londoner, would be accepted by any Life Insurance office, at a moderate rate, considering his age. The farmer thought of his own health, and it was with a pang that he fancied himself being probed by the civil-speaking Life Insurance doctor (a gentleman who seems to issue upon us applicants from out the muffled folding doors of Hades; taps us on the chest, once, twice, and forthwith writes down our fateful dates). Probably, Anthony would not have to pay a higher rate of interest than he.

"Are you insured, brother Tony?" the question escaped him.

"No, I ain't, brother William John;" Anthony went on nodding like an automaton set in motion. "There's two sides to that. I'm a long-lived man. Long-lived men don't insure; that is, unless they're fools. That's how the Offices thrive."

"Case of accident?" the farmer suggested.

"Oh! nothing happens to me," replied Anthony.

The farmer jumped on his legs, and yawned.

"Shall we take a turn in the garden, brother Tony?"

"With all my heart, brother William John."

The farmer had conscience to be ashamed of the fit of irritable vexation which had seized on him; and it was not till Anthony being asked the date of his birth, had declared himself twelve years his senior, that the farmer felt his speculations to be justified. Anthony was nearly a generation ahead. They walked about, and were seen from the windows touching one another on the shoulder in a brotherly way.

When they came back to the women, and tea, the farmer's mind was cooler, and all his reckonings had gone to mist. He was dejected over his tea.

"What is the matter, father?" said Rhoda.

"I'll tell you, my dear," Anthony replied for him. "He's envying me some one I want to ask me that question when I'm at my tea in London."

CHAPTER IV

THE TEXT FROM SCRIPTURE

Mr. Fleming kept his forehead from his daughter's good-night kiss until the room was cleared, after supper, and then embracing her very heartily, he informed her that her uncle had offered to pay her expenses on a visit to London, by which he contrived to hint that a golden path had opened to his girl, and at the same time entreated her to think nothing of it; to dismiss all expectations and dreams of impossible sums from her mind, and simply to endeavour to please her uncle, who had a right to his own, and a right to do what he liked with his own, though it were forty, fifty times as much as he possessed—and what that might amount to no one knew. In fact, as is the way with many experienced persons, in his attempt to give advice to another, he was very impressive in lecturing himself, and warned that other not to succumb to a temptation principally by indicating the natural basis of the allurement. Happily for young and for old, the intense insight of the young has much to distract or soften it. Rhoda thanked her father, and chose to think that she had listened to good and wise things.

"Your sister," he said—"but we won't speak of her. If I could part with you, my lass, I'd rather she was the one to come back."

"Dahlia would be killed by our quiet life now," said Rhoda.

"Ay," the farmer mused. "If she'd got to pay six men every Saturday night, she wouldn't complain o' the quiet. But, there—you neither of you ever took to farming or to housekeeping; but any gentleman might be proud to have one of you for a wife. I said so when you was girls. And if, you've been dull, my dear, what's the good o' society? Tea-cakes mayn't seem to cost money, nor a glass o' grog to neighbours; but once open the door to that sort o' thing and your reckoning goes. And what I said to your poor mother's true. I said: Our girls, they're mayhap not equals of the Hollands, the Nashaws, the Perrets, and the others about here—no; they're not equals, because the others are not equals o' them, maybe."

The yeoman's pride struggled out in this obscure way to vindicate his unneighbourliness and the seclusion of his daughters from the society of girls of their age and condition; nor was it hard for Rhoda to assure him, as she earnestly did, that he had acted rightly.

Rhoda, assisted by Mrs. Sumfit, was late in the night looking up what poor decorations she possessed wherewith to enter London, and be worthy of her sister's embrace, so that she might not shock the lady Dahlia had become.

"Depend you on it, my dear," said Mrs. Sumfit, "my Dahly's grown above him. That's nettles to your uncle, my dear. He can't abide it. Don't you see he can't? Some men's like that. Others 'd see you dressed like a princess, and not be satisfied. They vary so, the teasin' creatures! But one and all, whether they likes it or not, owns a woman's the better for bein' dressed in the fashion. What do grieve me to my insidest heart, it is your bonnet. What a bonnet that was lying beside her dear round arm in the po'trait, and her finger up making a dimple in her cheek, as if she was thinking of us in a sorrowful way. That's the arts o' being lady-like—look sad-like. How could we get a bonnet for you?"

"My own must do," said Rhoda.

"Yes, and you to look like lady and servant-gal a-goin' out for an airin'; and she to feel it! Pretty, that'd be!"

"She won't be ashamed of me," Rhoda faltered; and then hummed a little tune, and said firmly—"It's no use my trying to look like what I'm not."

"No, truly;" Mrs. Sumfit assented. "But it's your bein' behind the fashions what hurt me. As well you might be an old thing like me, for any pleasant looks you'll git. Now, the country—you're like in a coalhole for the matter o' that. While London, my dear, its pavement and gutter, and omnibus traffic; and if you're not in the fashion, the little wicked boys of the streets themselves 'll let you know it; they've got such eyes for fashions, they have. And I don't want my Dahly's sister to be laughed at, and called 'coal-scuttle,' as happened to me, my dear, believe it or not—and shoved aside, and said to— 'Who are you?' For she reely is nice-looking. Your uncle Anthony and Mr. Robert agreed upon that."

Rhoda coloured, and said, after a time, "It would please me if people didn't speak about my looks."

The looking-glass probably told her no more than that she was nice to the eye, but a young man who sees anything should not see like a mirror, and a girl's instinct whispers to her, that her image has not been taken to heart when she is accurately and impartially described by him.

The key to Rhoda at this period was a desire to be made warm with praise of her person. She beheld her face at times, and shivered. The face was so strange with its dark thick eyebrows, and peculiarly straight-gazing brown eyes; the level long red under-lip and curved upper; and the chin and nose, so unlike Dahlia's, whose nose was, after a little dip from the forehead, one soft line to its extremity, and whose chin seemed shaped to a cup. Rhoda's outlines were harder. There was a suspicion of a heavenward turn to her nose, and of squareness to her chin. Her face, when studied, inspired in its owner's mind a doubt of her being even nice to the eye, though she knew that in exercise, and when smitten by a blush, brightness and colour aided her claims. She knew also that her head was easily poised on her neck; and that her figure was reasonably good; but all this was unconfirmed knowledge, quickly shadowed by the doubt. As the sun is wanted to glorify the right features of a landscape, this girl thirsted for a dose of golden flattery. She felt, without envy of her sister, that Dahlia eclipsed her: and all she prayed for was that she might not be quite so much in the background and obscure.

But great, powerful London—the new universe to her spirit—was opening its arms to her. In her half sleep that night she heard the mighty thunder of the city, crashing, tumults of disordered harmonies, and the splendour of the lamp-lighted city appeared to hang up under a dark-blue heaven, removed from earth, like a fresh planet to which she was being beckoned.

At breakfast on the Sunday morning, her departure was necessarily spoken of in public. Robert talked to her exactly as he had talked to Dahlia, on the like occasion. He mentioned, as she remembered in one or two instances, the names of the same streets, and professed a similar anxiety as regarded driving her to the station and catching the train. "That's a thing which makes a man feel his strength's nothing," he said. "You can't stop it. I fancy I could stop a four-in-hand at full gallop. Mind, I only fancy I could; but when you come to do with iron and steam, I feel like a baby. You can't stop trains."

"You can trip 'em," said Anthony, a remark that called forth general laughter, and increased the impression that he was a man of resources.

Rhoda was vexed by Robert's devotion to his strength. She was going, and wished to go, but she wished to be regretted as well; and she looked at him more. He, on the contrary, scarcely looked at her at all. He threw verbal turnips, oats, oxen, poultry, and every possible melancholy matter-of-fact thing, about the table, described the farm and his fondness for it and the neighbourhood; said a farmer's life was best, and gave Rhoda a week in which to be tired of London.

She sneered in her soul, thinking "how little he knows of the constancy in the nature of women!" adding, "when they form attachments."

Anthony was shown at church, in spite of a feeble intimation he expressed, that it would be agreeable to him to walk about in the March sunshine, and see the grounds and the wild flowers, which never gave trouble, nor cost a penny, and were always pretty, and worth twenty of your artificial contrivances.

"Same as I say to Miss Dahly," he took occasion to remark; "but no!—no good. I don't believe women hear ye, when you talk sense of that kind. 'Look,' says I, 'at a violet.' 'Look,' says she, 'at a rose.' Well, what can ye say after that? She swears the rose looks best. You swear the violet costs least. Then there you have a battle between what it costs and how it looks."

Robert pronounced a conventional affirmative, when called on for it by a look from Anthony. Whereupon Rhoda cried out,—

"Dahlia was right—she was right, uncle."

"She was right, my dear, if she was a ten-thousander. She wasn't right as a farmer's daughter with poor expectations.—I'd say humble, if humble she were. As a farmer's daughter, she should choose the violet side. That's clear as day. One thing's good, I admit; she tells me she makes her own bonnets, and they're as good as milliners', and that's a proud matter to say of your own niece. And to buy dresses for herself, I suppose, she's sat down and she made dresses for fine ladies. I've found her at it. Save the money for the work, says I. What does she reply—she always has a reply: 'Uncle, I know the value of money better. 'You mean, you spend it,' I says to her. 'I buy more than it's worth,' says she. And I'll tell you what, Mr. Robert Armstrong, as I find your name to be, sir; if you beat women at talking, my lord! you're a clever chap."

Robert laughed. "I give in at the first mile."

"Don't think much of women—is that it, sir?"

"I'm glad to say I don't think of them at all."

"Do you think of one woman, now, Mr. Robert Armstrong?"

"I'd much rather think of two."

"And why, may I ask?"

"It's safer."

"Now, I don't exactly see that," said Anthony.

"You set one to tear the other," Robert explained.

"You're a Grand Turk Mogul in your reasonings of women, Mr. Robert Armstrong. I hope as your morals are sound, sir?"

They were on the road to church, but Robert could not restrain a swinging outburst.

He observed that he hoped likewise that his morals were sound.

"Because," said Anthony, "do you see, sir, two wives—"

"No, no; one wife," interposed Robert. "You said 'think about;' I'd 'think about' any number of women, if I was idle. But the woman you mean to make your wife, you go to at once, and don't 'think about' her or the question either."

"You make sure of her, do you, sir?"

"No: I try my luck; that is all."

"Suppose she won't have ye?"

"Then I wait for her."

"Suppose she gets married to somebody else?"

"Well, you know, I shouldn't cast eye on a woman who was a fool."

"Well, upon my—" Anthony checked his exclamation, returning to the charge with, "Just suppose, for the sake of supposing—supposing she was a fool, and gone and got married, and you thrown back'ard on one leg, starin' at the other, stupified-like?"

"I don't mind supposing it," said Robert. "Say, she's a fool. Her being a fool argues that I was one in making a fool's choice. So, she jilts me, and I get a pistol, or I get a neat bit of rope, or I take a clean header with a cannon-ball at my heels, or I go to the chemist's and ask for stuff to poison rats,— anything a fool'd do under the circumstances, it don't matter what."

Old Anthony waited for Rhoda to jump over a stile, and said to her,—

"He laughs at the whole lot of ye."

"Who?" she asked, with betraying cheeks.

"This Mr. Robert Armstrong of yours."

"Of mine, uncle!"

"He don't seem to care a snap o' the finger for any of ye."

"Then, none of us must care for him, uncle."

"Now, just the contrary. That always shows a young fellow who's attending to his business. If he'd seen you boil potatoes, make dumplings, beds, tea, all that, you'd have had a chance. He'd have marched up to ye before you was off to London."

"Saying, 'You are the woman.'" Rhoda was too desperately tickled by the idea to refrain from uttering it, though she was angry, and suffering internal discontent. "Or else, 'You are the cook,'" she muttered, and shut, with the word, steel bars across her heart, calling him, mentally, names not justified by anything he had said or done—such as mercenary, tyrannical, and such like.

Robert was attentive to her in church. Once she caught him with his eyes on her face; but he betrayed no confusion, and looked away at the clergyman. When the text was given out, he found the place in his Bible, and handed it to her pointedly—"There shall be snares and traps unto you;" a line from Joshua. She received the act as a polite pawing civility; but when she was coming out of church, Robert saw that a blush swept over her face, and wondered what thoughts could be rising within her, unaware that girls catch certain meanings late, and suffer a fiery torture when these meanings are clear to them. Rhoda called up the pride of her womanhood that she might despise the man who had dared to distrust her. She kept her poppy colour throughout the day, so sensitive was this pride. But most she was angered, after reflection, by the doubts which Robert appeared to cast on Dahlia, in setting his finger upon that burning line of Scripture. It opened a whole black kingdom to her imagination, and first touched her visionary life with shade. She was sincere in her ignorance that the doubts were her own, but they lay deep in unawakened recesses of the soul; it was by a natural action of her reason that she transferred and forced them upon him who had chanced to make them visible.

CHAPTER V

THE SISTERS MEET

When young minds are set upon a distant object, they scarcely live for anything about them. The drive to the station and the parting with Robert, the journey to London, which had latterly seemed to her secretly-distressed anticipation like a sunken city—a place of wonder with the waters over it—all passed by smoothly; and then it became necessary to call a cabman, for whom, as he did her the service to lift her box, Rhoda felt a gracious respect, until a quarrel ensued between him and her uncle concerning sixpence;—a poor sum, as she thought; but representing, as Anthony impressed upon her understanding during the conflict of hard words, a principle. Those who can persuade themselves that they are fighting for a principle, fight strenuously, and maybe reckoned upon to overmatch combatants on behalf of a miserable small coin; so the cabman went away discomfited. He used such bad language that Rhoda had no pity for him, and hearing her uncle style it "the London tongue," she thought dispiritedly of Dahlia's having had to listen to it through so long a season. Dahlia was not at home; but Mrs. Wicklow, Anthony's landlady, undertook to make Rhoda comfortable, which operation she began by praising dark young ladies over fair ones, at the same time shaking Rhoda's arm that she might not fail to see a compliment was intended. "This is our London way," she said. But Rhoda was most disconcerted when she heard Mrs. Wicklow relate that her daughter and Dahlia were out together, and say, that she had no doubt they had found some pleasant and attentive gentleman for a companion, if they had not gone purposely to meet one. Her thoughts of her sister were perplexed, and London seemed a gigantic net around them both.

"Yes, that's the habit with the girls up here," said Anthony; "that's what fine bonnets mean."

Rhoda dropped into a bitter depth of brooding. The savage nature of her virgin pride was such that it gave her great suffering even to suppose that a strange gentleman would dare to address her sister. She half-fashioned the words on her lips that she had dreamed of a false Zion, and was being righteously punished. By-and-by the landlady's daughter returned home alone, saying, with a dreadful laugh, that Dahlia had sent her for her Bible; but she would give no explanation of the singular mission which had been entrusted to her, and she showed no willingness to attempt to fulfil it, merely repeating, "Her Bible!" with a vulgar exhibition of simulated scorn that caused Rhoda to shrink from her, though she would gladly have poured out a multitude of questions in the ear of one who had last been with her beloved. After a while, Mrs. Wicklow looked at the clock, and instantly became overclouded with an extreme gravity.

"Eleven! and she sent Mary Ann home for her Bible. This looks bad. I call it hypocritical, the idea of mentioning the Bible. Now, if she had said to Mary Ann, go and fetch any other book but a Bible!"

"It was mother's Bible," interposed Rhoda.

Mrs. Wicklow replied: "And I wish all young women to be as innocent as you, my dear. You'll get you to bed. You're a dear, mild, sweet, good young woman. I'm never deceived in character."

Vaunting her penetration, she accompanied Rhoda to Dahlia's chamber, bidding her sleep speedily, or that when her sister came they would be talking till the cock crowed hoarse.

"There's a poultry-yard close to us?" said Rhoda; feeling less at home when she heard that there was not.

The night was quiet and clear. She leaned her head out of the window, and heard the mellow Sunday evening roar of the city as of a sea at ebb. And Dahlia was out on the sea. Rhoda thought of it as she looked at the row of lamps, and listened to the noise remote, until the sight of stars was pleasant as the faces of friends. "People are kind here," she reflected, for her short experience of the landlady was good, and a young gentleman who had hailed a cab for her at the station, had a nice voice. He was fair. "I am dark," came a spontaneous reflection. She undressed, and half dozing over her beating heart in bed, heard the street door open, and leaped to think that her sister approached, jumping up in her bed to give ear to the door and the stairs, that were conducting her joy to her: but she quickly recomposed herself, and feigned sleep, for the delight of revelling in her sister's first wonderment. The door was flung wide, and Rhoda heard her name called by Dahlia's voice, and then there was a delicious silence, and she felt that Dahlia was coming up to her on tiptoe, and waited for her head to be stooped near, that she might fling out her arms, and draw the dear head to her bosom. But Dahlia came only to the bedside, without leaning over, and spoke of her looks, which held the girl quiet.

"How she sleeps! It's a country sleep!" Dahlia murmured. "She's changed, but it's all for the better. She's quite a woman; she's a perfect brunette; and the nose I used to laugh at suits her face and those black, thick eyebrows of hers; my pet! Oh, why is she here? What's meant by it? I knew nothing of her coming. Is she sent on purpose?"

Rhoda did not stir. The tone of Dahlia's speaking, low and almost awful to her, laid a flat hand on her, and kept her still.

"I came for my Bible," she heard Dahlia say. "I promised mother—oh, my poor darling mother! And Dody lying in my bed! Who would have thought of such things? Perhaps heaven does look after us and interfere. What will become of me? Oh, you pretty innocent in your sleep! I lie for hours, and can't sleep. She binds her hair in a knot on the pillow, just as she used to in the old farm days!"

Rhoda knew that her sister was bending over her now, but she was almost frigid, and could not move.

Dahlia went to the looking-glass. "How flushed I am!" she murmured. "No; I'm pale, quite white. I've lost my strength. What can I do? How could I take mother's Bible, and run from my pretty one, who expects me, and dreams she'll wake with me beside her in the morning! I can't—I can't If you love me, Edward, you won't wish it."

She fell into a chair, crying wildly, and muffling her sobs. Rhoda's eyelids grew moist, but wonder and the cold anguish of senseless sympathy held her still frost-bound. All at once she heard the window open. Some one spoke in the street below; some one uttered Dahlia's name. A deep bell swung a note of midnight.

"Go!" cried Dahlia.

The window was instantly shut.

The vibration of Dahlia's voice went through Rhoda like the heavy shaking of the bell after it had struck, and the room seemed to spin and hum. It was to her but another minute before her sister slid softly into the bed, and they were locked together.

CHAPTER VI

EDWARD AND ALGERNON

Boyne's bank was of the order of those old and firmly fixed establishments which have taken root with the fortunes of the country—are honourable as England's name, solid as her prosperity, and even as the flourishing green tree to shareholders: a granite house. Boyne himself had been disembodied for more than a century: Burt and Hamble were still of the flesh; but a greater than Burt or Hamble was Blancove—the Sir William Blancove, Baronet, of city feasts and charities, who, besides being a wealthy merchant, possessed of a very acute head for banking, was a scholarly gentleman, worthy of riches. His brother was Squire Blancove, of Wrexby; but between these two close relatives there existed no stronger feeling than what was expressed by open contempt of a mind dedicated to business on the one side, and quiet contempt of a life devoted to indolence on the other. Nevertheless, Squire Blancove, though everybody knew how deeply he despised his junior for his city-gained title and commercial occupation, sent him his son Algernon, to get the youth into sound discipline, if possible. This was after the elastic Algernon had, on the paternal intimation of his colonel, relinquished his cornetcy and military service. Sir William received the hopeful young fellow much in the spirit with which he listened to the tales of his brother's comments on his own line of conduct; that is to say, as homage to his intellectual superiority. Mr. Algernon was installed in the Bank, and sat down for a long career of groaning at the desk, with more complacency than was expected from him. Sir William forwarded excellent accounts to his brother of the behaviour of the heir to his estates. It was his way of rebuking the squire, and in return for it the squire, though somewhat comforted, despised his clerkly son, and lived to learn how very unjustly he did so. Adolescents, who have the taste for running into excesses, enjoy the breath of change as another form of excitement: change is a sort of debauch to them. They will delight infinitely in a simple country round of existence, in propriety and church-going, in the sensation of feeling innocent. There is little that does not enrapture them, if you tie them down to nothing, and let them try all. Sir William was deceived by his nephew. He would have taken him into his town-house; but his own son, Edward, who was studying for the Law, had chambers in the Temple, and Algernon, receiving an invitation from Edward, declared a gentle preference for the abode of his cousin. His allowance from his father was properly contracted to keep him from excesses, as the genius of his senior devised, and Sir William saw no objection to the scheme, and made none. The two dined with him about twice in the month.

Edward Blancove was three-and-twenty years old, a student by fits, and a young man given to be moody. He had powers of gaiety far eclipsing Algernon's, but he was not the same easy tripping sinner and flippant soul. He was in that yeasty condition of his years when action and reflection alternately usurp the mind; remorse succeeded dissipation, and indulgences offered the soporific to remorse. The friends of the two imagined that Algernon was, or would become, his evil genius. In reality, Edward was the perilous companion. He was composed of better stuff. Algernon was but an airy animal nature, the soul within him being an effervescence lightly let loose. Edward had a fatally serious spirit, and one of some strength. What he gave himself up to, he could believe to be correct, in the teeth of an opposing world, until he tired of it, when he sided as heartily with the world against his quondam self. Algernon might mislead, or point his cousin's passions for a time; yet if they continued their courses together, there was danger that Algernon would degenerate into a reckless subordinate—a minister, a valet, and be tempted unknowingly to do things in earnest, which is nothing less than perdition to this sort of creature.

But the key to young men is the ambition, or, in the place of it, the romantic sentiment nourished by them. Edward aspired to become Attorney-General of these realms, not a judge, you observe; for a judge is to the imagination of youthful minds a stationary being, venerable, but not active; whereas, your Attorney-General is always in the fray, and fights commonly on the winning side,—a point that renders his position attractive to sagacious youth. Algernon had other views. Civilization had tried him, and found him wanting; so he condemned it. Moreover, sitting now all day at a desk, he was civilization's drudge. No wonder, then, that his dream was of prairies, and primeval forests, and Australian wilds. He believed in his heart that he would be a man new made over there, and always looked forward to savage life as to a bath that would cleanse him, so that it did not much matter his being unclean for the present.

The young men had a fair cousin by marriage, a Mrs. Margaret Lovell, a widow. At seventeen she had gone with her husband to India, where Harry Lovell encountered the sword of a Sikh Sirdar, and tried the last of his much-vaunted swordsmanship, which, with his skill at the pistols, had served him better in two antecedent duels, for the vindication of his lovely and terrible young wife. He perished on the field, critically admiring the stroke to which he owed his death. A week after Harry's burial his widow was asked in marriage by his colonel. Captains, and a giddy subaltern likewise, disputed claims to possess her. She, however, decided to arrest further bloodshed by quitting the regiment. She always said that she left India to save her complexion; "and people don't know how very candid I am," she added, for the colonel above-mentioned was wealthy,—a man expectant of a title, and a good match, and she was laughed at when she thus assigned trivial reasons for momentous resolutions. It is a luxury to be candid; and perfect candour can do more for us than a dark disguise.

Mrs. Lovell's complexion was worth saving from the ravages of an Indian climate, and the persecution of claimants to her hand. She was golden and white, like an autumnal birch-tree—yellow hair, with warm-toned streaks in it, shading a fabulously fair skin. Then, too, she was tall, of a nervous build, supple and proud in motion, a brilliant horsewoman, and a most distinguished sitter in an easy drawing-room chair, which is, let me impress upon you, no mean quality. After riding out for hours with a sweet comrade, who has thrown the mantle of dignity half-way off her shoulders, it is perplexing, and mixed strangely of humiliation and ecstasy, to come upon her clouded majesty where she reclines as upon rose-hued clouds, in a mystic circle of restriction (she who laughed at your jokes, and capped them, two hours ago) a queen.

Between Margaret Lovell and Edward there was a misunderstanding, of which no one knew the nature, for they spoke in public very respectfully one of the other. It had been supposed that they were lovers once; but when lovers quarrel, they snarl, they bite, they worry; their eyes are indeed unveiled, and their mouths unmuzzled. Now Margaret said of Edward: "He is sure to rise; he has such good principles." Edward said of Margaret: "She only wants a husband who will keep her well in hand." These sentences scarcely carried actual compliments when you knew the speakers; but outraged lovers cannot talk in that style after they have broken apart. It is possible that Margaret and Edward conveyed to one another as sharp a sting as envenomed lovers attempt. Gossip had once betrothed them, but was now at fault. The lady had a small jointure, and lived partly with her uncle, Lord Elling, partly with Squire Blancove, her aunt's husband, and a little by herself, which was when she counted money in her purse, and chose to assert her independence. She had a name in the world. There is a fate attached to some women, from Helen of Troy downward, that blood is to be shed for them. One duel on behalf of a woman is a reputation to her for life; two are notoriety. If she is very young, can they be attributable to her? We charge them naturally to her overpowering beauty. It happened that Mrs. Lovell was beautiful. Under the light of the two duels her beauty shone as from an illumination of black flame. Boys adored Mrs. Lovell. These are moths. But more, the birds of air, nay, grave owls (who stand in this metaphor for whiskered experience) thronged, dashing at the apparition of terrible splendour. Was it her fault that she had a name in the world?

Mrs. Margaret Lovell's portrait hung in Edward's room. It was a photograph exquisitely coloured, and was on the left of a dark Judith, dark with a serenity of sternness. On the right hung another coloured photograph of a young lady, also fair; and it was a point of taste to choose between them. Do you like the hollowed lily's cheeks, or the plump rose's? Do you like a thinnish fall of golden hair, or an abundant cluster of nut-brown? Do you like your blonde with limpid blue eyes, or prefer an endowment of sunny hazel? Finally, are you taken by an air of artistic innocence winding serpentine about your heart's fibres; or is blushing simplicity sweeter to you? Mrs. Lovell's eyebrows were the faintly-marked trace of a perfect arch. The other young person's were thickish, more level; a full brown colour. She looked as if she had not yet attained to any sense of her being a professed beauty: but the fair widow was clearly bent upon winning you, and had a shy, playful intentness of aspect. Her pure white skin was flat on the bone; the lips came forward in a soft curve, and, if they were not artistically stained, were triumphantly fresh. Here, in any case, she beat her rival, whose mouth had the plebeian beauty's fault of being too straight in a line, and was not trained, apparently, to tricks of dainty pouting.

It was morning, and the cousins having sponged in pleasant cold water, arranged themselves for exercise, and came out simultaneously into the sitting-room, slippered, and in flannels. They nodded and went through certain curt greetings, and then Algernon stepped to a cupboard and tossed out the leather gloves. The room was large and they had a tolerable space for the work, when the breakfast-table had been drawn a little on one side. You saw at a glance which was the likelier man of the two, when they stood opposed. Algernon's rounded features, full lips and falling chin, were not a match, though he was quick on his feet, for the wary, prompt eyes, set mouth, and hardness of Edward. Both had stout muscle, but in Edward there was vigour of brain as well, which seemed to knit and inform his shape without which, in fact, a man is as a ship under no command. Both looked their best; as, when sparring, men always do look.

"Now, then," said Algernon, squaring up to his cousin in good style, "now's the time for that unwholesome old boy underneath to commence groaning."

"Step as light as you can," replied Edward, meeting him with the pretty motion of the gloves.

"I'll step as light as a French dancing-master. Let's go to Paris and learn the savate, Ned. It must be a new sensation to stand on one leg and knock a fellow's hat off with the other."

"Stick to your fists."

"Hang it! I wish your fists wouldn't stick to me so."

"You talk too much."

"Gad, I don't get puffy half so soon as you."

"I want country air."

"You said you were going out, old Ned."

"I changed my mind."

Saying which, Edward shut his teeth, and talked for two or three hot minutes wholly with his fists. The room shook under Algernon's boundings to right and left till a blow sent him back on the breakfast-table, shattered a cup on the floor, and bespattered his close flannel shirt with a funereal coffee-tinge.

"What the deuce I said to bring that on myself, I don't know," Algernon remarked as he rose. "Anything connected with the country disagreeable to you, Ned? Come! a bout of quiet scientific boxing, and none of these beastly rushes, as if you were singling me out of a crowd of magsmen. Did you go to church yesterday, Ned? Confound it, you're on me again, are you?"

And Algernon went on spouting unintelligible talk under a torrent of blows. He lost his temper and fought out at them; but as it speedily became evident to him that the loss laid him open to punishment, he prudently recovered it, sparred, danced about, and contrived to shake the room in a manner that caused Edward to drop his arms, in consideration for the distracted occupant of the chambers below. Algernon accepted the truce, and made it peace by casting off one glove.

"There! that's a pleasant morning breather," he said, and sauntered to the window to look at the river. "I always feel the want of it when I don't get it. I could take a thrashing rather than not on with the gloves to begin the day. Look at those boats! Fancy my having to go down to the city. It makes me feel like my blood circulating the wrong way. My father'll suffer some day, for keeping me at this low ebb of cash, by jingo!"

He uttered this with a prophetic fierceness.

"I cannot even scrape together enough for entrance money to a Club. It's sickening! I wonder whether I shall ever get used to banking work? There's an old clerk in our office who says he should feel ill if he missed a day. And the old porter beats him—bangs him to fits. I believe he'd die off if he didn't see the house open to the minute. They say that old boy's got a pretty niece; but he don't bring her to the office now. Reward of merit!—Mr. Anthony Hackbut is going to receive ten pounds a year extra. That's for his honesty. I wonder whether I could earn a reputation for the sake of a prospect of ten extra pounds to my salary. I've got a salary! hurrah! But if they keep me to my hundred and fifty per annum, don't let them trust me every day with the bags, as they do that old fellow. Some of the men say he's good to lend fifty pounds at a pinch.—Are the chops coming, Ned?"

"The chops are coming," said Edward, who had thrown on a boating-coat and plunged into a book, and spoke echoing.

"Here's little Peggy Lovell." Algernon faced this portrait. "It don't do her justice. She's got more life, more change in her, more fire. She's starting for town, I hear."

"She is starting for town," said Edward.

"How do you know that?" Algernon swung about to ask.

Edward looked round to him. "By the fact of your not having fished for a holiday this week. How did you leave her yesterday, Algy? Quite well, I hope."

The ingenuous face of the young gentleman crimsoned.

"Oh, she was well," he said. "Ha! I see there can be some attraction in your dark women."

"You mean that Judith? Yes, she's a good diversion." Edward gave a two-edged response. "What train did you come up by last night?"

"The last from Wrexby. That reminds me: I saw a young Judith just as I got out. She wanted a cab. I called it for her. She belongs to old Hackbut of the Bank—the old porter, you know. If it wasn't that there's always something about dark women which makes me think they're going to have a moustache, I should take to that girl's face."

Edward launched forth an invective against fair women.

"What have they done to you-what have they done?" said Algernon.

"My good fellow, they're nothing but colour. They've no conscience. If they swear a thing to you one moment, they break it the next. They can't help doing it. You don't ask a gilt weathercock to keep faith with anything but the wind, do you? It's an ass that trusts a fair woman at all, or has anything to do with the confounded set. Cleopatra was fair; so was Delilah; so is the Devil's wife. Reach me that book of Reports."

"By jingo!" cried Algernon, "my stomach reports that if provision doesn't soon approach—why don't you keep a French cook here, Ned? Let's give up the women, and take to a French cook."

Edward yawned horribly. "All in good time. It's what we come to. It's philosophy—your French cook! I wish I had it, or him. I'm afraid a fellow can't anticipate his years—not so lucky!"

"By Jove! we shall have to be philosophers before we breakfast!" Algernon exclaimed. "It's nine. I've to be tied to the stake at ten, chained and muzzled—a leetle-a dawg! I wish I hadn't had to leave the service. It was a vile conspiracy against me there, Ned. Hang all tradesmen! I sit on a stool, and add up figures. I work harder than a nigger in the office. That's my life: but I must feed. It's no use going to the office in a rage."

"Will you try on the gloves again?" was Edward's mild suggestion.

Algernon thanked him, and replied that he knew him. Edward hit hard when he was empty.

They now affected patience, as far as silence went to make up an element of that sublime quality. The chops arriving, they disdained the mask. Algernon fired his glove just over the waiter's head, and Edward put the ease to the man's conscience; after which they sat and ate, talking little. The difference between them was, that Edward knew the state of Algernon's mind and what was working within it, while the latter stared at a blank wall as regarded Edward's.

"Going out after breakfast, Ned?" said Algernon. "We'll walk to the city together, if you like."

Edward fixed one of his intent looks upon his cousin. "You're not going to the city to-day?"

"The deuce, I'm not!"

"You're going to dance attendance on Mrs. Lovell, whom it's your pleasure to call Peggy, when you're some leagues out of her hearing."

Algernon failed to command his countenance. He glanced at one of the portraits, and said, "Who is that girl up there? Tell us her name. Talking of Mrs. Lovell, has she ever seen it?"

"If you'll put on your coat, my dear Algy, I will talk to you about Mrs. Lovell." Edward kept his penetrative eyes on Algernon. "Listen to me: you'll get into a mess there."

"If I must listen, Ned, I'll listen in my shirt-sleeves, with all respect to the lady."

"Very well. The shirt-sleeves help the air of bravado. Now, you know that I've what they call 'knelt at her feet.' She's handsome. Don't cry out. She's dashing, and as near being a devil as any woman I ever met. Do you know why we broke? I'll tell you. Plainly, because I refused to believe that one of her men had insulted her. You understand what that means. I declined to be a chief party in a scandal."

"Declined to fight the fellow?" interposed Algernon. "More shame to you!"

"I think you're a year younger than I am, Algy. You have the privilege of speaking with that year's simplicity. Mrs. Lovell will play you as she played me. I acknowledge her power, and I keep out of her way. I don't bet; I don't care to waltz; I can't keep horses; so I don't lose much by the privation to which I subject myself."

"I bet, I waltz, and I ride. So," said Algernon, "I should lose tremendously."

"You will lose, mark my words."

"Is the lecture of my year's senior concluded?" said Algernon.

"Yes; I've done," Edward answered.

"Then I'll put on my coat, Ned, and I'll smoke in it. That'll give you assurance I'm not going near Mrs. Lovell, if anything will."

"That gives me assurance that Mrs. Lovell tolerates in you what she detests," said Edward, relentless in his insight; "and, consequently, gives me assurance that she finds you of particular service to her at present."

Algernon had a lighted match in his hand. He flung it into the fire. "I'm hanged if I don't think you have the confounded vanity to suppose she sets me as a spy upon you!"

A smile ran along Edward's lips. "I don't think you'd know it, if she did."

"Oh, you're ten years older; you're twenty," bawled Algernon, in an extremity of disgust. "Don't I know what game you're following up? Isn't it clear as day you've got another woman in your eye?"

"It's as clear as day, my good Algy, that you see a portrait hanging in my chambers, and you have heard Mrs. Lovell's opinion of the fact. So much is perfectly clear. There's my hand. I don't blame you. She's a clever woman, and like many of the sort, shrewd at guessing the worst. Come, take my hand. I tell you, I don't blame you. I've been little dog to her myself, and fetched and carried, and wagged my tail. It's charming while it lasts. Will you shake it?"

"Your tail, man?" Algernon roared in pretended amazement.

Edward eased him back to friendliness by laughing. "No; my hand."

They shook hands.

"All right," said Algernon. "You mean well. It's very well for you to preach virtue to a poor devil; you've got loose, or you're regularly in love."

"Virtue! by heaven!" Edward cried; "I wish I were entitled to preach it to any man on earth."

His face flushed. "There, good-bye, old fellow," he added.

"Go to the city. I'll dine with you to-night, if you like; come and dine with me at my Club. I shall be disengaged."

Algernon mumbled a flexible assent to an appointment at Edward's Club, dressed himself with care, borrowed a sovereign, for which he nodded his acceptance, and left him.

Edward set his brain upon a book of law.

It may have been two hours after he had sat thus in his Cistercian stillness, when a letter was delivered to him by one of the Inn porters. Edward read the superscription, and asked the porter who it was that brought it. Two young ladies, the porter said.

These were the contents:—

"I am not sure that you will ever forgive me. I cannot forgive myself when I think of that one word I was obliged to speak to you in the cold street, and nothing to explain why, and how much I love, you. Oh! how I love you! I cry while I write. I cannot help it. I was a sop of tears all night long, and oh! if you had seen my face in the morning. I am thankful you did not. Mother's Bible brought me home. It must have been guidance, for in my bed there lay my sister, and I could not leave her, I love her so. I could not have got down stairs again after seeing her there; and I had to say that cold word and shut the window on you. May I call you Edward still? Oh, dear Edward, do make allowance for me. Write kindly to me. Say you forgive me. I feel like a ghost to-day. My life seems quite behind me somewhere, and I hardly feel anything I touch. I declare to you, dearest one, I had no idea my sister was here. I was surprised when I heard her name mentioned by my landlady, and looked on the bed; suddenly my strength was gone, and it changed all that I was thinking. I never knew before that women were so weak, but now I see they are, and I only know I am at my Edward's mercy, and am stupid! Oh, so wretched and stupid. I shall not touch food till I hear from you. Oh, if, you are angry, write so; but do write. My suspense would make you pity me. I know I deserve your anger. It was not that I do not trust you, Edward. My mother in heaven sees my heart and that I trust, I trust my heart and everything I am and have to you. I would almost wish and wait to see you to-day in the Gardens, but my crying has made me such a streaked thing to look at. If I had rubbed my face with a scrubbing-brush, I could not look worse, and I cannot risk your seeing me. It would excuse you for hating me. Do you? Does he hate her? She loves you. She would die for you, dear Edward. Oh! I feel that if I was told to-day that I should die for you to-morrow, it would be happiness. I am dying—yes, I am dying till I hear from you.

"Believe me,
"Your tender, loving, broken-hearted,
"Dahlia."

There was a postscript:—

"May I still go to lessons?"

Edward finished the letter with a calmly perusing eye. He had winced triflingly at one or two expressions contained in it; forcible, perhaps, but not such as Mrs. Lovell smiling from the wall yonder would have used.

"The poor child threatens to eat no dinner, if I don't write to her," he said; and replied in a kind and magnanimous spirit, concluding—"Go to lessons, by all means."

Having accomplished this, he stood up, and by hazard fell to comparing the rival portraits; a melancholy and a comic thing to do, as you will find if you put two painted heads side by side, and set their merits contesting, and reflect on the contest, and to what advantages, personal, or of the artist's, the winner owes the victory. Dahlia had been admirably dealt with by the artist; the charm of pure ingenuousness without rusticity was visible in her face and figure. Hanging there on the wall, she was a match for Mrs. Lovell.

CHAPTER VII

GREAT NEWS FROM DAHLIA

Rhoda returned home the heavier for a secret that she bore with her. All through the first night of her sleeping in London, Dahlia's sobs, and tender hugs, and self-reproaches, had penetrated her dreams, and when the morning came she had scarcely to learn that Dahlia loved some one. The confession was made; but his name was reserved. Dahlia spoke of him with such sacredness of respect that she seemed lost in him, and like a creature kissing his feet. With tears rolling down her cheeks, and with moans of anguish, she spoke of the deliciousness of loving: of knowing one to whom she abandoned her will and her destiny, until, seeing how beautiful a bloom love threw upon the tearful worn face of her sister, Rhoda was impressed by a mystical veneration for this man, and readily believed him to be above all other men, if not superhuman: for she was of an age and an imagination to conceive a spiritual pre-eminence over the weakness of mortality. She thought that one who could so transform her sister, touch her with awe, and give her gracefulness and humility, must be what Dahlia said he was. She asked shyly for his Christian name; but even so little Dahlia withheld. It was his wish that Dahlia should keep silence concerning him.

"Have you sworn an oath?" said Rhoda, wonderingly.

"No, dear love," Dahlia replied; "he only mentioned what he desired."

Rhoda was ashamed of herself for thinking it strange, and she surrendered her judgement to be stamped by the one who knew him well.

As regarded her uncle, Dahlia admitted that she had behaved forgetfully and unkindly, and promised amendment. She talked of the Farm as of an old ruin, with nothing but a thin shade of memory threading its walls, and appeared to marvel vaguely that it stood yet. "Father shall not always want money," she said. She was particular in prescribing books for Rhoda to read; good authors, she emphasized, and named books of history, and poets, and quoted their verses. "For my darling will some day have a dear husband, and he must not look down on her." Rhoda shook her head, full sure that she could never be brought to utter such musical words naturally. "Yes, dearest, when you know what love is," said Dahlia, in an underbreath.

Could Robert inspire her with the power? Rhoda looked upon that poor homely young man half-curiously when she returned, and quite dismissed the notion. Besides she had no feeling for herself. Her passion was fixed upon her sister, whose record of emotions in the letters from London placed her beyond dull days and nights. The letters struck many chords. A less subservient reader would have set them down as variations of the language of infatuation; but Rhoda was responsive to every word and change of mood, from the, "I am unworthy, degraded, wretched," to "I am blest above the angels." If one letter said, "We met yesterday," Rhoda's heart beat on to the question, "Shall I see him again to-morrow?" And will she see him?—has she seen him?—agitated her and absorbed her thoughts.

So humbly did she follow her sister, without daring to forecast a prospect for her, or dream of an issue, that when on a summer morning a letter was brought in at the breakfast-table, marked "urgent and private," she opened it, and the first line dazzled her eyes—the surprise was a shock to her brain. She rose from her unfinished meal, and walked out into the wide air, feeling as if she walked on thunder.

The letter ran thus:—

"My Own Innocent!—I am married. We leave England to-day. I must not love you too much, for I have all my love to give to my Edward, my own now, and I am his trustingly for ever. But he will let me give you some of it—and Rhoda is never jealous. She shall have a great deal. Only I am frightened when I think how immense my love is for him, so that anything—everything he thinks right is right to me. I am not afraid to think so. If I were to try, a cloud would come over me—it does, if only I fancy for half a moment I am rash, and a straw. I cannot exist except through him. So I must belong to him, and his will is my law. My prayer at my bedside every night is that I may die for him. We used to think the idea of death so terrible! Do you remember how we used to shudder together at night when we thought of people lying in the grave? And now, when I think that perhaps I may some day die for him, I feel like a crying in my heart with joy.

"I have left a letter—sent it, I mean—enclosed to uncle for father. He will see Edward by-and-by. Oh! may heaven spare him from any grief. Rhoda will comfort him. Tell him how devoted I am. I am like drowned to everybody but one.

"We are looking on the sea. In half an hour I shall have forgotten the tread of English earth. I do not know that I breathe. All I know is a fear that I am flying, and my strength will not continue. That is when I am not touching his hand. There is France opposite. I shut my eyes and see the whole country, but it is like what I feel for Edward—all in dark moonlight. Oh! I trust him so! I bleed for him. I could make all my veins bleed out at a sad thought about him. And from France to Switzerland and Italy. The sea sparkles just as if it said 'Come to the sun;' and I am going. Edward calls. Shall I be punished for so much happiness? I am too happy, I am too happy.

"God bless my beloved at home! That is my chief prayer now. I shall think of her when I am in the cathedrals.

"Oh, my Father in heaven! bless them all! bless Rhoda! forgive me!

"I can hear the steam of the steamer at the pier. Here is Edward. He says I may send his love to you.

"Address:—

"Mrs. Edward Ayrton,
 "Poste Restante,
"Lausanne,
"Switzerland.

"P.S.—Lausanne is where—but another time, and I will always tell you the history of the places to instruct you, poor heart in dull England. Adieu! Good-bye and God bless my innocent at home, my dear sister. I love her. I never can forget her. The day is so lovely. It seems on purpose for us. Be sure you write on thin paper to Lausanne. It is on a blue lake; you see snow mountains, and now there is a bell ringing—kisses from me! we start. I must sign.

"Dahlia."

By the reading of this letter, Rhoda was caught vividly to the shore, and saw her sister borne away in the boat to the strange countries; she travelled with her, following her with gliding speed through a multiplicity of shifting scenes, opal landscapes, full of fire and dreams, and in all of them a great bell towered. "Oh, my sweet! my own beauty!" she cried in Dahlia's language. Meeting Mrs. Sumfit, she called her "Mother Dumpling," as Dahlia did of old, affectionately, and kissed her, and ran on to Master Gammon, who was tramping leisurely on to the oatfield lying on toward the millholms.

"My sister sends you her love," she said brightly to the old man. Master Gammon responded with no remarkable flash of his eyes, and merely opened his mouth and shut it, as when a duck divides its bill, but fails to emit the customary quack.

"And to you, little pigs; and to you, Mulberry; and you, Dapple; and you, and you, and you."

Rhoda nodded round to all the citizens of the farmyard; and so eased her heart of its laughing bubbles. After which, she fell to a meditative walk of demurer joy, and had a regret. It was simply that Dahlia's hurry in signing the letter, had robbed her of the delight of seeing "Dahlia Ayrton" written proudly out, with its wonderful signification of the change in her life.

That was a trifling matter; yet Rhoda felt the letter was not complete in the absence of the bridal name. She fancied Dahlia to have meant, perhaps, that she was Dahlia to her as of old, and not a stranger. "Dahlia ever; Dahlia nothing else for you," she heard her sister say. But how delicious and mournful, how terrible and sweet with meaning would "Dahlia Ayrton," the new name in the dear handwriting, have looked! "And I have a brother-in-law," she thought, and her cheeks tingled. The banks of fern and foxglove, and the green young oaks fringing the copse, grew rich in colour, as she reflected that this beloved unknown husband of her sister embraced her and her father as well; even the old bent beggarman on the sandy ridge, though he had a starved frame and carried pitiless faggots, stood illumined in a soft warmth. Rhoda could not go back to the house.

It chanced that the farmer that morning had been smitten with the virtue of his wife's opinion of Robert, and her parting recommendation concerning him.

"Have you a mind to either one of my two girls?" he put the question bluntly, finding himself alone with Robert.

Robert took a quick breath, and replied, "I have."

"Then make your choice," said the farmer, and tried to go about his business, but hung near Robert in the fields till he had asked: "Which one is it, my boy?"

Robert turned a blade of wheat in his mouth.

"I think I shall leave her to tell that," was his answer.

"Why, don't ye know which one you prefer to choose, man?" quoth Mr. Fleming.

"I mayn't know whether she prefers to choose me," said Robert.

The farmer smiled.

"You never can exactly reckon about them; that's true."

He was led to think: "Dahlia's the lass;" seeing that Robert had not had many opportunities of speaking with her.

"When my girls are wives, they'll do their work in the house," he pursued. "They may have a little bit o' property in land, ye know, and they may have a share in—in gold. That's not to be reckoned on. We're an old family, Robert, and I suppose we've our pride somewhere down. Anyhow, you can't look on my girls and not own they're superior girls. I've no notion of forcing them to clean, and dish up, and do dairying, if it's not to their turn. They're handy with th' needle. They dress conformably, and do the millinery themselves. And I know they say their prayers of a night. That I know, if that's a comfort to ye, and it should be, Robert. For pray, and you can't go far wrong; and it's particularly good for girls. I'll say no more."

At the dinner-table, Rhoda was not present. Mr. Fleming fidgeted, blamed her and excused her, but as Robert appeared indifferent about her absence, he was confirmed in his idea that Dahlia attracted his fancy.

They had finished dinner, and Master Gammon had risen, when a voice immediately recognized as the voice of Anthony Hackbut was heard in the front part of the house. Mr. Fleming went round to him with a dismayed face.

"Lord!" said Mrs. Sumfit, "how I tremble!"

Robert, too, looked grave, and got away from the house. The dread of evil news of Dahlia was common to them all; yet none had mentioned it, Robert conceiving that it would be impertinence on his part to do so; the farmer, that the policy of permitting Dahlia's continued residence in London concealed the peril; while Mrs. Sumfit flatly defied the threatening of a mischance to one so sweet and fair, and her favourite. It is the insincerity of persons of their class; but one need not lay stress on the wilfulness of uneducated minds. Robert walked across the fields, walking like a man with an object in view. As he dropped into one of the close lanes which led up to Wrexby Hall, he saw Rhoda standing under an oak, her white morning-dress covered with sun-spots. His impulse was to turn back, the problem, how to speak to her, not being settled within him. But the next moment his blood chilled; for he had perceived, though he had not felt simultaneously, that two gentlemen were standing near her, addressing her. And it was likewise manifest that she listened to them. These presently raised their hats and disappeared. Rhoda came on toward Robert.

"You have forgotten your dinner," he said, with a queer sense of shame at dragging in the mention of that meal.

"I have been too happy to eat," Rhoda replied.

Robert glanced up the lane, but she gave no heed to this indication, and asked: "Has uncle come?"

"Did you expect him?"

"I thought he would come."

"What has made you happy?"

"You will hear from uncle."

"Shall I go and hear what those—"

Robert checked himself, but it would have been better had he spoken out. Rhoda's face, from a light of interrogation, lowered its look to contempt.

She did not affect the feminine simplicity which can so prettily misunderstand and put by an implied accusation of that nature. Doubtless her sharp instinct served her by telling her that her contempt would hurt him shrewdly now. The foolishness of a man having much to say to a woman, and not knowing how or where the beginning of it might be, was perceptible about him. A shout from her father at the open garden-gate, hurried on Rhoda to meet him. Old Anthony was at Mr. Fleming's elbow.

"You know it? You have her letter, father?" said Rhoda, gaily, beneath the shadow of his forehead.

"And a Queen of the Egyptians is what you might have been," said Anthony, with a speculating eye upon Rhoda's dark bright face.

Rhoda put out her hand to him, but kept her gaze on her father.

William Fleeting relaxed the knot of his brows and lifted the letter.

"Listen all! This is from a daughter to her father."

And he read, oddly accentuating the first syllables of the sentences:—

Dear Father,—

"My husband will bring me to see you when I return to dear England. I ought to have concealed nothing, I know. Try to forgive me. I hope you will. I shall always think of you. God bless you!

"I am,
"Ever with respect,
"Your dearly loving Daughter,
"Dahlia."

"Dahlia Blank!" said the farmer, turning his look from face to face.

A deep fire of emotion was evidently agitating him, for the letter rustled in his hand, and his voice was uneven. Of this, no sign was given by his inexpressive features. The round brown eyes and the ruddy varnish on his cheeks were a mask upon grief, if not also upon joy.

"Dahlia—what? What's her name?" he resumed. "Here—'my husband will bring me to see you'—who's her husband? Has he got a name? And a blank envelope to her uncle here, who's kept her in comfort for so long! And this is all she writes to me! Will any one spell out the meaning of it?"

"Dahlia was in great haste, father," said Rhoda.

"Oh, ay, you!—you're the one, I know," returned the farmer. "It's sister and sister, with you."

"But she was very, very hurried, father. I have a letter from her, and I have only 'Dahlia' written at the end—no other name."

"And you suspect no harm of your sister."

"Father, how can I imagine any kind of harm?"

"That letter, my girl, sticks to my skull, as though it meant to say, 'You've not understood me yet.' I've read it a matter of twenty times, and I'm no nearer to the truth of it. But, if she's lying, here in this letter, what's she walking on? How long are we to wait for to hear? I give you my word, Robert, I'm feeling for you as I am for myself. Or, wasn't it that one? Is it this one?" He levelled his finger at Rhoda. "In any case, Robert, you'll feel for me as a father. I'm shut in a dark room with the candle blown out. I've heard of a sort of fear you have in that dilemmer, lest you should lay your fingers on edges of sharp knives, and if I think a step—if I go thinking a step, and feel my way, I do cut myself, and I bleed, I do. Robert, just take and say, it wasn't that one."

Such a statement would carry with it the confession that it was this one for whom he cared this scornful one, this jilt, this brazen girl who could make appointments with gentlemen, or suffer them to speak to her, and subsequently look at him with innocence and with anger.

"Believe me, Mr. Fleming, I feel for you as much as a man can," he said, uneasily, swaying half round as he spoke.

"Do you suspect anything bad?" The farmer repeated the question, like one who only wanted a confirmation of his own suspicions to see the fact built up. "Robert, does this look like the letter of a married woman? Is it daughter-like—eh, man? Help another: I can't think for myself—she ties my hands. Speak out."

Robert set his eyes on Rhoda. He would have given much to have been able to utter, "I do." Her face was like an eager flower straining for light; the very beauty of it swelled his jealous passion, and he flattered himself with his incapacity to speak an abject lie to propitiate her.

"She says she is married. We're bound to accept what she says."

That was his answer.

"Is she married?" thundered the farmer. "Has she been and disgraced her mother in her grave? What am I to think? She's my flesh and blood. Is she—"

"Oh, hush, father!" Rhoda laid her hand on his arm. "What doubt can there be of Dahlia? You have forgotten that she is always truthful. Come away. It is shameful to stand here and listen to unmanly things."

She turned a face of ashes upon Robert.

"Come away, father. She is our own. She is my sister. A doubt of her is an insult to us."

"But Robert don't doubt her—eh?" The farmer was already half distracted from his suspicions. "Have you any real doubt about the girl, Robert?"

"I don't trust myself to doubt anybody," said Robert.

"You don't cast us off, my boy?"

"I'm a labourer on the farm," said Robert, and walked away.

"He's got reason to feel this more 'n the rest of us, poor lad! It's a blow to him." With which the farmer struck his hand on Rhoda's shoulder.

"I wish he'd set his heart on a safer young woman."

Rhoda's shudder of revulsion was visible as she put her mouth up to kiss her father's cheek.

CHAPTER VIII

INTRODUCES MRS. LOVELL

That is Wrexby Hall, upon the hill between Fenhurst and Wrexby: the white square mansion, with the lower drawing-room windows one full bow of glass against the sunlight, and great single trees spotting the distant green slopes. From Queen Anne's Farm you could read the hour by the stretching of their shadows. Squire Blancove, who lived there, was an irascible, gouty man, out of humour with his time, and beginning, alas for him! to lose all true faith in his Port, though, to do him justice, he wrestled hard with this great heresy. His friends perceived the decay in his belief sooner than he did himself. He was sour in the evening as in the morning. There was no chirp in him when the bottle went round. He had never one hour of a humane mood to be reckoned on now. The day, indeed, is sad when we see the skeleton of the mistress by whom we suffer, but cannot abandon her. The squire drank, knowing that the issue would be the terrific, curse-begetting twinge in his foot; but, as he said, he was a man who stuck to his habits. It was over his Port that he had quarrelled with his rector on the subject of hopeful Algernon, and the system he adopted with that young man. This incident has something to do with Rhoda's story, for it was the reason why Mrs. Lovell went to Wrexby Church, the spirit of that lady leading her to follow her own impulses, which were mostly in opposition. So, when perchance she visited the Hall, she chose not to accompany the squire and his subservient guests to Fenhurst, but made a point of going down to the unoccupied Wrexby pew. She was a beauty, and therefore powerful; otherwise her act of nonconformity would have produced bad blood between her and the squire.

It was enough to have done so in any case; for now, instead of sitting at home comfortably, and reading off the week's chronicle of sport while he nursed his leg, the unfortunate gentleman had to be up and away to Fenhurst every Sunday morning, or who would have known that the old cause of his general abstention from Sabbath services lay in the detestable doctrine of Wrexby's rector?

Mrs. Lovell was now at the Hall, and it was Sunday morning after breakfast. The lady stood like a rival head among the other guests, listening, gloved and bonneted, to the bells of Wrexby, West of the hills, and of Fenhurst, Northeast. The squire came in to them, groaning over his boots, cross with his fragile wife, and in every mood for satire, except to receive it.

"How difficult it is to be gouty and good!" murmured Mrs. Lovell to the person next her.

"Well," said the squire, singling out his enemy, "you're going to that fellow, I suppose, as usual—eh?"

"Not 'as usual,'" replied Mrs. Lovell, sweetly; "I wish it were!"

"Wish it were, do you?—you find him so entertaining? Has he got to talking of the fashions?"

"He talks properly; I don't ask for more." Mrs. Lovell assumed an air of meekness under persecution.

"I thought you were Low Church."

"Lowly of the Church, I trust you thought," she corrected him. "But, for that matter, any discourse, plainly delivered, will suit me."

"His elocution's perfect," said the squire; "that is, before dinner."

"I have only to do with him before dinner, you know."

"Well, I've ordered a carriage out for you."

"That is very honourable and kind."

"It would be kinder if I contrived to keep you away from the fellow."

"Would it not be kinder to yourself," Mrs. Lovell swam forward to him in all tenderness, taking his hands, and fixing the swimming blue of her soft eyes upon him pathetically, "if you took your paper and your slippers, and awaited our return?"

The squire felt the circulating smile about the room. He rebuked the woman's audacity with a frown; "Tis my duty to set an example," he said, his gouty foot and irritable temper now meeting in a common fire.

"Since you are setting an example," rejoined the exquisite widow, "I have nothing more to say."

The squire looked what he dared not speak. A woman has half, a beauty has all, the world with her when she is self-contained, and holds her place; and it was evident that Mrs. Lovell was not one to abandon her advantages.

He snapped round for a victim, trying his wife first. Then his eyes rested upon Algernon.

"Well, here we are; which of us will you take?" he asked Mrs. Lovell in blank irony.

"I have engaged my cavalier, who is waiting, and will be as devout as possible." Mrs. Lovell gave Algernon a smile.

"I thought I hit upon the man," growled the squire. "You're going in to Wrexby, sir! Oh, go, by all means, and I shan't be astonished at what comes of it. Like teacher, like pupil!"

"There!" Mrs. Lovell gave Algernon another smile. "You have to bear the sins of your rector, as well as your own. Can you support it?"

The flimsy fine dialogue was a little above Algernon's level in the society of ladies; but he muttered, bowing, that he would endeavour to support it, with Mrs. Lovell's help, and this did well enough; after which, the slight strain on the intellects of the assemblage relaxed, and ordinary topics were discussed. The carriages came round to the door; gloves, parasols, and scent-bottles were securely grasped; whereupon the squire, standing bare-headed on the steps, insisted upon seeing the party of the opposition off first, and waited to hand Mrs. Lovell into her carriage, an ironic gallantry accepted by the lady with serenity befitting the sacred hour.

"Ah! my pencil, to mark the text for you, squire," she said, taking her seat; and Algernon turned back at her bidding, to get a pencil; and she, presenting a most harmonious aspect in the lovely landscape, reclined in the carriage as if, like the sweet summer air, she too were quieted by those holy bells, while the squire stood, fuming, bareheaded, and with boiling blood, just within the bounds of decorum on the steps. She was more than his match.

She was more than a match for most; and it was not a secret. Algernon knew it as well as Edward, or any one. She was a terror to the soul of the youth, and an attraction. Her smile was the richest flattery he could feel; the richer, perhaps, from his feeling it to be a thing impossible to fix. He had heard tales of her; he remembered Edward's warning; but he was very humbly sitting with her now, and very happy.

"I'm in for it," he said to his fair companion; "no cheque for me next quarter, and no chance of an increase. He'll tell me I've got a salary. A salary! Good Lord! what a man comes to! I've done for myself with the squire for a year."

"You must think whether you have compensation," said the lady, and he received it in a cousinly squeeze of his hand.

He was about to raise the lank white hand to his lips.

"Ah!" she said, "there would be no compensation to me, if that were seen;" and her dainty hand was withdrawn. "Now, tell me," she changed her tone. "How do the loves prosper?"

Algernon begged her not to call them 'loves.' She nodded and smiled.

"Your artistic admirations," she observed. "I am to see her in church, am I not? Only, my dear Algy, don't go too far. Rustic beauties are as dangerous as Court Princesses. Where was it you saw her first?"

"At the Bank," said Algernon.

"Really! at the Bank! So your time there is not absolutely wasted. What brought her to London, I wonder?"

"Well, she has an old uncle, a queer old fellow, and he's a sort of porter—money porter—in the Bank, awfully honest, or he might half break it some fine day, if he chose to cut and run. She's got a sister, prettier than this girl, the fellows say; I've never seen her. I expect I've seen a portrait of her, though."

"Ah!" Mrs. Lovell musically drew him on. "Was she dark, too?"

"No, she's fair. At least, she is in her portrait."

"Brown hair; hazel eyes?"

"Oh—oh! You guess, do you?"

"I guess nothing, though it seems profitable. That Yankee betting man 'guesses,' and what heaps of money he makes by it!"

"I wish I did," Algernon sighed. "All my guessing and reckoning goes wrong. I'm safe for next Spring, that's one comfort. I shall make twenty thousand next Spring."

"On Templemore?"

"That's the horse. I've got a little on Tenpenny Nail as well. But I'm quite safe on Templemore; unless the Evil Principle comes into the field."

"Is he so sure to be against you, if he does appear?" said Mrs. Lovell.

"Certain!" ejaculated Algernon, in honest indignation.

"Well, Algy, I don't like to have him on my side. Perhaps I will take a share in your luck, to make it—? to make it?"—She played prettily as a mistress teasing her lap-dog to jump for a morsel; adding: "Oh! Algy, you are not a Frenchman. To make it divine, sir! you have missed your chance."

"There's one chance I shouldn't like to miss," said the youth.

"Then, do not mention it," she counselled him. "And, seriously, I will take a part of your risk. I fear I am lucky, which is ruinous. We will settle that, by-and-by. Do you know, Algy, the most expensive position in the world is a widow's."

"You needn't be one very long," growled he.

"I'm so wretchedly fastidious, don't you see? And it's best not to sigh when we're talking of business, if you'll take me for a guide. So, the old man brought this pretty rustic Miss Rhoda to the Bank?"

"Once," said Algernon. "Just as he did with her sister. He's proud of his nieces; shows them and then hides them. The fellows at the Bank never saw her again."

"Her name is—?"

"Dahlia."

"Ah, yes!—Dahlia. Extremely pretty. There are brown dahlias—dahlias of all colours. And the portrait of this fair creature hangs up in your chambers in town?"

"Don't call them my chambers," Algernon protested.

"Your cousin's, if you like. Probably Edward happened to be at the Bank when fair Dahlia paid her visit. Once seems to have been enough for both of you."

Algernon was unread in the hearts of women, and imagined that Edward's defection from Mrs. Lovell's sway had deprived him of the lady's sympathy and interest in his fortunes.

"Poor old Ned's in some scrape, I think," he said.

"Where is he?" the lady asked, languidly.

"Paris."

"Paris? How very odd! And out of the season, in this hot weather. It's enough to lead me to dream that he has gone over—one cannot realize why."

"Upon my honour!" Algernon thumped on his knee; "by jingo!" he adopted a less compromising interjection; "Ned's fool enough. My idea is, he's gone and got married."

Mrs. Lovell was lying back with the neglectful grace of incontestable beauty; not a line to wrinkle her smooth soft features. For one sharp instant her face was all edged and puckered, like the face of a fair witch. She sat upright.

"Married! But how can that be when we none of us have heard a word of it?"

"I daresay you haven't," said Algernon; "and not likely to. Ned's the closest fellow of my acquaintance. He hasn't taken me into his confidence, you maybe sure; he knows I'm too leaky. There's no bore like a secret! I've come to my conclusion in this affair by putting together a lot of little incidents and adding them up. First, I believe he was at the Bank when that fair girl was seen there. Secondly, from the description the fellows give of her, I should take her to be the original of the portrait. Next, I know that Rhoda has a fair sister who has run for it. And last, Rhoda has had a letter from her sister, to say she's away to the Continent and is married. Ned's in Paris. Those are my facts, and I give you my reckoning of them."

Mrs. Lovell gazed at Algernon for one long meditative moment.

"Impossible," she exclaimed. "Edward has more brains than heart." And now the lady's face was scarlet. "How did this Rhoda, with her absurd name, think of meeting you to tell you such stuff? Indeed, there's a simplicity in some of these young women—" She said the remainder to herself.

"She's really very innocent and good," Algernon defended Rhoda, "she is. There isn't a particle of nonsense in her. I first met her in town, as I stated, at the Bank; just on the steps, and we remembered I had called a cab for her a little before; and I met her again by accident yesterday."

"You are only a boy in their hands, my cousin Algy!" said Mrs. Lovell.

Algernon nodded with a self-defensive knowingness. "I fancy there's no doubt her sister has written to her that she's married. It's certain she has. She's a blunt sort of girl; not one to lie, not even for a sister or a lover, unless she had previously made up her mind to it. In that case, she wouldn't stick at much."

"But, do you know," said Mrs. Lovell—"do you know that Edward's father would be worse than yours over such an act of folly? He would call it an offence against common sense, and have no mercy for it. He would be vindictive on principle. This story of yours cannot be true. Nothing reconciles it."

"Oh, Sir Billy will be rusty; that stands to reason," Algernon assented. "It mayn't be true. I hope it isn't. But Ned has a madness for fair women. He'd do anything on earth for them. He loses his head entirely."

"That he may have been imprudent—" Mrs. Lovell thus blushingly hinted at the lesser sin of his deceiving and ruining the girl.

"Oh, it needn't be true," said Algernon; and with meaning, "Who's to blame if it is?"

Mrs. Lovell again reddened. She touched Algernon's fingers.

"His friends mustn't forsake him, in any case."

"By Jove! you are the right sort of woman," cried Algernon.

It was beyond his faculties to divine that her not forsaking of Edward might haply come to mean something disastrous to him. The touch of Mrs. Lovell's hand made him forget Rhoda in a twinkling. He detained it, audaciously, even until she frowned with petulance and stamped her foot.

There was over her bosom a large cameo-brooch, representing a tomb under a palm-tree, and the figure of a veiled woman with her head bowed upon the tomb. This brooch was falling, when Algernon caught it. The pin tore his finger, and in the energy of pain he dashed the brooch to her feet, with immediate outcries of violent disgust at himself and exclamations for pardon. He picked up the brooch. It was open. A strange, discoloured, folded substance lay on the floor of the carriage. Mrs. Lovell gazed down at it, and then at him, ghastly pale. He lifted it by one corner, and the diminutive folded squares came out, revealing a strip of red-stained handkerchief.

Mrs. Lovell grasped it, and thrust it out of sight.

She spoke as they approached the church-door: "Mention nothing of this to a soul, or you forfeit my friendship for ever."

When they alighted, she was smiling in her old affable manner.

CHAPTER IX

ROBERT INTERVENES

Some consideration for Robert, after all, as being the man who loved her, sufficed to give him rank as a more elevated kind of criminal in Rhoda's sight, and exquisite torture of the highest form was administered to him. Her faith in her sister was so sure that she could half pardon him for the momentary harm he had done to Dahlia with her father; but, judging him by the lofty standard of one who craved to be her husband, she could not pardon his unmanly hesitation and manner of speech. The old and deep grievance in her heart as to what men thought of women, and as to the harshness of men, was stirred constantly by the remembrance of his irresolute looks, and his not having dared to speak nobly for Dahlia, even though he might have had, the knavery to think evil. As the case stood, there was still mischief to counteract. Her father had willingly swallowed a drug, but his suspicions only slumbered, and she could not instil her own vivid hopefulness and trust into him. Letters from Dahlia came regularly. The first, from Lausanne, favoured Rhoda's conception of her as of a happy spirit resting at celestial stages of her ascent upward through spheres of ecstacy. Dahlia could see the snow-mountains in a flying glimpse; and again, peacefully seated, she could see the snow-mountains reflected in clear blue waters from her window, which, Rhoda thought, must be like heaven. On these inspired occasions, Robert presented the form of a malignant serpent in her ideas. Then Dahlia made excursions upon glaciers with her beloved, her helpmate, and had slippings and tumblings—little earthly casualties which gave a charming sense of reality to her otherwise miraculous flight. The Alps were crossed: Italy was beheld. A profusion of "Oh's!" described Dahlia's impressions of Italy; and "Oh! the heat!" showed her to be mortal, notwithstanding the sublime exclamations. Como received the blissful couple. Dahlia wrote from Como:—

"Tell father that gentlemen in my Edward's position cannot always immediately proclaim their marriage to the world. There are reasons. I hope he has been very angry with me: then it will be soon over, and we shall be—but I cannot look back. I shall not look back till we reach Venice. At Venice, I know I shall see you all as clear as day; but I cannot even remember the features of my darling here."

Her Christian name was still her only signature.

The thin blue-and-pink paper, and the foreign postmarks—testifications to Dahlia's journey not being a fictitious event, had a singular deliciousness for the solitary girl at the Farm. At times, as she turned them over, she was startled by the intoxication of her sentiments, for the wild thought would come, that many, many whose passionate hearts she could feel as her own, were ready to abandon principle and the bondage to the hereafter, for such a long delicious gulp of divine life. Rhoda found herself more than once brooding on the possible case that Dahlia had done this thing.

The fit of languor came on her unawares, probing at her weakness, and blinding her to the laws and duties of earth, until her conscious womanhood checked it, and she sprang from the vision in a spasm of terror, not knowing how far she had fallen.

After such personal experiences, she suffered great longings to be with her sister, that the touch of her hand, the gaze of her eyes, the tone of Dahlia's voice, might make her sure of her sister's safety.

Rhoda's devotions in church were frequently distracted by the occupants of the Blancove pew. Mrs. Lovell had the habit of looking at her with an extraordinary directness, an expressionless dissecting scrutiny, that was bewildering and confusing to the country damsel. Algernon likewise bestowed marked attention on her. Some curious hints had been thrown out to her by this young gentleman on the day when he ventured to speak to her in the lane, which led her to fancy distantly that he had some acquaintance with Dahlia's husband, or that he had heard of Dahlia.

It was clear to Rhoda that Algernon sought another interview. He appeared in the neighbourhood of the farm on Saturdays, and on Sundays he was present in the church, sometimes with Mrs. Lovell, and sometimes without a companion. His appearance sent her quick wits travelling through many scales of possible conduct: and they struck one ringing note:—she thought that by the aid of this gentleman a lesson might be given to Robert's mean nature. It was part of Robert's punishment to see that she was not unconscious of Algernon's admiration.

The first letter from Venice consisted of a series of interjections in praise of the poetry of gondolas, varied by allusions to the sad smell of the low tide water, and the amazing quality of the heat; and then Dahlia wrote more composedly:—

"Titian the painter lived here, and painted ladies, who sat to him without a bit of garment on, and indeed, my darling, I often think it was more comfortable for the model than for the artist. Even modesty seems too hot a covering for human creatures here. The sun strikes me down. I am ceasing to have a complexion. It is pleasant to know that my Edward is still proud of me. He has made acquaintance with some of the officers here, and seems pleased at the compliments they pay me.

"They have nice manners, and white uniforms that fit them like a kid glove. I am Edward's 'resplendent wife.' A colonel of one of the regiments invited him to dinner (speaking English), 'with your resplendent wife.' Edward has no mercy for errors of language, and he would not take me. Ah! who knows how strange men are! Never think of being happy unless you can always be blind. I see you all at home—Mother Dumpling and all—as I thought I should when I was to come to Venice.

"Persuade—do persuade father that everything will be well. Some persons are to be trusted. Make him feel it. I know that I am life itself to Edward. He has lived as men do, and he can judge, and he knows that there never was a wife who brought a heart to her husband like mine to him. He wants to think, or he wants to smoke, and he leaves me; but, oh! when he returns, he can scarcely believe that he has me, his joy is so great. He looks like a glad thankful child, and he has the manliest of faces. It is generally thoughtful; you might think it hard, at first sight.

"But you must be beautiful to please some men. You will laugh—I have really got the habit of talking to my face and all myself in the glass. Rhoda would think me cracked. And it is really true that I was never so humble about my good looks. You used to spoil me at home—you and that wicked old Mother Dumpling, and our own dear mother, Rhoda—oh! mother, mother! I wish I had always thought of you looking down on me! You made me so vain—much more vain than I let you see I was. There were times when it is quite true I thought myself a princess. I am not worse-looking now, but I suppose I desire to be so beautiful that nothing satisfies me.

"A spot on my neck gives me a dreadful fright. If my hair comes out much when I comb it, it sets my heart beating; and it is a daily misery to me that my hands are larger than they should be, belonging to Edward's 'resplendent wife.' I thank heaven that you and I always saw the necessity of being careful of our fingernails. My feet are of moderate size, though they are not French feet, as Edward says. No: I shall never dance. He sent me to the dancing-master in London, but it was too late. But I have been complimented on my walking, and that seems to please Edward. He does not dance (or mind dancing) himself, only he does not like me to miss one perfection. It is his love. Oh! if I have seemed to let you suppose he does not love me as ever, do not think it. He is most tender and true to me. Addio! I am signora, you are signorina.

"They have such pretty manners to us over here. Edward says they think less of women: I say they think more. But I feel he must be right. Oh, my dear, cold, loving, innocent sister! put out your arms; I shall feel them round me, and kiss you, kiss you for ever!"

Onward from city to city, like a radiation of light from the old farm-house, where so little of it was, Dahlia continued her journey; and then, without a warning, with only a word to say that she neared Rome, the letters ceased. A chord snapped in Rhoda's bosom. While she was hearing from her sister almost weekly, her confidence was buoyed on a summer sea. In the silence it fell upon a dread. She had no answer in her mind for her father's unspoken dissatisfaction, and she had to conceal her cruel anxiety. There was an interval of two months: a blank fell charged with apprehension that was like the humming of a toneless wind before storm; worse than the storm, for any human thing to bear.

Rhoda was unaware that Robert, who rarely looked at her, and never sought to speak a word to her when by chance they met and were alone, studied each change in her face, and read its signs. He was left to his own interpretation of them, but the signs he knew accurately. He knew that her pride had sunk, and that her heart was desolate. He believed that she had discovered her sister's misery.

One day a letter arrived that gave her no joyful colouring, though it sent colour to her cheeks. She opened it, evidently not knowing the handwriting; her eyes ran down the lines hurriedly. After a time she went upstairs for her bonnet.

At the stile leading into that lane where Robert had previously seen her, she was stopped by him.

"No farther," was all that he said, and he was one who could have interdicted men from advancing.

"Why may I not go by you?" said Rhoda, with a woman's affected humbleness.

Robert joined his hands. "You go no farther, Miss Rhoda, unless you take me with you."

"I shall not do that, Mr. Robert."

"Then you had better return home."

"Will you let me know what reasons you have for behaving in this manner to me?"

"I'll let you know by-and-by," said Robert. "At present, You'll let the stronger of the two have his way."

He had always been so meek and gentle and inoffensive, that her contempt had enjoyed free play, and had never risen to anger; but violent anger now surged against him, and she cried, "Do you dare to touch me?" trying to force her passage by.

Robert caught her softly by the wrist. There stood at the same time a full-statured strength of will in his eyes, under which her own fainted.

"Go back," he said; and she turned that he might not see her tears of irritation and shame. He was treating her as a child; but it was to herself alone that she could defend herself. She marvelled that when she thought of an outspoken complaint against him, her conscience gave her no support.

"Is there no freedom for a woman at all in this world?" Rhoda framed the bitter question.

Rhoda went back as she had come. Algernon Blancove did the same. Between them stood Robert, thinking, "Now I have made that girl hate me for life."

It was in November that a letter, dated from London, reached the farm, quickening Rhoda's blood anew. "I am alive," said Dahlia; and she said little more, except that she was waiting to see her sister, and bade her urgently to travel up alone. Her father consented to her doing so. After a consultation with Robert, however, he determined to accompany her.

"She can't object to see me too," said the farmer; and Rhoda answered "No." But her face was bronze to Robert when they took their departure.

CHAPTER X

DAHLIA IS NOT VISIBLE

Old Anthony was expecting them in London. It was now winter, and the season for theatres; so, to show his brother-in-law the fun of a theatre was one part of his projected hospitality, if Mr. Fleming should haply take the hint that he must pay for himself.

Anthony had laid out money to welcome the farmer, and was shy and fidgety as a girl who anticipates the visit of a promising youth, over his fat goose for next day's dinner, his shrimps for this day's tea, and his red slice of strong cheese, called of Cheshire by the reckless butter-man, for supper.

He knew that both Dahlia and Rhoda must have told the farmer that he was not high up in Boyne's Bank, and it fretted him to think that the mysterious respect entertained for his wealth by the farmer, which delighted him with a novel emotion, might be dashed by what the farmer would behold.

During his last visit to the farm, Anthony had talked of the Funds more suggestively than usual. He had alluded to his own dealings in them, and to what he would do and would not do under certain contingencies; thus shadowing out, dimly luminous and immense, what he could do, if his sagacity prompted the adventure. The farmer had listened through the buzzing of his uncertain grief, only sighing for answer. "If ever you come up to London, brother William John," said Anthony, "you mind you go about arm-in-arm with me, or you'll be judging by appearances, and says you, 'Lor', what a thousander fellow this is!' and 'What a millioner fellow that is!' You'll be giving your millions and your thousands to the wrong people, when they haven't got a penny. All London 'll be topsy-turvy to you, unless you've got a guide, and he'll show you a shabby-coated, head-in-the-gutter old man 'll buy up the lot. Everybody that doesn't know him says—look at him! but they that knows him—hats off, I can tell you. And talk about lords! We don't mind their coming into the city, but they know the scent of cash. I've had a lord take off his hat to me. It's a fact, I have."

In spite of the caution Anthony had impressed upon his country relative, that he should not judge by appearances, he was nevertheless under an apprehension that the farmer's opinion of him, and the luxurious, almost voluptuous, enjoyment he had of it, were in peril. When he had purchased the well-probed fat goose, the shrimps, and the cheese, he was only half-satisfied. His ideas shot boldly at a bottle of wine, and he employed a summer-lighted evening in going a round of wine-merchants' placards, and looking out for the cheapest bottle he could buy. And he would have bought one—he had sealing-wax of his own and could have stamped it with the office-stamp of Boyne's Bank for that matter, to make it as dignified and costly as the vaunted red seals and green seals of the placards—he would have bought one, had he not, by one of his lucky mental illuminations, recollected that it was within his power to procure an order to taste wine at the Docks, where you may get as much wine as you like out of big sixpenny glasses, and try cask after cask, walking down gas-lit paths between the huge bellies of wine which groan to be tapped and tried, that men may know them. The idea of paying two shillings and sixpence for one miserable bottle vanished at the richly-coloured prospect. "That'll show him something of what London is," thought Anthony; and a companion thought told him in addition that the farmer, with a skinful of wine, would emerge into the open air imagining no small things of the man who could gain admittance into those marvellous caverns. "By George! it's like a boy's story-book," cried Anthony, in his soul, and he chuckled over the vision of the farmer's amazement—acted it with his arms extended, and his hat unseated, and plunged into wheezy fits of laughter.

He met his guests at the station. Mr. Fleming was soberly attired in what, to Anthony's London eye, was a curiosity costume; but the broad brim of the hat, the square cut of the brown coat, and the leggings, struck him as being very respectable, and worthy of a presentation at any Bank in London.

"You stick to a leather purse, brother William John?" he inquired, with an artistic sentiment for things in keeping.

"I do," said the farmer, feeling seriously at the button over it.

"All right; I shan't ask ye to show it in the street," Anthony rejoined, and smote Rhoda's hand as it hung.

"Glad to see your old uncle—are ye?"

Rhoda replied quietly that she was, but had come with the principal object of seeing her sister.

"There!" cried Anthony, "you never get a compliment out of this gal. She gives ye the nut, and you're to crack it, and there maybe, or there mayn't be, a kernel inside—she don't care."

"But there ain't much in it!" the farmer ejaculated, withdrawing his fingers from the button they had been teasing for security since Anthony's question about the purse.

"Not much—eh! brother William John?" Anthony threw up a puzzled look. "Not much baggage—I see that—" he exclaimed; "and, Lord be thanked! no trunks. Aha, my dear"—he turned to Rhoda—"you remember your lesson, do ye? Now, mark me—I'll remember you for it. Do you know, my dear," he said to Rhoda confidentially, "that sixpenn'orth of chaff which I made the cabman pay for—there was the cream of it!—that was better than Peruvian bark to my constitution. It was as good to me as a sniff of sea-breeze and no excursion expenses. I'd like another, just to feel young again, when I'd have backed myself to beat—cabmen? Ah! I've stood up, when I was a young 'un, and shut up a Cheap Jack at a fair. Circulation's the soul o' chaff. That's why I don't mind tackling cabmen—they sit all day, and all they've got to say is 'rat-tat,' and they've done. But I let the boys roar. I know what I was when a boy myself. I've got devil in me—never you fear—but it's all on the side of the law. Now, let's off, for the gentlemen are starin' at you, which won't hurt ye, ye know, but makes me jealous."

Before the party moved away from the platform, a sharp tussle took place between Anthony and the farmer as to the porterage of the bulky bag; but it being only half-earnest, the farmer did not put out his strength, and Anthony had his way.

"I rather astonished you, brother William John," he said, when they were in the street.

The farmer admitted that he was stronger than he looked.

"Don't you judge by appearances, that's all," Anthony remarked, setting down the bag to lay his finger on one side of his nose for impressiveness.

"Now, there we leave London Bridge to the right, and we should away to the left, and quiet parts." He seized the bag anew. "Just listen. That's the roaring of cataracts of gold you hear, brother William John. It's a good notion, ain't it? Hark!—I got that notion from one of your penny papers. You can buy any amount for a penny, now-a-days—poetry up in a corner, stories, tales o' temptation—one fellow cut his lucky with his master's cash, dashed away to Australia, made millions, fit to be a lord, and there he was! liable to the law! and everybody bowing their hats and their heads off to him, and his knees knocking at the sight of a policeman—a man of a red complexion, full habit of body, enjoyed his dinner and his wine, and on account of his turning white so often, they called him—'sealing-wax and Parchment' was one name; 'Carrots and turnips' was another; 'Blumonge and something,' and so on. Fancy his having to pay half his income in pensions to chaps who could have had him out of his town or country mansion and popped into gaol in a jiffy. And found out at last! Them tales set you thinking. Once I was an idle young scaramouch. But you can buy every idea that's useful to you for a penny. I tried the halfpenny journals. Cheapness ain't always profitable. The moral is, Make your money, and you may buy all the rest."

Discoursing thus by the way, and resisting the farmer's occasional efforts to relieve him of the bag, with the observation that appearances were deceiving, and that he intended, please his Maker, to live and turn over a little more interest yet, Anthony brought them to Mrs. Wicklow's house. Mrs. Wicklow promised to put them into the track of the omnibuses running toward Dahlia's abode in the Southwest, and Mary Ann Wicklow, who had a burning desire in her bosom to behold even the outside shell of her friend's new grandeur, undertook very disinterestedly to accompany them. Anthony's strict injunction held them due at a lamp-post outside Boyne's Bank, at half-past three o'clock in the afternoon.

"My love to Dahly," he said. "She was always a head and shoulders over my size. Tell her, when she rolls by in her carriage, not to mind me. I got my own notions of value. And if that Mr. Ayrton of hers 'll bank at Boyne's, I'll behave to him like a customer. This here's the girl for my money." He touched Rhoda's arm, and so disappeared.

The farmer chided her for her cold manner to her uncle, murmuring aside to her: "You heard what he said." Rhoda was frozen with her heart's expectation, and insensible to hints or reproof. The people who entered the omnibus seemed to her stale phantoms bearing a likeness to every one she had known, save to her beloved whom she was about to meet, after long separation.

She marvelled pityingly at the sort of madness which kept the streets so lively for no reasonable purpose. When she was on her feet again, she felt for the first time, that she was nearing the sister for whom she hungered, and the sensation beset her that she had landed in a foreign country. Mary Ann Wicklow chattered all the while to the general ear. It was her pride to be the discoverer of Dahlia's terrace.

"Not for worlds would she enter the house," she said, in a general tone; she knowing better than to present herself where downright entreaty did not invite her.

Rhoda left her to count the numbers along the terrace-walk, and stood out in the road that her heart might select Dahlia's habitation from the other hueless residences. She fixed upon one, but she was wrong, and her heart sank. The fair Mary Ann fought her and beat her by means of a careful reckoning, as she remarked,—

"I keep my eyes open; Number 15 is the corner house, the bow-window, to a certainty."

Gardens were in front of the houses; or, to speak more correctly, strips of garden walks. A cab was drawn up close by the shrub-covered iron gate leading up to No. 15. Mary Ann hurried them on, declaring that they might be too late even now at a couple of dozen paces distant, seeing that London cabs, crawlers as they usually were, could, when required, and paid for it, do their business like lightning. Her observation was illustrated the moment after they had left her in the rear; for a gentleman suddenly sprang across the pavement, jumped into a cab, and was whirled away, with as much apparent magic to provincial eyes, as if a pantomimic trick had been performed. Rhoda pressed forward a step in advance of her father.

"It may have been her husband," she thought, and trembled. The curtains up in the drawing-room were moved as by a hand; but where was Dahlia's face? Dahlia knew that they were coming, and she was not on the look-out for them!—a strange conflict of facts, over which Rhoda knitted her black brows, so that she looked menacing to the maid opening the door, whose "Oh, if you please, Miss," came in contact with "My sister—Mrs.—, she expects me. I mean, Mrs.—" but no other name than "Dahlia" would fit itself to Rhoda's mouth.

"Ayrton," said the maid, and recommenced, "Oh, if you please, Miss, and you are the young lady, Mrs. Ayrton is very sorry, and have left word, would you call again to-morrow, as she have made a pressing appointment, and was sure you would excuse her, but her husband was very anxious for her to go, and could not put it off, and was very sorry, but would you call again to-morrow at twelve o'clock? and punctually she would be here."

The maid smiled as one who had fairly accomplished the recital of her lesson. Rhoda was stunned.

"Is Mrs. Ayrton at home?—Not at home?" she said.

"No: don't ye hear?" quoth the farmer, sternly.

"She had my letter—do you know?" Rhoda appealed to the maid.

"Oh, yes, Miss. A letter from the country."

"This morning?"

"Yes, Miss; this morning."

"And she has gone out? What time did she go out? When will she be in?"

Her father plucked at her dress. "Best not go making the young woman repeat herself. She says, nobody's at home to ask us in. There's no more, then, to trouble her for."

"At twelve o'clock to-morrow?" Rhoda faltered.

"Would you, if you please, call again at twelve o'clock to-morrow, and punctually she would be here," said the maid.

The farmer hung his head and turned. Rhoda followed him from the garden. She was immediately plied with queries and interjections of wonderment by Miss Wicklow, and it was not until she said: "You saw him go out, didn't you?—into the cab?" that Rhoda awakened to a meaning in her gabble.

Was it Dahlia's husband whom they had seen? And if so, why was Dahlia away from her husband? She questioned in her heart, but not for an answer, for she allowed no suspicions to live. The farmer led on with his plodding country step, burdened shoulders, and ruddy-fowled, serious face, not speaking to Rhoda, who had no desire to hear a word from him, and let him be. Mary Ann steered him and called from behind the turnings he was to take, while she speculated aloud to Rhoda upon the nature of the business that had torn Dahlia from the house so inopportunely. At last she announced that she knew what it was, but Rhoda failed to express curiosity. Mary Ann was driven to whisper something about strange things in the way of purchases. At that moment the farmer threw up his umbrella, shouting for a cab, and Rhoda ran up to him,—

"Oh, father, why do we want to ride?"

"Yes, I tell ye!" said the farmer, chafing against his coat-collar.

"It is an expense, when we can walk, father."

"What do I care for th' expense? I shall ride." He roared again for a cab, and one came that took them in; after which, the farmer, not being spoken to, became gravely placid as before. They were put down at Boyne's Bank. Anthony was on the look-out, and signalled them to stand away some paces from the door. They were kept about a quarter of an hour waiting between two tides of wayfarers, which hustled them one way and another, when out, at last, came the old, broad, bent figure, with little finicking steps, and hurried past them head foremost, his arms narrowed across a bulgy breast. He stopped to make sure that they were following, beckoned with his chin, and proceeded at a mighty rate. Marvellous was his rounding of corners, his threading of obstructions, his skilful diplomacy with passengers. Presently they lost sight of him, and stood bewildered; but while they were deliberating they heard his voice. He was above them, having issued from two swinging bright doors; and he laughed and nodded, as he ran down the steps, and made signs, by which they were to understand that he was relieved of a weight.

"I've done that twenty year of my life, brother William John," he said. "Eh? Perhaps you didn't guess I was worth some thousands when I got away from you just now? Let any chap try to stop me! They may just as well try to stop a railway train. Steam's up, and I'm off."

He laughed and wiped his forehead. Slightly vexed at the small amount of discoverable astonishment on the farmer's face, he continued,—

"You don't think much of it. Why, there ain't another man but myself Boyne's Bank would trust. They've trusted me thirty year:—why shouldn't they go on trusting me another thirty year? A good character, brother William John, goes on compound-interesting, just like good coin. Didn't you feel a sort of heat as I brushed by you—eh? That was a matter of one-two-three-four" Anthony watched the farmer as his voice swelled up on the heightening numbers: "five-six-six thousand pounds, brother William John. People must think something of a man to trust him with that sum pretty near every day of their lives, Sundays excepted—eh? don't you think so?"

He dwelt upon the immense confidence reposed in him, and the terrible temptation it would be to some men, and how they ought to thank their stars that they were never thrown in the way of such a temptation, of which he really thought nothing at all—nothing! until the farmer's countenance was lightened of its air of oppression, for a puzzle was dissolved in his brain. It was now manifest to him that Anthony was trusted in this extraordinary manner because the heads and managers of Boyne's Bank knew the old man to be possessed of a certain very respectable sum: in all probability they held it in their coffers for safety and credited him with the amount. Nay, more; it was fair to imagine that the guileless old fellow, who conceived himself to be so deep, had let them get it all into their hands without any suspicion of their prominent object in doing so.

Mr. Fleming said, "Ah, yes, surely."

He almost looked shrewd as he smiled over Anthony's hat. The healthy exercise of his wits relieved his apprehensive paternal heart; and when he mentioned that Dahlia had not been at home when he called, he at the same time sounded his hearer for excuses to be raised on her behalf, himself clumsily suggesting one or two, as to show that he was willing to swallow a very little for comfort.

"Oh, of course!" said Anthony, jeeringly. "Out? If you catch her in, these next three or four days, you'll be lucky. Ah, brother William John!"

The farmer, half frightened by Anthony's dolorous shake of his head, exclaimed: "What's the matter, man?"

"How proud I should be if only you was in a way to bank at Boyne's!"

"Ah!" went the farmer in his turn, and he plunged his chin deep in his neckerchief.

"Perhaps some of your family will, some day, brother William John."

"Happen, some of my family do, brother Anthony!"

"Will is what I said, brother William John; if good gals, and civil, and marry decently—eh?" and he faced about to Rhoda who was walking with Miss Wicklow. "What does she look so down about, my dear? Never be down. I don't mind you telling your young man, whoever he is; and I'd like him to be a strapping young six-footer I've got in my eye, who farms. What does he farm with to make farming answer now-a-days? Why, he farms with brains. You'll find that in my last week's Journal, brother William John, and thinks I, as I conned it—the farmer ought to read that! You may tell any young man you like, my dear, that your old uncle's fond of ye."

On their arrival home, Mrs. Wicklow met them with a letter in her hand. It was for Rhoda from Dahlia, saying that Dahlia was grieved to the heart to have missed her dear father and her darling sister. But her husband had insisted upon her going out to make particular purchases, and do a dozen things; and he was extremely sorry to have been obliged to take her away, but she hoped to see her dear sister and her father very, very soon. She wished she were her own mistress that she might run to them, but men when they are husbands require so much waiting on that she could never call five minutes her own. She would entreat them to call tomorrow, only she would then be moving to her new lodgings. "But, oh! my dear, my blessed Rhoda!" the letter concluded, "do keep fast in your heart that I do love you so, and pray that we may meet soon, as I pray it every night and all day long. Beg father to stop till we meet. Things will soon be arranged. They must. Oh! oh, my Rhoda, love! how handsome you have grown. It is very well to be fair for a time, but the brunettes have the happiest lot. They last, and when we blonde ones cry or grow thin, oh! what objects we become!"

There were some final affectionate words, but no further explanations.

The wrinkles again settled on the farmer's mild, uncomplaining forehead.

Rhoda said: "Let us wait, father."

When alone, she locked the letter against her heart, as to suck the secret meaning out of it. Thinking over it was useless; except for this one thought: how did her sister know she had grown very handsome? Perhaps the housemaid had prattled.

CHAPTER XI

AN INDICATIVE DUET IN A MINOR KEY

Dahlia, the perplexity to her sister's heart, lay stretched at full length upon the sofa of a pleasantly furnished London drawing-room, sobbing to herself, with her handkerchief across her eyes. She had cried passion out, and sobbed now for comfort.

She lay in her rich silken dress like the wreck of a joyful creature, while the large red Winter sun rounded to evening, and threw deep-coloured beams against the wall above her head. They touched the nut-brown hair to vivid threads of fire: but she lay faceless. Utter languor and the dread of looking at her eyelids in the glass kept her prostrate.

So, the darkness closed her about; the sickly gas-lamps of the street showing her as a shrouded body.

A girl came in to spread the cloth for dinner, and went through her duties with the stolidity of the London lodging-house maidservant, poking a clogged fire to perdition, and repressing a songful spirit.

Dahlia knew well what was being done; she would have given much to have saved her nostrils from the smell of dinner; it was a great immediate evil to her sickened senses; but she had no energy to call out, nor will of any kind. The odours floated to her, and passively she combated them.

At first she was nearly vanquished; the meat smelt so acrid, the potatoes so sour; each afflicting vegetable asserted itself peculiarly; and the bread, the salt even, on the wings of her morbid fancy, came steaming about her, subtle, penetrating, thick, and hateful, like the pressure of a cloud out of which disease is shot.

Such it seemed to her, till she could have shrieked; but only a few fresh tears started down her cheeks, and she lay enduring it.

Dead silence and stillness hung over the dinner-service, when the outer door below was opened, and a light foot sprang up the stairs.

There entered a young gentleman in evening dress, with a loose black wrapper drooping from his shoulders.

He looked on the table, and then glancing at the sofa, said:

"Oh, there she is!" and went to the window and whistled.

After a minute of great patience, he turned his face back to the room again, and commenced tapping his foot on the carpet.

"Well?" he said, finding these indications of exemplary self-command unheeded. His voice was equally powerless to provoke a sign of animation. He now displaced his hat, and said, "Dahlia!"

She did not move.

"I am here to very little purpose, then," he remarked.

A guttering fall of her bosom was perceptible.

"For heaven's sake, take away that handkerchief, my good child! Why have you let your dinner get cold? Here," he lifted a cover; "here's roast-beef. You like it—why don't you eat it? That's only a small piece of the general inconsistency, I know. And why haven't they put champagne on the table for you? You lose your spirits without it. If you took it when these moody fits came on—but there's no advising a woman to do anything for her own good. Dahlia, will you do me the favour to speak two or three words with me before I go? I would have dined here, but I have a man to meet me at the Club. Of what mortal service is it shamming the insensible? You've produced the required effect, I am as uncomfortable as I need be. Absolutely!"

"Well," seeing that words were of no avail, he summed up expostulation and reproach in this sigh of resigned philosophy: "I am going. Let me see—I have my Temple keys?—yes! I am afraid that even when you are inclined to be gracious and look at me, I shall not, be visible to you for some days. I start for Lord Elling's to-morrow morning at five. I meet my father there by appointment. I'm afraid we shall have to stay over Christmas. Good-bye." He paused. "Good-bye, my dear."

Two or three steps nearer the door, he said, "By the way, do you want anything? Money?—do you happen to want any money? I will send a blank cheque tomorrow. I have sufficient for both of us. I shall tell the landlady to order your Christmas dinner. How about wine? There is champagne, I know, and bottled ale. Sherry? I'll drop a letter to my wine-merchant; I think the sherry's running dry."

Her sense of hearing was now afflicted in as gross a manner as had been her sense of smell. She could not have spoken, though her vitality had pressed for speech. It would have astonished him to hear that his solicitude concerning provender for her during his absence was not esteemed a kindness; for surely it is a kindly thing to think of it; and for whom but for one for whom he cared would he be counting the bottles to be left at her disposal, insomuch that the paucity of the bottles of sherry in the establishment distressed his mental faculties?

"Well, good-bye," he said, finally. The door closed.

Had Dahlia's misery been in any degree simulated, her eyes now, as well as her ears, would have taken positive assurance of his departure. But with the removal of her handkerchief, the loathsome sight of the dinner-table would have saluted her, and it had already caused her suffering enough. She chose to remain as she was, saying to herself, "I am dead;" and softly revelling in that corpse-like sentiment. She scarcely knew that the door had opened again.

"Dahlia!"

She heard her name pronounced, and more entreatingly, and closer to her.

"Dahlia, my poor girl!" Her hand was pressed. It gave her no shudders.

"I am dead," she mentally repeated, for the touch did not run up to her heart and stir it.

"Dahlia, do be reasonable! I can't leave you like this. We shall be separated for some time. And what a miserable fire you've got here! You have agreed with me that we are acting for the best. It's very hard on me I try what I can to make you comf—happy; and really, to see you leaving your dinner to get cold! Your hands are like ice. The meat won't be eatable. You know I'm not my own master. Come, Dahly, my darling!"

He gently put his hand to her chin, and then drew away the handkerchief.

Dahlia moaned at the exposure of her tear-stained face, she turned it languidly to the wall.

"Are you ill, my dear?" he asked.

Men are so considerately practical! He begged urgently to be allowed to send for a doctor.

But women, when they choose to be unhappy, will not accept of practical consolations! She moaned a refusal to see the doctor.

Then what can I do for her? he naturally thought, and he naturally uttered it.

"Say good-bye to me," he whispered. "And my pretty one will write to me. I shall reply so punctually! I don't like to leave her at Christmas; and she will give me a line of Italian, and a little French—mind her accents, though!—and she needn't attempt any of the nasty German—kshrra-kouzzra-kratz!—which her pretty lips can't do, and won't do; but only French and Italian. Why, she learnt to speak Italian! 'La dolcezza ancor dentro me suona.' Don't you remember, and made such fun of it at first? 'Amo zoo;' 'no amo me?' my sweet!"

This was a specimen of the baby-lover talk, which is charming in its season, and maybe pleasantly cajoling to a loving woman at all times, save when she is in Dahlia's condition. It will serve even then, or she will pass it forgivingly, as not the food she for a moment requires; but it must be purely simple in its utterance, otherwise she detects the poor chicanery, and resents the meanness of it. She resents it with unutterable sickness of soul, for it is the language of what were to her the holiest hours of her existence, which is thus hypocritically used to blind and rock her in a cradle of deception. If corrupt, she maybe brought to answer to it all the same, and she will do her part of the play, and babble words, and fret and pout deliciously; and the old days will seem to be revived, when both know they are dead; and she will thereby gain any advantage she is seeking.

But Dahlia's sorrow was deep: her heart was sound. She did not even perceive the opportunity offered to her for a wily performance. She felt the hollowness of his speech, and no more; and she said, "Good-bye, Edward."

He had been on one knee. Springing cheerfully to his feet, "Good-bye, darling," he said. "But I must see her sit to table first. Such a wretched dinner for her!" and he mumbled, "By Jove, I suppose I shan't get any at all myself!" His watch confirmed it to him that any dinner which had been provided for him at the Club would be spoilt.

"Never mind," he said aloud, and examined the roast-beef ruefully, thinking that, doubtless, it being more than an hour behind the appointed dinner-time at the Club, his guest must now be gone.

For a minute or so he gazed at the mournful spectacle. The potatoes looked as if they had committed suicide in their own steam. There were mashed turnips, with a glazed surface, like the bright bottom of a tin pan. One block of bread was by the lonely plate. Neither hot nor cold, the whole aspect of the dinner-table resisted and repelled the gaze, and made no pretensions to allure it.

The thought of partaking of this repast endowed him with a critical appreciation of its character, and a gush of charitable emotion for the poor girl who had such miserable dishes awaiting her, arrested the philosophic reproof which he could have administered to one that knew so little how a dinner of any sort should be treated. He strode to the windows, pulled down the blind he had previously raised, rang the bell, and said,—

"Dahlia, there—I'm going to dine with you, my love. I've rung the bell for more candles. The room shivers. That girl will see you, if you don't take care. Where is the key of the cupboard? We must have some wine out. The champagne, at all events, won't be flat."

He commenced humming the song of complacent resignation. Dahlia was still inanimate, but as the door was about to open, she rose quickly and sat in a tremble on the sofa, concealing her face.

An order was given for additional candles, coals, and wood. When the maid had disappeared Dahlia got on her feet, and steadied herself by the wall, tottering away to her chamber.

"Ah, poor thing!" ejaculated the young man, not without an idea that the demonstration was unnecessary. For what is decidedly disagreeable is, in a young man's calculation concerning women, not necessary at all,—quite the reverse. Are not women the flowers which decorate sublunary life? It is really irritating to discover them to be pieces of machinery, that for want of proper oiling, creak, stick, threaten convulsions, and are tragic and stir us the wrong way. However, champagne does them good: an admirable wine—a sure specific for the sex!

He searched around for the keys to get at a bottle and uncork it forthwith. The keys were on the mantelpiece a bad comment on Dahlia's housekeeping qualities; but in the hurry of action let it pass. He welcomed the candles gladly, and soon had all the cupboards in the room royally open.

Bustle is instinctively adopted by the human race as the substitute of comfort. He called for more lights, more plates, more knives and forks. He sent for ice the maid observed that it was not to be had save at a distant street: "Jump into a cab—champagne's nothing without ice, even in Winter," he said, and rang for her as she was leaving the house, to name a famous fishmonger who was sure to supply the ice.

The establishment soon understood that Mr. Ayrton intended dining within those walls. Fresh potatoes were put on to boil. The landlady came up herself to arouse the fire. The maid was for a quarter of an hour hovering between the order to get ice and the execution of immediate commands. One was that she should take a glass of champagne to Mrs. Ayrton in her room. He drank off one himself. Mrs. Ayrton's glass being brought back untouched, he drank that off likewise, and as he became more exhilarated, was more considerate for her, to such a degree, that when she appeared he seized her hands and only jestingly scolded her for her contempt of sound medicine, declaring, in spite of her protestations, that she was looking lovely, and so they sat down to their dinner, she with an anguished glance at the looking-glass as she sank in her chair.

"It's not bad, after all," said he, drenching his tasteless mouthful of half-cold meat with champagne. "The truth is, that Clubs spoil us. This is Spartan fare. Come, drink with me, my dearest. One sip."

She was coaxed by degrees to empty a glass. She had a gentle heart, and could not hold out long against a visible lively kindliness. It pleased him that she should bow to him over fresh bubbles; and they went formally through the ceremony, and she smiled. He joked and laughed and talked, and she eyed him a faint sweetness. He perceived now that she required nothing more than the restoration of her personal pride, and setting bright eyes on her, hazarded a bold compliment.

Dahlia drooped like a yacht with idle sails struck by a sudden blast, that dips them in the salt; but she raised her face with the full bloom of a blush: and all was plain sailing afterward.

"Has my darling seen her sister?" he asked softly.

Dahlia answered, "No," in the same tone.

Both looked away.

"She won't leave town without seeing you?"

"I hope—I don't know. She—she has called at our last lodgings twice."

"Alone?"

"Yes; I think so."

Dahlia kept her head down, replying; and his observation of her wavered uneasily.

"Why not write to her, then?"

"She will bring father."

The sob thickened in her throat; but, alas for him who had at first, while she was on the sofa, affected to try all measures to revive her, that I must declare him to know well how certain was his mastery over her, when his manner was thoroughly kind. He had not much fear of her relapsing at present.

"You can't see your father?"

"No."

"But, do. It's best."

"I can't."

"Why not?"

"Not—" she hesitated, and clasped her hands in her lap.

"Yes, yes; I know," said he; "but still! You could surely see him. You rouse suspicions that need not exist. Try another glass, my dear."

"No more."

"Well; as I was saying, you force him to think—and there is no necessity for it. He maybe as hard on this point as you say; but now and then a little innocent deception maybe practised. We only require to gain time. You place me in a very hard position. I have a father too. He has his own idea of things. He's a proud man, as I've told you; tremendously ambitious, and he wants to push me, not only at the bar, but in the money market matrimonial. All these notions I have to contend against. Things can't be done at once. If I give him a shock—well, we'll drop any consideration of the consequences. Write to your sister to tell her to bring your father. If they make particular inquiries—very unlikely I think—but, if they do, put them at their ease."

She sighed.

"Why was my poor darling so upset, when I came in?" said he.

There was a difficulty in her speaking. He waited with much patient twiddling of bread crumbs; and at last she said:

"My sister called twice at my—our old lodgings. The second time, she burst into tears. The girl told me so."

"But women cry so often, and for almost anything, Dahlia."

"Rhoda cries with her hands closed hard, and her eyelids too."

"Well, that maybe her way."

"I have only seen her cry once, and that was when mother was dying, and asked her to fetch a rose from the garden. I met her on the stairs. She was like wood. She hates crying. She loves me so."

The sympathetic tears rolled down Dahlia's cheeks.

"So, you quite refuse to see your father?" he asked.

"Not yet!"

"Not yet," he repeated.

At the touch of scorn in his voice, she exclaimed:

"Oh, Edward! not yet, I cannot. I know I am weak. I can't meet him now. If my Rhoda had come alone, as I hoped—! but he is with her. Don't blame me, Edward. I can't explain. I only know that I really have not the power to see him."

Edward nodded. "The sentiment some women put into things is inexplicable," he said. "Your sister and father will return home. They will have formed their ideas. You know how unjust they will be. Since, however, the taste is for being a victim—eh?"

London lodging-house rooms in Winter when the blinds are down, and a cheerless fire is in the grate, or when blinds are up and street-lamps salute the inhabitants with uncordial rays, are not entertaining places of residence for restless spirits. Edward paced about the room. He lit a cigar and puffed at it fretfully.

"Will you come and try one of the theatres for an hour?" he asked.

She rose submissively, afraid to say that she thought she should look ill in the staring lights; but he, with great quickness of perception, rendered her task easier by naming the dress she was to wear, the jewels, and the colour of the opera cloak. Thus prompted, Dahlia went to her chamber, and passively attired herself, thankful to have been spared the pathetic troubles of a selection of garments from her wardrobe. When she came forth, Edward thought her marvellously beautiful.

Pity that she had no strength of character whatever, nor any pointed liveliness of mind to match and wrestle with his own, and cheer the domestic hearth! But she was certainly beautiful. Edward kissed her hand in commendation. Though it was practically annoying that she should be sad, the hue and spirit of sadness came home to her aspect. Sorrow visited her tenderly falling eyelids like a sister.

BOOK II

CHAPTER XII

AT THE THEATRE

Edward's engagement at his Club had been with his unfortunate cousin Algernon; who not only wanted a dinner but 'five pounds or so' (the hazy margin which may extend illimitably, or miserably contract, at the lender's pleasure, and the necessity for which shows the borrower to be dancing on Fortune's tight-rope above the old abyss).

"Over claret," was to have been the time for the asking; and Algernon waited dinnerless until the healthy-going minutes distended and swelled monstrous and horrible as viper-bitten bodies, and the venerable Signior, Time, became of unhealthy hue. For this was the first dinner which, during the whole course of the young man's career, had ever been failing to him. Reflect upon the mournful gap! He could scarcely believe in his ill-luck. He suggested it to himself with an inane grin, as one of the far-away freaks of circumstances that had struck him—and was it not comical?

He waited from the hour of six till the hour of seven. He compared clocks in the hall and the room. He changed the posture of his legs fifty times. For a while he wrestled right gallantly with the apparent menace of the Fates that he was to get no dinner at all that day; it seemed incredibly derisive, for, as I must repeat, it had never happened to him by any accident before. "You are born—you dine." Such appeared to him to be the positive regulation of affairs, and a most proper one,—of the matters of course following the birth of a young being.

By what frightful mischance, then, does he miss his dinner? By placing the smallest confidence in the gentlemanly feeling of another man! Algernon deduced this reply accurately from his own experience, and whether it can be said by other "undined" mortals, does not matter in the least. But we have nothing to do with the constitutionally luckless: the calamitous history of a simple empty stomach is enough. Here the tragedy is palpable. Indeed, too sadly so, and I dare apply but a flash of the microscope to the rageing dilemmas of this animalcule. Five and twenty minutes had signalled their departure from the hour of seven, when Algernon pronounced his final verdict upon Edward's conduct by leaving the Club. He returned to it a quarter of an hour later, and lingered on in desperate mood till eight.

He had neither watch in his pocket, nor ring on his finger, nor disposable stud in his shirt. The sum of twenty-one pence was in his possession, and, I ask you, as he asked himself, how is a gentleman to dine upon that? He laughed at the notion. The irony of Providence sent him by a cook's shop, where the mingled steam of meats and puddings rushed out upon the wayfarer like ambushed bandits, and seized him and dragged him in, or sent him qualmish and humbled on his way.

Two little boys had flattened their noses to the whiteness of winkles against the jealously misty windows. Algernon knew himself to be accounted a generous fellow, and remembering his reputation, he, as to hint at what Fortune might do in his case, tossed some coppers to the urchins, who ducked to the pavement and slid before the counter, in a flash, with never a "thank ye" or the thought of it.

Algernon was incapable of appreciating this childish faith in the beneficence of the unseen Powers who feed us, which, I must say for him, he had shared in a very similar manner only two hours ago. He laughed scornfully: "The little beggars!" considering in his soul that of such is humanity composed: as many a dinnerless man has said before, and will again, to point the speech of fools. He continued strolling on, comparing the cramped misty London aspect of things with his visionary free dream of the glorious prairies, where his other life was: the forests, the mountains, the endless expanses; the horses, the flocks, the slipshod ease of language and attire; and the grog-shops. Aha! There could be no mistake about him as a gentleman and a scholar out there! Nor would Nature shut up her pocket and demand innumerable things of him, as civilization did. This he thought in the vengefulness of his outraged mind.

Not only had Algernon never failed to dine every day of his life: he had no recollection of having ever dined without drinking wine. His conception did not embrace the idea of a dinner lacking wine. Possibly he had some embodied understanding that wine did not fall to the lot of every fellow upon earth: he had heard of gullets unrefreshed even by beer: but at any rate he himself was accustomed to better things, and he did not choose to excavate facts from the mass of his knowledge in order to reconcile himself to the miserable chop he saw for his dinner in the distance—a spot of meat in the arctic circle of a plate, not shone upon by any rosy-warming sun of a decanter!

But metaphorical language, though nothing other will convey the extremity of his misery, or the form of his thoughts, must be put aside.

"Egad, and every friend I have is out of town!" he exclaimed, quite willing to think it part of the plot.

He stuck his hands in his pockets, and felt vagabond-like and reckless. The streets were revelling in their winter muck. The carriages rolling by insulted him with their display of wealth.

He had democratic sentiments regarding them. Oh for a horse upon the boundless plains! he sighed to his heart. He remembered bitterly how he had that day ridden his stool at the bank, dreaming of his wilds, where bailiff never ran, nor duns obscured the firmament.

And then there were theatres here—huge extravagant places! Algernon went over to an entrance of one, to amuse his mind, cynically criticizing the bill. A play was going forward within, that enjoyed great popular esteem, "The Holly Berries." Seeing that the pit was crammed, Algernon made application to learn the state of the boxes, but hearing that one box was empty, he lost his interest in the performance.

As he was strolling forth, his attention was taken by a noise at the pit-doors, which swung open, and out tumbled a tough little old man with a younger one grasping his coat-collar, who proclaimed that he would sicken him of pushing past him at the end of every act.

"You're precious fond of plays," sneered the junior.

"I'm fond of everything I pay for, young fellow," replied the shaken senior; "and that's a bit of enjoyment you've got to learn—ain't it?"

"Well, don't you knock by me again, that's all," cried the choleric youth.

"You don't think I'm likely to stop in your company, do you?"

"Whose expense have you been drinking at?"

"My country's, young fellow; and mind you don't soon feed at the table. Let me go."

Algernon's hunger was appeased by the prospect of some excitement, and seeing a vicious shake administered to the old man by the young one, he cried, "Hands off!" and undertook policeman's duty; but as he was not in blue, his authoritative mandate obtained no respect until he had interposed his fist.

When he had done so, he recognized the porter at Boyne's Bank, whose enemy retired upon the threat that there should be no more pushing past him to get back to seats for the next act.

"I paid," said Anthony; "and you're a ticketer, and you ticketers sha' n't stop me. I'm worth a thousand of you. Holloa, sir," he cried to Algernon; "I didn't know you. I'm much obliged. These chaps get tickets given 'm, and grow as cocky in a theatre as men who pay. He never had such wine in him as I've got.

That I'd swear. Ha! ha! I come out for an airing after every act, and there's a whole pitfall of ticketers yelling and tearing, and I chaff my way through and back clean as a red-hot poker."

Anthony laughed, and rolled somewhat as he laughed.

"Come along, sir, into the street," he said, boring on to the pavement. "It's after office hours. And, ha! ha! what do you think? There's old farmer in there, afraid to move off his seat, and the girl with him, sticking to him tight, and a good girl too. She thinks we've had too much. We been to the Docks, wine-tasting: Port—Sherry: Sherry—Port! and, ha! ha! 'what a lot of wine!' says farmer, never thinking how much he's taking on board. 'I guessed it was night,' says farmer, as we got into the air, and to see him go on blinking, and stumbling, and saying to me, 'You stand wine, brother Tony!' I'm blest if I ain't bottled laughter. So, says I, 'come and see "The Holly Berries," brother William John; it's the best play in London, and a suitable winter piece.' 'Is there a rascal hanged in the piece?' says he. 'Oh, yes!' I let him fancy there was, and he—ha! ha! old farmer's sticking to his seat, solemn as a judge, waiting for the gallows to come on the stage."

A thought quickened Algernon's spirit. It was a notorious secret among the young gentlemen who assisted in maintaining the prosperity of Boyne's Bank, that the old porter—the "Old Ant," as he was called—possessed money, and had no objection to put out small sums for a certain interest. Algernon mentioned casually that he had left his purse at home; and "by the way," said he, "have you got a few sovereigns in your pocket?"

"What! and come through that crush, sir?" Anthony negatived the question decisively with a reference to his general knowingness.

Algernon pressed him; saying at last, "Well, have you got one?"

"I don't think I've been such a fool," said Anthony, feeling slowly about his person, and muttering as to the changes that might possibly have been produced in him by the Docks.

"Confound it, I haven't dined!" exclaimed Algernon, to hasten his proceedings; but at this, Anthony eyed him queerly. "What have you been about then, sir?"

"Don't you see I'm in evening dress? I had an appointment to dine with a friend. He didn't keep it. I find I've left my purse in my other clothes."

"That's a bad habit, sir," was Anthony's comment. "You don't care much for your purse."

"Much for my purse, be hanged!" interjected Algernon.

"You'd have felt it, or you'd have heard it, if there 'd been any weight in it," Anthony remarked.

"How can you hear paper?"

"Oh, paper's another thing. You keep paper in your mind, don't you—eh? Forget pound notes? Leave pound notes in a purse? And you Sir William's nephew, sir, who'd let you bank with him and put down everything in a book, so that you couldn't forget, or if you did, he'd remember for you; and you might change your clothes as often as not, and no fear of your losing a penny."

Algernon shrugged disgustedly, and was giving the old man up as a bad business, when Anthony altered his manner. "Oh! well, sir, I don't mind letting you have what I've got. I'm out for fun. Bother affairs!"

The sum of twenty shillings was handed to Algernon, after he had submitted to the indignity of going into a public-house, and writing his I.O.U. for twenty-three to Anthony Hackbut, which included interest. Algernon remonstrated against so needless a formality; but Anthony put the startling supposition to him, that he might die that night. He signed the document, and was soon feeding and drinking his wine. This being accomplished, he took some hasty puffs of tobacco, and returned to the theatre, in the hope that the dark girl Rhoda was to be seen there; for now that he had dined, Anthony's communication with regard to the farmer and his daughter became his uppermost thought, and a young man's uppermost thought is usually the propelling engine to his actions.

By good chance, and the aid of a fee, he obtained a front seat, commanding an excellent side-view of the pit, which sat wrapt in contemplation of a Christmas scene snow, ice, bare twigs, a desolate house, and a woman shivering—one of man's victims.

It is a good public, that of Britain, and will bear anything, so long as villany is punished, of which there was ripe promise in the oracular utterances of a rolling, stout, stage-sailor, whose nose, to say nothing of his frankness on the subject, proclaimed him his own worst enemy, and whose joke, by dint of repetition, had almost become the joke of the audience too; for whenever he appeared, there was agitation in pit and gallery, which subsided only on his jovial thundering of the familiar sentence; whereupon laughter ensued, and a quieting hum of satisfaction.

It was a play that had been favoured with a great run. Critics had once objected to it, that it was made to subsist on scenery, a song, and a stupid piece of cockneyism pretending to be a jest, that was really no more than a form of slapping the public on the back. But the public likes to have its back slapped, and critics, frozen by the Medusa-head of Success, were soon taught manners. The office of critic is now, in fact, virtually extinct; the taste for tickling and slapping is universal and imperative; classic appeals to the intellect, and passions not purely domestic, have grown obsolete. There are captains of the legions, but no critics. The mass is lord.

And behold our friend the sailor of the boards, whose walk is even as two meeting billows, appears upon the lonely moor, and salts that uninhabited region with nautical interjections. Loose are his hose in one part, tight in another, and he smacks them. It is cold; so let that be his excuse for showing the bottom of his bottle to the glittering spheres. He takes perhaps a sturdier pull at the liquor than becomes a manifest instrument of Providence, whose services may be immediately required; but he informs us that his ship was never known not to right itself when called upon.

He is alone in the world, he tells us likewise. If his one friend, the uplifted flask, is his enemy, why then he feels bound to treat his enemy as his friend. This, with a pathetic allusion to his interior economy, which was applauded, and the remark "Ain't that Christian?" which was just a trifle risky; so he secured pit and gallery at a stroke by a surpassingly shrewd blow at the bishops of our Church, who are, it can barely be contested, in foul esteem with the multitude—none can say exactly, for what reason—and must submit to be occasionally offered up as propitiatory sacrifices.

This good sailor was not always alone in the world. A sweet girl, whom he describes as reaching to his kneecap, and pathetically believes still to be of the same height, once called him brother Jack. To hear that name again from her lips, and a particular song!—he attempts it ludicrously, yet touchingly withal.

Hark! Is it an echo from a spirit in the frigid air?

The song trembled with a silver ring to the remotest corners of the house.

At that moment the breathless hush of the audience was flurried by hearing "Dahlia" called from the pit.

Algernon had been spying among the close-packed faces for a sight of Rhoda. Rhoda was now standing up amid gathering hisses and outcries. Her eyes were bent on a particular box, across which a curtain was hastily being drawn. "My sister!" she sent out a voice of anguish, and remained with clasped hands and twisted eyebrows, looking toward that one spot, as if she would have flown to it. She was wedged in the mass, and could not move.

The exclamation heard had belonged to brother Jack, on the stage, whose burst of fraternal surprise and rapture fell flat after it, to the disgust of numbers keenly awakened for the sentiment of this scene.

Roaring accusations that she was drunk; that she had just escaped from Bedlam for an evening; that she should be gagged and turned headlong out, surrounded her; but she stood like a sculptured figure, vital in her eyes alone. The farmer put his arm about his girl's waist. The instant, however, that Anthony's head uprose on the other side of her, the evil reputation he had been gaining for himself all through the evening produced a general clamour, over which the gallery played, miauling, and yelping like dogs that are never to be divorced from a noise. Algernon feared mischief. He quitted his seat, and ran out into the lobby.

Half-a-dozen steps, and he came in contact with some one, and they were mutually drenched with water by the shock. It was his cousin Edward, bearing a glass in his hand.

Algernon's wrath at the sight of this offender was stimulated by the cold bath; but Edward cut him short.

"Go in there;" he pointed to a box-door. "A lady has fainted. Hold her up till I come."

No time was allowed for explanation. Algernon passed into the box, and was alone with an inanimate shape in blue bournous. The uproar in the theatre raged; the whole pit was on its legs and shouting. He lifted the pallid head over one arm, miserably helpless and perplexed, but his anxiety concerning Rhoda's personal safety in that sea of strife prompted him to draw back the curtain a little, and he stood exposed. Rhoda perceived him. She motioned with both her hands in dumb supplication. In a moment the curtain closed between them. Edward's sharp white face cursed him mutely for his folly, while he turned and put the water to Dahlia's lips, and touched her forehead with it.

"What's the matter?" whispered Algernon.

"We must get her out as quick as we can. This is the way with women! Come! she's recovering." Edward nursed her sternly as he spoke.

"If she doesn't, pretty soon, we shall have the pit in upon us," said Algernon. "Is she that girl's sister?"

"Don't ask damned questions."

Dahlia opened her eyes, staring placidly.

"Now you can stand up, my dear. Dahlia! all's well. Try," said Edward.

She sighed, murmuring, "What is the time?" and again, "What noise is it?"

Edward coughed in a vexed attempt at tenderness, using all his force to be gentle with her as he brought her to her feet. The task was difficult amid the threatening storm in the theatre, and cries of "Show the young woman her sister!" for Rhoda had won a party in the humane public.

"Dahlia, in God's name give me your help!" Edward called in her ear.

The fair girl's eyelids blinked wretchedly in protestation of her weakness. She had no will either way, and suffered herself to be led out of the box, supported by the two young men.

"Run for a cab," said Edward; and Algernon went ahead.

He had one waiting for them as they came out. They placed Dahlia on a seat with care, and Edward, jumping in, drew an arm tightly about her. "I can't cry," she moaned.

The cab was driving off as a crowd of people burst from the pit-doors, and Algernon heard the voice of Farmer Fleming, very hoarse. He had discretion enough to retire.

CHAPTER XIII

THE FARMER SPEAKS

Robert was to drive to the station to meet Rhoda and her father returning from London, on a specified day. He was eager to be asking cheerful questions of Dahlia's health and happiness, so that he might dispel the absurd general belief that he had ever loved the girl, and was now regretting her absence; but one look at Rhoda's face when she stepped from the railway carriage kept him from uttering a word on that subject, and the farmer's heavier droop and acceptance of a helping hand into the cart, were signs of bad import.

Mr. Fleming made no show of grief, like one who nursed it. He took it to all appearance as patiently as an old worn horse would do, although such an outward submissiveness will not always indicate a placid spirit in men. He talked at stale intervals of the weather and the state of the ground along the line of rail down home, and pointed in contempt or approval to a field here and there; but it was as one who no longer had any professional interest in the tilling of the land.

Doubtless he was trained to have no understanding of a good to be derived by his communicating what he felt and getting sympathy. Once, when he was uncertain, and a secret pride in Dahlia's beauty and accomplishments had whispered to him that her flight was possibly the opening of her road to a higher fortune, he made a noise for comfort, believing in his heart that she was still to be forgiven. He knew better now. By holding his peace he locked out the sense of shame which speech would have stirred within him.

"Got on pretty smooth with old Mas' Gammon?" he expressed his hope; and Robert said, "Capitally. We shall make something out of the old man yet, never fear."

Master Gammon was condemned to serve at the ready-set tea-table as a butt for banter; otherwise it was apprehended well that Mrs. Sumfit would have scorched the ears of all present, save the happy veteran of the furrows, with repetitions of Dahlia's name, and wailings about her darling, of whom no one spoke. They suffered from her in spite of every precaution.

"Well, then, if I'm not to hear anything dooring meals—as if I'd swallow it and take it into my stomach!—I'll wait again for what ye've got to tell," she said, and finished her cup at a gulp, smoothing her apron.

The farmer then lifted his head.

"Mother, if you've done, you'll oblige me by going to bed," he said. "We want the kitchen."

"A-bed?" cried Mrs. Sumfit, with instantly ruffled lap.

"Upstairs, mother; when you've done—not before."

"Then bad's the noos! Something have happened, William. You 'm not going to push me out? And my place is by the tea-pot, which I cling to, rememberin' how I seen her curly head grow by inches up above the table and the cups. Mas' Gammon," she appealed to the sturdy feeder, "five cups is your number?"

Her hope was reduced to the prolonging of the service of tea, with Master Gammon's kind assistance.

"Four, marm," said her inveterate antagonist, as he finished that amount, and consequently put the spoon in his cup.

Mrs. Sumfit rolled in her chair.

"O Lord, Mas' Gammon! Five, I say; and never a cup less so long as here you've been."

"Four, marm. I don't know," said Master Gammon, with a slow nod of his head, "that ever I took five cups of tea at a stretch. Not runnin'."

"I do know, Mas' Gammon. And ought to: for don't I pour out to ye? It's five you take, and please, your cup, if you'll hand it over."

"Four's my number, marm," Master Gammon reiterated resolutely. He sat like a rock.

"If they was dumplins," moaned Mrs. Sumfit, "not four, no, nor five, 'd do till enough you'd had, and here we might stick to our chairs, but you'd go on and on; you know you would."

"That's eatin', marm;" Master Gammon condescended to explain the nature of his habits. "I'm reg'lar in my drinkin'."

Mrs. Sumfit smote her hands together. "O Lord, Mas' Gammon, the wearisomest old man I ever come across is you. More tea's in the pot, and it ain't watery, and you won't be comfortable. May you get forgiveness from above! is all I say, and I say no more. Mr. Robert, perhaps you'll be so good as let me help you, sir? It's good tea; and my Dody," she added, cajolingly, "my home girl 'll tell us what she saw. I'm pinched and starved to hear."

"By-and-by, mother," interposed the farmer; "tomorrow." He spoke gently, but frowned.

Both Rhoda and Robert perceived that they were peculiarly implicated in the business which was to be discussed without Mrs. Sumfit's assistance. Her father's manner forbade Rhoda from making any proposal for the relief of the forlorn old woman.

"And me not to hear to-night about your play-going!" sighed Mrs. Sumfit. "Oh, it's hard on me. I do call it cruel. And how my sweet was dressed—like as for a Ball."

She saw the farmer move his foot impatiently.

"Then, if nobody drinks this remaining cup, I will," she pursued.

No voice save her own was heard till the cup was emptied, upon which Master Gammon, according to his wont, departed for bed to avoid the seduction of suppers, which he shunned as apoplectic, and Mrs. Sumfit prepared, in a desolate way, to wash the tea-things, but the farmer, saying that it could be done in the morning, went to the door and opened it for her.

She fetched a great sigh and folded her hands resignedly. As she was passing him to make her miserable enforced exit, the heavy severity of his face afflicted her with a deep alarm; she fell on her knees, crying,—

"Oh, William! it ain't for sake of hearin' talk; but you, that went to see our Dahly, the blossom, 've come back streaky under the eyes, and you make the house feel as if we neighboured Judgement Day. Down to tea you set the first moment, and me alone with none of you, and my love for my girl known well to you. And now to be marched off! How can I go a-bed and sleep, and my heart jumps so? It ain't Christian to ask me to. I got a heart, dear, I have. Do give a bit of comfort to it. Only a word of my Dahly to me."

The farmer replied: "Mother, let's have no woman's nonsense. What we've got to bear, let us bear. And you go on your knees to the Lord, and don't be a heathen woman, I say. Get up. There's a Bible in your bedroom. Find you out comfort in that."

"No, William, no!" she sobbed, still kneeling: "there ain't a dose o' comfort there when poor souls is in the dark, and haven't got patience for passages. And me and my Bible!—how can I read it, and not know my ailing, and a'stract one good word, William? It'll seem only the devil's shootin' black lightnings across the page, as poor blessed granny used to say, and she believed witches could do it to you in her time, when they was evil-minded. No! To-night I look on the binding of the Holy Book, and I don't, and I won't, I sha' n't open it."

This violent end to her petition was wrought by the farmer grasping her arm to bring her to her feet.

"Go to bed, mother."

"I shan't open it," she repeated, defiantly. "And it ain't," she gathered up her comfortable fat person to assist the words "it ain't good—no, not the best pious ones—I shall, and will say it! as is al'ays ready to smack your face with the Bible."

"Now, don't ye be angry," said the farmer.

She softened instantly.

"William, dear, I got fifty-seven pounds sterling, and odd shillings, in a Savings-bank, and that I meant to go to Dahly, and not to yond' dark thing sitting there so sullen, and me in my misery; I'd give it to you now for news of my darlin'. Yes, William; and my poor husband's cottage, in Sussex—seventeen pound per annum. That, if you'll be goodness itself, and let me hear a word."

"Take her upstairs," said the farmer to Rhoda, and Rhoda went by her and took her hands, and by dint of pushing from behind and dragging in front, Mrs. Sumfit, as near on a shriek as one so fat and sleek could be, was ejected. The farmer and Robert heard her struggles and exclamations along the passage, but her resistance subsided very suddenly.

"There's power in that girl," said the farmer, standing by the shut door.

Robert thought so, too. It affected his imagination, and his heart began to beat sickeningly.

"Perhaps she promised to speak—what has happened, whatever that may be," he suggested.

"Not she; not she. She respects my wishes."

Robert did not ask what had happened.

Mr. Fleming remained by the door, and shut his mouth from a further word till he heard Rhoda's returning footstep. He closed the door again behind her, and went up to the square deal table, leaned his body forward on the knuckles of his trembling fist, and said, "We're pretty well broken up, as it is. I've lost my taste for life."

There he paused. Save by the shining of a wet forehead, his face betrayed nothing of the anguish he suffered. He looked at neither of them, but sent his gaze straight away under labouring brows to an arm of the fireside chair, while his shoulders drooped on the wavering support of his hard-shut hands. Rhoda's eyes, ox-like, as were her father's, smote full upon Robert's, as in a pang of apprehension of what was about to be uttered.

It was a quick blaze of light, wherein he saw that the girl's spirit was not with him. He would have stopped the farmer at once, but he had not the heart to do it, even had he felt in himself strength to attract an intelligent response from that strange, grave, bovine fixity of look, over which the human misery sat as a thing not yet taken into the dull brain.

"My taste for life," the old man resumed, "that's gone. I didn't bargain at set-out to go on fighting agen the world. It's too much for a man o' my years. Here's the farm. Shall 't go to pieces?—I'm a farmer of thirty year back—thirty year back, and more: I'm about no better'n a farm labourer in our time, which is to-day. I don't cost much. I ask to be fed, and to work for it, and to see my poor bit o' property safe, as handed to me by my father. Not for myself, 't ain't; though perhaps there's a bottom of pride there too, as in most things. Say it's for the name. My father seems to demand of me out loud, 'What ha' ye done with Queen Anne's Farm, William?' and there's a holler echo in my ears. Well; God wasn't merciful to give me a son. He give me daughters."

Mr. Fleming bowed his head as to the very weapon of chastisement.

"Daughters!" He bent lower.

His hearers might have imagined his headless address to them to be also without a distinct termination, for he seemed to have ended as abruptly as he had begun; so long was the pause before, with a wearied lifting of his body, he pursued, in a sterner voice:

"Don't let none interrupt me." His hand was raised as toward where Rhoda stood, but he sent no look with it; the direction was wide of her.

The aspect of the blank blind hand motioning to the wall away from her, smote an awe through her soul that kept her dumb, though his next words were like thrusts of a dagger in her side.

"My first girl—she's brought disgrace on this house. She's got a mother in heaven, and that mother's got to blush for her. My first girl's gone to harlotry in London."

It was Scriptural severity of speech. Robert glanced quick with intense commiseration at Rhoda. He saw her hands travel upward till they fixed in at her temples with crossed fingers, making the pressure of an iron band for her head, while her lips parted, and her teeth, and cheeks, and eyeballs were all of one whiteness. Her tragic, even, in and out breathing, where there was no fall of the breast, but the air was taken and given, as it were the square blade of a sharp-edged sword, was dreadful to see. She had the look of a risen corpse, recalling some one of the bloody ends of life.

The farmer went on,—

"Bury her! Now you here know the worst. There's my second girl. She's got no stain on her; if people 'll take her for what she is herself. She's idle. But I believe the flesh on her bones she'd wear away for any one that touched her heart. She's a temper. But she's clean both in body and in spirit, as I believe, and say before my God. I—what I'd pray for is, to see this girl safe. All I have shall go to her. That is, to the man who will—won't be ashamed—marry her, I mean!"

The tide of his harshness failed him here, and he began to pick his words, now feeble, now emphatic, but alike wanting in natural expression, for he had reached a point of emotion upon the limits of his nature, and he was now wilfully forcing for misery and humiliation right and left, in part to show what a black star Providence had been over him.

"She'll be grateful. I shall be gone. What disgrace I bring to their union, as father of the other one also, will, I'm bound to hope, be buried with me in my grave; so that this girl's husband shan't have to complain that her character and her working for him ain't enough to cover any harm he's like to think o' the connexion. And he won't be troubled by relationships after that.

"I used to think Pride a bad thing. I thank God we've all got it in our blood—the Flemings. I thank God for that now, I do. We don't face again them as we offend. Not, that is, with the hand out. We go. We're seen no more. And she'll be seen no more. On that, rely.

"I want my girl here not to keep me in the fear of death. For I fear death while she's not safe in somebody's hands—kind, if I can get him for her. Somebody—young or old!"

The farmer lifted his head for the first time, and stared vacantly at Robert.

"I'd marry her," he said, "if I was knowing myself dying now or to-morrow morning, I'd marry her, rather than leave her alone—I'd marry her to that old man, old Gammon."

The farmer pointed to the ceiling. His sombre seriousness cloaked and carried even that suggestive indication to the possible bridegroom's age and habits, and all things associated with him, through the gates of ridicule; and there was no laughter, and no thought of it.

"It stands to reason for me to prefer a young man for her husband. He'll farm the estate, and won't sell it; so that it goes to our blood, if not to a Fleming. If, I mean, he's content to farm soberly, and not play Jack o' Lantern tricks across his own acres. Right in one thing's right, I grant; but don't argue right in all. It's right only in one thing. Young men, when they've made a true hit or so, they're ready to think it's themselves that's right."

This was of course a reminder of the old feud with Robert, and sufficiently showed whom the farmer had in view for a husband to Rhoda, if any doubt existed previously.

Having raised his eyes, his unwonted power of speech abandoned him, and he concluded, wavering in look and in tone,—

"I'd half forgotten her uncle. I've reckoned his riches when I cared for riches. I can't say th' amount; but, all—I've had his word for it—all goes to this—God knows how much!—girl. And he don't hesitate to say she's worth a young man's fancying. May be so. It depends upon ideas mainly, that does. All goes to her. And this farm.—I wish ye good-night."

He gave them no other sign, but walked in his oppressed way quietly to the inner door, and forth, leaving the rest to them.

CHAPTER XIV

BETWEEN RHODA AND ROBERT

The two were together, and all preliminary difficulties had been cleared for Robert to say what he had to say, in a manner to make the saying of it well-nigh impossible. And yet silence might be misinterpreted by her. He would have drawn her to his heart at one sign of tenderness. There came none. The girl was frightfully torn with a great wound of shame. She was the first to speak.

"Do you believe what father says of my sister?"

"That she—?" Robert swallowed the words. "No!" and he made a thunder with his fist.

"No!" She drank up the word. "You do not? No! You know that Dahlia is innocent?"

Rhoda was trembling with a look for the asseveration; her pale face eager as a cry for life; but the answer did not come at once hotly as her passion for it demanded. She grew rigid, murmuring faintly: "speak! Do speak!"

His eyes fell away from hers. Sweet love would have wrought in him to think as she thought, but she kept her heart closed from him, and he stood sadly judicial, with a conscience of his own, that would not permit him to declare Dahlia innocent, for he had long been imagining the reverse.

Rhoda pressed her hands convulsively, moaning, "Oh!" down a short deep breath.

"Tell me what has happened?" said Robert, made mad by that reproachful agony of her voice. "I'm in the dark. I'm not equal to you all. If Dahlia's sister wants one to stand up for her, and defend her, whatever she has done or not done, ask me. Ask me, and I'll revenge her. Here am I, and I know nothing, and you despise me because—don't think me rude or unkind. This hand is yours, if you will. Come, Rhoda. Or, let me hear the case, and I'll satisfy you as best I can. Feel for her? I feel for her as you do. You don't want me to stand a liar to your question? How can I speak?"

A woman's instinct at red heat pierces the partial disingenuousness which Robert could only have avoided by declaring the doubts he entertained. Rhoda desired simply to be supported by his conviction of her sister's innocence, and she had scorn of one who would not chivalrously advance upon the risks of right and wrong, and rank himself prime champion of a woman belied, absent, and so helpless. Besides, there was but one virtue possible in Rhoda's ideas, as regarded Dahlia: to oppose facts, if necessary, and have her innocent perforce, and fight to the death them that dared cast slander on the beloved head.

Her keen instinct served her so far.

His was alive when she refused to tell him what had taken place during their visit to London.

She felt that a man would judge evil of the circumstances. Her father and her uncle had done so: she felt that Robert would. Love for him would have prompted her to confide in him absolutely. She was not softened by love; there was no fire on her side to melt and make them run in one stream, and they could not meet.

"Then, if you will not tell me," said Robert, "say what you think of your father's proposal? He meant that I may ask you to be my wife. He used to fancy I cared for your sister. That's false. I care for her—yes; as my sister too; and here is my hand to do my utmost for her, but I love you, and I've loved you for some time. I'd be proud to marry you and help on with the old farm. You don't love me yet—which is a pretty hard thing for me to see to be certain of. But I love you, and I trust you. I like the stuff you're made of— and nice stuff I'm talking to a young woman," he added, wiping his forehead at the idea of the fair and flattering addresses young women expect when they are being wooed.

As it was, Rhoda listened with savage contempt of his idle talk. Her brain was beating at the mystery and misery wherein Dahlia lay engulfed. She had no understanding for Robert's sentimentality, or her father's requisition. Some answer had to be given, and she said,—

"I'm not likely to marry a man who supposes he has anything to pardon."

"I don't suppose it," cried Robert.

"You heard what father said."

"I heard what he said, but I don't think the same. What has Dahlia to do with you?"

He was proceeding to rectify this unlucky sentence. All her covert hostility burst out on it.

"My sister?—what has my sister to do with me?—you mean!—you mean—you can only mean that we are to be separated and thought of as two people; and we are one, and will be till we die. I feel my sister's hand in mine, though she's away and lost. She is my darling for ever and ever. We're one!"

A spasm of anguish checked the girl.

"I mean," Robert resumed steadily, "that her conduct, good or bad, doesn't touch you. If it did, it'd be the same to me. I ask you to take me for your husband. Just reflect on what your father said, Rhoda."

The horrible utterance her father's lips had been guilty of flashed through her, filling her with mastering vindictiveness, now that she had a victim.

"Yes! I'm to take a husband to remind me of what he said."

Robert eyed her sharpened mouth admiringly; her defence of her sister had excited his esteem, wilfully though she rebutted his straightforward earnestness and he had a feeling also for the easy turns of her neck, and the confident poise of her figure.

"Ha! well!" he interjected, with his eyebrows queerly raised, so that she could make nothing of his look. It seemed half maniacal, it was so ridged with bright eagerness.

"By heaven! the task of taming you—that's the blessing I'd beg for in my prayers! Though you were as wild as a cat of the woods, by heaven! I'd rather have the taming of you than go about with a leash of quiet"—he checked himself—"companions."

Such was the sudden roll of his tongue, that she was lost in the astounding lead he had taken, and stared.

"You're the beauty to my taste, and devil is what I want in a woman! I can make something out of a girl with a temper like yours. You don't know me, Miss Rhoda. I'm what you reckon a good young man. Isn't that it?"

Robert drew up with a very hard smile.

"I would to God I were! Mind, I feel for you about your sister. I like you the better for holding to her through thick and thin. But my sheepishness has gone, and I tell you I'll have you whether you will or no. I can help you and you can help me. I've lived here as if I had no more fire in me than old Gammon snoring on his pillow up aloft; and who kept me to it? Did you see I never touched liquor? What did you guess from that?—that I was a mild sort of fellow? So I am: but I haven't got that reputation in other parts. Your father 'd like me to marry you, and I'm ready. Who kept me to work, so that I might learn to farm, and be a man, and be able to take a wife? I came here—I'll tell you how. I was a useless dog. I ran from home and served as a trooper. An old aunt of mine left me a little money, which just woke me up and gave me a lift of what conscience I had, and I bought myself out.

"I chanced to see your father's advertisement—came, looked at you all, and liked you—brought my traps and settled among you, and lived like a good young man. I like peace and orderliness, I find. I always thought I did, when I was dancing like mad to hell. I know I do now, and you're the girl to keep me to it. I've learnt that much by degrees. With any other, I should have been playing the fool, and going my old ways, long ago. I should have wrecked her, and drunk to forget. You're my match. By-and-by you'll know, me yours! You never gave me, or anybody else that I've seen, sly sidelooks.

"Come! I'll speak out now I'm at work. I thought you at some girl's games in the Summer. You went out one day to meet a young gentleman. Offence or no offence, I speak and you listen. You did go out. I was in love with you then, too. I saw London had been doing its mischief. I was down about it. I felt that he would make nothing of you, but I chose to take the care of you, and you've hated me ever since.

"That Mr. Algernon Blancove's a rascal. Stop! You'll say as much as you like presently. I give you a warning—the man's a rascal. I didn't play spy on your acts, but your looks. I can read a face like yours, and it's my home, my home!—by heaven, it is. Now, Rhoda, you know a little more of me. Perhaps I'm more of a man than you thought. Marry another, if you will; but I'm the man for you, and I know it, and you'll go wrong if you don't too. Come! let your father sleep well. Give me your hand."

All through this surprising speech of Robert's, which was a revelation of one who had been previously dark to her, she had steeled her spirit as she felt herself being borne upon unexpected rapids, and she marvelled when she found her hand in his.

Dismayed, as if caught in a trap, she said,—

"You know I've no love for you at all."

"None—no doubt," he answered.

The fit of verbal energy was expended, and he had become listless, though he looked frankly at her and assumed the cheerfulness which was failing within him.

"I wish to remain as I am," she faltered, surprised again by the equally astonishing recurrence of humility, and more spiritually subdued by it. "I've no heart for a change. Father will understand. I am safe."

She ended with a cry: "Oh! my dear, my own sister! I wish you were safe. Get her here to me and I'll do what I can, if you're not hard on her. She's so beautiful, she can't do wrong. My Dahlia's in some trouble. Mr. Robert, you might really be her friend?"

"Drop the Mister," said Robert.

"Father will listen to you," she pleaded. "You won't leave us? Tell him you know I am safe. But I haven't a feeling of any kind while my sister's away. I will call you Robert, if you like." She reached her hand forth.

"That's right," he said, taking it with a show of heartiness: "that's a beginning, I suppose."

She shrank a little in his sensitive touch, and he added: "Oh never fear. I've spoken out, and don't do the thing too often. Now you know me, that's enough. I trust you, so trust me. I'll talk to your father. I've got a dad of my own, who isn't so easily managed. You and I, Rhoda—we're about the right size for a couple. There—don't be frightened! I was only thinking—I'll let go your hand in a minute. If Dahlia's to be found, I'll find her. Thank you for that squeeze. You'd wake a dead man to life, if you wanted to. To-morrow I set about the business. That's settled. Now your hand's loose. Are you going to say good night? You must give me your hand again for that. What a rough fellow I must seem to you! Different from the man you thought I was? I'm just what you choose to make me, Rhoda; remember that. By heaven! go at once, for you're an armful—"

She took a candle and started for the door.

"Aha! you can look fearful as a doe. Out! make haste!"

In her hurry at his speeding gestures, the candle dropped; she was going to pick it up, but as he approached, she stood away frightened.

"One kiss, my girl," he said. "Don't keep me jealous as fire. One! and I'm a plighted man. One!—or I shall swear you know what kisses are. Why did you go out to meet that fellow? Do you think there's no danger in it? Doesn't he go about boasting of it now, and saying—that girl! But kiss me and I'll forget it; I'll forgive you. Kiss me only once, and I shall be certain you don't care for him. That's the thought maddens me outright. I can't bear it now I've seen you look soft. I'm stronger than you, mind." He caught her by the waist.

"Yes," Rhoda gasped, "you are. You are only a brute."

"A brute's a lucky dog, then, for I've got you!"

"Will you touch me?"

"You're in my power."

"It's a miserable thing, Robert."

"Why don't you struggle, my girl? I shall kiss you in a minute."

"You're never my friend again."

"I'm not a gentleman, I suppose!"

"Never! after this."

"It isn't done. And first you're like a white rose, and next you're like a red. Will you submit?"

"Oh! shame!" Rhoda uttered.

"Because I'm not a gentleman?"

"You are not."

"So, if I could make you a lady—eh? the lips 'd be ready in a trice. You think of being made a lady—a lady!"

His arm relaxed in the clutch of her figure.

She got herself free, and said: "We saw Mr. Blancove at the theatre with Dahlia."

It was her way of meeting his accusation that she had cherished an ambitious feminine dream.

He, to hide a confusion that had come upon him, was righting the fallen candle.

"Now I know you can be relied on; you can defend yourself," he said, and handed it to her, lighted. "You keep your kisses for this or that young gentleman. Quite right. You really can defend yourself. That's all I was up to. So let us hear that you forgive me. The door's open. You won't be bothered by me any more; and don't hate me overmuch."

"You might have learned to trust me without insulting me, Robert," she said.

"Do you fancy I'd take such a world of trouble for a kiss of your lips, sweet as they are?"

His blusterous beginning ended in a speculating glance at her mouth.

She saw it would be wise to accept him in his present mood, and go; and with a gentle "Good night," that might sound like pardon, she passed through the doorway.

CHAPTER XV

A VISIT TO WREXBY HALL

Next day, while Squire Blancove was superintending the laying down of lines for a new carriage drive in his park, as he walked slowly up the green slope he perceived Farmer Fleming, supported by a tall young man; and when the pair were nearer, he had the gratification of noting likewise that the worthy yeoman was very much bent, as with an acute attack of his well-known chronic malady of a want of money.

The squire greatly coveted the freehold of Queen Anne's Farm. He had made offers to purchase it till he was tired, and had gained for himself the credit of being at the bottom of numerous hypothetical cabals to injure and oust the farmer from his possession. But if Naboth came with his vineyard in his hand, not even Wrexby's rector (his quarrel with whom haunted every turn in his life) could quote Scripture against him for taking it at a proper valuation.

The squire had employed his leisure time during service in church to discover a text that might be used against him in the event of the farmer's reduction to a state of distress, and his, the squire's, making the most of it. On the contrary, according to his heathenish reading of some of the patriarchal doings, there was more to be said in his favour than not, if he increased his territorial property: nor could he, throughout the Old Testament, hit on one sentence that looked like a personal foe to his projects, likely to fit into the mouth of the rector of Wrexby.

"Well, farmer," he said, with cheerful familiarity, "winter crops looking well? There's a good show of green in the fields from my windows, as good as that land of yours will allow in heavy seasons."

To this the farmer replied, "I've not heart or will to be round about, squire. If you'll listen to me—here, or where you give command."

"Has it anything to do with pen and paper, Fleming? In that case you'd better be in my study," said the squire.

"I don't know that it have. I don't know that it have." The farmer sought Robert's face.

"Best where there's no chance of interruption," Robert counselled, and lifted his hat to the squire.

"Eh? Well, you see I'm busy." The latter affected a particular indifference, that in such cases, when well acted (as lords of money can do—squires equally with usurers), may be valued at hundreds of pounds in the pocket. "Can't you put it off? Come again to-morrow."

"To-morrow's a day too late," said the farmer, gravely. Whereto replying, "Oh! well, come along in, then," the squire led the way.

"You're two to one, if it's a transaction," he said, nodding to Robert to close the library door. "Take seats. Now then, what is it? And if I make a face, just oblige me by thinking nothing about it, for my gout's beginning to settle in the leg again, and shoots like an electric telegraph from purgatory."

He wheezed and lowered himself into his arm-chair; but the farmer and Robert remained standing, and the farmer spoke:—

"My words are going to be few, squire. I've got a fact to bring to your knowledge, and a question to ask."

Surprise, exaggerated on his face by a pain he had anticipated, made the squire glare hideously.

"Confound it, that's what they say to a prisoner in the box. Here's a murder committed:—Are you the guilty person? Fact and question! Well, out with 'em, both together."

"A father ain't responsible for the sins of his children," said the farmer.

"Well, that's a fact," the squire emphasized. "I've always maintained it; but, if you go to your church, farmer—small blame to you if you don't; that fellow who preaches there—I forget his name—stands out for just the other way. You are responsible, he swears. Pay your son's debts, and don't groan over it:— He spent the money, and you're the chief debtor; that's his teaching. Well: go on. What's your question?"

"A father's not to be held responsible for the sins of his children, squire. My daughter's left me. She's away. I saw my daughter at the theatre in London. She saw me, and saw her sister with me. She disappeared. It's a hard thing for a man to be saying of his own flesh and blood. She disappeared. She went, knowing her father's arms open to her. She was in company with your son."

The squire was thrumming on the arm of his chair. He looked up vaguely, as if waiting for the question to follow, but meeting the farmer's settled eyes, he cried, irritably, "Well, what's that to me?"

"What's that to you, squire?"

"Are you going to make me out responsible for my son's conduct? My son's a rascal—everybody knows that. I paid his debts once, and I've finished with him. Don't come to me about the fellow. If there's a greater curse than the gout, it's a son."

"My girl," said the farmer, "she's my flesh and blood, and I must find her, and I'm here to ask you to make your son tell me where she's to be found. Leave me to deal with that young man—leave you me! but I want my girl."

"But I can't give her to you," roared the squire, afflicted by his two great curses at once. "Why do you come to me? I'm not responsible for the doings of the dog. I'm sorry for you, if that's what you want to know. Do you mean to say that my son took her away from your house?"

"I don't do so, Mr. Blancove. I'm seeking for my daughter, and I see her in company with your son."

"Very well, very well," said the squire; "that shows his habits; I can't say more. But what has it got to do with me?"

The farmer looked helplessly at Robert.

"No, no," the squire sung out, "no interlopers, no interpreting here. I listen to you. My son—your daughter. I understand that, so far. It's between us two. You've got a daughter who's gone wrong somehow: I'm sorry to hear it. I've got a son who never went right; and it's no comfort to me, upon my word. If you were to see the bills and the letters I receive! but I don't carry my grievances to my neighbours. I should think, Fleming, you'd do best, if it's advice you're seeking, to keep it quiet. Don't make a noise about it. Neighbours' gossip I find pretty well the worst thing a man has to bear, who's unfortunate enough to own children."

The farmer bowed his head with that bitter humbleness which characterized his reception of the dealings of Providence toward him.

"My neighbours 'll soon be none at all," he said. "Let 'em talk. I'm not abusing you, Mr. Blancove. I'm a broken man: but I want my poor lost girl, and, by God, responsible for your son or not, you must help me to find her. She may be married, as she says. She mayn't be. But I must find her."

The squire hastily seized a scrap of paper on the table and wrote on it.

"There!" he handed the paper to the farmer; "that's my son's address, 'Boyne's Bank, City, London.' Go to him there, and you'll find him perched on a stool, and a good drubbing won't hurt him. You've my hearty permission, I can assure you: you may say so. 'Boyne's Bank.' Anybody will show you the place. He's a rascally clerk in the office, and precious useful, I dare swear. Thrash him, if you think fit."

"Ay," said the farmer, "Boyne's Bank. I've been there already. He's absent from work, on a visit down into Hampshire, one of the young gentlemen informed me; Fairly Park was the name of the place: but I came to you, Mr. Blancove; for you're his father."

"Well now, my good Fleming, I hope you think I'm properly punished for that fact." The squire stood up with horrid contortions.

Robert stepped in advance of the farmer.

"Pardon me, sir," he said, though the squire met his voice with a prodigious frown; "this would be an ugly business to talk about, as you observe. It would hurt Mr. Fleming in these parts of the country, and he would leave it, if he thought fit; but you can't separate your name from your son's—begging you to excuse the liberty I take in mentioning it—not in public: and your son has the misfortune to be well known in one or two places where he was quartered when in the cavalry. That matter of the jeweller—"

"Hulloa," the squire exclaimed, in a perturbation.

"Why, sir, I know all about it, because I was a trooper in the regiment your son, Mr. Algernon Blancove, quitted: and his name, if I may take leave to remark so, won't bear printing. How far he's guilty before Mr. Fleming we can't tell as yet; but if Mr. Fleming holds him guilty of an offence, your son 'll bear the consequences, and what's done will be done thoroughly. Proper counsel will be taken, as needn't be said. Mr. Fleming applied to you first, partly for your sake as well as his own. He can find friends, both to advise and to aid him."

"You mean, sir," thundered the squire, "that he can find enemies of mine, like that infernal fellow who goes by the title of Reverend, down below there. That'll do, that will do; there's some extortion at the bottom of this. You're putting on a screw."

"We're putting on a screw, sir," said Robert, coolly.

"Not a penny will you get by it."

Robert flushed with heat of blood.

"You don't wish you were a young man half so much as I do just now," he remarked, and immediately they were in collision, for the squire made a rush to the bell-rope, and Robert stopped him. "We're going," he said; "we don't want man-servants to show us the way out. Now mark me, Mr. Blancove, you've insulted an old man in his misery: you shall suffer for it, and so shall your son, whom I know to be a rascal worthy of transportation. You think Mr. Fleming came to you for money. Look at this old man, whose only fault is that he's too full of kindness; he came to you just for help to find his daughter, with whom your rascal of a son was last seen, and you swear he's come to rob you of money. Don't you know yourself a fattened cur, squire though you be, and called gentleman? England's a good place, but you make England a hell to men of spirit. Sit in your chair, and don't ever you, or any of you cross my path; and speak a word to your servants before we're out of the house, and I stand in the hall and give 'em your son's history, and make Wrexby stink in your nostril, till you're glad enough to fly out of it. Now, Mr. Fleming, there's no more to be done here; the game lies elsewhere."

Robert took the farmer by the arm, and was marching out of the enemy's territory in good order, when the squire, who had presented many changeing aspects of astonishment and rage, arrested them with a call. He began to say that he spoke to Mr. Fleming, and not to the young ruffian of a bully whom the farmer had brought there: and then asked in a very reasonable manner what he could do—what measures he could adopt to aid the farmer in finding his child. Robert hung modestly in the background while the farmer laboured on with a few sentences to explain the case, and finally the squire said, that his foot permitting (it was an almost pathetic reference to the weakness of flesh), he would go down to Fairly on the day following and have a personal interview with his son, and set things right, as far as it lay in his power, though he was by no means answerable for a young man's follies.

He was a little frightened by the farmer's having said that Dahlia, according to her own declaration was married, and therefore himself the more anxious to see Mr. Algernon, and hear the truth from his estimable offspring, whom he again stigmatized as a curse terrible to him as his gouty foot, but nevertheless just as little to be left to his own devices. The farmer bowed to these observations; as also when the squire counselled him, for his own sake, not to talk of his misfortune all over the parish.

"I'm not a likely man for that, squire; but there's no telling where gossips get their crumbs. It's about. It's about."

"About my son?" cried the squire.

"My daughter!"

"Oh, well, good-day," the squire resumed more cheerfully. "I'll go down to Fairly, and you can't ask more than that."

When the farmer was out of the house and out of hearing, he rebuked Robert for the inconsiderate rashness of his behaviour, and pointed out how he, the farmer, by being patient and peaceful, had attained to the object of his visit. Robert laughed without defending himself.

"I shouldn't ha' known ye," the farmer repeated frequently; "I shouldn't ha' known ye, Robert."

"No, I'm a trifle changed, may be," Robert agreed. "I'm going to claim a holiday of you. I've told Rhoda that if Dahlia's to be found, I'll find her, and I can't do it by sticking here. Give me three weeks. The land's asleep. Old Gammon can hardly turn a furrow the wrong way. There's nothing to do, which is his busiest occupation, when he's not interrupted at it."

"Mas' Gammon's a rare old man," said the farmer, emphatically.

"So I say. Else, how would you see so many farms flourishing!"

"Come, Robert: you hit th' old man hard; you should learn to forgive."

"So I do, and a telling blow's a man's best road to charity. I'd forgive the squire and many another, if I had them within two feet of my fist."

"Do you forgive my girl Rhoda for putting of you off?"

Robert screwed in his cheek.

"Well, yes, I do," he said. "Only it makes me feel thirsty, that's all."

The farmer remembered this when they had entered the farm.

"Our beer's so poor, Robert," he made apology; "but Rhoda shall get you some for you to try, if you like. Rhoda, Robert's solemn thirsty."

"Shall I?" said Rhoda, and she stood awaiting his bidding.

"I'm not a thirsty subject," replied Robert. "You know I've avoided drink of any kind since I set foot on this floor. But when I drink," he pitched his voice to a hard, sparkling heartiness, "I drink a lot, and the stuff must be strong. I'm very much obliged to you, Miss Rhoda, for what you're so kind as to offer to satisfy my thirst, and you can't give better, and don't suppose that I'm complaining; but your father's right, it is rather weak, and wouldn't break the tooth of my thirst if I drank at it till Gammon left off thinking about his dinner."

With that he announced his approaching departure.

The farmer dropped into his fireside chair, dumb and spiritless. A shadow was over the house, and the inhabitants moved about their domestic occupations silent as things that feel the thunder-cloud. Before sunset Robert was gone on his long walk to the station, and Rhoda felt a woman's great envy of the liberty of a man, who has not, if it pleases him not, to sit and eat grief among familiar images, in a home that furnishes its altar-flame.

CHAPTER XVI

AT FAIRLY PARK

Fairly, Lord Elling's seat in Hampshire, lay over the Warbeach river; a white mansion among great oaks, in view of the summer sails and winter masts of the yachting squadron. The house was ruled, during the congregation of the Christmas guests, by charming Mrs. Lovell, who relieved the invalid Lady of the house of the many serious cares attending the reception of visitors, and did it all with ease. Under her sovereignty the place was delightful, and if it was by repute pleasanter to young men than to any other class, it will be admitted that she satisfied those who are loudest in giving tongue to praise.

Edward and Algernon journeyed down to Fairly together, after the confidence which the astute young lawyer had been compelled to repose in his cousin. Sir William Blancove was to be at Fairly, and it was at his father's pointed request that Edward had accepted Mrs. Lovell's invitation. Half in doubt as to the lady's disposition toward him, Edward eased his heart with sneers at the soft, sanguinary graciousness they were to expect, and racked mythology for spiteful comparisons; while Algernon vehemently defended her with a battering fire of British adjectives in superlative. He as much as hinted, under instigation, that he was entitled to defend her; and his claim being by-and-by yawningly allowed by Edward, and presuming that he now had Edward in his power and need not fear him, he exhibited his weakness in the guise of a costly gem, that he intended to present to Mrs. Lovell—an opal set in a cross pendant from a necklace; a really fine opal, coquetting with the lights of every gem that is known: it shot succinct red flashes, and green, and yellow; the emerald, the amethyst, the topaz lived in it, and a remote ruby; it was veined with lightning hues, and at times it slept in a milky cloud, innocent of fire, quite maidenlike.

"That will suit her," was Edward's remark.

"I didn't want to get anything common," said Algernon, making the gem play before his eyes.

"A pretty stone," said Edward.

"Do you think so?"

"Very pretty indeed."

"Harlequin pattern."

"To be presented to Columbine!"

"The Harlequin pattern is of the best sort, you know. Perhaps you like the watery ones best? This is fresh from Russia. There's a set I've my eye on. I shall complete it in time. I want Peggy Lovell to wear the jolliest opals in the world. It's rather nice, isn't it?"

"It's a splendid opal," said Edward.

"She likes opals," said Algernon.

"She'll take your meaning at once," said Edward.

"How? I'll be hanged if I know what my meaning is, Ned."

"Don't you know the signification of your gift?"

"Not a bit."

"Oh! you'll be Oriental when you present it."

"The deuce I shall!"

"It means, 'You're the prettiest widow in the world.'"

"So she is. I'll be right there, old boy."

"And, 'You're a rank, right-down widow, and no mistake; you're everything to everybody; not half so innocent as you look: you're green as jealousy, red as murder, yellow as jaundice, and put on the whiteness of a virgin when you ought to be blushing like a penitent.' In short, 'You have no heart of your own, and you pretend to possess half a dozen: you're devoid of one steady beam, and play tricks with every scale of colour: you're an arrant widow, and that's what you are.' An eloquent gift, Algy."

"Gad, if it means all that, it'll be rather creditable to me," said Algernon. "Do opals mean widows?"

"Of course," was the answer.

"Well, she is a widow, and I suppose she's going to remain one, for she's had lots of offers. If I marry a girl I shall never like her half as much as Peggy Lovell. She's done me up for every other woman living. She never lets me feel a fool with her; and she has a way, by Jove, of looking at me, and letting me know she's up to my thoughts and isn't angry. What's the use of my thinking of her at all? She'd never go to the Colonies, and live in a log but and make cheeses, while I tore about on horseback gathering cattle."

"I don't think she would," observed Edward, emphatically; "I don't think she would."

"And I shall never have money. Confound stingy parents! It's a question whether I shall get Wrexby: there's no entail. I'm heir to the governor's temper and his gout, I dare say. He'll do as he likes with the estate. I call it beastly unfair."

Edward asked how much the opal had cost.

"Oh, nothing," said Algernon; "that is, I never pay for jewellery."

Edward was curious to know how he managed to obtain it.

"Why, you see," Algernon explained, "they, the jewellers—I've got two or three in hand—the fellows are acquainted with my position, and they speculate on my expectations. There is no harm in that if they like it. I look at their trinkets, and say, 'I've no money;' and they say, 'Never mind;' and I don't mind much. The understanding is, that I pay them when I inherit."

"In gout and bad temper?"

"Gad, if I inherit nothing else, they'll have lots of that for indemnification. It's a good system, Ned; it enables a young fellow like me to get through the best years of his life—which I take to be his youth—

without that squalid poverty bothering him. You can make presents, and wear a pin or a ring, if it takes your eye. You look well, and you make yourself agreeable; and I see nothing to complain of in that."

"The jewellers, then, have established an institution to correct one of the errors of Providence."

"Oh! put it in your long-winded way, if you like," said Algernon; "all I know is, that I should often have wanted a five-pound note, if—that is, if I hadn't happened to be dressed like a gentleman. With your prospects, Ned, I should propose to charming Peggy tomorrow morning early. We mustn't let her go out of the family. If I can't have her, I'd rather you would."

"You forget the incumbrances on one side," said Edward, his face darkening.

"Oh! that's all to be managed," Algernon rallied him. "Why, Ned, you'll have twenty thousand a-year, if you have a penny; and you'll go into Parliament, and give dinners, and a woman like Peggy Lovell 'd intrigue for you like the deuce."

"A great deal too like," Edward muttered.

"As for that pretty girl," continued Algernon; but Edward peremptorily stopped all speech regarding Dahlia. His desire was, while he made holiday, to shut the past behind a brazen gate; which being communicated sympathetically to his cousin, the latter chimed to it in boisterous shouts of anticipated careless jollity at Fairly Park, crying out how they would hunt and snap fingers at Jews, and all mortal sorrows, and have a fortnight, or three weeks, perhaps a full month, of the finest life possible to man, with good horses, good dinners, good wines, good society, at command, and a queen of a woman to rule and order everything. Edward affected a disdainful smile at the prospect; but was in reality the weaker of the two in his thirst for it.

They arrived at Fairly in time to dress for dinner, and in the drawing-room Mrs. Lovell sat to receive them. She looked up to Edward's face an imperceptible half-second longer than the ordinary form of welcome accords—one of the looks which are nothing at all when there is no spiritual apprehension between young people, and are so much when there is. To Algernon, who was gazing opals on her, she simply gave her fingers. At her right hand, was Sir John Capes, her antique devotee; a pure milky-white old gentleman, with sparkling fingers, who played Apollo to his Daphne, and was out of breath. Lord Suckling, a boy with a boisterous constitution, and a guardsman, had his place near her left hand, as if ready to seize it at the first whisper of encouragement or opportunity. A very little lady of seventeen, Miss Adeline Gosling, trembling with shyness under a cover of demureness, fell to Edward's lot to conduct down to dinner, where he neglected her disgracefully. His father, Sir William, was present at the table, and Lord Elling, with whom he was in repute as a talker and a wit. Quickened with his host's renowned good wine (and the bare renown of a wine is inspiriting), Edward pressed to be brilliant. He had an epigrammatic turn, and though his mind was prosaic when it ran alone, he could appear inventive and fanciful with the rub of other minds. Now, at a table where good talking is cared for, the triumphs of the excelling tongue are not for a moment to be despised, even by the huge appetite of the monster Vanity. For a year, Edward had abjured this feast. Before the birds appeared and the champagne had ceased to make its circle, he felt that he was now at home again, and that the term of his wandering away from society was one of folly. He felt the joy and vigour of a creature returned to his element. Why had he ever quitted it? Already he looked back upon Dahlia from a prodigious distance. He knew that there was something to be smoothed over; something written in the book of facts which had to be smeared out, and he seemed to do it, while he drank the babbling wine and heard himself talk. Not one man at that table, as he reflected, would consider the bond which held him in any serious degree binding. A lady is one thing, and a girl of the class Dahlia had sprung from altogether another. He could not help imagining the sort of appearance she would make there; and the thought even was a momentary clog upon his tongue. How he used to despise these people! Especially he had despised the young men as brainless cowards in regard to their views of women and conduct toward them. All that was changed. He fancied now that they, on the contrary, would despise him, if only they could be aware of the lingering sense he entertained of his being in bondage under a sacred obligation to a farmer's daughter.

But he had one thing to discover, and that was, why Sir William had made it a peculiar request that he should come to meet him here. Could the desire possibly be to reconcile him with Mrs. Lovell? His common sense rejected the idea at once: Sir William boasted of her wit and tact, and admired her beauty, but Edward remembered his having responded tacitly to his estimate of her character, and Sir William was not the man to court the alliance of his son with a woman like Mrs. Lovell. He perceived that his father and the fair widow frequently took counsel together. Edward laughed at the notion that the grave senior had himself become fascinated, but without utterly scouting it, until he found that the little lady whom he had led to dinner the first day, was an heiress; and from that, and other indications, he exactly divined the nature of his father's provident wishes. But this revelation rendered Mrs. Lovell's behaviour yet more extraordinary. Could it be credited that she was abetting Sir William's schemes with all her woman's craft? "Has she," thought Edward, "become so indifferent to me as to care for my welfare?" He determined to put her to the test. He made love to Adeline Gosling. Nothing that he did disturbed the impenetrable complacency of Mrs. Lovell. She threw them together as she shuffled the guests. She really seemed to him quite indifferent enough to care for his welfare. It was a point in the mysterious ways of women, or of widows, that Edward's experience had not yet come across. All the parties immediately concerned were apparently so desperately acquiescing in his suit, that he soon grew uneasy. Mrs. Lovell not only shuffled him into places with the raw heiress, but with the child's mother; of whom he spoke to Algernon as of one too strongly breathing of matrimony to appease the cravings of an eclectic mind.

"Make the path clear for me, then," said Algernon, "if you don't like the girl. Pitch her tales about me. Say, I've got a lot in me, though I don't let it out. The game's up between you and Peggy Lovell, that's clear. She don't forgive you, my boy."

"Ass!" muttered Edward, seeing by the light of his perception, that he was too thoroughly forgiven.

A principal charm of the life at Fairly to him was that there was no one complaining. No one looked reproach at him. If a lady was pale and reserved, she did not seem to accuse him, and to require coaxing. All faces here were as light as the flying moment, and did not carry the shadowy weariness of years, like that burdensome fair face in the London lodging-house, to which the Fates had terribly attached themselves. So, he was gay. He closed, as it were, a black volume, and opened a new and a bright one. Young men easily fancy that they may do this, and that when the black volume is shut the tide is stopped. Saying, "I was a fool," they believe they have put an end to the foolishness. What father teaches them that a human act once set in motion flows on for ever to the great account? Our deathlessness is in what we do, not in what we are. Comfortable Youth thinks otherwise.

The days at a well-ordered country-house, where a divining lady rules, speed to the measure of a waltz, in harmonious circles, dropping like crystals into the gulfs of Time, and appearing to write nothing in his book. Not a single hinge of existence is heard to creak. There is no after-dinner bill. You are waited on, without being elbowed by the humanity of your attendants. It is a civilized Arcadia. Only, do not desire, that you may not envy. Accept humbly what rights of citizenship are accorded to you upon entering. Discard the passions when you cross the threshold. To breathe and to swallow merely, are the duties which should prescribe your conduct; or, such is the swollen condition of the animal in this enchanted region, that the spirit of man becomes dangerously beset.

Edward breathed and swallowed, and never went beyond the prescription, save by talking. No other junior could enter the library, without encountering the scorn of his elders; so he enjoyed the privilege of hearing all the scandal, and his natural cynicism was plentifully fed. It was more of a school to him than he knew.

These veterans, in their arm-chairs, stripped the bloom from life, and showed it to be bare bones: They took their wisdom for an experience of the past: they were but giving their sensations in the present. Not to perceive this, is Youth's, error when it hears old gentlemen talking at their ease.

On the third morning of their stay at Fairly, Algernon came into Edward's room with a letter in his hand.

"There! read that!" he said. "It isn't ill-luck; it's infernal persecution! What, on earth!—why, I took a close cab to the station. You saw me get out of it. I'll swear no creditor of mine knew I was leaving London. My belief is that the fellows who give credit have spies about at every railway terminus in the kingdom. They won't give me three days' peace. It's enough to disgust any man with civilized life; on my soul, it is!"

Edward glanced at the superscription of the letter. "Not posted," he remarked.

"No; delivered by some confounded bailiff, who's been hounding me."

"Bailiffs don't generally deal in warnings."

"Will you read it!" Algernon shouted.

The letter ran thus:—

"Mr. Algernon Blancove,—

"The writer of this intends taking the first opportunity of meeting you, and gives you warning, you will have to answer his question with a Yes or a No; and speak from your conscience. The respectfulness of his behaviour to you as a gentleman will depend upon that."

Algernon followed his cousin's eye down to the last letter in the page.

"What do you think of it?" he asked eagerly.

Edward's broad thin-lined brows were drawn down in gloom. Mastering some black meditation in his brain, he answered Algernon's yells for an opinion,—

"I think—well, I think bailiffs have improved in their manners, and show you they are determined to belong to the social march in an age of universal progress. Nothing can be more comforting."

"But, suppose this fellow comes across me?"

"Don't know him."

"Suppose he insists on knowing me?"

"Don't know yourself."

"Yes; but hang it! if he catches hold of me?"

"Shake him off."

"Suppose he won't let go?"

"Cut him with your horsewhip."

"You think it's about a debt, then?"

"Intimidation, evidently."

"I shall announce to him that the great Edward Blancove is not to be intimidated. You'll let me borrow your name, old Ned. I've stood by you in my time. As for leaving Fairly, I tell you I can't. It's too delightful to be near Peggy Lovell."

Edward smiled with a peculiar friendliness, and Algernon went off, very well contented with his cousin.

CHAPTER XVII

A YEOMAN OF THE OLD BREED

Within a mile of Fairly Park lay the farm of another yeoman; but he was of another character. The Hampshireman was a farmer of renown in his profession; fifth of a family that had cultivated a small domain of one hundred and seventy acres with sterling profit, and in a style to make Sutton the model of a perfect farm throughout the country. Royal eyes had inspected his pigs approvingly; Royal wits had taken hints from Jonathan Eccles in matters agricultural; and it was his comforting joke that he had taught his Prince good breeding. In return for the service, his Prince had transformed a lusty Radical into a devoted Royalist. Framed on the walls of his parlours were letters from his Prince, thanking him for specimen seeds and worthy counsel: veritable autograph letters of the highest value. The Prince had steamed up the salt river, upon which the Sutton harvests were mirrored, and landed on a spot marked in honour of the event by a broad grey stone; and from that day Jonathan Eccles stood on a pinnacle of pride, enabling him to see horizons of despondency hitherto unknown to him. For he had a son, and the son was a riotous devil, a most wild young fellow, who had no taste for a farmer's life, and openly declared his determination not to perpetuate the Sutton farm in the hands of the Eccleses, by running off one day and entering the ranks of the British army.

Those framed letters became melancholy objects for contemplation, when Jonathan thought that no posterity of his would point them out gloryingly in emulation. Man's aim is to culminate; but it is the saddest thing in the world to feel that we have accomplished it. Mr. Eccles shrugged with all the philosophy he could summon, and transferred his private disappointment to his country, whose agricultural day was, he said, doomed. "We shall be beaten by those Yankees." He gave Old England twenty years of continued pre-eminence (due to the impetus of the present generation of Englishmen), and then, said he, the Yankees will flood the market. No more green pastures in Great Britain; no pretty clean-footed animals; no yellow harvests; but huge chimney pots everywhere; black earth under black vapour, and smoke-begrimed faces. In twenty years' time, sooty England was to be a gigantic manufactory, until the Yankees beat us out of that field as well; beyond which Jonathan Eccles did not care to spread any distinct border of prophecy; merely thanking the Lord that he should then be under grass. The decay of our glory was to be edged with blood; Jonathan admitted that there would be stuff in the fallen race to deliver a sturdy fight before they went to their doom.

For this prodigious curse, England had to thank young Robert, the erratic son of Jonathan.

It was now two years since Robert had inherited a small legacy of money from an aunt, and spent it in waste, as the farmer bitterly supposed. He was looking at some immense seed-melons in his garden, lying about in morning sunshine—a new feed for sheep, of his own invention,—when the call of the wanderer saluted his ears, and he beheld his son Robert at the gate.

"Here I am, sir," Robert sang out from the exterior.

"Stay there, then," was his welcome.

They were alike in their build and in their manner of speech. The accost and the reply sounded like reports from the same pistol. The old man was tall, broad-shouldered, and muscular—a grey edition of the son, upon whose disorderly attire he cast a glance, while speaking, with settled disgust. Robert's necktie streamed loose; his hair was uncombed; a handkerchief dangled from his pocket. He had the look of the prodigal, returned with impudence for his portion instead of repentance.

"I can't see how you are, sir, from this distance," said Robert, boldly assuming his privilege to enter.

"Are you drunk?" Jonathan asked, as Robert marched up to him.

"Give me your hand, sir."

"Give me an answer first. Are you drunk?"

Robert tried to force the complacent aspect of a mind unabashed, but felt that he made a stupid show before that clear-headed, virtuously-living old, man of iron nerves. The alternative to flying into a passion, was the looking like a fool.

"Come, father," he said, with a miserable snigger, like a yokel's smile; "here I am at last. I don't say, kill the fatted calf, and take a lesson from Scripture, but give me your hand. I've done no man harm but myself—damned if I've done a mean thing anywhere! and there's no shame to you in shaking your son's hand after a long absence."

Jonathan Eccles kept both hands firmly in his pockets.

"Are you drunk?" he repeated.

Robert controlled himself to answer, "I'm not."

"Well, then, just tell me when you were drunk last."

"This is a pleasant fatherly greeting!" Robert interjected.

"You get no good by fighting shy of a simple question, Mr. Bob," said Jonathan.

Robert cried querulously, "I don't want to fight shy of a simple question."

"Well, then; when were you drunk last? answer me that."

"Last night."

Jonathan drew his hand from his pocket to thump his leg.

"I'd have sworn it!"

All Robert's assurance had vanished in a minute, and he stood like a convicted culprit before his father.

"You know, sir, I don't tell lies. I was drunk last night. I couldn't help it."

"No more could the little boy."

"I was drunk last night. Say, I'm a beast."

"I shan't!" exclaimed Jonathan, making his voice sound as a defence to this vile charge against the brutish character.

"Say, I'm worse than a beast, then," cried Robert, in exasperation. "Take my word that it hasn't happened to me to be in that state for a year and more. Last night I was mad. I can't give you any reasons. I thought I was cured but I've trouble in my mind, and a tide swims you over the shallows—so I felt. Come, sir—father, don't make me mad again."

"Where did you get the liquor?" inquired Jonathan.

"I drank at 'The Pilot.'"

"Ha! there's talk there of 'that damned old Eccles' for a month to come—'the unnatural parent.' How long have you been down here?"

"Eight and twenty hours."

"Eight and twenty hours. When are you going?"

"I want lodging for a night."

"What else?"

"The loan of a horse that'll take a fence."

"Go on."

"And twenty pounds."

"Oh!" said Jonathan. "If farming came as easy to you as face, you'd be a prime agriculturalist. Just what I thought! What's become of that money your aunt Jane was fool enough to bequeath to you?"

"I've spent it."

"Are you a Deserter?"

For a moment Robert stood as if listening, and then white grew his face, and he swayed and struck his hands together. His recent intoxication had unmanned him.

"Go in—go in," said his father in some concern, though wrath was predominant.

"Oh, make your mind quiet about me." Robert dropped his arms. "I'm weakened somehow—damned weak, I am—I feel like a woman when my father asks me if I've been guilty of villany. Desert? I wouldn't desert from the hulks. Hear the worst, and this is the worst: I've got no money—I don't owe a penny, but I haven't got one."

"And I won't give you one," Jonathan appended; and they stood facing one another in silence.

A squeaky voice was heard from the other side of the garden hedge of clipped yew.

"Hi! farmer, is that the missing young man?" and presently a neighbour, by name John Sedgett, came trotting through the gate, and up the garden path.

"I say," he remarked, "here's a rumpus. Here's a bobbery up at Fairly. Oh! Bob Eccles! Bob Eccles! At it again!"

Mr. Sedgett shook his wallet of gossip with an enjoying chuckle. He was a thin-faced creature, rheumy of eye, and drawing his breath as from a well; the ferret of the village for all underlying scandal and tattle, whose sole humanity was what he called pitifully 'a peakin' at his chest, and who had retired from his business of grocer in the village upon the fortune brought to him in the energy and capacity of a third wife to conduct affairs, while he wandered up and down and knitted people together—an estimable office in a land where your house is so grievously your castle.

"What the devil have you got in you now?" Jonathan cried out to him.

Mr. Sedgett was seized by his complaint and demanded commiseration, but, recovering, he chuckled again.

"Oh, Bob Eccles! Don't you never grow older? And the first day down among us again, too. Why, Bob, as a military man, you ought to acknowledge your superiors. Why, Stephen Bilton, the huntsman, says, Bob, you pulled the young gentleman off his horse—you on foot, and him mounted. I'd ha' given pounds to be there. And ladies present! Lord help us! I'm glad you're returned, though. These melons of the farmer's, they're a wonderful invention; people are speaking of 'em right and left, and says, says they, Farmer Eccles, he's best farmer going—Hampshire ought to be proud of him—he's worth two of any others: that they are fine ones! And you're come back to keep 'em up, eh, Bob? Are ye, though, my man?"

"Well, here I am, Mr. Sedgett," said Robert, "and talking to my father."

"Oh! I wouldn't be here to interrupt ye for the world." Mr. Sedgett made a show of retiring, but Jonathan insisted upon his disburdening himself of his tale, saying: "Damn your raw beginnings, Sedgett! What's been up? Nobody can hurt me."

"That they can't, neighbour; nor Bob neither, as far as stand up man to man go. I give him three to one—Bob Eccles! He took 'em when a boy. He may, you know, he may have the law agin him, and by George! if he do—why, a man's no match for the law. No use bein' a hero to the law. The law masters every man alive; and there's law in everything, neighbour Eccles; eh, sir? Your friend, the Prince, owns to it, as much as you or me. But, of course, you know what Bob's been doing. What I dropped in to ask was, why did ye do it, Bob? Why pull the young gentleman off his horse? I'd ha' given pounds to be there!"

"Pounds o' tallow candles don't amount to much," quoth Robert.

"That's awful bad brandy at 'The Pilot,'" said Mr. Sedgett, venomously.

"Were you drunk when you committed this assault?" Jonathan asked his son.

"I drank afterwards," Robert replied.

"'Pilot' brandy's poor consolation," remarked Mr. Sedgett.

Jonathan had half a mind to turn his son out of the gate, but the presence of Sedgett advised him that his doings were naked to the world.

"You kicked up a shindy in the hunting-field—what about? Who mounted ye?"

Robert remarked that he had been on foot.

"On foot—eh? on foot!" Jonathan speculated, unable to realize the image of his son as a foot-man in the hunting-field, or to comprehend the insolence of a pedestrian who should dare to attack a mounted huntsman. "You were on foot? The devil you were on foot! Foot? And caught a man out of his saddle?"

Jonathan gave up the puzzle. He laid out his fore finger decisively,—

"If it's an assault, mind, you stand damages. My land gives and my land takes my money, and no drunken dog lives on the produce. A row in the hunting-field's un-English, I call it."

"So it is, sir," said Robert.

"So it be, neighbour," said Mr. Sedgett.

Whereupon Robert took his arm, and holding the scraggy wretch forward, commanded him to out with what he knew.

"Oh, I don't know no more than what I've told you." Mr. Sedgett twisted a feeble remonstrance of his bones, that were chiefly his being, at the gripe; "except that you got hold the horse by the bridle, and wouldn't let him go, because the young gentleman wouldn't speak as a gentleman, and—oh! don't squeeze so hard—"

"Out with it!" cried Robert.

"And you said, Steeve Bilton said, you said, 'Where is she?' you said, and he swore, and you swore, and a lady rode up, and you pulled, and she sang out, and off went the gentleman, and Steeve said she said, 'For shame.'"

"And it was the truest word spoken that day!" Robert released him. "You don't know much, Mr. Sedgett; but it's enough to make me explain the cause to my father, and, with your leave, I'll do so."

Mr. Sedgett remarked: "By all means, do;" and rather preferred that his wits should be accused of want of brightness, than that he should miss a chance of hearing the rich history of the scandal and its origin. Something stronger than a hint sent him off at a trot, hugging in his elbows.

"The postman won't do his business quicker than Sedgett 'll tap this tale upon every door in the parish," said Jonathan.

"I can only say I'm sorry, for your sake;" Robert was expressing his contrition, when his father caught him up,—

"Who can hurt me?—my sake? Have I got the habits of a sot?—what you'd call 'a beast!' but I know the ways o' beasts, and if you did too, you wouldn't bring them in to bear your beastly sins. Who can hurt me?—You've been quarrelling with this young gentleman about a woman—did you damage him?"

"If knuckles could do it, I should have brained him, sir," said Robert.

"You struck him, and you got the best of it?"

"He got the worst of it any way, and will again."

"Then the devil take you for a fool! why did you go and drink I could understand it if you got licked. Drown your memory, then, if that filthy soaking's to your taste; but why, when you get the prize, we'll say, you go off headlong into a manure pond?—There! except that you're a damned idiot!" Jonathan struck the air, as to observe that it beat him, but for the foregoing elucidation: thundering afresh, "Why did you go and drink?"

"I went, sir, I went—why did I go?" Robert slapped his hand despairingly to his forehead. "What on earth did I go for?—because I'm at sea, I suppose. Nobody cares for me. I'm at sea, and no rudder to steer me. I suppose that's it. So, I drank. I thought it best to take spirits on board. No; this was the reason—I remember: that lady, whoever she was, said something that stung me. I held the fellow under her eyes, and shook him, though she was begging me to let him off. Says she—but I've drunk it clean out of my mind."

"There, go in and look at yourself in the glass," said Jonathan.

"Give me your hand first,"—Robert put his own out humbly.

"I'll be hanged if I do," said Jonathan firmly. "Bed and board you shall have while I'm alive, and a glass to look at yourself in; but my hand's for decent beasts. Move one way or t' other: take your choice."

Seeing Robert hesitate, he added, "I shall have a damned deal more respect for you if you toddle." He waved his hand away from the premises.

"I'm sorry you've taken so to swearing of late, sir," said Robert.

"Two flints strike fire, my lad. When you keep distant, I'm quiet enough in my talk to satisfy your aunt Anne."

"Look here, sir; I want to make use of you, so I'll go in."

"Of course you do," returned Jonathan, not a whit displeased by his son's bluntness; "what else is a father good for? I let you know the limit, and that's a brick wall; jump it, if you can. Don't fancy it's your aunt Jane you're going in to meet."

Robert had never been a favourite with his aunt Anne, who was Jonathan's housekeeper.

"No, poor old soul! and may God bless her in heaven!" he cried.

"For leaving you what you turned into a thundering lot of liquor to consume—eh?"

"For doing all in her power to make a man of me; and she was close on it—kind, good old darling, that she was! She got me with that money of hers to the best footing I've been on yet—bless her heart, or her memory, or whatever a poor devil on earth may bless an angel for! But here I am."

The fever in Robert blazed out under a pressure of extinguishing tears.

"There, go along in," said Jonathan, who considered drunkenness to be the main source of water in a man's eyes. "It's my belief you've been at it already this morning."

Robert passed into the house in advance of his father, whom he quite understood and appreciated. There was plenty of paternal love for him, and a hearty smack of the hand, and the inheritance of the farm, when he turned into the right way. Meantime Jonathan was ready to fulfil his parental responsibility, by sheltering, feeding, and not publicly abusing his offspring, of whose spirit he would have had a higher opinion if Robert had preferred, since he must go to the deuce, to go without troubling any of his relatives; as it was, Jonathan submitted to the infliction gravely. Neither in speech nor in tone did he solicit from the severe maiden, known as Aunt Anne, that snub for the wanderer whom he introduced, which, when two are agreed upon the infamous character of a third, through whom they are suffering, it is always agreeable to hear. He said, "Here, Anne; here's Robert. He hasn't breakfasted."

"He likes his cold bath beforehand," said Robert, presenting his cheek to the fleshless, semi-transparent woman.

Aunt Anne divided her lips to pronounce a crisp, subdued "Ow!" to Jonathan after inspecting Robert; and she shuddered at sight of Robert, and said "Ow!" repeatedly, by way of an interjectory token of comprehension, to all that was uttered; but it was a horrified "No!" when Robert's cheek pushed nearer.

"Then, see to getting some breakfast for him," said Jonathan. "You're not anyway bound to kiss a drunken—"

"Dog's the word, sir," Robert helped him. "Dogs can afford it. I never saw one in that state; so they don't lose character."

He spoke lightly, but dejection was in his attitude. When his aunt Anne had left the room, he exclaimed,—

"By jingo! women make you feel it, by some way that they have. She's a religious creature. She smells the devil in me."

"More like, the brandy," his father responded.

"Well! I'm on the road, I'm on the road!" Robert fetched a sigh.

"I didn't make the road," said his father.

"No, sir; you didn't. Work hard: sleep sound that's happiness. I've known it for a year. You're the man I'd imitate, if I could. The devil came first the brandy's secondary. I was quiet so long. I thought myself a safe man."

He sat down and sent his hair distraught with an effort at smoothing it.

"Women brought the devil into the world first. It's women who raise the devil in us, and why they—"

He thumped the table just as his aunt Anne was preparing to spread the cloth.

"Don't be frightened, woman," said Jonathan, seeing her start fearfully back. "You take too many cups of tea, morning and night—hang the stuff!"

"Never, never till now have you abused me, Jonathan," she whimpered, severely.

"I don't tell you to love him; but wait on him. That's all. And I'll about my business. Land and beasts—they answer to you."

Robert looked up.

"Land and beasts! They sound like blessed things. When next I go to church, I shall know what old Adam felt. Go along, sir. I shall break nothing in the house."

"You won't go, Jonathan?" begged the trembling spinster.

"Give him some of your tea, and strong, and as much of it as he can take—he wants bringing down," was Jonathan's answer; and casting a glance at one of the framed letters, he strode through the doorway, and Aunt Anne was alone with the flushed face and hurried eyes of her nephew, who was to her little better than a demon in the flesh. But there was a Bible in the room.

An hour later, Robert was mounted and riding to the meet of hounds.

CHAPTER XVIII

AN ASSEMBLY AT THE PILOT INN

A single night at the Pilot Inn had given life and vigour to Robert's old reputation in Warbeach village, as the stoutest of drinkers and dear rascals throughout a sailor-breeding district, where Dibdin was still thundered in the ale-house, and manhood in a great degree measured by the capacity to take liquor on board, as a ship takes ballast. There was a profound affectation of deploring the sad fact that he drank as hard as ever, among the men, and genuine pity expressed for him by the women of Warbeach; but his fame was fresh again. As the Spring brings back its flowers, Robert's presence revived his youthful deeds. There had not been a boxer in the neighbourhood like Robert Eccles, nor such a champion in all games, nor, when he set himself to it, such an invincible drinker. It was he who thrashed the brute, Nic Sedgett, for stabbing with his clasp-knife Harry Boulby, son of the landlady of the Pilot Inn; thrashed him publicly, to the comfort of all Warbeach. He had rescued old Dame Garble from her burning cottage, and made his father house the old creature, and worked at farming, though he hated it, to pay for her subsistence. He vindicated the honour of Warbeach by drinking a match against a Yorkshire skipper till four o'clock in the morning, when it was a gallant sight, my boys, to see Hampshire steadying the defeated North-countryman on his astonished zigzag to his flattish-bottomed billyboy, all in the cheery sunrise on the river—yo-ho! ahoy!

Glorious Robert had tried, first the sea, and then soldiering. Now let us hope he'll settle to farming, and follow his rare old father's ways, and be back among his own people for good. So chimed the younger ones, and many of the elder.

Danish blood had settled round Warbeach. To be a really popular hero anywhere in Britain, a lad must still, I fear, have something of a Scandinavian gullet; and if, in addition to his being a powerful drinker, he is pleasant in his cups, and can sing, and forgive, be freehanded, and roll out the grand risky phrases of a fired brain, he stamps himself, in the apprehension of his associates, a king.

Much of the stuff was required to deal King Robert of Warbeach the capital stroke, and commonly he could hold on till a puff of cold air from the outer door, like an admonitory messenger, reminded him that he was, in the greatness of his soul, a king of swine; after which his way of walking off, without a word to anybody, hoisting his whole stature, while others were staggering, or roaring foul rhymes, or feeling consciously mortal in their sensation of feverishness, became a theme for admiration; ay, and he was fresh as an orchard apple in the morning! there lay his commandership convincingly. What was proved overnight was confirmed at dawn.

Mr. Robert had his contrast in Sedgett's son, Nicodemus Sedgett, whose unlucky Christian name had assisted the wits of Warbeach in bestowing on him a darkly-luminous relationship. Young Nic loved also to steep his spirit in the bowl; but, in addition to his never paying for his luxury, he drank as if in emulation of the colour of his reputed patron, and neighbourhood to Nic Sedgett was not liked when that young man became thoughtful over his glass.

The episode of his stabbing the landlady's son Harry clung to him fatally. The wound was in the thigh, and nothing serious. Harry was up and off to sea before Nic had ceased to show the marks of Robert's vengeance upon him; but blood-shedding, even on a small scale, is so detested by Englishmen, that Nic never got back to his right hue in the eyes of Warbeach. None felt to him as to a countryman, and it may be supposed that his face was seen no more in the house of gathering, the Pilot Inn.

He rented one of the Fairly farms, known as the Three-Tree Farm, subsisting there, men fancied, by the aid of his housekeeper's money. For he was of those evil fellows who disconcert all righteous prophecy, and it was vain for Mrs. Boulby and Warbeach village to declare that no good could come to him, when Fortune manifestly kept him going.

He possessed the rogue's most serviceable art: in spite of a countenance that was not attractive, this fellow could, as was proved by evidence, make himself pleasing to women. "The truth of it is," said Mrs. Boulby, at a loss for any other explanation, and with a woman's love of sharp generalization, "it's because my sex is fools."

He had one day no money to pay his rent, and forthwith (using for the purpose his last five shillings, it was said) advertized for a housekeeper; and before Warbeach had done chuckling over his folly, an agreeable woman of about thirty-five was making purchases in his name; she made tea, and the evening brew for such friends as he could collect, and apparently paid his rent for him, after a time; the distress was not in the house three days. It seemed to Warbeach an erratic proceeding on the part of Providence, that Nic should ever be helped to swim; but our modern prophets have small patience, and summon Destiny to strike without a preparation of her weapons or a warning to the victim.

More than Robert's old occasional vice was at the bottom of his popularity, as I need not say. Let those who generalize upon ethnology determine whether the ancient opposition of Saxon and Norman be at an end; but it is certain, to my thinking, that when a hero of the people can be got from the common popular stock, he is doubly dear. A gentleman, however gallant and familiar, will hardly ever be as much beloved, until he dies to inform a legend or a ballad: seeing that death only can remove the peculiar distinctions and distances which the people feel to exist between themselves and the gentleman-class, and which, not to credit them with preternatural discernment, they are carefully taught to feel. Dead Britons are all Britons, but live Britons are not quite brothers.

It was as the son of a yeoman, showing comprehensible accomplishments, that Robert took his lead. He was a very brave, a sweet-hearted, and a handsome young man, and he had very chivalrous views of life, that were understood by a sufficient number under the influence of ale or brandy, and by a few in default of that material aid; and they had a family pride in him. The pride was mixed with fear, which threw over it a tender light, like a mother's dream of her child. The people, I have said, are not so lost in self-contempt as to undervalue their best men, but it must be admitted that they rarely produce young fellows wearing the undeniable chieftain's stamp, and the rarity of one like Robert lent a hue of sadness to him in their thoughts.

Fortune, moreover, the favourer of Nic Sedgett, blew foul whichever the way Robert set his sails. He would not look to his own advantage; and the belief that man should set his little traps for the liberal hand of his God, if he wishes to prosper, rather than strive to be merely honourable in his Maker's eye, is almost as general among poor people as it is with the moneyed classes, who survey them from their height.

When jolly Butcher Billing, who was one of the limited company which had sat with Robert at the Pilot last night, reported that he had quitted the army, he was hearkened to dolefully, and the feeling was universal that glorious Robert had cut himself off from his pension and his hospital.

But when gossip Sedgett went his rounds, telling that Robert was down among them again upon the darkest expedition their minds could conceive, and rode out every morning for the purpose of encountering one of the gentlemen up at Fairly, and had already pulled him off his horse and laid him in the mud, calling him scoundrel and challenging him either to yield his secret or to fight; and that he followed him, and was out after him publicly, and matched himself against that gentleman, who had all the other gentlemen, and the earl, and the law to back him, the little place buzzed with wonder and alarm. Faint hearts declared that Robert was now done for. All felt that he had gone miles beyond the mark. Those were the misty days when fogs rolled up the salt river from the winter sea, and the sun lived but an hour in the clotted sky, extinguished near the noon.

Robert was seen riding out, and the tramp of his horse was heard as he returned homeward. He called no more at the Pilot. Darkness and mystery enveloped him. There were nightly meetings under Mrs. Boulby's roof, in the belief that he could not withstand her temptations; nor did she imprudently discourage them; but the woman at last overcame the landlady within her, and she wailed: "He won't come because of the drink. Oh! why was I made to sell liquor, which he says sends him to the devil, poor blessed boy? and I can't help begging him to take one little drop. I did, the first night he was down, forgetting his ways; he looked so desperate, he did, and it went on and went on, till he was primed, and me proud to see him get out of his misery. And now he hates the thought of me."

In her despair she encouraged Sedgett to visit her bar and parlour, and he became everywhere a most important man.

Farmer Eccles's habits of seclusion (his pride, some said), and more especially the dreaded austere Aunt Anne, who ruled that household, kept people distant from the Warbeach farm-house, all excepting Sedgett, who related that every night on his return, she read a chapter from the Bible to Robert, sitting up for him patiently to fulfil her duty; and that the farmer's words to his son had been: "Rest here; eat and drink, and ride my horse; but not a penny of my money do you have."

By the help of Steeve Bilton, the Fairly huntsman, Sedgett was enabled to relate that there was a combination of the gentlemen against Robert, whose behaviour none could absolutely approve, save the landlady and jolly Butcher Billing, who stuck to him with a hearty blind faith.

"Did he ever," asked the latter, "did Bob Eccles ever conduct himself disrespectful to his superiors? Wasn't he always found out at his wildest for to be right—to a sensible man's way of thinking?—though not, I grant ye, to his own interests—there's another tale." And Mr. Billing's staunch adherence to the hero of the village was cried out to his credit when Sedgett stated, on Stephen Bilton's authority, that Robert's errand was the defence of a girl who had been wronged, and whose whereabout, that she might be restored to her parents, was all he wanted to know. This story passed from mouth to mouth, receiving much ornament in the passage. The girl in question became a lady; for it is required of a mere common girl that she should display remarkable character before she can be accepted as the fitting companion of a popular hero. She became a young lady of fortune, in love with Robert, and concealed by the artifice of the offending gentleman whom Robert had challenged. Sedgett told this for truth, being instigated to boldness of invention by pertinacious inquiries, and the dignified sense which the whole story hung upon him.

Mrs. Boulby, who, as a towering woman, despised Sedgett's weak frame, had been willing to listen till she perceived him to be but a man of fiction, and then she gave him a flat contradiction, having no esteem for his custom.

"Eh! but, Missis, I can tell you his name—the gentleman's name," said Sedgett, placably. "He's a Mr. Algernon Blancove, and a cousin by marriage, or something, of Mrs. Lovell."

"I reckon you're right about that, goodman," replied Mrs. Boulby, with intuitive discernment of the true from the false, mingled with a desire to show that she was under no obligation for the news. "All t' other's a tale of your own, and you know it, and no more true than your rigmaroles about my brandy, which is French; it is, as sure as my blood's British."

"Oh! Missis," quoth Sedgett, maliciously, "as to tales, you've got witnesses enough it crassed chann'l. Aha! Don't bring 'em into the box. Don't you bring 'em into ne'er a box."

"You mean to say, Mr. Sedgett, they won't swear?"

"No, Missis; they'll swear, fast and safe, if you teach 'em. Dashed if they won't run the Pilot on a rock with their swearin'. It ain't a good habit."

"Well, Mr. Sedgett, the next time you drink my brandy and find the consequences bad, you let me hear of it."

"And what'll you do, Missis, may be?"

Listeners were by, and Mrs. Boulby cruelly retorted; "I won't send you home to your wife;" which created a roar against this hen-pecked man.

"As to consequences, Missis, it's for your sake I'm looking at them," Sedgett said, when he had recovered from the blow.

"You say that to the Excise, Mr. Sedgett; it, belike, 'll make 'em sorry."

"Brandy's your weak point, it appears, Missis."

"A little in you would stiffen your back, Mr. Sedgett."

"Poor Bob Eccles didn't want no stiffening when he come down first," Sedgett interjected.

At which, flushing enraged, Mrs. Boulby cried: "Mention him, indeed! And him and you, and that son of your'n—the shame of your cheeks if people say he's like his father. Is it your son, Nic Sedgett, thinks to inform against me, as once he swore to, and to get his wage that he may step out of a second bankruptcy? and he a farmer! You let him know that he isn't feared by me, Sedgett, and there's one here to give him a second dose, without waiting for him to use clasp-knives on harmless innocents."

"Pacify yourself, ma'am, pacify yourself," remarked Sedgett, hardened against words abroad by his endurance of blows at home. "Bob Eccles, he's got his hands full, and he, maybe, 'll reach the hulks before my Nic do, yet. And how 'm I answerable for Nic, I ask you?"

"More luck to you not to be, I say; and either, Sedgett, you does woman's work, gossipin' about like a cracked bell-clapper, or men's the biggest gossips of all, which I believe; for there's no beating you at your work, and one can't wish ill to you, knowing what you catch."

"In a friendly way, Missis,"—Sedgett fixed on the compliment to his power of propagating news—"in a friendly way. You can't accuse me of leavin' out the 'I' in your name, now, can you? I make that observation,"—the venomous tattler screwed himself up to the widow insinuatingly, as if her understanding could only be seized at close quarters, "I make that observation, because poor Dick Boulby, your lamented husband—eh! poor Dick! You see, Missis, it ain't the tough ones last longest: he'd sing, 'I'm a Sea Booby,' to the song, 'I'm a green Mermaid:' poor Dick! 'a-shinin' upon the sea-deeps.' He kept the liquor from his head, but didn't mean it to stop down in his leg."

"Have you done, Mr. Sedgett?" said the widow, blandly.

"You ain't angry, Missis?"

"Not a bit, Mr. Sedgett; and if I knock you over with the flat o' my hand, don't you think so."

Sedgett threw up the wizened skin of his forehead, and retreated from the bar. At a safe distance, he called: "Bad news that about Bob Eccles swallowing a blow yesterday!"

Mrs. Boulby faced him complacently till he retired, and then observed to those of his sex surrounding her, "Don't 'woman-and-dog-and-walnut-tree' me! Some of you men 'd be the better for a drubbing every day of your lives. Sedgett yond' 'd be as big a villain as his son, only for what he gets at home."

That was her way of replying to the Parthian arrow; but the barb was poisoned. The village was at fever heat concerning Robert, and this assertion that he had swallowed a blow, produced almost as great a consternation as if a fleet of the enemy had been reported off Sandy Point.

Mrs. Boulby went into her parlour and wrote a letter to Robert, which she despatched by one of the loungers about the bar, who brought back news that three of the gentlemen of Fairly were on horseback, talking to Farmer Eccles at his garden gate. Affairs were waxing hot. The gentlemen had only to threaten Farmer Eccles, to make him side with his son, right or wrong. In the evening, Stephen Bilton, the huntsman, presented himself at the door of the long parlour of the Pilot, and loud cheers were his greeting from a full company.

"Gentlemen all," said Stephen, with dapper modesty; and acted as if no excitement were current, and he had nothing to tell.

"Well, Steeve?" said one, to encourage him.

"How about Bob, to-day?" said another.

Before Stephen had spoken, it was clear to the apprehension of the whole room that he did not share the popular view of Robert. He declined to understand who was meant by "Bob." He played the questions off; and then shrugged, with, "Oh, let's have a quiet evening."

It ended in his saying, "About Bob Eccles? There, that's summed up pretty quick—he's mad."

"Mad!" shouted Warbeach.

"That's a lie," said Mrs. Boulby, from the doorway.

"Well, mum, I let a lady have her own opinion." Stephen nodded to her. "There ain't a doubt as t' what the doctors 'd bring him in I ain't speaking my ideas alone. It's written like the capital letters in a newspaper. Lunatic's the word! And I'll take a glass of something warm, Mrs. Boulby. We had a stiff run to-day."

"Where did ye kill, Steeve?" asked a dispirited voice.

"We didn't kill at all: he was one of those 'longshore dog-foxes,' and got away home on the cliff." Stephen thumped his knee. "It's my belief the smell o' sea gives 'em extra cunning."

"The beggar seems to have put ye out rether—eh, Steeve?"

So it was generally presumed: and yet the charge of madness was very staggering; madness being, in the first place, indefensible, and everybody's enemy when at large; and Robert's behaviour looked extremely like it. It had already been as a black shadow haunting enthusiastic minds in the village, and there fell a short silence, during which Stephen made his preparations for filling and lighting a pipe.

"Come; how do you make out he's mad?"

Jolly Butcher Billing spoke; but with none of the irony of confidence.

"Oh!" Stephen merely clapped both elbows against his sides.

Several pairs of eyes were studying him. He glanced over them in turn, and commenced leisurely the puff contemplative.

"Don't happen to have a grudge of e'er a kind against old Bob, Steeve?"

"Not I!"

Mrs. Boulby herself brought his glass to Stephen, and, retreating, left the parlour-door open.

"What causes you for to think him mad, Steeve?"

A second "Oh!" as from the heights dominating argument, sounded from Stephen's throat, half like a grunt. This time he condescended to add,—

"How do you know when a dog's gone mad? Well, Robert Eccles, he's gone in like manner. If you don't judge a man by his actions, you've got no means of reckoning. He comes and attacks gentlemen, and swears he'll go on doing it."

"Well, and what does that prove?" said jolly Butcher Billing.

Mr. William Moody, boatbuilder, a liver-complexioned citizen, undertook to reply.

"What does that prove? What does that prove when the midshipmite was found with his head in the mixedpickle jar? It proved that his head was lean, and t' other part was rounder."

The illustration appeared forcible, but not direct, and nothing more was understood from it than that Moody, and two or three others who had been struck by the image of the infatuated young naval officer, were going over to the enemy. The stamp of madness upon Robert's acts certainly saved perplexity, and was the easiest side of the argument. By this time Stephen had finished his glass, and the effect was seen.

"Hang it!" he exclaimed, "I don't agree he deserves shooting. And he may have had harm done to him. In that case, let him fight. And I say, too, let the gentleman give him satisfaction."

"Hear! hear!" cried several.

"And if the gentleman refuse to give him satisfaction in a fair stand-up fight, I say he ain't a gentleman, and deserves to be treated as such. My objection's personal. I don't like any man who spoils sport, and ne'er a rascally vulpeci' spoils sport as he do, since he's been down in our parts again. I'll take another brimmer, Mrs. Boulby."

"To be sure you will, Stephen," said Mrs. Boulby, bending as in a curtsey to the glass; and so soft with him that foolish fellows thought her cowed by the accusation thrown at her favourite.

"There's two questions about they valpecies, Master Stephen," said Farmer Wainsby, a farmer with a grievance, fixing his elbow on his knee for serious utterance. "There's to ask, and t' ask again. Sport, I grant ye. All in doo season. But," he performed a circle with his pipe stem, and darted it as from the centre thereof toward Stephen's breast, with the poser, "do we s'pport thieves at public expense for them to keep thievin'—black, white, or brown—no matter, eh? Well, then, if the public wunt bear it, dang me if I can see why individles shud bear it. It ent no manner o' reason, net as I can see; let gentlemen have their opinion, or let 'em not. Foxes be hanged!"

Much slow winking was interchanged. In a general sense, Farmer Wainsby's remarks were held to be un-English, though he was pardoned for them as one having peculiar interests at stake.

"Ay, ay! we know all about that," said Stephen, taking succour from the eyes surrounding him.

"And so, may be, do we," said Wainsby.

"Fox-hunting 'll go on when your great-grandfather's your youngest son, farmer; or t' other way."

"I reckon it'll be a stuffed fox your chil'ern 'll hunt, Mr. Steeve; more straw in 'em than bow'ls."

"If the country," Stephen thumped the table, "were what you'd make of it, hang me if my name 'd long be Englishman!"

"Hear, hear, Steeve!" was shouted in support of the Conservative principle enunciated by him.

"What I say is, flesh and blood afore foxes!"

Thus did Farmer Wainsby likewise attempt a rallying-cry; but Stephen's retort, "Ain't foxes flesh and blood?" convicted him of clumsiness, and, buoyed on the uproar of cheers, Stephen pursued, "They are; to kill 'em in cold blood's beast-murder, so it is. What do we do? We give 'em a fair field—a fair field and no favour! We let 'em trust to the instincts Nature, she's given 'em; and don't the old woman know best? If they cap, get away, they win the day. All's open, and honest, and aboveboard. Kill your rats and kill your rabbits, but leave foxes to your betters. Foxes are gentlemen. You don't understand? Be hanged if they ain't! I like the old fox, and I don't like to see him murdered and exterminated, but die the death of a gentleman, at the hands of gentlemen—"

"And ladies," sneered the farmer.

All the room was with Stephen, and would have backed him uproariously, had he not reached his sounding period without knowing it, and thus allowed his opponent to slip in that abominable addition.

"Ay, and ladies," cried the huntsman, keen at recovery. "Why shouldn't they? I hate a field without a woman in it; don't you? and you? and you? And you, too, Mrs. Boulby? There you are, and the room looks better for you—don't it, lads? Hurrah!"

The cheering was now aroused, and Stephen had his glass filled again in triumph, while the farmer meditated thickly over the ruin of his argument from that fatal effort at fortifying it by throwing a hint to the discredit of the sex, as many another man has meditated before.

"Eh! poor old Bob!" Stephen sighed and sipped. "I can cry that with any of you. It's worse for me to see than for you to hear of him. Wasn't I always a friend of his, and said he was worthy to be a gentleman, many a time? He's got the manners of a gentleman now; offs with his hat, if there's a lady present, and such a neat way of speaking. But there, acting's the thing, and his behaviour's beastly bad! You can't call it no other. There's two Mr. Blancoves up at Fairly, relations of Mrs. Lovell's—whom I'll take the liberty of calling My Beauty, and no offence meant: and it's before her that Bob only yesterday rode up—one of the gentlemen being Mr. Algernon, free of hand and a good seat in the saddle, t' other's Mr. Edward; but Mr. Algernon, he's Robert Eccles's man—up rides Bob, just as we was tying Mr. Reenard's brush to the pommel of the lady's saddle, down in Ditley Marsh; and he bows to the lady. Says he—but he's mad, stark mad!"

Stephen resumed his pipe amid a din of disappointment that made the walls ring and the glasses leap.

"A little more sugar, Stephen?" said Mrs. Boulby, moving in lightly from the doorway.

"Thank ye, mum; you're the best hostess that ever breathed."

"So she be; but how about Bob?" cried her guests—some asking whether he carried a pistol or flourished a stick.

"Ne'er a blessed twig, to save his soul; and there's the madness written on him;" Stephen roared as loud as any of them. "And me to see him riding in the ring there, and knowing what the gentleman had sworn to do if he came across the hunt; and feeling that he was in the wrong! I haven't got a oath to swear how mad I was. Fancy yourselves in my place. I love old Bob. I've drunk with him; I owe him obligations from since I was a boy up'ard; I don't know a better than Bob in all England. And there he was: and says to Mr. Algernon, 'You know what I'm come for.' I never did behold a gentleman so pale—shot all over his cheeks as he was, and pinkish under the eyes; if you've ever noticed a chap laid hands on by detectives in plain clothes. Smack at Bob went Mr. Edward's whip."

"Mr. Algernon's," Stephen was corrected.

"Mr. Edward's, I tell ye—the cousin. And right across the face. My Lord! it made my blood tingle."

A sound like the swish of a whip expressed the sentiments of that assemblage at the Pilot.

"Bob swallowed it?"

"What else could he do, the fool? He had nothing to help him but his hand. Says he, 'That's a poor way of trying to stop me. My business is with this gentleman;' and Bob set his horse at Mr. Algernon, and Mrs. Lovell rode across him with her hand raised; and just at that moment up jogged the old gentleman, Squire Blancove, of Wrexby: and Robert Eccles says to him, 'You might have saved your son something by keeping your word.' It appears according to Bob, that the squire had promised to see his son, and settle matters. All Mrs. Lovell could do was hardly enough to hold back Mr. Edward from laying out at Bob. He was like a white devil, and speaking calm and polite all the time. Says Bob, 'I'm willing to take one when I've done with the other;' and the squire began talking to his son, Mrs. Lovell to Mr. Edward, and the rest of the gentlemen all round poor dear old Bob, rather bullying—like for my blood; till Bob couldn't help being nettled, and cried out, 'Gentlemen, I hold him in my power, and I'm silent so long as there's a chance of my getting him to behave like a man with human feelings.' If they'd gone at him then, I don't think I could have let him stand alone: an opinion's one thing, but blood's another, and I'm distantly related to Bob; and a man who's always thinking of the value of his place, he ain't worth it. But Mrs. Lovell, she settled the case—a lady, Farmer Wainsby, with your leave. There's the good of having a lady present on the field. That's due to a lady!"

"Happen she was at the bottom of it," the farmer returned Stephen's nod grumpily.

"How did it end, Stephen, my lad?" said Butcher Billing, indicating a "never mind him."

"It ended, my boy, it ended like my glass here—hot and strong stuff, with sugar at the bottom. And I don't see this, so glad as I saw that, my word of honour on it! Boys all!" Stephen drank the dregs.

Mrs. Boulby was still in attendance. The talk over the circumstances was sweeter than the bare facts, and the replenished glass enabled Stephen to add the picturesque bits of the affray, unspurred by a surrounding eagerness of his listeners—too exciting for imaginative effort. In particular, he dwelt on Robert's dropping the reins and riding with his heels at Algernon, when Mrs. Lovell put her horse in his way, and the pair of horses rose like waves at sea, and both riders showed their horsemanship, and Robert an adroit courtesy, for which the lady thanked him with a bow of her head.

"I got among the hounds, pretending to pacify them, and call 'em together," said Stephen, "and I heard her say—just before all was over, and he turned off—I heard her say: 'Trust this to me: I will meet you.' I'll swear to them exact words, though there was more, and a 'where' in the bargain, and that I didn't hear. Aha! by George! thinks I, old Bob, you're a lucky beggar, and be hanged if I wouldn't go mad too for a minute or so of short, sweet, private talk with a lovely young widow lady as ever the sun did shine upon so boldly—oho!

You've seen a yacht upon the sea,
She dances and she dances, O!
As fair is my wild maid to me...

Something about 'prances, O!' on her horse, you know, or you're a hem'd fool if you don't. I never could sing; wish I could! It's the joy of life! It's utterance! Hey for harmony!"

"Eh! brayvo! now you're a man, Steeve! and welcomer and welcomest; yi—yi, O!" jolly Butcher Billing sang out sharp. "Life wants watering. Here's a health to Robert Eccles, wheresoever and whatsoever! and ne'er a man shall say of me I didn't stick by a friend like Bob. Cheers, my lads!"

Robert's health was drunk in a thunder, and praises of the purity of the brandy followed the grand roar. Mrs. Boulby received her compliments on that head.

"'Pends upon the tide, Missis, don't it?" one remarked with a grin broad enough to make the slyness written on it easy reading.

"Ah! first a flow and then a ebb," said another.

"It's many a keg I plant i' the mud,
Coastguardsman, come! and I'll have your blood!"

Instigation cried, "Cut along;" but the defiant smuggler was deficient in memory, and like Steeve Bilton, was reduced to scatter his concluding rhymes in prose, as "something about;" whereat jolly Butcher Billing, a reader of song-books from a literary delight in their contents, scraped his head, and then, as if he had touched a spring, carolled,—

"In spite of all you Gov'ment pack,
I'll land my kegs of the good Cognyac"—

"though," he took occasion to observe when the chorus and a sort of cracker of irrelevant rhymes had ceased to explode; "I'm for none of them games. Honesty!—there's the sugar o' my grog."

"Ay, but you like to be cock-sure of the stuff you drink, if e'er a man did," said the boatbuilder, whose eye blazed yellow in this frothing season of song and fun.

"Right so, Will Moody!" returned the jolly butcher: "which means—not wrong this time!"

"Then, what's understood by your sticking prongs into your hostess here concerning of her brandy? Here it is—which is enough, except for discontented fellows."

"Eh, Missus?" the jolly butcher appealed to her, and pointed at Moody's complexion for proof.

It was quite a fiction that kegs of the good cognac were sown at low water, and reaped at high, near the river-gate of the old Pilot Inn garden; but it was greatly to Mrs. Boulby's interest to encourage the delusion which imaged her brandy thus arising straight from the very source, without villanous contact with excisemen and corrupting dealers; and as, perhaps, in her husband's time, the thing had happened, and still did, at rare intervals, she complacently gathered the profitable fame of her brandy being the best in the district.

"I'm sure I hope you're satisfied, Mr. Billing," she said.

The jolly butcher asked whether Will Moody was satisfied, and Mr. William Moody declaring himself thoroughly satisfied, "then I'm satisfied too!" said the jolly butcher; upon which the boatbuilder heightened the laugh by saying he was not satisfied at all; and to escape from the execrations of the majority, pleaded that it was because his glass was empty: thus making his peace with them. Every glass in the room was filled again.

The young fellows now loosened tongue; and Dick Curtis, the promising cricketer of Hampshire, cried, "Mr. Moody, my hearty! that's your fourth glass, so don't quarrel with me, now!"

"You!" Moody fired up in a bilious frenzy, and called him a this and that and t' other young vagabond; for which the company, feeling the ominous truth contained in Dick Curtis's remark more than its impertinence, fined Mr. Moody in a song. He gave the—

"So many young Captains have walked o'er my pate,
It's no wonder you see me quite bald, sir,"

with emphatic bitterness, and the company thanked him. Seeing him stand up as to depart, however, a storm of contempt was hurled at him; some said he was like old Sedgett, and was afraid of his wife; and some, that he was like Nic Sedgett, and drank blue.

"You're a bag of blue devils, oh dear! oh dear!"

sang Dick to the tune of "The Campbells are coming."

"I ask e'er a man present," Mr. Moody put out his fist, "is that to be borne? Didn't you," he addressed Dick Curtis,—"didn't you sing into my chorus—"

'It's no wonder to hear how you squall'd, sir?'

"You did!"

"Don't he,"—Dick addressed the company, "make Mrs. Boulby's brandy look ashamed of itself in his face? I ask e'er a gentleman present."

Accusation and retort were interchanged, in the course of which, Dick called Mr. Moody Nic Sedgett's friend; and a sort of criminal inquiry was held. It was proved that Moody had been seen with Nic Sedgett; and then three or four began to say that Nic Sedgett was thick with some of the gentlemen up at Fairly;—just like his luck! Stephen let it be known that he could confirm this fact; he having seen Mr. Algernon Blancove stop Nic on the road and talk to him.

"In that case," said Butcher Billing, "there's mischief in a state of fermentation. Did ever anybody see Nic and the devil together?"

"I saw Nic and Mr. Moody together," said Dick Curtis. "Well, I'm only stating a fact," he exclaimed, as Moody rose, apparently to commence an engagement, for which the company quietly prepared, by putting chairs out of his way: but the recreant took his advantage from the error, and got away to the door, pursued.

"Here's an example of what we lose in having no President," sighed the jolly butcher. "There never was a man built for the chair like Bob Eccles I say! Our evening's broke up, and I, for one, 'd ha' made it morning. Hark, outside; By Gearge! they're snowballing."

An adjournment to the front door brought them in view of a white and silent earth under keen stars, and Dick Curtis and the bilious boatbuilder, foot to foot, snowball in hand. A bout of the smart exercise made Mr. Moody laugh again, and all parted merrily, delivering final shots as they went their several ways.

"Thanks be to heaven for snowing," said Mrs. Boulby; "or when I should have got to my bed, Goodness only can tell!" With which, she closed the door upon the empty inn.

CHAPTER XIX

ROBERT SMITTEN LOW

The night was warm with the new-fallen snow, though the stars sparkled coldly. A fleet of South-westerly rainclouds had been met in mid-sky by a sharp puff from due North, and the moisture had descended like a woven shroud, covering all the land, the house-tops, and the trees.

Young Harry Boulby was at sea, and this still weather was just what a mother's heart wished for him. The widow looked through her bed-room window and listened, as if the absolute stillness must beget a sudden cry. The thought of her boy made her heart revert to Robert. She was thinking of Robert when the muffled sound of a horse at speed caused her to look up the street, and she saw one coming—a horse without a rider. The next minute he was out of sight.

Mrs. Boulby stood terrified. The silence of the night hanging everywhere seemed to call on her for proof that she had beheld a real earthly spectacle, and the dead thump of the hooves on the snow-floor in passing struck a chill through her as being phantom-like. But she had seen a saddle on the horse, and the stirrups flying, and the horse looked affrighted. The scene was too earthly in its suggestion of a tale of blood. What if the horse were Robert's? She tried to laugh at her womanly fearfulness, and had almost to suppress a scream in doing so. There was no help for it but to believe her brandy as good and efficacious as her guests did, so she went downstairs and took a fortifying draught; after which her blood travelled faster, and the event galloped swiftly into the recesses of time, and she slept.

While the morning was still black, and the streets without a sign of life, she was aroused by a dream of some one knocking at her grave-stone. "Ah, that brandy!" she sighed. "This is what a poor woman has to pay for custom!" Which we may interpret as the remorseful morning confession of a guilt she had been the victim of over night. She knew that good brandy did not give bad dreams, and was self-convicted. Strange were her sensations when the knocking continued; and presently she heard a voice in the naked street below call in a moan, "Mother!"

"My darling!" she answered, divided in her guess at its being Harry or Robert.

A glance from the open window showed Robert leaning in the quaint old porch, with his head bound by a handkerchief; but he had no strength to reply to a question at that distance, and when she let him in he made two steps and dropped forward on the floor.

Lying there, he plucked at her skirts. She was shouting for help, but with her ready apprehension of the pride in his character, she knew what was meant by his broken whisper before she put her ear to his lips, and she was silent, miserable sight as was his feeble efforts to rise on an elbow that would not straighten.

His head was streaming with blood, and the stain was on his neck and chest. He had one helpless arm; his clothes were torn as from a fierce struggle.

"I'm quite sensible," he kept repeating, lest she should relapse into screams.

"Lord love you for your spirit!" exclaimed the widow, and there they remained, he like a winged eagle, striving to raise himself from time to time, and fighting with his desperate weakness. His face was to the ground; after a while he was still. In alarm the widow stooped over him: she feared that he had given up his last breath; but the candle-light showed him shaken by a sob, as it seemed to her, though she could scarce believe it of this manly fellow. Yet it proved true; she saw the very tears. He was crying at his helplessness.

"Oh, my darling boy!" she burst out; "what have they done to ye? the cowards they are! but do now have pity on a woman, and let me get some creature to lift you to a bed, dear. And don't flap at me with your hand like a bird that's shot. You're quite, quite sensible, I know; quite sensible, dear; but for my sake, Robert, my Harry's good friend, only for my sake, let yourself be a carried to a clean, nice bed, till I get Dr. Bean to you. Do, do."

Her entreaties brought on a succession of the efforts to rise, and at last, getting round on his back, and being assisted by the widow, he sat up against the wall. The change of posture stupified him with a dizziness. He tried to utter the old phrase, that he was sensible, but his hand beat at his forehead before the words could be shaped.

"What pride is when it's a man!" the widow thought, as he recommenced the grievous struggle to rise on his feet; now feeling them up to the knee with a questioning hand, and pausing as if in a reflective wonder, and then planting them for a spring that failed wretchedly; groaning and leaning backward, lost in a fit of despair, and again beginning, patient as an insect imprisoned in a circle.

The widow bore with his man's pride, until her nerves became afflicted by the character of his movements, which, as her sensations conceived them, were like those of a dry door jarring loose. She caught him in her arms: "It's let my back break, but you shan't fret to death there, under my eyes, proud or humble, poor dear," she said, and with a great pull she got him upright. He fell across her shoulder with so stiff a groan that for a moment she thought she had done him mortal injury.

"Good old mother," he said boyishly, to reassure her.

"Yes; and you'll behave to me like a son," she coaxed him.

They talked as by slow degrees the stairs were ascended.

"A crack o' the head, mother—a crack o' the head," said he.

"Was it the horse, my dear?"

"A crack o' the head, mother."

"What have they done to my boy Robert?"

"They've,"—he swung about humorously, weak as he was and throbbing with pain—"they've let out some of your brandy, mother...got into my head."

"Who've done it, my dear?"

"They've done it, mother."

"Oh, take care o' that nail at your foot; and oh, that beam to your poor poll—poor soul! he's been and hurt himself again. And did they do it to him? and what was it for?" she resumed in soft cajolery.

"They did it, because—"

"Yes, my dear; the reason for it?"

"Because, mother, they had a turn that way."

"Thanks be to Above for leaving your cunning in you, my dear," said the baffled woman, with sincere admiration. "And Lord be thanked, if you're not hurt bad, that they haven't spoilt his handsome face," she added.

In the bedroom, he let her partially undress him, refusing all doctor's aid, and commanding her to make no noise about him and then he lay down and shut his eyes, for the pain was terrible—galloped him and threw him with a shock—and galloped him and threw him again, whenever his thoughts got free for a moment from the dizzy aching.

"My dear," she whispered, "I'm going to get a little brandy."

She hastened away upon this mission.

He was in the same posture when she returned with bottle and glass.

She poured out some, and made much of it as a specific, and of the great things brandy would do; but he motioned his hand from it feebly, till she reproached him tenderly as perverse and unkind.

"Now, my dearest boy, for my sake—only for my sake. Will you? Yes, you will, my Robert!"

"No brandy, mother."

"Only one small thimbleful?"

"No more brandy for me!"

"See, dear, how seriously you take it, and all because you want the comfort."

"No brandy," was all he could say.

She looked at the label on the bottle. Alas! she knew whence it came, and what its quality. She could cheat herself about it when herself only was concerned—but she wavered at the thought of forcing it upon Robert as trusty medicine, though it had a pleasant taste, and was really, as she conceived, good enough for customers.

She tried him faintly with arguments in its favour; but his resolution was manifested by a deaf ear.

With a perfect faith in it she would, and she was conscious that she could, have raised his head and poured it down his throat. The crucial test of her love for Robert forbade the attempt. She burst into an uncontrollable fit of crying.

"Halloa! mother," said Robert, opening his eyes to the sad candlelight surrounding them.

"My darling boy! whom I do love so; and not to be able to help you! What shall I do—what shall I do!"

With a start, he cried, "Where's the horse!"

"The horse?"

"The old dad 'll be asking for the horse to-morrow."

"I saw a horse, my dear, afore I turned to my prayers at my bedside, coming down the street without his rider. He came like a rumble of deafness in my ears. Oh, my boy, I thought, Is it Robert's horse?— knowing you've got enemies, as there's no brave man has not got 'em—which is our only hope in the God of heaven!"

"Mother, punch my ribs."

He stretched himself flat for the operation, and shut his mouth.

"Hard, mother!—and quick!—I can't hold out long."

"Oh! Robert," moaned the petrified woman "strike you?"

"Straight in the ribs. Shut your fist and do it—quick."

"My dear!—my boy!—I haven't the heart to do it!"

"Ah!" Robert's chest dropped in; but tightening his muscles again, he said, "now do it—do it!"

"Oh! a poke at a poor fire puts it out, dear. And make a murderess of me, you call mother! Oh! as I love the name, I'll obey you, Robert. But!—there!"

"Harder, mother."

"There!—goodness forgive me!"

"Hard as you can—all's right."

"There!—and there!—oh!—mercy!"

"Press in at my stomach."

She nerved herself to do his bidding, and, following his orders, took his head in her hands, and felt about it. The anguish of the touch wrung a stifled scream from him, at which she screamed responsive. He laughed, while twisting with the pain.

"You cruel boy, to laugh at your mother," she said, delighted by the sound of safety in that sweet human laughter. "Hey! don't ye shake your brain; it ought to lie quiet. And here's the spot of the wicked blow—

and him in love—as I know he is! What would she say if she saw him now? But an old woman's the best nurse—ne'er a doubt of it."

She felt him heavy on her arm, and knew that he had fainted. Quelling her first impulse to scream, she dropped him gently on the pillow, and rapped to rouse up her maid.

The two soon produced a fire and hot water, bandages, vinegar in a basin, and every crude appliance that could be thought of, the maid followed her mistress's directions with a consoling awe, for Mrs. Boulby had told her no more than that a man was hurt.

"I do hope, if it's anybody, it's that ther' Moody," said the maid.

"A pretty sort of a Christian you think yourself, I dare say," Mrs. Boulby replied.

"Christian or not, one can't help longin' for a choice, mum. We ain't all hands and knees."

"Better for you if you was," said the widow. "It's tongues, you're to remember, you're not to be. Now come you up after me—and you'll not utter a word. You'll stand behind the door to do what I tell you. You're a soldier's daughter, Susan, and haven't a claim to be excitable."

"My mother was given to faints," Susan protested on behalf of her possible weakness.

"You may peep." Thus Mrs. Boulby tossed a sop to her frail woman's nature.

But for her having been appeased by the sagacious accordance of this privilege, the maid would never have endured to hear Robert's voice in agony, and to think that it was really Robert, the beloved of Warbeach, who had come to harm. Her apprehensions not being so lively as her mistress's, by reason of her love being smaller, she was more terrified than comforted by Robert's jokes during the process of washing off the blood, cutting the hair from the wound, bandaging and binding up the head.

His levity seemed ghastly; and his refusal upon any persuasion to see a doctor quite heathenish, and a sign of one foredoomed.

She believed that his arm was broken, and smarted with wrath at her mistress for so easily taking his word to the contrary. More than all, his abjuration of brandy now when it would do him good to take it, struck her as an instance of that masculine insanity in the comprehension of which all women must learn to fortify themselves. There was much whispering in the room, inarticulate to her, before Mrs. Boulby came out; enjoining a rigorous silence, and stating that the patient would drink nothing but tea.

"He begged," she said half to herself, "to have the window blinds up in the morning, if the sun wasn't strong, for him to look on our river opening down to the ships."

"That looks as if he meant to live," Susan remarked.

"He!" cried the widow, "it's Robert Eccles. He'd stand on his last inch."

"Would he, now!" ejaculated Susan, marvelling at him, with no question as to what footing that might be.

"Leastways," the widow hastened to add, "if he thought it was only devils against him. I've heard him say, 'It's a fool that holds out against God, and a coward as gives in to the devil;' and there's my Robert painted by his own hand."

"But don't that bring him to this so often, Mum?" Susan ruefully inquired, joining teapot and kettle.

"I do believe he's protected," said the widow.

With the first morning light Mrs. Boulby was down at Warbeach Farm, and being directed to Farmer Eccles in the stables, she found the sturdy yeoman himself engaged in grooming Robert's horse.

"Well, Missis," he said, nodding to her; "you win, you see. I thought you would; I'd have sworn you would. Brandy's stronger than blood, with some of our young fellows."

"If you please, Mr. Eccles," she replied, "Robert's sending of me was to know if the horse was unhurt and safe."

"Won't his legs carry him yet, Missis?"

"His legs have been graciously spared, Mr. Eccles; it's his head."

"That's where the liquor flies, I'm told."

"Pray, Mr. Eccles, believe me when I declare he hasn't touched a drop of anything but tea in my house this past night."

"I'm sorry for that; I'd rather have him go to you. If he takes it, let him take it good; and I'm given to understand that you've a reputation that way. Just tell him from me, he's at liberty to play the devil with himself, but not with my beasts."

The farmer continued his labour.

"No, you ain't a hard man, surely," cried the widow. "Not when I say he was sober, Mr. Eccles; and was thrown, and made insensible?"

"Never knew such a thing to happen to him, Missis, and, what's more, I don't believe it. Mayhap you're come for his things: his Aunt Anne's indoors, and she'll give 'em up, and gladly. And my compliments to Robert, and the next time he fancies visiting Warbeach, he'd best forward a letter to that effect."

Mrs. Boulby curtseyed humbly. "You think bad of me, sir, for keeping a public; but I love your son as my own, and if I might presume to say so, Mr. Eccles, you will be proud of him too before you die. I know no more than you how he fell yesterday, but I do know he'd not been drinking, and have got bitter bad enemies."

"And that's not astonishing, Missis."

"No, Mr. Eccles; and a man who's brave besides being good soon learns that."

"Well spoken, Missis."

"Is Robert to hear he's denied his father's house?"

"I never said that, Mrs. Boulby. Here's my principle—My house is open to my blood, so long as he don't bring downright disgrace on it, and then any one may claim him that likes I won't give him money, because I know of a better use for it; and he shan't ride my beasts, because he don't know how to treat 'em. That's all."

"And so you keep within the line of your duty, sir," the widow summed his speech.

"So I hope to," said the farmer.

"There's comfort in that," she replied.

"As much as there's needed," said he.

The widow curtseyed again. "It's not to trouble you, sir, I called. Robert—thanks be to Above!—is not hurt serious, though severe."

"Where's he hurt?" the farmer asked rather hurriedly.

"In the head, it is."

"What have you come for?"

"First, his best hat."

"Bless my soul!" exclaimed the farmer. "Well, if that 'll mend his head it's at his service, I'm sure."

Sick at his heartlessness, the widow scattered emphasis over her concluding remarks. "First, his best hat, he wants; and his coat and clean shirt; and they mend the looks of a man, Mr. Eccles; and it's to look well is his object: for he's not one to make a moan of himself, and doctors may starve before he'd go to any of them. And my begging prayer to you is, that when you see your son, you'll not tell him I let you know his head or any part of him was hurt. I wish you good morning, Mr. Eccles."

"Good morning to you, Mrs. Boulby. You're a respectable woman."

"Not to be soaped," she murmured to herself in a heat.

The apparently medicinal articles of attire were obtained from Aunt Anne, without a word of speech on the part of that pale spinster. The deferential hostility between the two women acknowledged an intervening chasm. Aunt Anne produced a bundle, and placed the hat on it, upon which she had neatly pinned a tract, "The Drunkard's Awakening!" Mrs. Boulby glanced her eye in wrath across this superscription, thinking to herself, "Oh, you good people! how you make us long in our hearts for trouble with you." She controlled the impulse, and mollified her spirit on her way home by distributing stray leaves of the tract to the outlying heaps of rubbish, and to one inquisitive pig, who was looking up from a badly-smelling sty for what the heavens might send him.

She found Robert with his arm doubled over a basin, and Susan sponging cold water on it.

"No bones broken, mother!" he sang out. "I'm sound; all right again. Six hours have done it this time. Is it a thaw? You needn't tell me what the old dad has been saying. I shall be ready to breakfast in half an hour."

"Lord, what a big arm it is!" exclaimed the widow. "And no wonder, or how would you be a terror to men? You naughty boy, to think of stirring! Here you'll lie."

"Ah, will I?" said Robert: and he gave a spring, and sat upright in the bed, rather white with the effort, which seemed to affect his mind, for he asked dubiously, "What do I look like, mother?"

She brought him the looking-glass, and Susan being dismissed, he examined his features.

"Dear!" said the widow, sitting down on the bed; "it ain't much for me to guess you've got an appointment."

"At twelve o'clock, mother."

"With her?" she uttered softly.

"It's with a lady, mother."

"And so many enemies prowling about, Robert, my dear! Don't tell me they didn't fall upon you last night. I said nothing, but I'd swear it on the Book. Do you think you can go?"

"Why, mother, I go by my feelings, and there's no need to think at all, or God knows what I should think."

The widow shook her head. "Nothing 'll stop you, I suppose?"

"Nothing inside of me will, mother."

"Doesn't she but never mind. I've no right to ask, Robert; and if I have curiosity, it's about last night, and why you should let villains escape. But there's no accounting for a man's notions; only, this I say, and I do say it, Nic Sedgett, he's at the bottom of any mischief brewed against you down here. And last night Stephen Bilton, or somebody, declared that Nic Sedgett had been seen up at Fairly."

"Selling eggs, mother. Why shouldn't he? We mustn't complain of his getting an honest livelihood."

"He's black-blooded, Robert; and I never can understand why the Lord did not make him a beast in face. I'm told that creature's found pleasing by the girls."

"Ugh, mother, I'm not."

"She won't have you, Robert?"

He laughed. "We shall see to-day."

"You deceiving boy!" cried the widow; "and me not know it's Mrs. Lovell you're going to meet! and would to heaven she'd see the worth of ye, for it's a born lady you ought to marry."

"Just feel in my pockets, mother, and you won't be so ready with your talk of my marrying. And now I'll get up. I feel as if my legs had to learn over again how to bear me. The old dad, bless his heart! gave me sound wind and limb to begin upon, so I'm not easily stumped, you see, though I've been near on it once or twice in my life."

Mrs. Boulby murmured, "Ah! are you still going to be at war with those gentlemen, Robert?"

He looked at her steadily, while a shrewd smile wrought over his face, and then taking her hand, he said, "I'll tell you a little; you deserve it, and won't tattle. My curse is, I'm ashamed to talk about my feelings; but there's no shame in being fond of a girl, even if she refuses to have anything to say to you, is there? No, there isn't. I went with my dear old aunt's money to a farmer in Kent, and learnt farming; clear of the army first, by—But I must stop that burst of swearing. Half the time I've been away, I was there. The farmer's a good, sober, downhearted man—a sort of beaten Englishman, who don't know it, tough, and always backing. He has two daughters: one went to London, and came to harm, of a kind. The other I'd prick this vein for and bleed to death, singing; and she hates me! I wish she did. She thought me such a good young man! I never drank; went to bed early, was up at work with the birds. Mr. Robert Armstrong! That changeing of my name was like a lead cap on my head. I was never myself with it, felt hang-dog—it was impossible a girl could care for such a fellow as I was. Mother, just listen: she's dark as a gipsy. She's the faithfullest, stoutest-hearted creature in the world. She has black hair, large brown eyes; see her once! She's my mate. I could say to her, 'Stand there; take guard of a thing;' and I could be dead certain of her—she'd perish at her post. Is the door locked? Lock the door; I won't be seen when I speak of her. Well, never mind whether she's handsome or not. She isn't a lady; but she's my lady; she's the woman I could be proud of. She sends me to the devil! I believe a woman 'd fall in love with her cheeks, they are so round and soft and kindly coloured. Think me a fool; I am. And here am I, away from her, and I feel that any day harm may come to her, and she 'll melt, and be as if the devils of hell were mocking me. Who's to keep harm from her when I'm away? What can I do but drink and forget? Only now, when I wake up from it, I'm a crawling wretch at her feet. If I had her feet to kiss! I've never kissed her—never! And no man has kissed her. Damn my head! here's the ache coming on. That's my last oath, mother. I wish there was a Bible handy, but I'll try and stick to it without. My God! when I think of her, I fancy everything on earth hangs still and doubts what's to happen. I'm like a wheel, and go on spinning. Feel my pulse now. Why is it I can't stop it? But there she is, and I could crack up this old world to know what's coming. I was mild as milk all those days I was near her. My comfort is, she don't know me. And that's my curse too! If she did, she'd know as clear as day I'm her mate, her match, the man for her. I am, by heaven!—that's an oath permitted. To see the very soul I want, and to miss her! I'm down here, mother; she loves her sister, and I must learn where her sister's to be found. One of those gentlemen up at Fairly's the guilty man. I don't say which; perhaps I don't know. But oh, what a lot of lightnings I see in the back of my head!"

Robert fell back on the pillow. Mrs. Boulby wiped her eyes. Her feelings were overwhelmed with mournful devotion to the passionate young man; and she expressed them practically: "A rump-steak would never digest in his poor stomach!"

He seemed to be of that opinion too, for when, after lying till eleven, he rose and appeared at the breakfast-table, he ate nothing but crumbs of dry bread. It was curious to see his precise attention to the neatness of his hat and coat, and the nervous eye he cast upon the clock, while brushing and accurately fixing these garments. The hat would not sit as he was accustomed to have it, owing to the bruise on his head, and he stood like a woman petulant with her milliner before the glass; now pressing the hat down till the pain was insufferable, and again trying whether it presented him acceptably in the enforced style of his wearing it. He persisted in this, till Mrs. Boulby's exclamation of wonder admonished him of the ideas received by other eyes than his own. When we appear most incongruous, we are often exposing the key to our characters; and how much his vanity, wounded by Rhoda, had to do with his proceedings down at Warbeach, it were unfair to measure just yet, lest his finer qualities be cast into shade, but to what degree it affected him will be seen.

Mrs. Boulby's persuasions induced him to take a stout silver-topped walking-stick of her husband's, a relic shaped from the wood of the Royal George; leaning upon which rather more like a Naval pensioner than he would have cared to know, he went forth to his appointment with the lady.

CHAPTER XX

MRS. LOVELL SHOWS A TAME BRUTE

The park-sward of Fairly, white with snow, rolled down in long sweeps to the salt water: and under the last sloping oak of the park there was a gorse-bushed lane, green in Summer, but now bearing cumbrous blossom—like burdens of the crisp snow-fall. Mrs. Lovell sat on horseback here, and alone, with her gauntleted hand at her waist, charmingly habited in tone with the landscape. She expected a cavalier, and did not perceive the approach of a pedestrian, but bowed quietly when Robert lifted his hat.

"They say you are mad. You see, I trust myself to you."

"I wish I could thank you for your kindness, madam."

"Are you ill?"

"I had a fall last night, madam."

The lady patted her horse's neck.

"I haven't time to inquire about it. You understand that I cannot give you more than a minute."

She glanced at her watch.

"Let us say five exactly. To begin: I can't affect to be ignorant of the business which brings you down here. I won't pretend to lecture you about the course you have taken; but, let me distinctly assure you, that the gentleman you have chosen to attack in this extraordinary manner, has done no wrong to you or to any one. It is, therefore, disgracefully unjust to single him out. You know he cannot possibly fight you. I speak plainly."

"Yes, madam," said Robert. "I'll answer plainly. He can't fight a man like me. I know it. I bear him no ill-will. I believe he's innocent enough in this matter, as far as acts go."

"That makes your behaviour to him worse!"

Robert looked up into her eyes.

"You are a lady. You won't be shocked at what I tell you."

"Yes, yes," said Mrs. Lovell, hastily: "I have learnt—I am aware of the tale. Some one has been injured or, you think so. I don't accuse you of madness, but, good heavens! what means have you been pursuing! Indeed, sir, let your feelings be as deeply engaged as possible, you have gone altogether the wrong way to work."

"Not if I have got your help by it, madam."

"Gallantly spoken."

She smiled with a simple grace. The next moment she consulted her watch.

"Time has gone faster than I anticipated. I must leave you. Let this be our stipulation:"

She lowered her voice.

"You shall have the address you require. I will undertake to see her myself, when next I am in London. It will be soon. In return, sir, favour me with your word of honour not to molest this gentleman any further. Will you do that? You may trust me."

"I do, madam, with all my soul!" said Robert.

"That's sufficient. I ask no more. Good morning."

Her parting bow remained with him like a vision. Her voice was like the tinkling of harp-strings about his ears. The colour of her riding-habit this day, harmonious with the snow-faced earth, as well as the gentle mission she had taken upon herself, strengthened his vivid fancy in blessing her as something quite divine.

He thought for the first time in his life bitterly of the great fortune which fell to gentlemen in meeting and holding equal converse with so adorable a creature; and he thought of Rhoda as being harshly earthly; repulsive in her coldness as that black belt of water contrasted against the snow on the shores.

He walked some paces in the track of Mrs. Lovell's horse, till his doing so seemed too presumptuous, though to turn the other way and retrace his steps was downright hateful: and he stood apparently in profound contemplation of a ship of war and the trees of the forest behind the masts. Either the fatigue of standing, or emotion, caused his head to throb, so that he heard nothing, not even men's laughter; but looking up suddenly, he beheld, as in a picture, Mrs. Lovell with some gentlemen walking their horses toward him. The lady gazed softly over his head, letting her eyes drop a quiet recognition in passing; one or two of the younger gentlemen stared mockingly.

Edward Blancove was by Mrs. Lovell's side. His eyes fixed upon Robert with steady scrutiny, and Robert gave him a similar inspection, though not knowing why. It was like a child's open look, and he was feeling childish, as if his brain had ceased to act. One of the older gentlemen, with a military aspect, squared his shoulders, and touching an end of his moustache, said, half challengingly,—

"You are dismounted to-day?"

"I have only one horse," Robert simply replied.

Algernon Blancove came last. He neither spoke nor looked at his enemy, but warily clutched his whip. All went by, riding into line some paces distant; and again they laughed as they bent forward to the lady, shouting.

"Odd, to have out the horses on a day like this," Robert thought, and resumed his musing as before. The lady's track now led him homeward, for he had no will of his own. Rounding the lane, he was surprised to see Mrs. Boulby by the hedge. She bobbed like a beggar woman, with a rueful face.

"My dear," she said, in apology for her presence, "I shouldn't ha' interfered, if there was fair play. I'm Englishwoman enough for that. I'd have stood by, as if you was a stranger. Gentlemen always give fair play before a woman. That's why I come, lest this appointment should ha' proved a pitfall to you. Now you'll come home, won't you; and forgive me?"

"I'll come to the old Pilot now, mother," said Robert, pressing her hand.

"That's right; and ain't angry with me for following of you?"

"Follow your own game, mother."

"I did, Robert; and nice and vexed I am, if I'm correct in what I heard say, as that lady and her folk passed, never heeding an old woman's ears. They made a bet of you, dear, they did."

"I hope the lady won," said Robert, scarce hearing.

"And it was she who won, dear. She was to get you to meet her, and give up, and be beaten like, as far as I could understand their chatter; gentlefolks laugh so when they talk; and they can afford to laugh, for they has the best of it. But I'm vexed; just as if I'd felt big and had burst. I want you to be peaceful, of course I do; but I don't like my boy made a bet of."

"Oh, tush, mother," said Robert impatiently.

"I heard 'em, my dear; and complimenting the lady they was, as they passed me. If it vexes you my thinking it, I won't, dear; I reelly won't. I see it lowers you, for there you are at your hat again. It is lowering, to be made a bet of. I've that spirit, that if you was well and sound, I'd rather have you fighting 'em. She's a pleasant enough lady to look at, not a doubt; small-boned, and slim, and fair."

Robert asked which way they had gone.

"Back to the stables, my dear; I heard 'em say so, because one gentleman said that the spectacle was over, and the lady had gained the day; and the snow was balling in the horses' feet; and go they'd better, before my lord saw them out. And another said, you were a wild man she'd tamed; and they said, you ought to wear a collar, with Mrs. Lovell's, her name, graved on it. But don't you be vexed; you may guess they're not my Robert's friends. And, I do assure you, Robert, your hat's neat, if you'd only let it be comfortable: such fidgeting worries the brim. You're best in appearance—and I always said it— when stripped for boxing. Hats are gentlemen's things, and becomes them like as if a title to their heads; though you'd bear being Sir Robert, that you would; and for that matter, your hat is agreeable to behold, and not like the run of our Sunday hats; only you don't seem easy in it. Oh, oh! my tongue's a yard too long. It's the poor head aching, and me to forget it. It's because you never will act invalidy; and I remember how handsome you were one day in the field behind our house, when you boxed a wager with Simon Billet, the waterman; and you was made a bet of then, for my husband betted on you; and that's what made me think of comparisons of you out of your hat and you in it."

Thus did Mrs. Boulby chatter along the way. There was an eminence a little out of the road, overlooking the Fairly stables. Robert left her and went to this point, from whence he beheld the horsemen with the grooms at the horses' heads.

"Thank God, I've only been a fool for five minutes!" he summed up his sensations at the sight. He shut his eyes, praying with all his might never to meet Mrs. Lovell more. It was impossible for him to combat the suggestion that she had befooled him; yet his chivalrous faith in women led him to believe, that as she knew Dahlia's history, she would certainly do her best for the poor girl, and keep her word to him. The throbbing of his head stopped all further thought. It had become violent. He tried to gather his ideas, but the effort was like that of a light dreamer to catch the sequence of a dream, when blackness follows close up, devouring all that is said and done. In despair, he thought with kindness of Mrs. Boulby's brandy.

"Mother," he said, rejoining her, "I've got a notion brandy can't hurt a man when he's in bed. I'll go to bed, and you shall brew me some; and you'll let no one come nigh me; and if I talk light-headed, it's blank paper and scribble, mind that."

The widow promised devoutly to obey all his directions; but he had begun to talk light-headed before he was undressed. He called on the name of a Major Waring, of whom Mrs. Boulby had heard him speak tenderly as a gentleman not ashamed to be his friend; first reproaching him for not being by, and then by the name of Percy, calling to him endearingly, and reproaching himself for not having written to him.

"Two to one, and in the dark!" he kept moaning "and I one to twenty, Percy, all in broad day. Was it fair, I ask?"

Robert's outcries became anything but "blank paper and scribble" to the widow, when he mentioned Nic Sedgett's name, and said: "Look over his right temple he's got my mark a second time."

Hanging by his bedside, Mrs. Boulby strung together, bit by bit, the history of that base midnight attack, which had sent her glorious boy bleeding to her. Nic Sedgett; she could understand, was the accomplice of one of the Fairly gentlemen; but of which one, she could not discover, and consequently set him down as Mr. Algernon Blancove.

By diligent inquiry, she heard that Algernon had been seen in company with the infamous Nic, and likewise that the countenance of Nicodemus was reduced to accept the consolation of a poultice, which was confirmation sufficient. By nightfall Robert was in the doctor's hands, unconscious of Mrs. Boulby's breach of agreement. His father and his aunt were informed of his condition, and prepared, both of them, to bow their heads to the close of an ungodly career. It was known over Warbeach, that Robert lay in danger, and believed that he was dying.

BOOK III

CHAPTER XXI

GIVES A GLIMPSE OF WHAT POOR VILLANIES THE STORY CONTAINS

Mrs. Boulby's ears had not deceived her; it had been a bet: and the day would have gone disastrously with Robert, if Mrs. Lovell had not won her bet. What was heroism to Warbeach, appeared very outrageous blackguardism up at Fairly. It was there believed by the gentlemen, though rather against evidence, that the man was a sturdy ruffian, and an infuriated sot. The first suggestion was to drag him before the magistrates; but against this Algernon protested, declaring his readiness to defend himself, with so vehement a magnanimity, that it was clearly seen the man had a claim on him. Lord Elling, however, when he was told of these systematic assaults upon one of his guests, announced his resolve to bring the law into operation. Algernon heard it as the knell to his visit.

He was too happy, to go away willingly; and the great Jew City of London was exceedingly hot for him at that period; but to stay and risk an exposure of his extinct military career, was not possible. In his despair, he took Mrs. Lovell entirely into his confidence; in doing which, he only filled up the outlines of what she already knew concerning Edward. He was too useful to the lady for her to afford to let him go. No other youth called her "angel" for listening complacently to strange stories of men and their dilemmas; no one fetched and carried for her like Algernon; and she was a woman who cherished dog-like adoration, and could not part with it. She had also the will to reward it.

At her intercession, Robert was spared an introduction to the magistrates. She made light of his misdemeanours, assuring everybody that so splendid a horseman deserved to be dealt with differently from other offenders. The gentlemen who waited upon Farmer Eccles went in obedience to her orders.

Then came the scene on Ditley Marsh, described to that assembly at the Pilot, by Stephen Bilton, when she perceived that Robert was manageable in silken trammels, and made a bet that she would show him tamed. She won her bet, and saved the gentlemen from soiling their hands, for which they had conceived a pressing necessity, and they thanked her, and paid their money over to Algernon, whom she constituted her treasurer. She was called "the man-tamer," gracefully acknowledging the compliment. Colonel Barclay, the moustachioed horseman, who had spoken the few words to Robert in passing, now remarked that there was an end of the military profession.

"I surrender my sword," he said gallantly.

Another declared that ladies would now act in lieu of causing an appeal to arms.

"Similia similibus, &c.," said Edward. "They can, apparently, cure what they originate."

"Ah, the poor sex!" Mrs. Lovell sighed. "When we bring the millennium to you, I believe you will still have a word against Eve."

The whole parade back to the stables was marked by pretty speeches.

"By Jove! but he ought to have gone down on his knees, like a horse when you've tamed him," said Lord Suckling, the young guardsman.

"I would mark a distinction between a horse and a brave man, Lord Suckling," said the lady; and such was Mrs. Lovell's dignity when an allusion to Robert was forced on her, and her wit and ease were so admirable, that none of those who rode with her thought of sitting in judgement on her conduct. Women can make for themselves new spheres, new laws, if they will assume their right to be eccentric as an unquestionable thing, and always reserve a season for showing forth like the conventional women of society.

The evening was Mrs. Lovell's time for this important re-establishment of her position; and many a silly youth who had sailed pleasantly with her all the day, was wrecked when he tried to carry on the topics where she reigned the lady of the drawing-room. Moreover, not being eccentric from vanity, but simply to accommodate what had once been her tastes, and were now her necessities, she avoided slang, and all the insignia of eccentricity.

Thus she mastered the secret of keeping the young men respectfully enthusiastic; so that their irrepressible praises did not (as is usual when these are in acclamation) drag her to their level; and the female world, with which she was perfectly feminine, and as silkenly insipid every evening of her life as was needed to restore her reputation, admitted that she belonged to it, which is everything to an adventurous spirit of that sex: indeed, the sole secure basis of operations.

You are aware that men's faith in a woman whom her sisters discountenance, and partially repudiate, is uneasy, however deeply they may be charmed. On the other hand, she maybe guilty of prodigious oddities without much disturbing their reverence, while she is in the feminine circle.

But what fatal breath was it coming from Mrs. Lovell that was always inflaming men to mutual animosity? What encouragement had she given to Algernon, that Lord Suckling should be jealous of him? And what to Lord Suckling, that Algernon should loathe the sight of the young lord? And why was each desirous of showing his manhood in combat before an eminent peacemaker?

Edward laughed—"Ah-ha!" and rubbed his hands as at a special confirmation of his prophecy, when Algernon came into his room and said, "I shall fight that fellow Suckling. Hang me if I can stand his impudence! I want to have a shot at a man of my own set, just to let Peggy Lovell see! I know what she thinks."

"Just to let Mrs. Lovell see!" Edward echoed. "She has seen it lots of times, my dear Algy. Come; this looks lively. I was sure she would soon be sick of the water-gruel of peace."

"I tell you she's got nothing to do with it, Ned. Don't be confoundedly unjust. She didn't tell me to go and seek him. How can she help his whispering to her? And then she looks over at me, and I swear I'm not going to be defended by a woman. She must fancy I haven't got the pluck of a flea. I know what her idea of young fellows is. Why, she said to me, when Suckling went off from her, the other day, 'These are our Guards.' I shall fight him."

"Do," said Edward.

"Will you take a challenge?"

"I'm a lawyer, Mr. Mars."

"You won't take a challenge for a friend, when he's insulted?"

"I reply again, I am a lawyer. But this is what I'll do, if you like. I'll go to Mrs. Lovely and inform her that it is your desire to gain her esteem by fighting with pistols. That will accomplish the purpose you seek. It will possibly disappoint her, for she will have to stop the affair; but women are born to be disappointed—they want so much."

"I'll fight him some way or other," said Algernon, glowering; and then his face became bright: "I say, didn't she manage that business beautifully this morning? Not another woman in the world could have done it."

"Oh, Una and the Lion! Mrs. Valentine and Orson! Did you bet with the rest?" his cousin asked.

"I lost my tenner; but what's that!"

"There will be an additional five to hand over to the man Sedgett. What's that!"

"No, hang it!" Algernon shouted.

"You've paid your ten for the shadow cheerfully. Pay your five for the substance."

"Do you mean to say that Sedgett—" Algernon stared.

"Miracles, if you come to examine them, Algy, have generally had a pathway prepared for them; and the miracle of the power of female persuasion exhibited this morning was not quite independent of the preliminary agency of a scoundrel."

"So that's why you didn't bet." Algernon signified the opening of his intelligence with his eyelids, pronouncing "by jingos" and "by Joves," to ease the sudden rush of ideas within him. "You might have let me into the secret, Ned. I'd lose any number of tens to Peggy Lovell, but a fellow don't like to be in the dark."

"Except, Algy, that when you carry light, you're a general illuminator. Let the matter drop. Sedgett has saved you from annoyance. Take him his five pounds."

"Annoyance be hanged, my good Ned!" Algernon was aroused to reply. "I don't complain, and I've done my best to stand in front of you; and as you've settled the fellow, I say nothing; but, between us two, who's the guilty party, and who's the victim?"

"Didn't he tell you he had you in his power?"

"I don't remember that he did."

"Well, I heard him. The sturdy cur refused to be bribed, so there was only one way of quieting him; and you see what a thrashing does for that sort of beast. I, Algy, never abandon a friend; mark that. Take the five pounds to Sedgett."

Algernon strode about the room. "First of all, you stick me up in a theatre, so that I'm seen with a girl; and then you get behind me, and let me be pelted," he began grumbling. "And ask a fellow for money, who hasn't a farthing! I shan't literally have a farthing till that horse 'Templemore' runs; and then, by George! I'll pay my debts. Jews are awful things!"

"How much do you require at present?" said Edward, provoking his appetite for a loan.

"Oh, fifty—that is, just now. More like a thousand when I get to town. And where it's to come from! but never mind. 'Pon my soul, I pity the fox I run down here. I feel I'm exactly in his case in London. However, if I can do you any service, Ned—"

Edward laughed. "You might have done me the service of not excusing yourself to the squire when he came here, in such a way as to implicate me."

"But I was so tremendously badgered, Ned."

"You had a sort of gratification in letting the squire crow over his brother. And he did crow for a time."

"On my honour, Ned, as to crowing! he went away cursing at me. Peggy Lovell managed it somehow for you. I was really awfully badgered."

"Yes; but you know what a man my father is. He hasn't the squire's philosophy in those affairs."

"'Pon my soul, Mr. Ned, I never guessed it before; but I rather fancy you got clear with Sir Billy the banker by washing in my basin—eh, did you?"

Edward looked straight at his cousin, saying, "You deserved worse than that. You were treacherous. You proved you were not to be trusted; and yet, you see, I trust you. Call it my folly. Of course (and I don't mind telling you) I used my wits to turn the point of the attack. I may be what they call unscrupulous when I'm surprised. I have to look to money as well as you; and if my father thought it went in a—what he considers—wrong direction, the source would be choked by paternal morality. You betrayed me. Listen."

"I tell you, Ned, I merely said to my governor—"

"Listen to me. You betrayed me. I defended myself; that is, I've managed so that I may still be of service to you. It was a near shave; but you now see the value of having a character with one's father. Just open my writing-desk there, and toss out the cheque-book. I confess I can't see why you should have objected—but let that pass. How much do you want? Fifty? Say forty-five, and five I'll give you to pay to Sedgett—making fifty. Eighty before, and fifty—one hundred and thirty. Write that you owe me that sum, on a piece of paper. I can't see why you should wish to appear so uncommonly virtuous."

Algernon scribbled the written acknowledgment, which he despised himself for giving, and the receiver for taking, but was always ready to give for the money, and said, as he put the cheque in his purse: "It was this infernal fellow completely upset me. If you were worried by a bull-dog, by Jove, Ned, you'd lose your coolness. He bothered my head off. Ask me now, and I'll do anything on earth for you. My back's broad. Sir Billy can't think worse of me than he does. Do you want to break positively with that pretty rival to Peggy L.? I've got a scheme to relieve you, my poor old Ned, and make everybody happy. I'll lay the foundations of a fresh and brilliant reputation for myself."

Algernon took a chair. Edward was fathoms deep in his book.

The former continued: "I'd touch on the money-question last, with any other fellow than you; but you always know that money's the hinge, and nothing else lifts a man out of a scrape. It costs a stiff pull on your banker, and that reminds me, you couldn't go to Sir Billy for it; you'd have to draw in advance, by degrees anyhow, look here:—There are lots of young farmers who want to emigrate and want wives and money. I know one. It's no use going into particulars, but it's worth thinking over. Life is made up of mutual help, Ned. You can help another fellow better than yourself. As for me, when I'm in a hobble, I give you my word of honour, I'm just like a baby, and haven't an idea at my own disposal. The same with others. You can't manage without somebody's assistance. What do you say, old boy?"

Edward raised his head from his book. "Some views of life deduced from your private experience?" he observed; and Algernon cursed at book-worms, who would never take hints, and left him.

But when he was by himself, Edward pitched his book upon the floor and sat reflecting. The sweat started on his forehead. He was compelled to look into his black volume and study it. His desire was to act humanely and generously; but the question inevitably recurred: "How can I utterly dash my prospects in the world?" It would be impossible to bring Dahlia to great houses; and he liked great houses and the charm of mixing among delicately-bred women. On the other hand, lawyers have married beneath them—married cooks, housemaids, governesses, and so forth. And what has a lawyer to do with a dainty lady, who will constantly distract him with finicking civilities and speculations in unprofitable regions? What he does want is a woman amiable as a surface of parchment, serviceable as his inkstand; one who will be like the wig in which he closes his forensic term, disreputable from overwear, but suited to the purpose.

"Ah! if I meant to be nothing but a lawyer!" Edward stopped the flow of this current in Dahlia's favour. His passion for her was silent. Was it dead? It was certainly silent. Since Robert had come down to play his wild game of persecution at Fairly, the simple idea of Dahlia had been Edward's fever. He detested brute force, with a finely-witted man's full loathing; and Dahlia's obnoxious champion had grown to be associated in his mind with Dahlia. He swept them both from his recollection abhorrently, for in his recollection he could not divorce them. He pretended to suppose that Dahlia, whose only reproach to him was her suffering, participated in the scheme to worry him. He could even forget her beauty—forget all, save the unholy fetters binding him. She seemed to imprison him in bare walls. He meditated on her character. She had no strength. She was timid, comfort-loving, fond of luxury, credulous, preposterously conventional; that is, desirous more than the ordinary run of women of being hedged about and guarded by ceremonies—"mere ceremonies," said Edward, forgetting the notion he entertained of women not so protected. But it may be, that in playing the part of fool and coward, we cease to be mindful of the absolute necessity for sheltering the weak from that monstrous allied army, the cowards and the fools. He admitted even to himself that he had deceived her, at the same time denouncing her unheard-of capacity of belief, which had placed him in a miserable hobble, and that was the truth.

Now, men confessing themselves in a miserable hobble, and knowing they are guilty of the state of things lamented by them, intend to drown that part of their nature which disturbs them by its outcry. The submission to a tangle that could be cut through instantaneously by any exertion of a noble will, convicts them. They had better not confide, even to their secret hearts, that they are afflicted by their conscience and the generosity of their sentiments, for it will be only to say that these high qualities are on the failing side. Their inclination, under the circumstances, is generally base, and no less a counsellor than uncorrupted common sense, when they are in such a hobble, will sometimes advise them to be base. But, in admitting the plea which common sense puts forward on their behalf, we may fairly ask them to be masculine in their baseness. Or, in other words, since they must be selfish, let them be so without the poltroonery of selfishness. Edward's wish was to be perfectly just, as far as he could be now—just to himself as well; for how was he to prove of worth and aid to any one depending on him, if he stood crippled? Just, also, to his family; to his possible posterity; and just to Dahlia. His task was to reconcile the variety of justness due upon all sides. The struggle, we will assume, was severe, for he thought so; he thought of going to Dahlia and speaking the word of separation; of going to her family and stating his offence, without personal exculpation; thus masculine in baseness, he was in idea; but poltroonery triumphed, the picture of himself facing his sin and its victims dismayed him, and his struggle ended in his considering as to the fit employment of one thousand pounds in his possession, the remainder of a small legacy, hitherto much cherished.

A day later, Mrs. Lovell said to him: "Have you heard of that unfortunate young man? I am told that he lies in great danger from a blow on the back of his head. He looked ill when I saw him, and however mad he may be, I'm sorry harm should have come to one who is really brave. Gentle means are surely best. It is so with horses, it must be so with men. As to women, I don't pretend to unriddle them."

"Gentle means are decidedly best," said Edward, perceiving that her little dog Algy had carried news to her, and that she was setting herself to fathom him. "You gave an eminent example of it yesterday. I was so sure of the result that I didn't bet against you."

"Why not have backed me?"

The hard young legal face withstood the attack of her soft blue eyes, out of which a thousand needles flew, seeking a weak point in the mask.

"The compliment was, to incite you to a superhuman effort."

"Then why not pay the compliment?"

"I never pay compliments to transparent merit; I do not hold candles to lamps."

"True," said she.

"And as gentle means are so admirable, it would be as well to stop incision and imbruing between those two boys."

"Which?" she asked innocently.

"Suckling and Algy."

"Is it possible? They are such boys."

"Exactly of the kind to do it. Don't you know?" and Edward explained elaborately and cruelly the character of the boys who rushed into conflicts. Colour deep as evening red confused her cheeks, and she said, "We must stop them."

"Alas!" he shook his head; "if it's not too late."

"It never is too late."

"Perhaps not, when the embodiment of gentle means is so determined."

"Come; I believe they are in the billiard room now, and you shall see," she said.

The pair were found in the billiard room, even as a pair of terriers that remember a bone. Mrs. Lovell proposed a game, and offered herself for partner to Lord Suckling.

"Till total defeat do us part," the young nobleman acquiesced; and total defeat befell them. During the play of the balls, Mrs. Lovell threw a jealous intentness of observation upon all the strokes made by Algernon; saying nothing, but just looking at him when he did a successful thing. She winked at some quiet stately betting that went on between him and Lord Suckling.

They were at first preternaturally polite and formal toward one another; by degrees, the influence at work upon them was manifested in a thaw of their stiff demeanour, and they fell into curt dialogues, which Mrs. Lovell gave herself no concern to encourage too early.

Edward saw, and was astonished himself to feel that she had ceased to breathe that fatal inciting breath, which made men vindictively emulous of her favour, and mad to match themselves for a claim to the chief smile. No perceptible change was displayed. She was Mrs. Lovell still; vivacious and soft; flame-coloured, with the arrowy eyelashes; a pleasant companion, who did not play the woman obtrusively among men, and show a thirst for homage. All the difference appeared to be, that there was an absence as of some evil spiritual emanation.

And here a thought crossed him—one of the memorable little evanescent thoughts which sway us by our chance weakness; "Does she think me wanting in physical courage?"

Now, though the difference between them had been owing to a scornful remark that she had permitted herself to utter, on his refusal to accept a quarrel with one of her numerous satellites, his knowledge of her worship of brains, and his pride in his possession of the burdensome weight, had quite precluded his guessing that she might haply suppose him to be deficient in personal bravery. He was astounded by the reflection that she had thus misjudged him. It was distracting; sober-thoughted as he was by nature. He watched the fair simplicity of her new manner with a jealous eye. Her management of the two youths was exquisite; but to him, Edward, she had never condescended to show herself thus mediating and amiable. Why? Clearly, because she conceived that he had no virile fire in his composition. Did the detestable little devil think silly duelling a display of valour? Did the fair seraph think him anything less than a man?

How beautifully hung the yellow loop of her hair as she leaned over the board! How gracious she was and like a Goddess with these boys, as he called them! She rallied her partner, not letting him forget that he had the honour of being her partner; while she appeared envious of Algernon's skill, and talked to both and got them upon common topics, and laughed, and was like a fair English flower of womanhood; nothing deadly.

"There, Algy; you have beaten us. I don't think I'll have Lord Suckling for my partner any more," she said, putting up her wand, and pouting.

"You don't bear malice?" said Algernon, revived.

"There is my hand. Now you must play a game alone with Lord Suckling, and beat him; mind you beat him, or it will redound to my discredit."

With which, she and Edward left them.

"Algy was a little crestfallen, and no wonder," she said. "He is soon set up again. They will be good friends now."

"Isn't it odd, that they should be ready to risk their lives for trifles?"

Thus Edward tempted her to discuss the subject which he had in his mind.

She felt intuitively the trap in his voice.

"Ah, yes," she replied; "it must be because they know their lives are not precious."

So utterly at her mercy had he fallen, that her pronunciation of that word "precious" carried a severe sting to him, and it was not spoken with peculiar emphasis; on the contrary, she wished to indicate that she was of his way of thinking, as regarded this decayed method of settling disputes. He turned to leave her.

"You go to your Adeline, I presume," she said.

"Ah! that reminds me. I have never thanked you."

"For my good services? such as they are. Sir William will be very happy, and it was for him, a little more than for you, that I went out of my way to be a matchmaker."

"It was her character, of course, that struck you as being so eminently suited to mine."

"Can I tell what is the character of a girl? She is mild and shy, and extremely gentle. In all probability she has a passion for battles and bloodshed. I judged from your father's point of view. She has money, and you are to have money; and the union of money and money is supposed to be a good thing. And besides, you are variable, and off to-morrow what you are on to-day; is it not so? and heiresses are never jilted. Colonel Barclay is only awaiting your retirement. Le roi est mort; vive le roi! Heiresses may cry it like kingdoms."

"I thought," said Edward, meaningly, "the colonel had better taste."

"Do you not know that my friends are my friends because they are not allowed to dream they will do anything else? If they are taken poorly, I commend them to a sea-voyage—Africa, the North-West Passage, the source of the Nile. Men with their vanity wounded may discover wonders! They return friendly as before, whether they have done the Geographical Society a service or not. That is, they generally do."

"Then I begin to fancy I must try those latitudes."

"Oh! you are my relative."

He scarcely knew that he had uttered "Margaret."

She replied to it frankly, "Yes, Cousin Ned. You have made the voyage, you see, and have come back friends with me. The variability of opals! Ah! Sir John, you join us in season. We were talking of opals. Is the opal a gem that stands to represent women?"

Sir John Capes smoothed his knuckles with silken palms, and with courteous antique grin, responded, "It is a gem I would never dare to offer to a lady's acceptance."

"It is by repute unlucky; so you never can have done so."

"Exquisite!" exclaimed the veteran in smiles, "if what you deign to imply were only true!"

They entered the drawing-room among the ladies.

Edward whispered in Mrs. Lovell's ear, "He is in need of the voyage."

"He is very near it," she answered in the same key, and swam into general conversation.

Her cold wit, Satanic as the gleam of it struck through his mind, gave him a throb of desire to gain possession of her, and crush her.

CHAPTER XXII

EDWARD TAKES HIS COURSE

The writing of a letter to Dahlia had previously been attempted and abandoned as a sickening task. Like an idle boy with his holiday imposition, Edward shelved it among the nightmares, saying, "How can I sit down and lie to her!" and thinking that silence would prepare her bosom for the coming truth.

Silence is commonly the slow poison used by those who mean to murder love. There is nothing violent about it; no shock is given; Hope is not abruptly strangled, but merely dreams of evil, and fights with gradually stifling shadows. When the last convulsions come they are not terrific; the frame has been weakened for dissolution; love dies like natural decay. It seems the kindest way of doing a cruel thing. But Dahlia wrote, crying out her agony at the torture. Possibly your nervously organized natures require a modification of the method.

Edward now found himself able to conduct a correspondence. He despatched the following:—

"My Dear Dahlia,—Of course I cannot expect you to be aware of the bewildering occupations of a country house, where a man has literally not five minutes' time to call his own; so I pass by your reproaches. My father has gone at last. He has manifested an extraordinary liking for my society, and I am to join him elsewhere —perhaps run over to Paris (your city)—but at present for a few days I am my own master, and the first thing I do is to attend to your demands: not to write 'two lines,' but to give you a good long letter.

"What on earth makes you fancy me unwell? You know I am never unwell. And as to your nursing me— when has there ever been any need for it?

"You must positively learn patience. I have been absent a week or so, and you talk of coming down here and haunting the house! Such ghosts as you meet with strange treatment when they go about unprotected, let me give you warning. You have my full permission to walk out in the Parks for exercise. I think you are bound to do it, for your health's sake.

"Pray discontinue that talk about the alteration in your looks. You must learn that you are no longer a child. Cease to write like a child. If people stare at you, as you say, you are very well aware it is not because you are becoming plain. You do not mean it, I know; but there is a disingenuousness in remarks of this sort that is to me exceedingly distasteful. Avoid the shadow of hypocrisy. Women are subject to it—and it is quite innocent, no doubt. I won't lecture you.

"My cousin Algernon is here with me. He has not spoken of your sister. Your fears in that direction are quite unnecessary. He is attached to a female cousin of ours, a very handsome person, witty, and highly sensible, who dresses as well as the lady you talk about having seen one day in Wrexby Church. Her lady's-maid is a Frenchwoman, which accounts for it. You have not forgotten the boulevards?

"I wish you to go on with your lessons in French. Educate yourself, and you will rise superior to these distressing complaints. I recommend you to read the newspapers daily. Buy nice picture-books, if the papers are too matter-of-fact for you. By looking eternally inward, you teach yourself to fret, and the consequence is, or will be, that you wither. No constitution can stand it. All the ladies here take an interest in Parliamentary affairs. They can talk to men upon men's themes. It is impossible to explain to you how wearisome an everlasting nursery prattle becomes. The idea that men ought never to tire of it is founded on some queer belief that they are not mortal.

"Parliament opens in February. My father wishes me to stand for Selborough. If he or some one will do the talking to the tradesmen, and provide the beer and the bribes, I have no objection. In that case my Law goes to the winds. I'm bound to make a show of obedience, for he has scarcely got over my summer's trip. He holds me a prisoner to him for heaven knows how long—it may be months.

"As for the heiress whom he has here to make a match for me, he and I must have a pitched battle about her by and by. At present my purse insists upon my not offending him. When will old men understand young ones? I burn your letters, and beg you to follow the example. Old letters are the dreariest ghosts in the world, and you cannot keep more treacherous rubbish in your possession. A discovery would exactly ruin me.

"Your purchase of a black-velvet bonnet with pink ribands, was very suitable. Or did you write 'blue' ribands? But your complexion can bear anything.

"You talk of being annoyed when you walk out. Remember, that no woman who knows at all how to conduct herself need for one moment suffer annoyance.

"What is the 'feeling' you speak of? I cannot conceive any 'feeling' that should make you helpless when you consider that you are insulted. There are women who have natural dignity, and women who have none.

"You ask the names of the gentlemen here:—Lord Carey, Lord Wippern (both leave to-morrow), Sir John Capes, Colonel Barclay, Lord Suckling. The ladies:—Mrs. Gosling, Miss Gosling, Lady Carey. Mrs. Anybody—to any extent.

"They pluck hen's feathers all day and half the night. I see them out, and make my bow to the next batch of visitors, and then I don't know where I am.

"Read poetry, if it makes up for my absence, as you say. Repeat it aloud, minding the pulsation of feet. Go to the theatre now and then, and take your landlady with you. If she's a cat, fit one of your dresses on the servant-girl, and take her. You only want a companion—a dummy will do. Take a box and sit behind the curtain, back to the audience.

"I wrote to my wine-merchant to send Champagne and Sherry. I hope he did: the Champagne in pints and half-pints; if not, return them instantly. I know how Economy, sitting solitary, poor thing, would not dare to let the froth of a whole pint bottle fly out.

"Be an obedient girl and please me.

"Your stern tutor,

"Edward the First."

He read this epistle twice over to satisfy himself that it was a warm effusion, and not too tender; and it satisfied him. By a stretch of imagination, he could feel that it represented him to her as in a higher atmosphere, considerate for her, and not so intimate that she could deem her spirit to be sharing it. Another dose of silence succeeded this discreet administration of speech.

Dahlia replied with letter upon letter; blindly impassioned, and again singularly cold; but with no reproaches. She was studying, she said. Her head ached a little; only a little. She walked; she read poetry; she begged him to pardon her for not drinking wine. She was glad that he burnt her letters, which were so foolish that if she could have the courage to look at them after they were written, they would never be sent. He was slightly revolted by one exclamation: "How ambitious you are!"

"Because I cannot sit down for life in a London lodging-house!" he thought, and eyed her distantly as a poor good creature who had already accepted her distinctive residence in another sphere than his. From such a perception of her humanity, it was natural that his livelier sense of it should diminish. He felt that he had awakened; and he shook her off.

And now he set to work to subdue Mrs. Lovell. His own subjugation was the first fruit of his effort. It was quite unacknowledged by him: but when two are at this game, the question arises—"Which can live without the other?" and horrid pangs smote him to hear her telling musically of the places she was journeying to, the men she would see, and the chances of their meeting again before he was married to the heiress Adeline.

"I have yet to learn that I am engaged to her," he said. Mrs. Lovell gave him a fixed look,—

"She has a half-brother."

He stepped away in a fury.

"Devil!" he muttered, absolutely muttered it, knowing that he fooled and frowned like a stage-hero in stagey heroics. "You think to hound me into this brutal stupidity of fighting, do you? Upon my honour," he added in his natural manner, "I believe she does, though!"

But the look became his companion. It touched and called up great vanity in his breast, and not till then could he placably confront the look. He tried a course of reading. Every morning he was down in the library, looking old in an arm-chair over his book; an intent abstracted figure.

Mrs. Lovell would enter and eye him carelessly; utter little commonplaces and go forth. The silly words struck on his brain. The book seemed hollow; sounded hollow as he shut it. This woman breathed of active striving life. She was a spur to black energies; a plumed glory; impulsive to chivalry. Everything she said and did held men in scales, and approved or rejected them.

Intoxication followed this new conception of her. He lost altogether his right judgement; even the cooler after-thoughts were lost. What sort of man had Harry been, her first husband? A dashing soldier, a quarrelsome duellist, a dull dog. But, dull to her? She, at least, was reverential to the memory of him.

She lisped now and then of "my husband," very prettily, and with intense provocation; and yet she worshipped brains. Evidently she thirsted for that rare union of brains and bravery in a man, and would never surrender till she had discovered it. Perhaps she fancied it did not exist. It might be that she took Edward as the type of brains, and Harry of bravery, and supposed that the two qualities were not to be had actually in conjunction.

Her admiration of his (Edward's) wit, therefore, only strengthened the idea she entertained of his deficiency in that other companion manly virtue.

Edward must have been possessed, for he ground his teeth villanously in supposing himself the victim of this outrageous suspicion. And how to prove it false? How to prove it false in a civilized age, among sober-living men and women, with whom the violent assertion of bravery would certainly imperil his claim to brains? His head was like a stew-pan over the fire, bubbling endlessly.

He railed at her to Algernon, and astonished the youth, who thought them in a fair way to make an alliance. "Milk and capsicums," he called her, and compared her to bloody mustard-haired Saxon Queens of history, and was childishly spiteful. And Mrs. Lovell had it all reported to her, as he was-quite aware.

"The woman seeking for an anomaly wants a master."

With this pompous aphorism, he finished his reading of the fair Enigma.

Words big in the mouth serve their turn when there is no way of satisfying the intelligence.

To be her master, however, one must not begin by writhing as her slave.

The attempt to read an inscrutable woman allows her to dominate us too commandingly. So the lordly mind takes her in a hard grasp, cracks the shell, and drawing forth the kernel, says, "This was all the puzzle."

Doubtless it is the fate which women like Mrs. Lovell provoke. The truth was, that she could read a character when it was under her eyes; but its yesterday and to-morrow were a blank. She had no imaginative hold on anything. For which reason she was always requiring tangible signs of virtues that she esteemed.

The thirst for the shows of valour and wit was insane with her; but she asked for nothing that she herself did not give in abundance, and with beauty super-added. Her propensity to bet sprang of her passion for combat; she was not greedy of money, or reckless in using it; but a difference of opinion arising, her instinct forcibly prompted her to back her own. If the stake was the risk of a lover's life, she was ready to put down the stake, and would have marvelled contemptuously at the lover complaining. "Sheep! sheep!" she thought of those who dared not fight, and had a wavering tendency to affix the epithet to those who simply did not fight.

Withal, Mrs. Lovell was a sensible person; clearheaded and shrewd; logical, too, more than the run of her sex: I may say, profoundly practical. So much so, that she systematically reserved the after-years for enlightenment upon two or three doubts of herself, which struck her in the calm of her spirit, from time to time.

"France," Edward called her, in one of their colloquies.

It was an illuminating title. She liked the French (though no one was keener for the honour of her own country in opposition to them), she liked their splendid boyishness, their unequalled devotion, their merciless intellects; the oneness of the nation when the sword is bare and pointing to chivalrous enterprise.

She liked their fine varnish of sentiment, which appears so much on the surface that Englishmen suppose it to have nowhere any depth; as if the outer coating must necessarily exhaust the stock, or as if what is at the source of our being can never be made visible.

She had her imagination of them as of a streaming banner in the jaws of storm, with snows among the cloud-rents and lightning in the chasms:—which image may be accounted for by the fact that when a girl she had in adoration kissed the feet of Napoleon, the giant of the later ghosts of history.

It was a princely compliment. She received it curtseying, and disarmed the intended irony. In reply, she called him "Great Britain." I regret to say that he stood less proudly for his nation. Indeed, he flushed. He remembered articles girding at the policy of peace at any price, and half felt that Mrs. Lovell had meant to crown him with a Quaker's hat. His title fell speedily into disuse; but, "Yes, France," and "No, France," continued, his effort being to fix the epithet to frivolous allusions, from which her ingenuity rescued it honourably.

Had she ever been in love? He asked her the question. She stabbed him with so straightforward an affirmative that he could not conceal the wound.

"Have I not been married?" she said.

He began to experience the fretful craving to see the antecedents of the torturing woman spread out before him. He conceived a passion for her girlhood. He begged for portraits of her as a girl. She showed him the portrait of Harry Lovell in a locket. He held the locket between his fingers. Dead Harry was kept very warm. Could brains ever touch her emotions as bravery had done?

"Where are the brains I boast of?" he groaned, in the midst of these sensational extravagances.

The lull of action was soon to be disturbed. A letter was brought to him.

He opened it and read—

"Mr. Edward Blancove,—When you rode by me under Fairly Park, I did not know you. I can give you a medical certificate that since then I have been in the doctor's hands. I know you now. I call upon you to meet me, with what weapons you like best, to prove that you are not a midnight assassin. The place shall be where you choose to appoint. If you decline I will make you publicly acknowledge what you have done. If you answer, that I am not a gentleman and you are one, I say that you have attacked me in the dark, when I was on horseback, and you are now my equal, if I like to think so. You will not talk about the law after that night. The man you employed I may punish or I may leave, though he struck the blow. But I will meet you. To-morrow, a friend of mine, who is a major in the army, will be down here, and will call on you from me; or on any friend of yours you are pleased to name. I will not let you escape. Whether I shall face a guilty man in you, God knows; but I know I have a right to call upon you to face me.

"I am, Sir,

"Yours truly,

"Robert Eccles."

Edward's face grew signally white over the contents of this unprecedented challenge. The letter had been brought in to him at the breakfast table. "Read it, read it," said Mrs. Lovell, seeing him put it by; and he had read it with her eyes on him.

The man seemed to him a man of claws, who clutched like a demon. Would nothing quiet him? Edward thought of bribes for the sake of peace; but a second glance at the letter assured his sagacious mind that bribes were powerless in this man's case; neither bribes nor sticks were of service. Departure from Fairly would avail as little: the tenacious devil would follow him to London; and what was worse, as a hound from Dahlia's family he was now on the right scent, and appeared to know that he was. How was a scandal to be avoided? By leaving Fairly instantly for any place on earth, he could not avoid leaving the man behind; and if the man saw Mrs. Lovell again, her instincts as a woman of her class were not to be trusted. As likely as not she would side with the ruffian; that is, she would think he had been wronged— perhaps think that he ought to have been met. There is the democratic virus secret in every woman; it was predominant in Mrs. Lovell, according to Edward's observation of the lady. The rights of individual manhood were, as he angrily perceived, likely to be recognized by her spirit, if only they were stoutly asserted; and that in defiance of station, of reason, of all the ideas inculcated by education and society.

"I believe she'll expect me to fight him," he exclaimed. At least, he knew she would despise him if he avoided the brutal challenge without some show of dignity.

On rising from the table, he drew Algernon aside. It was an insufferable thought that he was compelled to take his brainless cousin into his confidence, even to the extent of soliciting his counsel, but there was no help for it. In vain Edward asked himself why he had been such an idiot as to stain his hands with the affair at all. He attributed it to his regard for Algernon. Having commonly the sway of his passions, he was in the habit of forgetting that he ever lost control of them; and the fierce black mood, engendered by Robert's audacious persecution, had passed from his memory, though it was now recalled in full force.

"See what a mess you drag a man into," he said.

Algernon read a line of the letter. "Oh, confound this infernal fellow!" he shouted, in sickly wonderment; and snapped sharp, "drag you into the mess? Upon my honour, your coolness, Ned, is the biggest part about you, if it isn't the best."

Edward's grip fixed on him, for they were only just out of earshot of Mrs. Lovell. They went upstairs, and Algernon read the letter through.

"'Midnight assassin,'" he repeated; "by Jove! how beastly that sounds. It's a lie that you attacked him in the dark, Ned—eh?"

"I did not attack him at all," said Edward. "He behaved like a ruffian to you, and deserved shooting like a mad dog."

"Did you, though," Algernon persisted in questioning, despite his cousin's manifest shyness of the subject "did you really go out with that man Sedgett, and stop this fellow on horseback? He speaks of a blow. You didn't strike him, did you, Ned? I mean, not a hit, except in self-defence?"

Edward bit his lip, and shot a level reflective side-look, peculiar to him when meditating. He wished his cousin to propose that Mrs. Lovell should see the letter. He felt that by consulting with her, he could bring her to apprehend the common sense of the position, and be so far responsible for what he might do, that she would not dare to let her heart be rebellious toward him subsequently. If he himself went to her it would look too much like pleading for her intercession. The subtle directness of the woman's spirit had to be guarded against at every point.

He replied to Algernon,—

"What I did was on your behalf. Oblige me by not interrogating me. I give you my positive assurance that I encouraged no unmanly assault on him."

"That'll do, that'll do," said Algernon, eager not to hear more, lest there should come an explanation of what he had heard. "Of course, then, this fellow has no right—the devil's in him! If we could only make him murder Sedgett and get hanged for it! He's got a friend who's a major in the army? Oh, come, I say; this is pitching it too stiff. I shall insist upon seeing his commission. Really, Ned, I can't advise. I'll stand by you, that you may be sure of—stand by you; but what the deuce to say to help you! Go before the magistrate.... Get Lord Elling to issue a warrant to prevent a breach of the peace. No; that won't do. This quack of a major in the army's to call to-morrow. I don't mind, if he shows his credentials all clear, amusing him in any manner he likes. I can't see the best scheme. Hang it, Ned, it's very hard upon me to ask me to do the thinking. I always go to Peggy Lovell when I'm bothered. There—Mrs. Lovell! Mistress Lovell! Madame! my Princess Lovell, if you want me to pronounce respectable titles to her name. You're too proud to ask a woman to help you, ain't you, Ned?"

"No," said Edward, mildly. "In some cases their wits are keen enough. One doesn't like to drag her into such a business."

"Hm," went Algernon. "I don't think she's so innocent of it as you fancy."

"She's very clever," said Edward.

"She's awfully clever!" cried Algernon. He paused to give room for more praises of her, and then pursued:

"She's so kind. That's what you don't credit her for. I'll go and consult her, if positively you don't mind. Trust her for keeping it quiet. Come, Ned, she's sure to hit upon the right thing. May I go?"

"It's your affair, more than mine," said Edward.

"Have it so, if you like," returned the good-natured fellow. "It's worth while consulting her, just to see how neatly she'll take it. Bless your heart, she won't know a bit more than you want her to know. I'm off to her now." He carried away the letter.

Edward's own practical judgement would have advised his instantly sending a short reply to Robert, explaining that he was simply in conversation with the man Sedgett, when Robert, the old enemy of the latter, rode by, and, that while regretting Sedgett's proceedings, he could not be held accountable for them. But it was useless to think of acting in accordance with his reason. Mrs. Lovell was queen, and sat in reason's place. It was absolutely necessary to conciliate her approbation of his conduct in this dilemma, by submitting to the decided unpleasantness of talking with her on a subject that fevered him, and of allowing her to suppose he required the help of her sagacity. Such was the humiliation imposed upon him. Further than this he had nothing to fear, for no woman could fail to be overborne by the masculine force of his brain in an argument. The humiliation was bad enough, and half tempted him to think that his old dream of working as a hard student, with fair and gentle Dahlia ministering to his comforts, and too happy to call herself his, was best. Was it not, after one particular step had been taken, the manliest life he could have shaped out? Or did he imagine it so at this moment, because he was a coward, and because pride, and vanity, and ferocity alternately had to screw him up to meet the consequences of his acts, instead of the great heart?

If a coward, Dahlia was his home, his refuge, his sanctuary. Mrs. Lovell was perdition and its scorching fires to a man with a taint of cowardice in him.

Whatever he was, Edward's vanity would not permit him to acknowledge himself that. Still, he did not call on his heart to play inspiriting music. His ideas turned to subterfuge. His aim was to keep the good opinion of Mrs. Lovell while he quieted Robert; and he entered straightway upon that very perilous course, the attempt, for the sake of winning her, to bewilder and deceive a woman's instincts.

CHAPTER XXIII

MAJOR PERCY WARING

Over a fire in one of the upper sitting-rooms of the Pilot Inn, Robert sat with his friend, the beloved friend of whom he used to speak to Dahlia and Rhoda, too proudly not to seem betraying the weaker point of pride. This friend had accepted the title from a private soldier of his regiment; to be capable of doing which, a man must be both officer and gentleman in a sterner and less liberal sense than is expressed by that everlasting phrase in the mouth of the military parrot. Major Percy Waring, the son of a clergyman, was a working soldier, a slayer, if you will, from pure love of the profession of arms, and all the while the sweetest and gentlest of men. I call him a working soldier in opposition to the parading soldier, the coxcomb in uniform, the hero by accident, and the martial boys of wealth and station, who are of the army of England. He studied war when the trumpet slumbered, and had no place but in the field when it sounded. To him the honour of England was as a babe in his arms: he hugged it like a mother. He knew the military history of every regiment in the service. Disasters even of old date brought groans from him. This enthusiastic face was singularly soft when the large dark eyes were set musing. The cast of it being such, sometimes in speaking of a happy play of artillery upon congregated masses, an odd effect was produced. Ordinarily, the clear features were reflective almost to sadness, in the absence of animation; but an exulting energy for action would now and then light them up. Hilarity of spirit did not belong to him. He was, nevertheless, a cheerful talker, as could be seen in the glad ear given to him by Robert. Between them it was "Robert" and "Percy." Robert had rescued him from drowning on the East Anglian shore, and the friendship which ensued was one chief reason for Robert's quitting the post of trooper and buying himself out. It was against Percy's advice, who wanted to purchase a commission for him; but the humbler man had the sturdy scruples of his rank regarding money, and his romantic illusions being dispersed by an experience of the absolute class-distinctions in the service, Robert; that he might prevent his friend from violating them, made use of his aunt's legacy to obtain release. Since that date they had not met; but their friendship was fast. Percy had recently paid a visit to Queen Anne's Farm, where he had seen Rhoda and heard of Robert's departure. Knowing

Robert's birthplace, he had come on to Warbeach, and had seen Jonathan Eccles, who referred him to Mrs. Boulby, licenced seller of brandy, if he wished to enjoy an interview with Robert Eccles.

"The old man sent up regularly every day to inquire how his son was faring on the road to the next world," said Robert, laughing. "He's tough old English oak. I'm just to him what I appear at the time. It's better having him like that than one of your jerky fathers, who seem to belong to the stage of a theatre. Everybody respects my old dad, and I can laugh at what he thinks of me. I've only to let him know I've served an apprenticeship in farming, and can make use of some of his ideas—sound! every one of 'em; every one of 'em sound! And that I say of my own father."

"Why don't you tell him?" Percy asked.

"I want to forget all about Kent and drown the county," said Robert. "And I'm going to, as far as my memory's concerned."

Percy waited for some seconds. He comprehended perfectly this state of wilfulness in an uneducated sensitive man.

"She has a steadfast look in her face, Robert. She doesn't look as if she trifled. I've really never seen a finer, franker girl in my life, if faces are to be trusted."

"It's t' other way. There's no trifling in her case. She's frank. She fires at you point blank."

"You never mentioned her in your letters to me, Robert."

"No. I had a suspicion from the first I was going to be a fool about the girl."

Percy struck his hand.

"You didn't do quite right."

"Do you say that?"

Robert silenced him with this question, for there was a woman in Percy's antecedent history.

The subject being dismissed, they talked more freely. Robert related the tale of Dahlia, and of his doings at Fairly.

"Oh! we agree," he said, noting a curious smile that Percy could not smooth out of sight. "I know it was odd conduct. I do respect my superiors; but, believe me or not, Percy, injury done to a girl makes me mad, and I can't hold back; and she's the sister of the girl you saw. By heaven! if it weren't for my head getting blind now when my blood boils, I've the mind to walk straight up to the house and screw the secret out of one of them. What I say is—Is there a God up aloft? Then, he sees all, and society is vapour, and while I feel the spirit in me to do it, I go straight at my aim."

"If, at the same time, there's no brandy in you," said Percy, "which would stop your seeing clear or going straight."

The suggestion was a cruel shock. Robert nodded. "That's true. I suppose it's my bad education that won't let me keep cool. I'm ashamed of myself after it. I shout and thunder, and the end of it is, I go away and think about the same of Robert Eccles that I've frightened other people into thinking. Perhaps you'll think me to blame in this case? One of those Mr. Blancoves—not the one you've heard of—struck me on the field before a lady. I bore it. It was part of what I'd gone out to meet. I was riding home late at night, and he stood at the corner of the lane, with an old enemy of mine, and a sad cur that is! Sedgett's his name—Nic, the Christian part of it. There'd just come a sharp snowfall from the north, and the moonlight shot over the flying edge of the rear-cloud; and I saw Sedgett with a stick in his hand; but the gentleman had no stick. I'll give Mr. Edward Blancove credit for not meaning to be active in a dastardly assault.

"But why was he in consultation with my enemy? And he let my enemy—by the way, Percy, you dislike that sort of talk of 'my enemy,' I know. You like it put plain and simple: but down in these old parts again, I catch at old habits; and I'm always a worse man when I haven't seen you for a time. Sedgett, say. Sedgett, as I passed, made a sweep at my horse's knees, and took them a little over the fetlock. The beast reared. While I was holding on he swung a blow at me, and took me here."

Robert touched his head. "I dropped like a horse-chestnut from the tree. When I recovered, I was lying in the lane. I think I was there flat, face to the ground, for half an hour, quite sensible, looking at the pretty colour of my blood on the snow. The horse was gone. I just managed to reel along to this place, where there's always a home for me. Now, will you believe it possible? I went out next day: I saw Mr. Edward Blancove, and I might have seen a baby and felt the same to it. I didn't know him a bit. Yesterday morning your letter was sent up from Sutton farm. Somehow, the moment I'd read it, I remembered his face. I sent him word there was a matter to be settled between us. You think I was wrong?"

Major Waring had set a deliberately calculating eye on him.

"I want to hear more," he said.

"You think I have no claim to challenge a man in his position?"

"Answer me first, Robert. You think this Mr. Blancove helped, or instigated this man Sedgett in his attack upon you?"

"I haven't a doubt that he did."

"It's not plain evidence."

"It's good circumstantial evidence."

"At any rate, you are perhaps justified in thinking him capable of this: though the rule is, to believe nothing against a gentleman until it is flatly proved—when we drum him out of the ranks. But, if you can fancy it true, would you put yourself upon an equal footing with him?"

"I would," said Robert.

"Then you accept his code of morals."

"That's too shrewd for me: but men who preach against duelling, or any kind of man-to-man in hot earnest, always fence in that way."

"I detest duelling," Major Waring remarked. "I don't like a system that permits knaves and fools to exercise a claim to imperil the lives of useful men. Let me observe, that I am not a preacher against it. I think you know my opinions; and they are not quite those of the English magistrate, and other mild persons who are wrathful at the practice upon any pretence. Keep to the other discussion. You challenge a man—you admit him your equal. But why do I argue with you? I know your mind as well as my own. You have some other idea in the background."

"I feel that he's the guilty man," said Robert.

"You feel called upon to punish him."

"No. Wait: he will not fight; but I have him and I'll hold him. I feel he's the man who has injured this girl, by every witness of facts that I can bring together; and as for the other young fellow I led such a dog's life down here, I could beg his pardon. This one's eye met mine. I saw it wouldn't have stopped short of murder—opportunity given. Why? Because I pressed on the right spring. I'm like a woman in seeing some things. He shall repent. By—! Slap me on the face, Percy. I've taken to brandy and to swearing. Damn the girl who made me forget good lessons! Bless her heart, I mean. She saw you, did she? Did she colour when she heard your name?"

"Very much," said Major Waring.

"Was dressed in—?"

"Black, with a crimson ribbon round the collar."

Robert waved the image from his eyes.

"I'm not going to dream of her. Peace, and babies, and farming, and pride in myself with a woman by my side—there! You've seen her—all that's gone. I might as well ask the East wind to blow West. Her face is set the other way. Of course, the nature and value of a man is shown by how he takes this sort of pain; and hark at me! I'm yelling. I thought I was cured. I looked up into the eyes of a lady ten times sweeter—when?—somewhen! I've lost dates. But here's the girl at me again. She cuddles into me—slips her hand into my breast and tugs at strings there. I can't help talking to you about her, now we've got over the first step. I'll soon give it up.

"She wore a red ribbon? If it had been Spring, you'd have seen roses. Oh! what a stanch heart that girl has. Where she sets it, mind! Her life where that creature sets her heart! But, for me, not a penny of comfort! Now for a whole week of her, day and night, in that black dress with the coloured ribbon. On she goes: walking to church; sitting at table; looking out of the window!

"Will you believe I thought those thick eyebrows of hers ugly once—a tremendous long time ago. Yes; but what eyes she has under them! And if she looks tender, one corner of her mouth goes quivering; and the eyes are steady, so that it looks like some wonderful bit of mercy.

"I think of that true-hearted creature praying and longing for her sister, and fearing there's shame—that's why she hates me. I wouldn't say I was certain her sister had not fallen into a pit. I couldn't. I was an idiot. I thought I wouldn't be a hypocrite. I might have said I believed as she did. There she stood ready to be taken—ready to have given herself to me, if I had only spoken a word! It was a moment of heaven, and God the Father could not give it to me twice The chance has gone.

"Oh! what a miserable mad dog I am to gabble on in this way.—Come in! come in, mother."

Mrs. Boulby entered, with soft footsteps, bearing a letter.

"From the Park," she said, and commenced chiding Robert gently, to establish her right to do it with solemnity.

"He will talk, sir. He's one o' them that either they talk or they hang silent, and no middle way will they take; and the doctor's their foe, and health they despise; and since this cruel blow, obstinacy do seem to have been knocked like a nail into his head so fast, persuasion have not a atom o' power over him."

"There must be talking when friends meet, ma'am," said Major Waring.

"Ah!" returned the widow, "if it wouldn't be all on one side."

"I've done now, mother," said Robert.

Mrs. Boulby retired, and Robert opened the letter.

It ran thus:—

"Sir, I am glad you have done me the favour of addressing me temperately, so that I am permitted to clear myself of an unjust and most unpleasant imputation. I will, if you please, see you, or your friend; to whom perhaps I shall better be able to certify how unfounded is the charge you bring against me. I will call upon you at the Pilot Inn, where I hear that you are staying; or, if you prefer it, I will attend to any appointment you may choose to direct elsewhere. But it must be immediate, as the term of my residence in this neighbourhood is limited.

"I am,

"Sir,

"Yours obediently,

"Edward Blancove."

Major Waning read the lines with a critical attention.

"It seems fair and open," was his remark.

"Here," Robert struck his breast, "here's what answers him. What shall I do? Shall I tell him to come?"

"Write to say that your friend will meet him at a stated place."

Robert saw his prey escaping. "I'm not to see him?"

"No. The decent is the right way in such cases. You must leave it to me. This will be the proper method between gentlemen."

"It appears to my idea," said Robert, "that gentlemen are always, somehow, stopped from taking the straight-ahead measure."

"You," Percy rejoined, "are like a civilian before a fortress. Either he finds it so easy that he can walk into it, or he gives it up in despair as unassailable. You have followed your own devices, and what have you accomplished?"

"He will lie to you smoothly."

"Smoothly or not, if I discover that he has spoken falsely, he is answerable to me."

"To me, Percy."

"No; to me. He can elude you; and will be acquitted by the general verdict. But when he becomes answerable to me, his honour, in the conventional, which is here the practical, sense, is at stake, and I have him."

"I see that. Yes; he can refuse to fight me," Robert sighed. "Hey, Lord! it's a heavy world when we come to methods. But will you, Percy, will you put it to him at the end of your fist—'Did you deceive the girl, and do you know where the girl now is?' Why, great heaven! we only ask to know where she is. She may have been murdered. She's hidden from her family. Let him confess, and let him go."

Major Waring shook his head. "You see like a woman perhaps, Robert. You certainly talk like a woman. I will state your suspicions. When I have done so, I am bound to accept his reply. If we discover it to have been false, I have my remedy."

"Won't you perceive, that it isn't my object to punish him by and by, but to tear the secret out of him on the spot—now—instantly," Robert cried.

"I perceive your object, and you have experienced some of the results of your system. It's the primitive action of an appeal to the god of combats, that is exploded in these days. You have no course but to take his word."

"She said"—Robert struck his knee—"she said I should have the girl's address. She said she would see her. She pledged that to me. I'm speaking of the lady up at Fairly. Come! things get clearer. If she knows where Dahlia is, who told her? This Mr. Algernon—not Edward Blancove—was seen with Dahlia in a box at the Playhouse. He was there with Dahlia, yet I don't think him the guilty man. There's a finger of light upon that other."

"Who is this lady?" Major Waring asked, with lifted eyebrows.

"Mrs. Lovell."

At the name, Major Waring sat stricken.

"Lovell!" he repeated, under his breath. "Lovell! Was she ever in India?"

"I don't know, indeed."

"Is she a widow?"

"Ay; that I've heard."

"Describe her."

Robert entered upon the task with a dozen headlong exclamations, and very justly concluded by saying that he could give no idea of her; but his friend apparently had gleaned sufficient.

Major Waring's face was touched by a strange pallor, and his smile had vanished. He ran his fingers through his hair, clutching it in a knot, as he sat eyeing the red chasm in the fire, where the light of old days and wild memories hangs as in a crumbling world.

Robert was aware of there being a sadness in Percy's life, and that he had loved a woman and awakened from his passion. Her name was unknown to him. In that matter, his natural delicacy and his deference to Percy had always checked him from sounding the subject closely. He might be, as he had said, keen as a woman where his own instincts were in action; but they were ineffective in guessing at the cause for Percy's sudden depression.

"She said—this lady, Mrs. Lovell, whoever she may be—she said you should have the girl's address:— gave you that pledge of her word?" Percy spoke, half meditating. "How did this happen? When did you see her?"

Robert related the incident of his meeting with her, and her effort to be a peacemaker, but made no allusion to Mrs. Boulby's tale of the bet.

"A peacemaker!" Percy interjected. "She rides well?"

"Best horsewoman I ever saw in my life," was Robert's ready answer.

Major Waring brushed at his forehead, as in impatience of thought.

"You must write two letters: one to this Mrs. Lovell. Say, you are about to leave the place, and remind her of her promise. It's incomprehensible; but never mind. Write that first. Then to the man. Say that your friend—by the way, this Mrs. Lovell has small hands, has she? I mean, peculiarly small? Did you notice, or not? I may know her. Never mind. Write to the man. Say—don't write down my name—say that I will meet him." Percy spoke on as in a dream. "Appoint any place and hour. To-morrow at ten, down by the river—the bridge. Write briefly. Thank him for his offer to afford you explanations. Don't argue it with me any more. Write both the letters straight off."

His back was to Robert as he uttered the injunction. Robert took pen and paper, and did as he was bidden, with all the punctilious obedience of a man who consents perforce to see a better scheme abandoned.

One effect of the equality existing between these two of diverse rank in life and perfect delicacy of heart, was, that the moment Percy assumed the lead, Robert never disputed it. Muttering simply that he was incapable of writing except when he was in a passion, he managed to produce what, in Percy's eyes, were satisfactory epistles, though Robert had horrible misgivings in regard to his letter to Mrs. Lovell— the wording of it, the cast of the sentences, even down to the character of the handwriting. These missives were despatched immediately.

"You are sure she said that?" Major Waring inquired more than once during the afternoon, and Robert assured him that Mrs. Lovell had given him her word. He grew very positive, and put it on his honour that she had said it.

"You may have heard incorrectly."

"I've got the words burning inside me," said Robert.

They walked together, before dark, to Sutton Farm, but Jonathan Eccles was abroad in his fields, and their welcome was from Mistress Anne, whom Major Waring had not power to melt; the moment he began speaking praise of Robert, she closed her mouth tight and crossed her wrists meekly.

"I see," said Major Waring, as they left the farm, "your aunt is of the godly who have no forgiveness."

"I'm afraid so," cried Robert. "Cold blood never will come to an understanding with hot blood, and the old lady's is like frozen milk. She's right in her way, I dare say. I don't blame her. Her piety's right enough, take it as you find it."

Mrs. Boulby had a sagacious notion that gentlemen always dined well every day of their lives, and claimed that much from Providence as their due. She had exerted herself to spread a neat little repast for Major Waring, and waited on the friends herself; grieving considerably to observe that the major failed in his duty as a gentleman, as far as the relish of eating was concerned.

"But," she said below at her bar, "he smokes the beautifullest—smelling cigars, and drinks coffee made in his own way. He's very particular." Which was reckoned to be in Major Waring's favour.

The hour was near midnight when she came into the room, bearing another letter from the Park. She thumped it on the table, ruffling and making that pretence at the controlling of her bosom which precedes a feminine storm. Her indignation was caused by a communication delivered by Dick Curtis, in the parlour underneath, to the effect that Nicodemus Sedgett was not to be heard of in the neighbourhood.

Robert laughed at her, and called her Hebrew woman—eye-for-eye and tooth-for-tooth woman.

"Leave real rascals to the Lord above, mother. He's safe to punish them. They've stepped outside the chances. That's my idea. I wouldn't go out of my way to kick them—not I! It's the half-and-half villains we've got to dispose of. They're the mischief, old lady."

Percy, however, asked some questions about Sedgett, and seemed to think his disappearance singular. He had been examining the handwriting of the superscription to the letter. His face was flushed as he tossed it for Robert to open. Mrs. Boulby dropped her departing curtsey, and Robert read out, with odd pauses and puzzled emphasis:

"Mrs. Lovell has received the letter which Mr. Robert Eccles has addressed to her, and regrets that a misconception should have arisen from anything that was uttered during their interview. The allusions are obscure, and Mrs. Lovell can only remark, that she is pained if she at all misled Mr. Eccles in what she either spoke or promised. She is not aware that she can be of any service to him. Should such an occasion present itself, Mr. Eccles may rest assured that she will not fail to avail herself of it, and do her utmost to redeem a pledge to which he has apparently attached a meaning she can in no way account for or comprehend."

When Robert had finished, "It's like a female lawyer," he said. "That woman speaking, and that woman writing, they're two different creatures—upon my soul, they are! Quick, sharp, to the point, when she speaks; and read this! Can I venture to say of a lady, she's a liar?"

"Perhaps you had better not," said Major Waring, who took the letter in his hand and seemed to study it. After which he transferred it to his pocket.

"To-morrow? To-morrow's Sunday," he observed. "We will go to church to-morrow." His eyes glittered.

"Why, I'm hardly in the mood," Robert protested. "I haven't had the habit latterly."

"Keep up the habit," said Percy. "It's a good thing for men like you."

"But what sort of a fellow am I to be showing myself there among all the people who've been talking about me—and the people up at Fairly!" Robert burst out in horror of the prospect. "I shall be a sight among the people. Percy, upon my honour, I don't think I well can. I'll read the Bible at home if you like."

"No; you'll do penance," said Major Waring.

"Are you meaning it?"

"The penance will be ten times greater on my part, believe me."

Robert fancied him to be referring to some idea of mocking the interposition of religion.

"Then we'll go to Upton Church," he said. "I don't mind it at Upton."

"I intend to go to the church attended by 'The Family,' as we say in our parts; and you must come with me to Warbeach."

Clasping one hand across his forehead, Robert cried, "You couldn't ask me to do a thing I hate so much. Go, and sit, and look sheepish, and sing hymns with the people I've been badgering; and everybody seeing me! How can it be anything to you like what it is to me?"

"You have only to take my word for it that it is, and far more," said Major Waring, sinking his voice. "Come; it won't do you any harm to make an appointment to meet your conscience now and then. You will never be ruled by reason, and your feelings have to teach you what you learn. At any rate, it's my request."

This terminated the colloquy upon that topic. Robert looked forward to a penitential Sabbath-day.

"She is a widow still," thought Major Waring, as he stood alone in his bed-room, and, drawing aside the curtains of his window, looked up at the white moon.

CHAPTER XXIV

WARBEACH VILLAGE CHURCH

When the sun takes to shining in winter, and the Southwest to blowing, the corners of the earth cannot hide from him—the mornings are like halls full of light. Robert had spent his hopes upon a wet day that would have kept the congregation sparse and the guests at Fairly absent from public devotions.

He perceived at once that he was doomed to be under everybody's eyes when he walked down the aisle, for everybody would attend the service on such a morning as this.

Already he had met his conscience, in so far as that he shunned asking Percy again what was the reason for their going to church, and he had not the courage to petition to go in the afternoon instead of the morning.

The question, "Are you ashamed of yourself, then?" sang in his ears as a retort ready made.

There was no help for it; so he set about assisting his ingenuity to make the best appearance possible— brushing his hat and coat with extraordinary care.

Percy got him to point out the spot designated for the meeting, and telling him to wait in the Warbeach churchyard, or within sight of it, strolled off in the direction of the river. His simple neatness and quiet gentlemanly air abashed Robert, and lured him from his intense conception of abstract right and wrong, which had hitherto encouraged and incited him, so that he became more than ever crestfallen at the prospect of meeting the eyes of the church people, and with the trembling sensitiveness of a woman who weighs the merits of a lover when passion is having one of its fatal pauses, he looked at himself, and compared himself with the class of persons he had outraged, and tried to think better of himself, and to justify himself, and sturdily reject comparisons. They would not be beaten back. His enemies had never suggested them, but they were forced on him by the aspect of his friend.

Any man who takes the law into his own hands, and chooses to stand against what is conventionally deemed fitting:—against the world, as we say, is open to these moods of degrading humility. Robert waited for the sound of the bells with the emotions of a common culprit. Could he have been driven to the church and deposited suddenly in his pew, his mind would have been easier.

It was the walking there, the walking down the aisle, the sense of his being the fellow who had matched himself against those well-attired gentlemen, which entirely confused him. And not exactly for his own sake—for Percy's partly. He sickened at the thought of being seen by Major Waring's side. His best suit and his hat were good enough, as far as they went, only he did not feel that he wore them—he could not divine how it was—with a proper air, an air of signal comfort. In fact, the graceful negligence of an English gentleman's manner had been unexpectedly revealed to him; and it was strange, he reflected, that Percy never appeared to observe how deficient he was, and could still treat him as an equal, call him by his Christian name, and not object to be seen with him in public.

Robert did not think at the same time that illness had impoverished his blood. Your sensational beings must keep a strong and a good flow of blood in their veins to be always on a level with the occasion which they provoke. He remembered wonderingly that he had used to be easy in gait and ready of wit when walking from Queen Anne's Farm to Wrexby village church. Why was he a different creature now? He could not answer the question.

Two or three of his Warbeach acquaintances passed him in the lanes. They gave him good day, and spoke kindly, and with pleasant friendly looks.

Their impression when they left him was that he was growing proud.

The jolly butcher of Warbeach, who had a hearty affection for him, insisted upon clapping his hand, and showing him to Mrs. Billing, and showing their two young ones to Robert. With a kiss to the children, and a nod, Robert let them pass.

Here and there, he was hailed by young fellows who wore their hats on one side, and jaunty-fashioned coats—Sunday being their own bright day of exhibition. He took no notice of the greetings.

He tried to feel an interest in the robins and twittering wrens, and called to mind verses about little birds, and kept repeating them, behind a face that chilled every friendly man who knew him.

Moody the boat-builder asked him, with a stare, if he was going to church, and on Robert's replying that perhaps he was, said "I'm dashed!" and it was especially discouraging to one in Robert's condition.

Further to inspirit him, he met Jonathan Eccles, who put the same question to him, and getting the same answer, turned sharp round and walked homeward.

Robert had a great feeling of relief when the bells were silent, and sauntered with a superior composure round the holly and laurel bushes concealing the church. Not once did he ponder on the meeting between Major Waring and Mr. Edward Blancove, until he beheld the former standing alone by the churchyard gate, and then he thought more of the empty churchyard and the absence of carriages, proclaiming the dreadful admonition that he must immediately consider as to the best way of comporting himself before an observant and censorious congregation.

Major Waring remarked, "You are late."

"Have I kept you waiting?" said Robert.

"Not long. They are reading the lessons."

"Is it full inside?"

"I dare say it is."

"You have seen him, I suppose?"

"Oh yes; I have seen him."

Percy was short in his speech, and pale as Robert had never seen him before. He requested hastily to be told the situation of Lord Elling's pew.

"Don't you think of going into the gallery?" said Robert, but received no answer, and with an inward moan of "Good God! they'll think I've come here in a sort of repentance," he found himself walking down the aisle; and presently, to his amazement, settled in front of the Fairly pew, and with his eyes on Mrs. Lovell.

What was the matter with her? Was she ill? Robert forgot his own tribulation in an instant. Her face was like marble, and as she stood with the prayer-book in her hand, her head swayed over it: her lips made a faint effort at smiling, and she sat quietly down, and was concealed. Algernon and Sir John Capes were in the pew beside her, as well as Lady Elling, who, with a backward-turned hand and disregarding countenance, reached out her smelling-bottle.

"Is this because she fancies I know of her having made a bet of me?" thought Robert, and it was not his vanity prompted the supposition, though his vanity was awakened by it. "Or is she ashamed of her falsehood?" he thought again, and forgave her at the sight of her sweet pale face. The singing of the hymns made her evident suffering seem holy as a martyr's. He scarce had the power to conduct himself reverently, so intense was his longing to show her his sympathy.

"That is Mrs. Lovell—did you see her just now?" he whispered.

"Ah?" said Major Waring.

"I'm afraid she has fainted."

"Possibly."

But Mrs. Lovell had not fainted. She rose when the time for rising came again, and fixing her eyes with a grave devotional collectedness upon the vicar at his reading-desk, looked quite mistress of herself—but mistress of herself only when she kept them so fixed. When they moved, it was as if they had relinquished some pillar of support, and they wavered; livid shades chased her face, like the rain-clouds on a grey lake-water. Some one fronting her weighed on her eyelids. This was evident. Robert thought her a miracle of beauty. She was in colour like days he had noted thoughtfully: days with purple storm, and with golden horizon edges. She had on a bonnet of black velvet, with a delicate array of white lace, that was not suffered to disturb the contrast to her warm yellow hair. Her little gloved hands were both holding the book; at times she perused it, or, the oppression becoming unendurable, turned her gaze toward the corner of the chancel, and thence once more to her book. Robert rejected all idea of his being in any way the cause of her strange perturbation. He cast a glance at his friend. He had begun to nourish a slight suspicion; but it was too slight to bear up against Percy's self-possession; for, as he understood the story, Percy had been the sufferer, and the lady had escaped without a wound. How, then, if such were the case, would she be showing emotion thus deep, while he stood before her with perfect self-command?

Robert believed that if he might look upon that adorable face for many days together, he could thrust Rhoda's from his memory. The sermon was not long enough for him; and he was angry with Percy for rising before there was any movement for departure in the Fairly pew. In the doorway of the church Percy took his arm, and asked him to point out the family tombstone. They stood by it, when Lady Elling and Mrs. Lovell came forth and walked to the carriage, receiving respectful salutes from the people of Warbeach.

"How lovely she is!" said Robert.

"Do you think her handsome?" said Major Waring.

"I can't understand such a creature dying." Robert stepped over an open grave.

The expression of Percy's eyes was bitter.

"I should imagine she thinks it just as impossible."

The Warbeach villagers waited for Lady Elling's carriage to roll away, and with a last glance at Robert, they too went off in gossiping groups. Robert's penance was over, and he could not refrain from asking what good his coming to church had done.

"I can't assist you," said Percy. "By the way, Mr. Blancove denies everything. He thinks you mad. He promises, now that you have adopted reasonable measures, to speak to his cousin, and help, as far as he can, to discover the address you are in search of."

"That's all?" cried Robert.

"That is all."

"Then where am I a bit farther than when I began?"

"You are only at the head of another road, and a better one."

"Oh, why do I ever give up trusting to my right hand—" Robert muttered.

But the evening brought a note to him from Algernon Blancove. It contained a dignified condemnation of Robert's previous insane behaviour, and closed by giving Dahlia's address in London.

"How on earth was this brought about?" Robert now questioned.

"It's singular, is it not?" said Major blaring; "but if you want a dog to follow you, you don't pull it by the collar; and if you want a potato from the earth, you plant the potato before you begin digging. You are a soldier by instinct, my good Robert: your first appeal is to force. I, you see, am a civilian: I invariably try the milder methods. Do you start for London tonight? I remain. I wish to look at the neighbourhood."

Robert postponed his journey to the morrow, partly in dread of his approaching interview with Dahlia, but chiefly to continue a little longer by the side of him whose gracious friendship gladdened his life. They paid a second visit to Sutton Farm. Robert doggedly refused to let a word be said to his father about his having taken to farming, and Jonathan listened to all Major Waring said of his son like a man deferential to the accomplishment of speaking, but too far off to hear more than a chance word. He talked, in reply, quite cheerfully of the weather and the state of the ground; observed that the soil was a perpetual study, but he knew something of horses and dogs, and Yorkshiremen were like Jews in the trouble they took to over-reach in a bargain. "Walloping men is poor work, if you come to compare it with walloping Nature," he said, and explained that, according to his opinion, "to best a man at buying and selling was as wholesome an occupation as frowzlin' along the gutters for parings and strays." He himself preferred to go to the heart of things: "Nature makes you rich, if your object is to do the same for her. Yorkshire fellows never think except of making theirselves rich by fattening on your blood, like sheep-ticks." In fine, Jonathan spoke sensibly, and abused Yorkshire, without hesitating to confess that a certain Yorkshireman, against whom he had matched his wits in a purchase of horseflesh, had given him a lively recollection of the encounter.

Percy asked him what he thought of his country. "I'll tell you," said Jonathan; "Englishmen's business is to go to war with the elements, and so long as we fight them, we're in the right academy for learnin' how the game goes. Our vulnerability commences when we think we'll sit down and eat the fruits, and if I don't see signs o' that, set me mole-tunnelling. Self-indulgence is the ruin of our time."

This was the closest remark he made to his relations with Robert, who informed him that he was going to London on the following day. Jonathan shook his hand heartily, without troubling himself about any inquiries.

"There's so much of that old man in me," said Robert, when Percy praised him, on their return, "that I daren't call him a Prince of an old boy: and never a spot of rancour in his soul. Have a claim on him—and there's your seat at his table: take and offend him—there's your seat still. Eat and drink, but you don't get near his heart. I'll surprise him some day. He fancies he's past surprises."

"Well," said Percy, "you're younger than I am, and may think the future belongs to you."

Early next morning they parted. Robert was in town by noon. He lost no time in hurrying to the Western suburb. As he neared the house where he was to believe Dahlia to be residing, he saw a man pass through the leafless black shrubs by the iron gate; and when he came to the gate himself the man was at the door. The door opened and closed on this man. It was Nicodemus Sedgett, or Robert's eyes did him traitorous service. He knocked at the door violently, and had to knock a second and a third time. Dahlia was denied to him. He was told that Mrs. Ayrton had lived there, but had left, and her present address was unknown. He asked to be allowed to speak a word to the man who had just entered the house. No one had entered for the last two hours, was the reply. Robert had an impulse to rush by the stolid little female liar, but Percy's recent lesson to him acted as a restraint; though, had it been a brawny woman or a lacquey in his path, he would certainly have followed his natural counsel. He turned away, lingering outside till it was dusk and the bruise on his head gave great throbs, and then he footed desolately farther and farther from the house. To combat with evil in his own country village had seemed a simple thing enough, but it appeared a superhuman task in giant London.

CHAPTER XXV

OF THE FEARFUL TEMPTATION WHICH CAME UPON ANTHONY HACKBUT, AND OF HIS MEETING WITH DAHLIA

It requires, happily, many years of an ordinary man's life to teach him to believe in the exceeding variety and quantity of things money can buy: yet, when ingenuous minds have fully comprehended the potent character of the metal, they are likely enough to suppose that it will buy everything: after which comes the groaning anxiety to possess it.

This stage of experience is a sublime development in the great souls of misers. It is their awakening moment, and it is their first real sense of a harvest being in their hands. They have begun under the influence of the passion for hoarding, which is but a blind passion of the finger-ends. The idea that they have got together, bit by bit, a power, travels slowly up to their heavy brains. Once let it be grasped, however, and they clutch a god. They feed on everybody's hunger for it. And, let us confess, they have in that a mighty feast.

Anthony Hackbut was not a miser. He was merely a saving old man. His vanity was, to be thought a miser, envied as a miser. He lived in daily hearing of the sweet chink of gold, and loved the sound, but with a poetical love, rather than with the sordid desire to amass gold pieces. Though a saving old man, he had his comforts; and if they haunted him and reproached him subsequently, for indulging wayward appetites for herrings and whelks and other sea-dainties that render up no account to you when they have disappeared, he put by copper and silver continually, weekly and monthly, and was master of a sum.

He knew the breadth of this sum with accuracy, and what it would expand to this day come a year, and probably this day come five years. He knew it only too well. The sum took no grand leaps. It increased, but did not seem to multiply. And he was breathing in the heart of the place, of all places in the world, where money did multiply.

He was the possessor of twelve hundred pounds, solid, and in haven; that is, the greater part in the Bank of England, and a portion in Boyne's Bank. He had besides a few skirmishing securities, and some such bits of paper as Algernon had given him in the public-house on that remarkable night of his visit to the theatre.

These, when the borrowers were defaulters in their payments and pleaded for an extension of time, inspired him with sentiments of grandeur that the solid property could not impart. Nevertheless, the anti-poetical tendency within him which warred with the poetical, and set him reducing whatsoever he claimed to plain figures, made it but a fitful hour of satisfaction.

He had only to fix his mind upon Farmer Fleming's conception of his wealth, to feel the miserable smallness of what seemed legitimately his own; and he felt it with so poignant an emotion that at times his fears of death were excited by the knowledge of a dead man's impotence to suggest hazy margins in the final exposure of his property. There it would lie, dead as himself! contracted, coffined, contemptible!

What would the farmer think when he came to hear that his brother Tony's estate was not able to buy up Queen Anne's Farm?—when, in point of fact, he found that he had all along been the richer man of the two!

Anthony's comfort was in the unfaltering strength of his constitution. He permitted his estimate of it to hint at the probability of his outlasting his brother William John, to whom he wished no earthly ill, but only that he should not live with a mitigated veneration for him. He was really nourished by the farmer's gluttonous delight in his supposed piles of wealth. Sometimes, for weeks, he had the gift of thinking himself one of the Bank with which he had been so long connected; and afterward a wretched reaction set in.

It was then that his touch upon Bank money began to intoxicate him strangely. He had at times thousands hugged against his bosom, and his heart swelled to the money-bags immense. He was a dispirited, but a grateful creature, after he had delivered them up. The delirium came by fits, as if a devil lurked to surprise him.

"With this money," said the demon, "you might speculate, and in two days make ten times the amount."

To which Anthony answered: "My character's worth fifty times the amount."

Such was his reply, but he did not think it. He was honest, and his honesty had become a habit; but the money was the only thing which acted on his imagination; his character had attained to no sacred halo, and was just worth his annual income and the respect of the law for his person. The money fired his brain!

"Ah! if it was mine!" he sighed. "If I could call it mine for just forty or fifty hours! But it ain't, and I can't."

He fought dogged battles with the tempter, and beat him off again and again. One day he made a truce with him by saying that if ever the farmer should be in town of an afternoon he would steal ten minutes or so, and make an appointment with him somewhere and show him the money-bags without a word: let him weigh and eye them: and then the plan was for Anthony to talk of politics, while the farmer's mind was in a ferment.

With this arrangement the infernal Power appeared to be content, and Anthony was temporarily relieved of his trouble. In other words, the intermittent fever of a sort of harmless rascality was afflicting this old creature. He never entertained the notion of running clear away with the money entrusted to him.

Whither could an aged man fly? He thought of foreign places as of spots that gave him a shivering sense of its being necessary for him to be born again in nakedness and helplessness, if ever he was to see them and set foot on them.

London was his home, and clothed him about warmly and honourably, and so he said to the demon in their next colloquy.

Anthony had become guilty of the imprudence of admitting him to conferences and arguing with him upon equal terms. They tell us, that this is the imprudence of women under temptation; and perhaps

Anthony was pushed to the verge of the abyss from causes somewhat similar to those which imperil them, and employed the same kind of efforts in his resistance.

In consequence of this compromise, the demon by degrees took seat at his breakfast-table, when Mrs. Wicklow, his landlady, could hear Anthony talking in the tone of voice of one who was pushed to his sturdiest arguments. She conceived that the old man's head was softening.

He was making one of his hurried rushes with the porterage of money on an afternoon in Spring, when a young female plucked at his coat, and his wrath at offenders against the law kindled in a minute into fury.

"Hands off, minx!" he cried. "You shall be given in charge. Where's a policeman?"

"Uncle!" she said.

"You precious swindler in petticoats!" Anthony fumed.

But he had a queer recollection of her face, and when she repeated piteously: "Uncle!" he peered at her features, saying,—

"No!" in wonderment, several times.

Her hair was cut like a boy's. She was in common garments, with a close-shaped skull-cap and a black straw bonnet on her head; not gloved, of ill complexion, and with deep dark lines slanting down from the corners of her eyes. Yet the inspection convinced him that he beheld Dahlia, his remembering the niece. He was amazed; but speedily priceless trust in his arms, and the wickedness of the streets, he bade her follow him. She did so with some difficulty, for he ran, and dodged, and treated the world as his enemy, suddenly vanished, and appeared again breathing freely.

"Why, my girl?" he said: "Why, Dahl—Mrs. What's-your-name? Why, who'd have known you? Is that"—he got his eyes close to her hair; "is that the ladies' fashion now? 'Cause, if it is, our young street scamps has only got to buy bonnets, and—I say, you don't look the Pomp. Not as you used to, Miss Ma'am, I mean—no, that you don't. Well, what's the news? How's your husband?"

"Uncle," said Dahlia; "will you, please, let me speak to you somewhere?"

"Ain't we standing together?"

"Oh! pray, out of the crowd!"

"Come home with me, if my lodgings ain't too poor for you," said Anthony.

"Uncle, I can't. I have been unwell. I cannot walk far. Will you take me to some quiet place?"

"Will you treat me to a cab?" Anthony sneered vehemently.

"I have left off riding, uncle."

"What! Hulloa!" Anthony sang out. "Cash is down in the mouth at home, is it? Tell me that, now?"

Dahlia dropped her eyelids, and then entreated him once more to conduct her to a quiet place where they might sit together, away from noise. She was very earnest and very sad, not seeming to have much strength.

"Do you mind taking my arm?" said Anthony.

She leaned her hand on his arm, and he dived across the road with her, among omnibuses and cabs, shouting to them through the roar,—

"We're the Independence on two legs, warranted sound, and no competition;" and saying to Dahlia: "Lor' bless you! there's no retort in 'em, or I'd say something worth hearing. It's like poking lions in cages with raw meat, afore you get a chaffing-match out o' them. Some of 'em know me. They'd be good at it, those fellows. I've heard of good things said by 'em. But there they sit, and they've got no circulation—ain't ready, except at old women, or when they catch you in a mess, and getting the worst of it. Let me tell you; you'll never get manly chaff out of big bundles o' fellows with ne'er an atom o' circulation. The river's the place for that. I've heard uncommon good things on the river—not of 'em, but heard 'em. T' other's most part invention. And, they tell me, horseback's a prime thing for chaff. Circulation, again. Sharp and lively, I mean; not bawl, and answer over your back—most part impudence, and nothing else—and then out of hearing. That sort o' chaff's cowardly. Boys are stiff young parties—circulation—and I don't tackle them pretty often, 'xcept when I'm going like a ball among nine-pins. It's all a matter o' circulation. I say, my dear," Anthony addressed her seriously, "you should never lay hold o' my arm when you see me going my pace of an afternoon. I took you for a thief, and worse—I did. That I did. Had you been waiting to see me?"

"A little," Dahlia replied, breathless.

"You have been ill?"

"A little," she said.

"You've written to the farm? O' course you have!"

"Oh! uncle, wait," moaned Dahlia.

"But, ha' you been sick, and not written home?"

"Wait; please, wait," she entreated him.

"I'll wait," said Anthony; "but that's no improvement to queerness; and 'queer''s your motto. Now we cross London Bridge. There's the Tower that lived in times when no man was safe of keeping his own money, 'cause of grasping kings—all claws and crown. I'm Republican as far as 'none o' them'—goes. There's the ships. The sun rises behind 'em, and sets afore 'em, and you may fancy, if you like, there's always gold in their rigging. Gals o' your sort think I say, come! tell me, if you are a lady?"

"No, uncle, no!" Dahlia cried, and then drawing in her breath, added: "not to you."

"Last time I crossed this bridge with a young woman hanging on my arm, it was your sister; they say she called on you, and you wouldn't see her; and a gal so good and a gal so true ain't to be got for a sister every day in the year! What are you pulling me for?"

Dahlia said nothing, but clung to him with a drooping head, and so they hurried along, until Anthony stopped in front of a shop displaying cups and muffins at the window, and leprous-looking strips of bacon, and sausages that had angled for appetites till they had become pallid sodden things, like washed-out bait.

Into this shop he led her, and they took possession of a compartment, and ordered tea and muffins.

The shop was empty.

"It's one of the expenses of relationship," Anthony sighed, after probing Dahlia unsatisfactorily to see whether she intended to pay for both, or at least for herself; and finding that she had no pride at all. "My sister marries your father, and, in consequence—well! a muffin now and then ain't so very much. We'll forget it, though it is a breach, mind, in counting up afterwards, and two-pences every day's equal to a good big cannonball in the castle-wall at the end of the year. Have you written home?"

Dahlia's face showed the bright anguish of unshed tears.

"Uncle-oh! speak low. I have been near death. I have been ill for so long a time. I have come to you to hear about them—my father and Rhoda. Tell me what they are doing, and do they sleep and eat well, and are not in trouble? I could not write. I was helpless. I could not hold a pen. Be kind, dear uncle, and do not reproach me. Please, tell me that they have not been sorrowful."

A keenness shot from Anthony's eyes. "Then, where's your husband?" he asked.

She made a sad attempt at smiling. "He is abroad."

"How about his relations? Ain't there one among 'em to write for you when you're ill?"

"He... Yes, he has relatives. I could not ask them. Oh! I am not strong, uncle; if you will only leave following me so with questions; but tell me, tell me what I want to know."

"Well, then, you tell me where your husband banks," returned Anthony.

"Indeed, I cannot say."

"Do you," Anthony stretched out alternative fingers, "do you get money from him to make payments in gold, or, do you get it in paper?"

She stared as in terror of a pit-fall. "Paper," she said at a venture.

"Well, then, name your Bank."

There was no cunning in her eye as she answered: "I don't know any bank, except the Bank of England."

"Why the deuce didn't you say so at once—eh?" cried Anthony. "He gives you bank-notes. Nothing better in the world. And he a'n't been givin' you many lately—is that it? What's his profession, or business?"

"He is...he is no profession."

"Then, what is he? Is he a gentleman?"

"Yes," she breathed plaintively.

"Your husband's a gentleman. Eh?—and lost his money?"

"Yes."

"How did he lose it?"

The poor victim of this pertinacious interrogatory now beat about within herself for succour. "I must not say," she replied.

"You're going to try to keep a secret, are ye?" said Anthony; and she, in her relief at the pause to her torment, said: "I am," with a little infantile, withering half-smile.

"Well, you've been and kept yourself pretty secret," the old man pursued. "I suppose your husband's proud? He's proud, ain't he? He's of a family, I'll be bound. Is he of a family? How did he like your dressing up like a mill'ner gal to come down in the City and see me?"

Dahlia's guile was not ready. "He didn't mind," she said.

"He didn't mind, didn't he? He don't mind your cutting of your hair so?—didn't mind that?"

She shook her head. "No."

Anthony was down upon her like a hawk.

"Why, he's abroad!"

"Yes; I mean, he did not see me."

With which, in a minute, she was out of his grasp; but her heart beat thick, her lips were dry, and her thoughts were in disorder.

"Then, he don't know you've been and got shaved, and a poll like a turnip-head of a thief? That's something for him to learn, is it?"

The picture of her beauty gone, seared her eyes like heated brass. She caught Anthony's arm with one firm hand to hold him silent, and with the other hand covered her sight and let the fit of weeping pass.

When the tears had spent themselves, she relinquished her hold of the astonished old man, who leaned over the table to her, and dominated by the spirit of her touch, whispered, like one who had accepted a bond of secresy: "Th' old farmer's well. So's Rhoda—my darkie lass. They've taken on a bit. And then they took to religion for comfort. Th' old farmer attends Methody meetin's, and quotes Scriptur' as if he was fixed like a pump to the Book, and couldn't fetch a breath without quotin'. Rhoda's oftenest along with your rector's wife down there, and does works o' charity, sicknussin', readin'—old farmer does the preachin'. Old mother Sumfit's fat as ever, and says her money's for you. Old Gammon goes on eatin' of the dumplins. Hey! what a queer old ancient he is. He seems to me to belong to a time afore ever money was. That Mr. Robert's off...never been down there since he left, 'cause my darkie lass thought herself too good for him. So she is!—too good for anybody. They're going to leave the farm; sell, and come to London."

"Oh, no!" exclaimed Dahlia; "not going to leave the dear old farm, and our lane, and the old oaks, leading up to the heath. Are they? Father will miss it. Rhoda will mourn so. No place will ever be like that to them. I love it better than any place on earth."

"That's queer," said Anthony. "Why do you refuse to go, or won't let your husband take you down there; if you like the place that raving-like? But 'queer''s your motto. The truth is this—you just listen. Hear me—hush! I won't speak in a bawl. You're a reasonable being, and you don't—that's to say, you do understand, the old farmer feels it uncomfortable—"

"But I never helped him when I was there," said Dahlia, suddenly shrinking in a perceptible tremble of acute divination. "I was no use. I never helped him—not at all. I was no—no use!"

Anthony blinked his eyes, not knowing how it was that he had thus been thrown out of his direct road. He began again, in his circumlocutory delicacy: "Never mind; help or no help, what th' old farmer feels is—and quite nat'ral. There's sensations as a father, and sensations as a man; and what th' old farmer feels is—"

"But Rhoda has always been more to father than I have," Dahlia cried, now stretching forward with desperate courage to confront her uncle, distract his speech, and avert the saying of the horrible thing she dreaded. "Rhoda was everything to him. Mother perhaps took to me—my mother!"

The line of her long underlie drawn sharp to check her tears, stopped her speaking.

"All very well about Rhoda," said Anthony. "She's everything to me, too."

"Every—everybody loves her!" Dahlia took him up.

"Let 'em, so long as they don't do no harm to her," was Anthony's remark. There was an idea in this that he had said, and the light of it led off his fancy. It was some time before he returned to the attack.

"Neighbours gossip a good deal. O' course you know that."

"I never listen to them," said Dahlia, who now felt bare at any instant for the stab she saw coming.

"No, not in London; but country's different, and a man hearing of his child 'it's very odd!' and 'keepin' away like that!' and 'what's become of her?' and that sort of thing, he gets upset."

Dahlia swallowed in her throat, as in perfect quietude of spirit, and pretended to see no meaning for herself in Anthony's words.

But she said, inadvertently, "Dear father!" and it gave Anthony his opening.

"There it is. No doubt you're fond of him. You're fond o' th' old farmer, who's your father. Then, why not make a entry into the village, and show 'em? I loves my father, says you. I can or I can't bring my husband, you seems to say; but I'm come to see my old father. Will you go down to-morrow wi' me?"

"Oh!" Dahlia recoiled and abandoned all defence in a moan: "I can't—I can't!"

"There," said Anthony, "you can't. You confess you can't; and there's reason for what's in your father's mind. And he hearin' neighbours' gossip, and it comes to him by a sort of extractin'—'Where's her husband?' bein' the question; and 'She ain't got one,' the answer—it's nat'ral for him to leave the place. I never can tell him how you went off, or who's the man, lucky or not. You went off sudden, on a morning, after kissin' me at breakfast; and no more Dahly visible. And he suspects—he more'n suspects. Farm's up for sale. Th' old farmer thinks it's unbrotherly of me not to go and buy, and I can't make him see I don't understand land: it's about like changeing sovereigns for lumps o' clay, in my notions; and that ain't my taste. Long and the short is—people down there at Wrexby and all round say you ain't married. He ain't got a answer for 'em; it's cruel to hear, and crueller to think: he's got no answer, poor old farmer! and he's obliged to go inter exile. Farm's up for sale."

Anthony thumped with his foot conclusively.

"Say I'm not married!" said Dahlia, and a bad colour flushed her countenance. "They say—I'm not married. I am—I am. It's false. It's cruel of father to listen to them—wicked people! base—base people! I am married, uncle. Tell father so, and don't let him sell the farm. Tell him, I said I was married. I am. I'm respected. I have only a little trouble, and I'm sure others have too. We all have. Tell father not to leave. It breaks my heart. Oh! uncle, tell him that from me."

Dahlia gathered her shawl close, and set an irresolute hand upon her bonnet strings, that moved as if it had forgotten its purpose. She could say no more. She could only watch her uncle's face, to mark the effect of what she had said.

Anthony nodded at vacancy. His eyebrows were up, and did not descend from their elevation. "You see, your father wants assurances; he wants facts. They're easy to give, if give 'em you can. Ah, there's a weddin' ring on your finger, sure enough. Plain gold—and, Lord! how bony your fingers ha' got, Dahly. If you are a sinner, you're a bony one now, and that don't seem so bad to me. I don't accuse you, my dear. Perhaps I'd like to see your husband's banker's book. But what your father hears, is—You've gone wrong."

Dahlia smiled in a consummate simulation of scorn.

"And your father thinks that's true."

She smiled with an equal simulation of saddest pity.

"And he says this: 'Proof,' he says, 'proof's what I want, that she's an honest woman.' He asks for you to clear yourself. He says, 'It's hard for an old man'—these are his words 'it's hard for an old man to hear his daughter called...'"

Anthony smacked his hand tight on his open mouth.

He was guiltless of any intended cruelty, and Dahlia's first impulse when she had got her breath, was to soothe him. She took his hand. "Dear father! poor father! Dear, dear father!" she kept saying.

"Rhoda don't think it," Anthony assured her.

"No?" and Dahlia's bosom exulted up to higher pain.

"Rhoda declares you are married. To hear that gal fight for you—there's ne'er a one in Wrexby dares so much as hint a word within a mile of her."

"My Rhoda! my sister!" Dahlia gasped, and the tears came pouring down her face.

In vain Anthony lifted her tea-cup and the muffin-plate to her for consolation. His hushings and soothings were louder than her weeping. Incapable of resisting such a protest of innocence, he said, "And I don't think it, neither."

She pressed his fingers, and begged him to pay the people of the shop: at which sign of her being probably moneyless, Anthony could not help mumbling, "Though I can't make out about your husband, and why he lets ye be cropped—that he can't help, may be—but lets ye go about dressed like a mill'ner gal, and not afford cabs. Is he very poor?"

She bowed her head.

"Poor?"

"He is very poor."

"Is he, or ain't he, a gentleman?"

Dahlia seemed torn by a new anguish.

"I see," said Anthony. "He goes and persuades you he is, and you've been and found out he's nothin' o' the sort—eh? That'd be a way of accounting for your queerness, more or less. Was it that fellow that Wicklow gal saw ye with?"

Dahlia signified vehemently, "No."

"Then, I've guessed right; he turns out not to be a gentleman—eh, Dahly? Go on noddin', if ye like. Never mind the shop people; we're well-conducted, and that's all they care for. I say, Dahly, he ain't a gentleman? You speak out or nod your head. You thought you'd caught a gentleman and 'taint the case. Gentlemen ain't caught so easy. They all of 'em goes to school, and that makes 'em knowin'. Come; he ain't a gentleman?"

Dahlia's voice issued, from a terrible inward conflict, like a voice of the tombs. "No," she said.

"Then, will you show him to me? Let me have a look at him."

Pushed from misery to misery, she struggled within herself again, and again in the same hollow manner said, "Yes."

"You will?"

"Yes."

"Seein's believin'. If you'll show him to me, or me to him..."

"Oh! don't talk of it." Dahlia struck her fingers in a tight lock.

"I only want to set eye on him, my gal. Whereabouts does he live?"

"Down—down a great—very great way in the West."

Anthony stared.

She replied to the look: "In the West of London—a long way down."

"That's where he is?"

"Yes."

"I thought—hum!" went the old man suspiciously. "When am I to see him? Some day?"

"Yes; some day."

"Didn't I say, Sunday?"

"Next Sunday?"—Dahlia gave a muffled cry.

"Yes, next Sunday. Day after to-morrow. And I'll write off to-morrow, and ease th' old farmer's heart, and Rhoda 'll be proud for you. She don't care about gentleman—or no gentleman. More do th' old farmer. It's let us, live and die respectable, and not disgrace father nor mother. Old-fashioned's best-fashioned about them things, I think. Come, you bring him—your husband—to me on Sunday, if you object to my callin' on you. Make up your mind to."

"Not next Sunday—the Sunday after," Dahlia pleaded. "He is not here now."

"Where is he?" Anthony asked.

"He's in the country."

Anthony pounced on her, as he had done previously.

"You said to me he was abroad."

"In the country—abroad. Not—not in the great cities. I could not make known your wishes to him."

She gave this cool explanation with her eyelids fluttering timorously, and rose as she uttered it, but with faint and ill-supporting limbs, for during the past hour she had gone through the sharpest trial of her life, and had decided for the course of her life. Anthony was witless thereof, and was mystified by his incapability of perceiving where and how he had been deluded; but he had eaten all the muffin on the plate, and her rising proclaimed that she had no intention of making him call for another; which was satisfactory. He drank off her cup of tea at a gulp.

The waitress named the sum he was to pay, and receiving a meditative look in return for her air of expectancy after the amount had been laid on the table, at once accelerated their passage from the shop by opening the door.

"If ever I did give pennies, I'd give 'em to you," said Anthony, when he was out of her hearing. "Women beat men in guessing at a man by his face. Says she—you're honourable—you're legal—but prodigal ain't your portion. That's what she says, without the words, unless she's a reader. Now, then, Dahly, my lass, you take my arm. Buckle to. We'll to the West. Don't th' old farmer pronounce like 'toe' the West? We'll 'toe' the West. I can afford to laugh at them big houses up there.

"Where's the foundation, if one of them's sound? Why, in the City.

"I'll take you by our governor's house. You know—you know—don't ye, Dahly, know we been suspecting his nephew? 'cause we saw him with you at the theatre.

"I didn't suspect. I knew he found you there by chance, somehow. And I noticed your dress there. No wonder your husband's poor. He wanted to make you cut a figure as one of the handsomes, and that's as ruinous as cabs—ha! ha!"

Anthony laughed, but did not reveal what had struck him.

"Sir William Blancove's house is a first-rater. I've been in it. He lives in the library. All the other rooms— enter 'em, and if 'taint like a sort of, a social sepulchre! Dashed if he can get his son to live with him; though they're friends, and his son'll get all the money, and go into Parliament, and cut a shine, never fear.

"By the way, I've seen Robert, too. He called on me at the Bank. Asked after you.

"'Seen her?' says he.

"'No,' I says.

"'Ever see Mr. Edward Blancove here?' he says.

"I told him, I'd heard say, Mr. Edward was Continentalling. And then Robert goes off. His opinion is you ain't in England; 'cause a policeman he spoke to can't find you nowhere.

"'Come,' says I, 'let's keep our detectives to catch thieves, and not go distracting of 'em about a parcel o' women.'

"He's awfully down about Rhoda. She might do worse than take him. I don't think he's got a ounce of a chance now Religion's set in, though he's the mildest big 'un I ever come across. I forgot to haul him over about what he 'd got to say about Mr. Edward. I did remark, I thought—ain't I right?—Mr. Algernon's not the man?—eh? How come you in the theatre with him?"

Dahlia spoke huskily. "He saw me. He had seen me at home. It was an accident."

"Exactly how I put it to Robert. And he agreed with me. There's sense in that young man. Your husband wouldn't let you come to us there—eh? because he...why was that?"

Dahlia had it on her lips to say it "Because he was poorer than I thought;" but in the intensity of her torment, the wretchedness of this lie, revolted her. "Oh! for God's sake, uncle, give me peace about that."

The old man murmured: "Ay, ay;" and thought it natural that she should shun an allusion to the circumstance.

They crossed one of the bridges, and Dahlia stopped and said: "Kiss me, uncle."

"I ain't ashamed," said Anthony.

This being over, she insisted on his not accompanying her farther.

Anthony made her pledge her word of honour as a married woman, to bring her husband to the identical spot where they stood at three o'clock in the afternoon of Sunday week. She promised it.

"I'll write home to th' old farmer—a penny," said Anthony, showing that he had considered the outlay and was prepared for it.

"And uncle," she stipulated in turn, "they are not to see me yet. Very soon; but not yet. Be true to me, and come alone, or it will be your fault—I shall not appear. Now, mind. And beg them not to leave the farm. It will kill father. Can you not," she said, in the faded sweetness of her speech, "could you not buy it, and let father be your tenant, uncle? He would pay you regularly."

Anthony turned a rough shoulder on her.

"Good-bye, Dahly. You be a good girl, and all 'll go right. Old farmer talks about praying. If he didn't make it look so dark to a chap, I'd be ready to fancy something in that. You try it. You try, Dahly. Say a bit of a prayer to-night."

"I pray every night," Dahlia answered.

Her look of meek despair was hauntingly sad with Anthony on his way home.

He tracked her sorrowfulness to the want of money; and another of his terrific vague struggles with the money-demon set in.

CHAPTER XXVI

IN THE PARK

Sir William Blancove did business at his Bank till the hour of three in the afternoon, when his carriage conveyed him to a mews near the park of Fashion, where he mounted horse and obeyed the bidding of his doctor for a space, by cantering in a pleasant, portly, cock-horsey style, up and down the Row.

It was the day of the great race on Epsom Downs, and elderly gentlemen pricked by the doctors were in the ascendant in all London congregations on horseback.

Like Achilles (if the bilious Shade will permit the impudent comparison), they dragged their enemy, Gout, at their horses' heels for a term, and vengeance being accomplished went to their dinners and revived him.

Sir William was disturbed by his son's absence from England. A youth to whom a baronetcy and wealth are to be bequeathed is an important organism; and Sir William, though his faith reposed in his son, was averse to his inexplicably prolonged residence in the French metropolis, which, a school for many things, is not a school for the study of our Parliamentary system, and still less for that connubial career Sir William wished him to commence.

Edward's delightful cynical wit—the worldly man's profundity—and his apt quotations of the wit of others, would have continued to exercise their charm, if Sir William had not wanted to have him on the spot that he might answer certain questions pertinaciously put by Mama Gosling on behalf of her daughter.

"There is no engagement," Edward wrote; "let the maiden wait and discern her choice: let her ripen;" and he quoted Horace up to a point.

Nor could his father help smiling and completing the lines. He laughed, too, as he read the jog of a verse: "Were I to marry the Gosling, pray, which would be the goose?"

He laughed, but with a shade of disappointment in the fancy that he perceived a wearing away of the robust mental energy which had characterized his son: and Sir William knew the danger of wit, and how the sharp blade cuts the shoots of the sapling. He had thought that Edward was veritable tough oak, and had hitherto encouraged his light play with the weapon.

It became a question with him now, whether Wit and Ambition may dwell together harmoniously in a young man: whether they will not give such manifestation of their social habits as two robins shut in a cage will do: of which pretty birds one will presently be discovered with a slightly ruffled bosom amid the feathers of his defunct associate.

Thus painfully revolving matters of fact and feeling, Sir William cantered, and, like a cropped billow blown against by the wind, drew up in front of Mrs. Lovell, and entered into conversation with that lady, for the fine needles of whose brain he had the perfect deference of an experienced senior. She, however, did not give him comfort. She informed him that something was wrong with Edward; she could not tell what. She spoke of him languidly, as if his letters contained wearisome trifling.

"He strains to be Frenchy," she said. "It may be a good compliment for them to receive: it's a bad one for him to pay."

"Alcibiades is not the best of models," murmured Sir William. "He doesn't mention Miss Gosling."

"Oh dear, yes. I have a French acrostic on her name."

"An acrostic!"

A more contemptible form of mental exercise was not to be found, according to Sir William's judgement.

"An acrostic!" he made it guttural. "Well!"

"He writes word that he hears Moliere every other night. That can't harm him. His reading is principally Memoirs, which I think I have heard you call 'The backstairs of history.' We are dull here, and I should not imagine it to be a healthy place to dwell in, if the absence of friends and the presence of sunshine conspire to dullness. Algy, of course, is deep in accounts to-day?"

Sir William remarked that he had not seen the young man at the office, and had not looked for him; but the mention of Algernon brought something to his mind, and he said,—

"I hear he is continually sending messengers from the office to you during the day. You rule him with a rod of iron. Make him discontinue that practice. I hear that he despatched our old porter to you yesterday with a letter marked 'urgent.'"

Mrs. Lovell laughed pleadingly for Algernon.

"No; he shall not do it again. It occurred yesterday, and on no other occasion that I am aware of. He presumes that I am as excited as he is himself about the race—"

The lady bowed to a passing cavalier; a smarting blush dyed her face.

"He bets, does he!" said Sir William. "A young man, whose income, at the extreme limit, is two hundred pounds a year."

"May not the smallness of the amount in some degree account for the betting?" she asked whimsically. "You know, I bet a little—just a little. If I have but a small sum, I already regard it as a stake; I am tempted to bid it fly."

"In his case, such conduct puts him on the high road to rascality," said Sir William severely. "He is doing no good."

"Then the squire is answerable for such conduct, I think."

"You presume to say that he is so because he allows his son very little money to squander? How many young men have to contain their expenses within two hundred pounds a year!"

"Not sons of squires and nephews of baronets," said Mrs. Lovell. "Adieu! I think I see a carrier-pigeon flying overhead, and, as you may suppose, I am all anxiety."

Sir William nodded to her. He disliked certain of her ways; but they were transparent bits of audacity and restlessness pertaining to a youthful widow, full of natural dash; and she was so sweetly mistress of herself in all she did, that he never supposed her to be needing caution against excesses. Old gentlemen have their pets, and Mrs. Lovell was a pet of Sir William's.

She was on the present occasion quite mistress of herself, though the stake was large. She was mistress of herself when Lord Suckling, who had driven from the Downs and brushed all save a spot of white dust out of his baby moustache to make himself presentable, rode up to her to say that the horse Templemore was beaten, and that his sagacity in always betting against favourites would, in this last instance, transfer a "pot of money" from alien pockets to his own.

"Algy Blancove's in for five hundred to me," he said; adding with energy, "I hope you haven't lost? No, don't go and dash my jolly feeling by saying you have. It was a fine heat; neck-and-neck past the Stand. Have you?"

"A little," she confessed. "It's a failing of mine to like favourites. I'm sorry for Algy."

"I'm afraid he's awfully hit."

"What makes you think so?"

"He took it so awfully cool."

"That may mean the reverse."

"It don't with him. But, Mrs. Lovell, do tell me you haven't lost. Not much, is it? Because, I know there's no guessing, when you are concerned."

The lady trifled with her bridle-rein.

"I really can't tell you yet. I may have lost. I haven't won. I'm not cool-blooded enough to bet against favourites. Addio, son of Fortune! I'm at the Opera to-night."

As she turned her horse from Lord Suckling, the cavalier who had saluted her when she was with Sir William passed again. She made a signal to her groom, and sent the man flying in pursuit of him, while she turned and cantered. She was soon overtaken.

"Madam, you have done me the honour."

"I wish to know why it is your pleasure to avoid me, Major Waring?"

"In this place?"

"Wherever we may chance to meet."

"I must protest."

"Do not. The thing is evident."

They rode together silently.

Her face was toward the sunset. The light smote her yellow hair, and struck out her grave and offended look, as in a picture.

"To be condemned without a hearing!" she said. "The most dastardly criminal gets that. Is it imagined that I have no common feelings? Is it manly to follow me with studied insult? I can bear the hatred of fools. Contempt I have not deserved. Dead! I should be dead, if my conscience had once reproached me. I am a mark for slander, and brave men should beware of herding with despicable slanderers."

She spoke, gazing frontward all the while. The pace she maintained in no degree impeded the concentrated passion of her utterance.

But it was a more difficult task for him, going at that pace, to make explanations, and she was exquisitely fair to behold! The falling beams touched her with a mellow sweetness that kindled bleeding memories.

"If I defend myself?" he said.

"No. All I ask is that you should Accuse me. Let me know what I have done—done, that I have not been bitterly punished for? What is it? what is it? Why do you inflict a torture on me whenever you see me? Not by word, not by look. You are too subtle in your cruelty to give me anything I can grasp. You know how you wound me. And I am alone."

"That is supposed to account for my behaviour?"

She turned her face to him. "Oh, Major blaring! say nothing unworthy of yourself. That would be a new pain to me."

He bowed. In spite of a prepossessing anger, some little softness crept through his heart.

"You may conceive that I have dropped my pride," she said. "That is the case, or my pride is of a better sort."

"Madam, I fully hope and trust," said he.

"And believe," she added, twisting his words to the ironic tongue. "You certainly must believe that my pride has sunk low. Did I ever speak to you in this manner before?"

"Not in this manner, I can attest."

"Did I speak at all, when I was hurt?" She betrayed that he had planted a fresh sting.

"If my recollection serves me," said he, "your self-command was remarkable."

Mrs. Lovell slackened her pace.

"Your recollection serves you too well, Major Waring. I was a girl. You judged the acts of a woman. I was a girl, and you chose to put your own interpretation on whatever I did. You scourged me before the whole army. Was not that enough? I mean, enough for you? For me, perhaps not, for I have suffered since, and may have been set apart to suffer. I saw you in that little church at Warbeach; I met you in the lanes; I met you on the steamer; on the railway platform; at the review. Everywhere you kept up the look of my judge. You! and I have been 'Margaret' to you. Major Waring, how many a woman in my place would attribute your relentless condemnation of her to injured vanity or vengeance? In those days I trifled with everybody. I played with fire. I was ignorant of life. I was true to my husband; and because I was true, and because I was ignorant, I was plunged into tragedies I never suspected. This is to be what you call a coquette. Stamping a name saves thinking. Could I read my husband's temper? Would not a coquette have played her cards differently? There never was need for me to push my husband to a contest. I never had the power to restrain him. Now I am wiser; and now is too late; and now you sit in judgement on me. Why? It is not fair; it is unkind."

Tears were in her voice, though not in her eyes.

Major Waring tried to study her with the coolness of a man who has learnt to doubt the truth of women; but he had once yearned in a young man's frenzy of love to take that delicate shape in his arms, and he was not proof against the sedate sweet face and keen sad ring of the voice.

He spoke earnestly.

"You honour me by caring for my opinion. The past is buried. I have some forgiveness to ask. Much, when I think of it—very much. I did you a public wrong. From a man to a woman it was unpardonable. It is a blot on my career. I beg you humbly to believe that I repent it."

The sun was flaming with great wings red among the vapours; and in the recollection of the two, as they rode onward facing it, arose that day of the forlorn charge of English horse in the Indian jungle, the thunder and the dust, the fire and the dense knot of the struggle. And like a ghost sweeping across her eyeballs, Mrs. Lovell beheld, part in his English freshness, part ensanguined, the image of the gallant boy who had ridden to perish at the spur of her mad whim. She forgot all present surroundings.

"Percy!" she said.

"Madam?"

"Percy!"

"Margaret?"

"Oh, what an undying day, Percy!"

And then she was speechless.

CHAPTER XXVII

CONTAINS A STUDY OF A FOOL IN TROUBLE

The Park had been empty, but the opera-house was full; and in the brilliance of the lights and divine soaring of the music, the genius of Champagne luncheons discussed the fate of the horse Templemore; some, as a matter of remote history; some, as another delusion in horse-flesh the greater number, however, with a determination to stand by the beaten favourite, though he had fallen, and proclaim him the best of racers and an animal foully mishandled on the course. There were whispers, and hints, and assertions; now implicating the jockey, now the owner of Templemore. The Manchester party, and the Yorkshire party, and their diverse villanous tricks, came under review. Several offered to back Templemore at double the money they had lost, against the winner. A favourite on whom money has been staked, not only has friends, but in adversity he is still believed in; nor could it well be otherwise, for the money, no doubt, stands for faith, or it would never have been put up to the risks of a forfeit.

Foremost and wildest among the excited young men who animated the stalls, and rushed about the lobby, was Algernon. He was the genius of Champagne luncheon incarnate. On him devolves, for a time, the movement of this story, and we shall do well to contemplate him, though he may seem possibly to be worthless. What is worthless, if it be well looked at? Nay, the most worthless creatures are most serviceable for examination, when the microscope is applied to them, as a simple study of human mechanism. This youth is one of great Nature's tom-fools: an elegant young gentleman outwardly, of the very large class who are simply the engines of their appetites, and, to the philosophic eye, still run wild in woods, as did the primitive nobleman that made a noise in the earlier world.

Algernon had this day lost ten times more than he could hope to be in a position to pay within ten years, at the least, if his father continued to argue the matter against Providence, and live. He had lost, and might speedily expect to be posted in all good betting circles as something not pleasantly odoriferous for circles where there is no betting. Nevertheless, the youth was surcharged with gaiety. The soul of mingled chicken and wine illumined his cheeks and eyes. He laughed and joked about the horse—his horse, as he called Templemore—and meeting Lord Suckling, won five sovereigns of him by betting that the colours of one of the beaten horses, Benloo, were distinguished by a chocolate bar. The bet was referred to a dignified umpire, who, a Frenchman, drew his right hand down an imperial tuft of hair dependent from his chin, and gave a decision in Algernon's favour. Lord Suckling paid the money on the spot, and Algernon pocketed it exulting. He had the idea that it was the first start in his making head against the flood. The next instant he could have pitched himself upon the floor and bellowed. For, a soul of chicken and wine, lightly elated, is easily dashed; and if he had but said to Lord Suckling that, it might as well be deferred, the thing would have become a precedent, and his own debt might have been held back. He went on saying, as he rushed forward alone: "Never mind, Suckling. Oh, hang it! put it in your pocket;" and the imperative necessity for talking, and fancying what was adverse to fact, enabled him to feel for a time as if he had really acted according to the prompting of his wisdom. It amazed him to see people sitting and listening. The more he tried it, the more unendurable it became. Those sitters and loungers appeared like absurd petrifactions to him. If he abstained from activity for ever so short a term, he was tormented by a sense of emptiness; and, as he said to himself, a man who has eaten a chicken, and part of a game-pie, and drunk thereto Champagne all day, until the popping of the corks has become as familiar as minute-guns, he can hardly be empty. It was peculiar. He stood, just for the sake of investigating the circumstance—it was so extraordinary. The music rose in a triumphant swell. And now he was sure that he was not to be blamed for thinking this form of entertainment detestable. How could people pretend to like it? "Upon my honour!" he said aloud. The hypocritical nonsense of pretending to like opera-music disgusted him.

"Where is it, Algy?" a friend of his and Suckling's asked, with a languid laugh.

"Where's what?"

"Your honour."

"My honour? Do you doubt my honour?" Algernon stared defiantly at the inoffensive little fellow.

"Not in the slightest. Very sorry to, seeing that I have you down in my book."

"Latters? Ah, yes," said Algernon, musically, and letting his under-lip hang that he might restrain the impulse to bite it. "Fifty, or a hundred, is it? I lost my book on the Downs."

"Fifty; but wait till settling-day, my good fellow, and don't fiddle at your pockets as if I'd been touching you up for the money. Come and sup with me to-night."

Algernon muttered a queer reply in a good-tempered tone, and escaped him.

He was sobered by that naming of settling-day. He could now listen to the music with attention, if not with satisfaction. As he did so, the head of drowned memory rose slowly up through the wine-bubbles in his brain, and he flung out a far thought for relief: "How, if I were to leave England with that dark girl Rhoda at Wrexby, marry her like a man, and live a wild ramping life in the colonies?" A curtain closed on the prospect, but if memory was resolved that it would not be drowned, he had at any rate dosed it with something fresh to occupy its digestion.

His opera-glass had been scouring the house for a sight of Mrs. Lovell, and at last she appeared in Lord Elling's box.

"I can give you two minutes, Algy," she said, as he entered and found her opportunely alone. "We have lost, I hear. No interjection, pray. Let it be, fors l'honneur, with us. Come to me to-morrow. You have tossed trinkets into my lap. They were marks of esteem, my cousin. Take them in the same light back from me. Turn them into money, and pay what is most pressing. Then go to Lord Suckling. He is a good boy, and won't distress you; but you must speak openly to him at once. Perhaps he will help you. I will do my best, though whether I can, I have yet to learn."

"Dear Mrs. Lovell!" Algernon burst out, and the corners of his mouth played nervously.

He liked her kindness, and he was wroth at the projected return of his gifts. A man's gifts are an exhibition of the royalty of his soul, and they are the last things which should be mentioned to him as matters to be blotted out when he is struggling against ruin. The lady had blunt insight just then. She attributed his emotion to gratitude.

"The door may be opened at any minute," she warned him.

"It's not about myself," he said; "it's you. I believe I tempted you to back the beastly horse. And he would have won—a fair race, and he would have won easy. He was winning. He passed the stand a head ahead. He did win. It's a scandal to the Turf. There's an end of racing in England. It's up. They've done for themselves to-day. There's a gang. It's in the hands of confederates."

"Think so, if it consoles you," said Mrs. Lovell, "don't mention your thoughts, that is all."

"I do think so. Why should we submit to a robbery? It's a sold affair. That Frenchman, Baron Vistocq, says we can't lift our heads after it."

"He conducts himself with decency, I hope."

"Why, he's won!"

"Imitate him."

Mrs. Lovell scanned the stalls.

"Always imitate the behaviour of the winners when you lose," she resumed. "To speak of other things: I have had no letter of late from Edward. He should be anxious to return. I went this morning to see that unhappy girl. She consents."

"Poor creature," murmured Algernon; and added "Everybody wants money."

"She decides wisely; for it is the best she can do. She deserves pity, for she has been basely used."

"Poor old Ned didn't mean," Algernon began pleading on his cousin's behalf, when Mrs. Lovell's scornful eye checked the feeble attempt.

"I am a woman, and, in certain cases, I side with my sex."

"Wasn't it for you?"

"That he betrayed her? If that were so, I should be sitting in ashes."

Algernon's look plainly declared that he thought her a mystery.

The simplicity of his bewilderment made her smile.

"I think your colonies are the right place for you, Algy, if you can get an appointment; which must be managed by-and-by. Call on me to-morrow, as I said."

Algernon signified positively that he would not, and doggedly refused to explain why.

"Then I will call on you," said Mrs. Lovell.

He was going to say something angrily, when Mrs. Lovell checked him: "Hush! she is singing."

Algernon listened to the prima donna in loathing; he had so much to inquire about, and so much to relate: such a desire to torment and be comforted!

Before he could utter a word further, the door opened, and Major Waring appeared, and he beheld Mrs. Lovell blush strangely. Soon after, Lord Elling came in, and spoke the ordinary sentence or two concerning the day's topic—the horse Templemore. Algernon quitted the box. His ears were surcharged with sound entirely foreign to his emotions, and he strolled out of the house and off to his dingy chambers, now tenanted by himself alone, and there faced the sealed letters addressed to Edward, which had, by order, not been forwarded. No less than six were in Dahlia's handwriting. He had imagination sufficient to conceive the lamentations they contained, and the reproach they were to his own subserviency in not sending them. He looked at the postmarks. The last one was dated two months back.

"How can she have cared a hang for Ned, if she's ready to go and marry a yokel, for the sake of a home and respectability?" he thought, rather in scorn; and, having established this contemptuous opinion of one of the sex, he felt justified in despising all. "Just like women! They—no! Peggy Lovell isn't. She's a trump card, and she's a coquette—can't help being one. It's in the blood. I never saw her look so confoundedly lovely as when that fellow came into the box. One up, one down. Ned's away, and it's this fellow's turn. Why the deuce does she always think I'm a boy? or else, she pretends to. But I must give my mind to business."

He drew forth the betting-book which his lively fancy had lost on the Downs. Prompted by an afterthought, he went to the letter-box, saying,—

"Who knows? Wait till the day's ended before you curse your luck."

There was a foreign letter in it from Edward, addressed to him, and another addressed to "Mr. Blancuv," that he tore open and read with disgusted laughter. It was signed "N. Sedgett." Algernon read it twice over, for the enjoyment of his critical detection of the vile grammar, with many "Oh! by Joves!" and a concluding, "This is a curiosity!"

It was a countryman's letter, ill-spelt, involved, and of a character to give Algernon a fine scholarly sense of superiority altogether novel. Everybody abused Algernon for his abuse of common Queen's English in his epistles: but here was a letter in comparison with which his own were doctorial, and accordingly he fell upon it with an acrimonious rapture of pedantry known to dull wits that have by extraordinary hazard pounced on a duller.

"You're 'willing to forgeit and forgeive,' are you, you dog!" he exclaimed, half dancing. "You'd forge anything, you rascal, if you could disguise your hand—that, I don't doubt. You 'expeck the thousand pound to be paid down the day of my marriage,' do you, you impudent ruffian! 'according to agremint.' What a mercenary vagabond this is!"

Algernon reflected a minute. The money was to pass through his hands. He compressed a desire to dispute with Sedgett that latter point about the agreement, and opened Edward's letter.

It contained an order on a firm of attorneys to sell out so much Bank Stock and pay over one thousand pounds to Mr. A. Blancove.

The beautiful concision of style in this document gave Algernon a feeling of profound deference toward the law and its officers.

"Now, that's the way to Write!" he said.

CHAPTER XXVIII

EDWARD'S LETTER

Accompanying this pleasant, pregnant bit of paper, possessed of such admirable literary excellence, were the following flimsy lines from Edward's self, to Algernon incomprehensible.

As there is a man to be seen behind these lines in the dull unconscious process of transformation from something very like a villain to something by a few degrees more estimable, we may as well look at the letter in full.

It begins with a neat display of consideration for the person addressed, common to letters that are dictated by overpowering egoism:—

"Dear Algy,—I hope you are working and attending regularly to office business. Look to that and to your health at present. Depend upon it, there is nothing like work. Fix your teeth in it. Work is medicine. A truism! Truisms, whether they lie in the depths of thought, or on the surface, are at any rate the pearls of experience.

"I am coming home. Let me know the instant this affair is over. I can't tell why I wait here. I fall into lethargies. I write to no one but to you. Your supposition that I am one of the hangers-on of the coquette of her time, and that it is for her I am seeking to get free, is conceived with your usual discrimination. For Margaret Lovell? Do you imagine that I desire to be all my life kicking the beam, weighed in capricious scales, appraised to the direct nicety, petulantly taken up, probed for my weakest point, and then flung into the grate like a child's toy? That's the fate of the several asses who put on the long-eared Lovell-livery.

"All women are the same. Know one, know all. Aware of this, and too wise to let us study them successfully, Nature pretty language this is for you, Algy! I can do nothing but write nonsense. I am sick of life. I feel choked. After a month, Paris is sweet biscuit.

"I have sent you the order for the money. If it were two, or twenty, thousand pounds, it would be the same to me.

"I swear to heaven that my lowest cynical ideas of women, and the loathing with which their simply animal vagaries inspires a thoughtful man, are distanced and made to seem a benevolent criticism, by the actualities of my experience. I say that you cannot put faith in a woman. Even now, I do not—it's against reason—I do not believe that she—this Dahlia—means to go through with it. She is trying me. I have told her that she was my wife. Her self-respect—everything that keeps a woman's head up—must have induced her to think so. Why, she is not a fool! How can she mean to give herself to an ignorant country donkey? She does not: mark me. For her, who is a really—I may say, the most refined nature I have ever met, to affect this, and think of deceiving me, does not do credit to her wits—and she is not without her share.

"I did once mean that she should be honourably allied to me. It's comforting that the act is not the wife of the intention, or I should now be yoked to a mere thing of the seasons and the hours—a creature whose 'No' to-day is the 'Yes' of to-morrow. Women of this cast are sure to end comfortably for themselves, they are so obedient to the whips of Providence.

"But I tell you candidly, Algy, I believe she's pushing me, that she may see how far I will let her go. I do not permit her to play at this game with me." The difficulty is in teaching women that we are not constituted as they are, and that we are wilfully earnest, while they, who never can be so save under compulsion, carry it on with us, expecting that at a certain crisis a curtain will drop, and we shall take a deep breath, join hands, and exclaim, 'What an exciting play!'—weeping luxuriously. The actualities of life must be branded on their backs—you can't get their brains to apprehend them.

"Poor things! they need pity. I am ready to confess I did not keep my promise to her. I am very sorry she has been ill. Of course, having no brains—nothing but sensations wherewith to combat every new revolution of fortune, she can't but fall ill. But I think of her; and I wish to God I did not. She is going to enter her own sphere—though, mark me, it will turn out as I say, that, when it comes to the crisis, there will be shrieks and astonishment that the curtain doesn't fall and the whole resolve itself to what they call a dream in our language, a farce.

"I am astonished that there should be no letters for me. I can understand her not writing at first; but apparently she cherishes rancour. It is not like her. I can't help thinking there must be one letter from her, and that you keep it back. I remember that I told you when I left England I desired to have no letter forwarded to me, but I have repeatedly asked you since if there was a letter, and it appears to me that you have shuffled in your answer. I merely wish to know if there is a letter; because I am at present out in my study of her character. It seems monstrous that she should never have written! Don't you view it in that light? To be ready to break with me, without one good-bye!—it's gratifying, but I am astonished; for so gentle and tender a creature, such as I knew her, never existed to compare with her. Ce qui est bien la preuve que je ne la connaissais pas! I thought I did, which was my error. I have a fatal habit of trusting to my observation less than to my divining wit; and La Rochefoucauld is right: 'on est quelquefois un sot avec de l'esprit; mais on ne Pest jamais avec du jugement.' Well! better be deceived in a character than doubt it.

"This will soon be over. Then back to the dear old dusky chambers, with the pick and the axe in the mine of law, till I strike a gold vein, and follow it to the woolsack. I want peace. I begin to hate pleading. I hope to meet Death full-wigged. By my troth, I will look as grimly at him as he at me. Meantime, during a vacation, I will give you holiday (or better, in the February days, if I can spare time and Equity is dispensed without my aid), dine you, and put you in the whirl of Paris. You deserve a holiday. Nunc est bibendum! You shall sing it. Tell me what you think of her behaviour. You are a judge of women. I think I am developing nerves. In fact, work is what I need—a file to bite. And send me also the name of this man who has made the bargain—who is to be her husband. Give me a description of him. It is my duty to see that he has principle; at least we're bound to investigate his character, if it's really to go on. I wonder whether you will ever perceive the comedy of, life. I doubt whether a man is happier when he does perceive it. Perhaps the fact is, that he has by that time lost his power of laughter; except in the case of here and there a very tremendous philosopher.

"I believe that we comic creatures suffer more than your tragic personages. We, do you see, are always looking to be happy and comfortable; but in a tragedy, the doomed wretches are liver-complexioned from the opening act. Their laughter is the owl: their broadest smile is twilight. All the menacing horrors of an eclipse are ours, for we have a sun over us; but they are born in shades, with the tuck of a curtain showing light, and little can be taken from them; so that they find scarce any terrors in the inevitable final stroke. No; the comedy is painfullest. You and I, Algy, old bachelors, will earn the right just to chuckle. We will take the point of view of science, be the stage carpenters, and let the actors move on and off. By this, we shall learn to take a certain pride in the machinery. To become stage carpenter, is to attain to the highest rank within the reach of intellectual man. But your own machinery must be sound, or you can't look after that of the theatre. Don't over-tax thy stomach, O youth!

"And now, farewell, my worthy ass! You have been thinking me one through a fair half of this my letter, so I hasten to be in advance of you, by calling you one. You are one: I likewise am one. We are all one. The universal language is hee-haw, done in a grievous yawn.

"Yours,

"Edward B.

"P.S.—Don't fail to send a letter by the next post; then, go and see her; write again exactly what she says, and let me know the man's name. You will not lose a minute. Also, don't waste ink in putting Mrs. Lovell's name to paper: I desire not to hear anything of the woman."

Algernon read this letter in a profound mystification, marvelling how it could possibly be that Edward and Mrs. Lovell had quarrelled once more, and without meeting.

They had parted, he knew or supposed that he knew, under an engagement to arrange the preliminaries of an alliance, when Edward should return from France; in other words, when Edward had thrown grave-dust on a naughty portion of his past; severing an unwise connection. Such had certainly been Edward's view of the matter. But Mrs. Lovell had never spoken to Algernon on that subject. She had spoken willingly and in deep sympathy of Dahlia. She had visited her, pitied her, comforted her; and Algernon remembered that she had looked very keen and pinched about the mouth in alluding to Dahlia; but how she and Edward had managed to arrive at another misunderstanding was a prodigious puzzle to him; and why, if their engagement had snapped, each consented to let Dahlia's marriage (which was evidently distasteful to both) go on to the conclusion of the ceremony, he could not comprehend. There were, however, so many things in the world that he could not comprehend, and he had grown so accustomed, after an effort to master a difficulty, to lean his head back upon downy ignorance, that he treated this significant letter of Edward's like a tough lesson, and quietly put it by, together with every recommendation it contained. For all that was practical in it, it might just as well not have been written.

The value of the letter lies in the exhibition it presents of a rather mark-worthy young man, who has passed through the hands of a—(what I must call her; and in doing so, I ask pardon of all the Jack Cades of Letters, who, in the absence of a grammatical king and a government, sit as lords upon the English tongue) a crucible woman. She may be inexcusable herself; but you for you to be base, for you to be cowardly, even to betray a weakness, though it be on her behalf,—though you can plead that all you have done is for her, yea, was partly instigated by her,—it will cause her to dismiss you with the inexorable contempt of Nature, when she has tried one of her creatures and found him wanting.

Margaret Lovell was of this description: a woman fashioned to do both harm and good, and more of harm than of good; but never to sanction a scheme of evil or blink at it in alliance with another: a woman, in contact with whom you were soon resolved to your component elements. Separated from a certain fascination that there was for her in Edward's acerb wit, she saw that he was doing a dastardly thing in cold blood. We need not examine their correspondence. In a few weeks she had contrived to put a chasm between them as lovers. Had he remained in England, boldly facing his own evil actions, she would have been subjugated, for however keenly she might pierce to the true character of a man, the show of an unflinching courage dominated her; but his departure, leaving all the brutality to be done for him behind his back, filled this woman with a cutting spleen. It is sufficient for some men to know that they are seen through, in order to turn away in loathing from her whom they have desired; and when they do thus turn away, they not uncommonly turn with a rush of old affection to those who have generously trusted them in the days past, and blindly thought them estimable beings.

Algernon was by no means gifted to perceive whether this was the case with his cousin in Paris.

CHAPTER XXIX

FURTHERMORE OF THE FOOL

So long as the fool has his being in the world, he will be a part of every history, nor can I keep him from his place in a narrative that is made to revolve more or less upon its own wheels. Algernon went to bed, completely forgetting Edward and his own misfortunes, under the influence of the opiate of the order for one thousand pounds, to be delivered to him upon application. The morning found him calmly cheerful, until a little parcel was brought to his door, together with a note from Mrs. Lovell, explaining that the parcel contained those jewels, his precious gifts of what she had insultingly chosen to call "esteem" for her.

Algernon took it in his hand, and thought of flinging it through the window; but as the window happened to be open, he checked the impulse, and sent it with great force into a corner of the room: a perfectly fool-like proceeding, for the fool is, after his fashion, prudent, and will never, if he can help it, do himself thorough damage, that he may learn by it and be wiser.

"I never stand insult," he uttered, self-approvingly, and felt manlier. "No; not even from you, ma'am," he apostrophized Mrs. Lovell's portrait, that had no rival now upon the wall, and that gave him a sharp fight for the preservation of his anger, so bewitching she was to see. Her not sending up word that she wished him to come to her rendered his battle easier.

"It looks rather like a break between us," he said. "If so, you won't find me so obedient to your caprices, Mrs. Margaret L.; though you are a pretty woman, and know it. Smile away. I prefer a staunch, true sort of a woman, after all. And the colonies it must be, I begin to suspect." This set him conjuring before his eyes the image of Rhoda, until he cried, "I'll be hanged if the girl doesn't haunt me!" and considered the matter with some curiosity.

He was quickly away, and across the square of Lincoln's Inn Fields to the attorney's firm, where apparently his coming was expected, and he was told that the money would be placed in his hands on the following day. He then communicated with Edward, in the brief Caesarian tongue of the telegraph: "All right. Stay. Ceremony arranged." After which, he hailed a skimming cab, and pronouncing the word "Epsom," sank back in it, and felt in his breast-pocket for his cigar-case, without casting one glance of interest at the deep fit of cogitation the cabman had been thrown into by the suddenness of the order.

"Dash'd if it ain't the very thing I went and gone and dreamed last night," said the cabman, as he made his dispositions to commence the journey.

Certain boys advised him to whip it away as hard as he could, and he would come in the winner.

"Where shall I grub, sir?" the cabman asked through the little door above, to get some knowledge of the quality of his fare.

"Eat your 'grub' on the course," said Algernon.

"Ne'er a hamper to take up nowheres, is there, sir?"

"Do you like the sight of one?"

"Well, it ain't what I object to."

"Then go fast, my man, and you will soon see plenty."

"If you took to chaffin' a bit later in the day, it'd impart more confidence to my bosom," said the cabman; but this he said to that bosom alone.

"Ain't no particular colours you'd like me to wear, is there? I'll get a rosette, if you like, sir, and enter in triumph. Gives ye something to stand by. That's always my remark, founded on observation."

"Go to the deuce! Drive on," Algernon sang out. "Red, yellow, and green."

"Lobster, ale, and salad!" said the cabman, flicking his whip; "and good colours too. Tenpenny Nail's the horse. He's the colours I stick to." And off he drove, envied of London urchins, as mortals would have envied a charioteer driving visibly for Olympus.

Algernon crossed his arms, with the frown of one looking all inward.

At school this youth had hated sums. All arithmetical difficulties had confused and sickened him. But now he worked with indefatigable industry on an imaginary slate; put his postulate, counted probabilities, allowed for chances, added, deducted, multiplied, and unknowingly performed algebraic feats, till his brows were stiff with frowning, and his brain craved for stimulant.

This necessity sent his hand to his purse, for the calling of the cab had not been a premeditated matter. He discovered therein some half-crowns and a sixpence, the latter of which he tossed in contempt at some boys who were cheering the vehicles on their gallant career.

There was something desperately amusing to him in the thought that he had not even money enough to pay the cabman, or provide for a repast. He rollicked in his present poverty. Yesterday he had run down with a party of young guardsmen in a very royal manner; and yesterday he had lost. To-day he journeyed to the course poorer than many of the beggars he would find there; and by a natural deduction, to-day he was to win.

He whistled mad waltzes to the measure of the wheels. He believed that he had a star. He pitched his half-crowns to the turnpike-men, and sought to propitiate Fortune by displaying a signal indifference to small change; in which method of courting her he was perfectly serious. He absolutely rejected coppers. They "crossed his luck." Nor can we say that he is not an authority on this point: the Goddess certainly does not deal in coppers.

Anxious efforts at recollection perplexed him. He could not remember whether he had "turned his money" on looking at the last new moon. When had he seen the last new moon, and where? A cloud obscured it; he had forgotten. He consoled himself by cursing superstition. Tenpenny Nail was to gain the day in spite of fortune. Algernon said this, and entrenched his fluttering spirit behind common sense, but he found it a cold corner. The longing for Champagne stimulant increased in fervour. Arithmetic languished.

As he was going up the hill, the wheels were still for a moment, and hearing "Tenpenny Nail" shouted, he put forth his head, and asked what the cry was, concerning that horse.

"Gone lame," was the answer.

It hit the centre of his nerves, without reaching his comprehension, and all Englishmen being equal on Epsom Downs, his stare at the man who had spoken, and his sickly colour, exposed him to pungent remarks.

"Hullos! here's another Ninepenny—a penny short!" and similar specimens of Epsom wit, encouraged by the winks and retorts of his driver, surrounded him; but it was empty clamour outside. A rage of emotions drowned every idea in his head, and when he got one clear from the mass, it took the form of a bitter sneer at Providence, for cutting off his last chance of reforming his conduct and becoming good. What would he not have accomplished, that was brilliant, and beautiful, and soothing, but for this dead set against him!

It was clear that Providence cared "not a rap," whether he won or lost—was good or bad. One might just as well be a heathen; why not?

He jumped out of the cab (tearing his coat in the acts minor evil, but "all of a piece," as he said), and made his way to the Ring. The bee-swarm was thick as ever on the golden bough. Algernon heard no curses, and began to nourish hope again, as he advanced. He began to hope wildly that this rumour about the horse was a falsity, for there was no commotion, no one declaiming.

He pushed to enter the roaring circle, which the demand for an entrance-fee warned him was a privilege, and he stammered, and forgot the gentlemanly coolness commonly distinguishing him, under one of the acuter twinges of his veteran complaint of impecuniosity. And then the cabman made himself heard: a civil cabman, but without directions, and uncertain of his dinner and his pay, tolerably hot, also, from threading a crowd after a deaf gentleman. His half-injured look restored to Algernon his self-possession.

"Ah! there you are:—scurry away and fetch my purse out of the bottom of the cab. I've dropped it."

On this errand, the confiding cabman retired. Holding to a gentleman's purse is even securer than holding to a gentleman.

While Algernon was working his forefinger in his waistcoat-pocket reflectively, a man at his elbow said, with a show of familiar deference,—

"If it's any convenience to you, sir," and showed the rim of a gold piece 'twixt finger and thumb.

"All right," Algernon replied readily, and felt that he was known, but tried to keep his eyes from looking at the man's face; which was a vain effort. He took the money, nodded curtly, and passed in.

Once through the barrier, he had no time to be ashamed. He was in the atmosphere of challenges. He heard voices, and saw men whom not to challenge, or try a result with, was to acknowledge oneself mean, and to abandon the manliness of life. Algernon's betting-book was soon out and in operation. While thus engaged, he beheld faces passing and repassing that were the promise of luncheon and a loan; and so comfortable was the assurance thereof to him, that he laid the thought of it aside, quite in the background, and went on betting with an easy mind.

Small, senseless bets, they merely occupied him; and winning them was really less satisfactory than losing, which, at all events, had the merit of adding to the bulk of his accusation against the ruling Powers unseen.

Algernon was too savage for betting when the great race was run. He refused both at taunts and cajoleries; but Lord Suckling coming by, said "Name your horse," and, caught unawares, Algernon named Little John, one of the ruck, at a hazard. Lord Suckling gave him fair odds, asking: "In tens?—fifties?"

"Silver," shrugged Algernon, implacable toward Fortune; and the kindly young nobleman nodded, and made allowance for his ill-temper and want of spirit, knowing the stake he had laid on the favourite.

Little John startled the field by coming in first at a canter.

"Men have committed suicide for less than this" said Algernon within his lips, and a modest expression of submission to fate settled on his countenance. He stuck to the Ring till he was haggard with fatigue. His whole nature cried out for Champagne, and now he burst away from that devilish circle, looking about for Lord Suckling and a hamper. Food and a frothing drink were all that he asked from Fortune. It seemed to him that the concourse on the downs shifted in a restless way.

"What's doing, I wonder?" he thought aloud.

"Why, sir, the last race ain't generally fashionable," said his cabman, appearing from behind his shoulder. "Don't you happen to be peckish, sir?—'cause, luck or no luck, that's my case. I couldn't see, your purse, nowheres."

"Confound you! how you hang about me! What do you want?" Algernon cried; and answered his own question, by speeding the cabman to a booth with what money remained to him, and appointing a place of meeting for the return. After which he glanced round furtively to make sure that he was not in view of the man who had lent him the sovereign. It became evident that the Downs were flowing back to London.

He hurried along the lines of carriages, all getting into motion. The ghastly conviction overtook him that he was left friendless, to starve. Wherever he turned, he saw strangers and empty hampers, bottles, straw, waste paper—the ruins of the feast: Fate's irony meantime besetting him with beggars, who swallowed his imprecations as the earnest of coming charity in such places.

At last, he was brought almost to sigh that he might see the man who had lent him the sovereign, and his wish was hardly formed, when Nicodemus Sedgett approached, waving a hat encircled by preposterous wooden figures, a trifle less lightly attired than the ladies of the ballet, and as bold in the matter of leg as the female fashion of the period.

Algernon eyed the lumpy-headed, heavy-browed rascal with what disgust he had left in him, for one who came as an instrument of the Fates to help him to some poor refreshment. Sedgett informed him that he had never had such fun in his life.

"Just 'fore matrimony," he communicated in a dull whisper, "a fellow ought to see a bit o' the world, I says—don't you, sir? and this has been rare sport, that it has! Did ye find your purse, sir? Never mind 'bout that ther' pound. I'll lend you another, if ye like. How sh'll it be? Say the word."

Algernon was meditating, apparently on a remote subject. He nodded sharply.

"Yes. Call at my chambers to-morrow."

Another sovereign was transferred to him: but Sedgett would not be shaken off.

"I just wanted t' have a bit of a talk with you," he spoke low.

"Hang it! I haven't eaten all day," snapped the irritable young gentleman, fearful now of being seen in the rascal's company.

"You come along to the jolliest booth—I'll show it to you," said Sedgett, and lifted one leg in dancing attitude. "Come along, sir: the jolliest booth I ever was in, dang me if it ain't! Ale and music—them's my darlings!" the wretch vented his slang. "And I must have a talk with you. I'll stick to you. I'm social when I'm jolly, that I be: and I don't know a chap on these here downs. Here's the pint: Is all square? Am I t' have the cash in cash counted down, I asks? And is it to be before, or is it to be after, the ceremony? There! bang out! say, yes or no."

Algernon sent him to perdition with infinite heartiness, but he was dry, dispirited, and weak, and he walked on, Sedgett accompanying him. He entered a booth, and partook of ale and ham, feeling that he was in the dregs of calamity. Though the ale did some service in reviving, it did not cheer him, and he had a fit of moral objection to Sedgett's discourse.

Sedgett took his bluntness as a matter to be endured for the honour of hob-a-nobbing with a gentleman. Several times he recurred to the theme which he wanted, as he said, to have a talk upon.

He related how he had courted the young woman, "bashful-like," and had been so; for she was a splendid young woman; not so handsome now, as she used to be when he had seen her in the winter: but her illness had pulled her down and made her humble: they had cut her hair during the fever, which had taken her pride clean out of her; and when he had put the question to her on the evening of last Sunday, she had gone into a sort of faint, and he walked away with her affirmative locked up in his breast-pocket, and was resolved always to treat her well—which he swore to.

"Married, and got the money, and the lease o' my farm disposed of, I'm off to Australia and leave old England behind me, and thank ye, mother, thank ye! and we shan't meet again in a hurry. And what sort o' song I'm to sing for 'England is my nation, ain't come across me yet. Australia's such a precious big world; but that'll come easy in time. And there'll I farm, and damn all you gentlemen, if you come anigh me."

The eyes of the fellow were fierce as he uttered this; they were rendered fierce by a peculiar blackish flush that came on his brows and cheek-bones; otherwise, the yellow about the little brown dot in the centre of the eyeball had not changed; but the look was unmistakably savage, animal, and bad. He closed the lids on them, and gave a sort of churlish smile immediately afterward.

"Harmony's the game. You act fair, I act fair. I've kept to the condition. She don't know anything of my whereabouts—res'dence, I mean; and thinks I met you in her room for the first time. That's the truth, Mr. Blancove. And thinks me a sheepish chap, and I'm that, when I'm along wi' her. She can't make out how I come to call at her house and know her first. Gives up guessing, I suppose, for she's quiet about it; and I pitch her tales about Australia, and life out there. I've got her to smile, once or twice. She'll turn her hand to making cheeses, never you fear. Only, this I say. I must have the money. It's a thousand and a bargain. No thousand, and no wife for me. Not that I don't stand by the agreement. I'm solid."

Algernon had no power of encountering a human eye steadily, or he would have shown the man with a look how repulsive he was to a gentleman. His sensations grew remorseful, as if he were guilty of handing a victim to the wretch.

But the woman followed her own inclination, did she not? There was no compulsion: she accepted this man. And if she could do that, pity was wasted on her!

So thought he: and so the world would think of the poor forlorn soul striving to expiate her fault, that her father and sister might be at peace, without shame.

Algernon signified to Sedgett that the agreement was fixed and irrevocable on his part.

Sedgett gulped some ale.

"Hands on it," he said, and laid his huge hand open across the table.

This was too much.

"My word must satisfy you," said Algernon, rising.

"So it shall. So it do," returned Sedgett, rising with him. "Will you give it in writing?"

"I won't."

"That's blunt. Will you come and have a look at a sparring-match in yond' brown booth, sir?"

"I am going back to London."

"London and the theayter that's the fun, now, ain't it!" Sedgett laughed.

Algernon discerned his cabman and the conveyance ready, and beckoned him.

"Perhaps, sir," said Sedgett, "if I might make so bold—I don't want to speak o' them sovereigns—but I've got to get back too, and cash is run low. D' ye mind, sir? Are you kind-hearted?"

A constitutional habit of servility to his creditor when present before him signalized Algernon. He detested the man, but his feebleness was seized by the latter question, and he fancied he might, on the road to London, convey to Sedgett's mind that it would be well to split that thousand, as he had previously devised.

"Jump in," he said.

When Sedgett was seated, Algernon would have been glad to walk the distance to London to escape from the unwholesome proximity. He took the vacant place, in horror of it. The man had hitherto appeared respectful; and in Dahlia's presence he had seemed a gentle big fellow with a reverent, affectionate heart. Sedgett rallied him.

"You've had bad luck—that's wrote on your hatband. Now, if you was a woman, I'd say, tak' and go and have a peroose o' your Bible. That's what my young woman does; and by George! it's just like medicine to her—that 'tis! I've read out to her till I could ha' swallowed two quart o' beer at a gulp—I was that mortal thirsty. It don't somehow seem to improve men. It didn't do me no good. There was I, cursin' at the bother, down in my boots, like, and she with her hands in a knot, staring the fire out o' count'nance. They're weak, poor sort o' things."

The intolerable talk of the ruffian prompted Algernon to cry out, for relief,—

"A scoundrel like you must be past any good to be got from reading his Bible."

Sedgett turned his dull brown eyes on him, the thick and hateful flush of evil blood informing them with detestable malignity.

"Come; you be civil, if you're going to be my companion," he said. "I don't like bad words; they don't go down my windpipe. 'Scoundrel 's a name I've got a retort for, and if it hadn't been you, and you a gentleman, you'd have had it spanking hot from the end o' my fist. Perhaps you don't know what sort of a arm I've got? Just you feel that ther' muscle."

He doubled his arm, the knuckles of the fist toward Algernon's face.

"Down with it, you dog!" cried Algernon, crushing his hat as he started up.

"It'll come on your nose, if I downs with it, my lord," said Sedgett. "You've what they Londoners calls 'bonneted yourself.'"

He pulled Algernon by the coat-tail into his seat.

"Stop!" Algernon shouted to the cabman.

"Drive ahead!" roared Sedgett.

This signal of a dissension was heard along the main street of Epsom, and re-awakened the flagging hilarity of the road.

Algernon shrieked his commands; Sedgett thundered his. They tussled, and each having inflicted an unpleasant squeeze on the other, they came apart by mutual consent, and exchanged half-length blows. Overhead, the cabman—not merely a cabman, but an individual—flicked the flanks of his horse, and cocked his eye and head in answer to gesticulations from shop-doors and pavement.

"Let 'em fight it out, I'm impartial," he remarked; and having lifted his little observing door, and given one glance, parrot-wise, below, he shut away the troubled prospect of those mortals, and drove along benignly.

Epsom permitted it; but Ewell contained a sturdy citizen, who, smoking his pipe under his eaves, contemplative of passers-by, saw strife rushing on like a meteor. He raised the waxed end of his pipe, and with an authoritative motion of his head at the same time, pointed out the case to a man in a donkey-cart, who looked behind, saw pugnacity upon wheels, and manoeuvred a docile and wonderfully pretty-stepping little donkey in such a manner that the cabman was fain to pull up.

The combatants jumped into the road.

"That's right, gentlemen; I don't want to spile sport," said the donkey's man. "O' course you ends your Epsom-day with spirit."

"There's sunset on their faces," said the cabman. "Would you try a by-lane, gentlemen?"

But now the donkey's man had inspected the figures of the antagonistic couple.

"Taint fair play," he said to Sedgett. "You leave that gentleman alone, you, sir?"

The man with the pipe came up.

"No fighting," he observed. "We ain't going to have our roads disgraced. It shan't be said Englishmen don't know how to enjoy themselves without getting drunk and disorderly. You drop your fists."

The separation had to be accomplished by violence, for Algernon's blood was up.

A crowd was not long in collecting, which caused a stoppage of vehicles of every description.

A gentleman leaned from an open carriage to look at the fray critically, and his companion stretching his neck to do likewise, "Sedgett!" burst from his lips involuntarily.

The pair of original disputants (for there were many by this time) turned their heads simultaneously toward the carriage.

"Will you come on?" Sedgett roared, but whether to Algernon, or to one of the gentlemen, or one of the crowd, was indefinite. None responding, he shook with ox-like wrath, pushed among shoulders, and plunged back to his seat, making the cabman above bound and sway, and the cab-horse to start and antic.

Greatly to the amazement of the spectators, the manifest gentleman (by comparison) who had recently been at a pummelling match with him, and bore the stains of it, hung his head, stepped on the cab, and suffered himself to be driven away.

"Sort of a 'man-and-wife' quarrel," was the donkey's man's comment. "There's something as corks 'em up, and something uncorks 'em; but what that something is, I ain't, nor you ain't, man enough to inform the company."

He rubbed his little donkey's nose affectionately.

"Any gentleman open to a bet I don't overtake that ere Hansom within three miles o' Ewell?" he asked, as he took the rein.

But his little donkey's quality was famous in the neighbourhood.

"Come on, then," he said; "and show what you can do, without emilation, Master Tom."

Away the little donkey trotted.

BOOK IV

CHAPTER XXX

THE EXPIATION

Those two in the open carriage, one of whom had called out Sedgett's name, were Robert and Major Waring. When the cab had flown by, they fell back into their seats, and smoked; the original stipulation for the day having been that no harassing matter should be spoken of till nightfall.

True to this, Robert tried to think hard on the scene of his recent enjoyment. Horses were to him what music is to a poet, and the glory of the Races he had witnessed was still quick in heart, and partly counteracted his astonishment at the sight of his old village enemy in company with Algernon Blancove.

It was not astonishing at all to him that they should have quarrelled and come to blows; for he knew Sedgett well, and the imperative necessity for fighting him, if only to preserve a man's self-respect and the fair division of peace, when once he had been allowed to get upon terms sufficiently close to assert his black nature; but how had it come about? How was it that a gentleman could consent to appear publicly with such a fellow? He decided that it meant something, and something ominous—but what? Whom could it affect? Was Algernon Blancove such a poor creature that, feeling himself bound by certain dark dealings with Sedgett to keep him quiet, he permitted the bullying dog to hang to his coat-tail? It seemed improbable that any young gentleman should be so weak, but it might be the case; and "if so," thought Robert, "and I let him know I bear him no ill-will for setting Sedgett upon me, I may be doing him a service."

He remembered with pain Algernon's glance of savage humiliation upward, just before he turned to follow Sedgett into the cab; and considered that he ought in kindness to see him and make him comfortable by apologizing, as if he himself had no complaint to make.

He resolved to do it when the opportunity should come. Meantime, what on earth brought them together?

"How white the hedges are!" he said.

"There's a good deal of dust," Major Waring replied.

"I wasn't aware that cabs came to the races."

"They do, you see."

Robert perceived that Percy meant to fool him if he attempted a breach of the bond; but he longed so much for Percy's opinion of the strange alliance between Sedgett and Algernon Blancove, that at any cost he was compelled to say, "I can't get to the bottom of that."

"That squabble in the road?" said Percy. "We shall see two or three more before we reach home."

"No. What's the meaning of a gentleman consorting with a blackguard?" Robert persisted.

"One or the other has discovered an assimilation, I suppose," Percy gave answer. "That's an odd remark on returning from Epsom. Those who jump into the same pond generally come out the same colour."

Robert spoke low.

"Has it anything to do with the poor girl, do you think?"

"I told you I declined to think till we were home again. Confound it, man, have you no idea of a holiday?"

Robert puffed his tobacco-smoke.

"Let's talk of Mrs. Lovell," he said.

"That's not a holiday for me," Percy murmured but Robert's mind was too preoccupied to observe the tone, and he asked,—

"Is she to be trusted to keep her word faithfully this time?"

"Come," said Percy, "we haven't betted to-day. I'll bet you she will, if you like. Will you bet against it?"

"I won't. I can't nibble at anything. Betting's like drinking."

"But you can take a glass of wine. This sort of bet is much the same. However, don't; for you would lose."

"There," said Robert; "I've heard of being angry with women for fickleness, changeableness, and all sorts of other things. She's a lady I couldn't understand being downright angry with, and here's the reason—it ain't a matter of reason at all—she fascinates me. I do, I declare, clean forget Rhoda; I forget the girl, if only I see Mrs. Lovell at a distance. How's that? I'm not a fool, with nonsensical fancies of any kind. I know what loving a woman is; and a man in my position might be ass enough to—all sorts of things. It isn't that; it's fascination. I'm afraid of her. If she talks to me, I feel something like having gulped a bottle of wine. Some women you have a respect for; some you like or you love; some you despise: with her, I just feel I'm intoxicated."

Major Waring eyed him steadily. He said: "I'll unriddle it, if I can, to your comprehension. She admires you for what you are, and she lets you see it; I dare say she's not unwilling that you should see it. She has a worship for bravery: it's a deadly passion with her."

Robert put up a protesting blush of modesty, as became him. "Then why, if she does me the honour to think anything of me, does she turn against me?"

"Ah! now you go deeper. She is giving you what assistance she can; at present: be thankful, if you can be satisfied with her present doings. Perhaps I'll answer the other question by-and-by. Now we enter London, and our day is over. How did you like it?"

Robert's imagination rushed back to the downs.

"The race was glorious. I wish we could go at that pace in life; I should have a certainty of winning. How miserably dull the streets look; and the people creep along—they creep, and seem to like it. Horseback's my element."

They drove up to Robert's lodgings, where, since the Winter, he had been living austerely and recklessly; exiled by his sensitiveness from his two homes, Warbeach and Wrexby; and seeking over London for

Dahlia—a pensioner on his friend's bounty; and therein had lain the degrading misery to a man of his composition. Often had he thought of enlisting again, and getting drafted to a foreign station. Nothing but the consciousness that he was subsisting on money not his own would have kept him from his vice. As it was, he had lived through the months between Winter and Spring, like one threading his way through the tortuous lengths of a cavern; never coming to the light, but coming upon absurd mishaps in his effort to reach it. His adventures in London partook somewhat of the character of those in Warbeach, minus the victim; for whom two or three gentlemen in public thoroughfares had been taken. These misdemeanours, in the face of civil society, Robert made no mention of in his letters to Percy.

But there was light now, though at first it gave but a faint glimmer, in a lady's coloured envelope, lying on the sitting-room table. Robert opened it hurriedly, and read it; seized Dahlia's address, with a brain on fire, and said:

"It's signed 'Margaret Lovell.' This time she calls me 'Dear Sir.'"

"She could hardly do less," Percy remarked.

"I know: but there is a change in her. There's a summer in her writing now. She has kept her word, Percy. She's the dearest lady in the world. I don't ask why she didn't help me before."

"You acknowledge the policy of mild measures," said Major Waring.

"She's the dearest lady in the world," Robert repeated. He checked his enthusiasm. "Lord in heaven! what an evening I shall have."

The thought of his approaching interview with Dahlia kept him dumb.

As they were parting in the street, Major Waring said, "I will be here at twelve. Let me tell you this, Robert: she is going to be married; say nothing to dissuade her; it's the best she can do; take a manly view of it. Good-bye."

Robert was but slightly affected by the intelligence. His thoughts were on Dahlia as he had first seen her, when in her bloom, and the sister of his darling; now miserable; a thing trampled to earth! With him, pity for a victim soon became lost in rage at the author of the wrong, and as he walked along he reflected contemptuously on his feeble efforts to avenge her at Warbeach. She lived in a poor row of cottages, striking off from one of the main South-western suburb roads, not very distant from his own lodgings, at which he marvelled, as at a cruel irony. He could not discern the numbers, and had to turn up several of the dusky little strips of garden to read the numbers on the doors. A faint smell of lilac recalled the country and old days, and some church bells began ringing. The number of the house where he was to find Dahlia was seven. He was at the door of the house next to it, when he heard voices in the garden beside him.

A man said, "Then I have your answer?"

A woman said, "Yes; yes."

"You will not trust to my pledged honour?"

"Pardon me; not that. I will not live in disgrace."

"When I promise, on my soul, that the moment I am free I will set you right before the world?"

"Oh! pardon me."

"You will?"

"No; no! I cannot."

"You choose to give yourself to an obscure dog, who'll ill-treat you, and for whom you don't care a pin's-head; and why? that you may be fenced from gossip, and nothing more. I thought you were a woman above that kind of meanness. And this is a common countryman. How will you endure that kind of life? You were made for elegance and happiness: you shall have it. I met you before your illness, when you would not listen to me: I met you after. I knew you at once. Am I changed? I swear to you I have dreamed of you ever since, and love you. Be as faded as you like; be hideous, if you like; but come with me. You know my name, and what I am. Twice I have followed you, and found your name and address; twice I have written to you, and made the same proposal. And you won't trust to my honour? When I tell you I love you tenderly? When I give you my solemn assurance that you shall not regret it? You have been deceived by one man: why punish me? I know—I feel you are innocent and good. This is the third time that you have permitted me to speak to you: let it be final. Say you will trust yourself to me—trust in my honour. Say it shall be to-morrow. Yes; say the word. To-morrow. My sweet creature—do!"

The man spoke earnestly, but a third person and extraneous hearer could hardly avoid being struck by the bathetic conclusion. At least, in tone it bordered on a fall; but the woman did not feel it so.

She replied: "You mean kindly to me, sir. I thank you indeed, for I am very friendless. Oh! pardon me: I am quite—quite determined. Go—pray, forget me."

This was Dahlia's voice.

Robert was unconscious of having previously suspected it. Heartily ashamed of letting his ears be filled with secret talk, he went from the garden and crossed the street.

He knew this to be one of the temptations of young women in London.

Shortly after, the man came through the iron gateway of the garden. He passed under lamplight, and Robert perceived him to be a gentleman in garb.

A light appeared in the windows of the house. Now that he had heard her voice, the terrors of his interview were dispersed, and he had only plain sadness to encounter. He knocked at the door quietly. There was a long delay after he had sent in his name; but finally admission was given.

"If I had loved her!" groaned Robert, before he looked on her; but when he did look on her, affectionate pity washed the selfish man out of him. All these false sensations, peculiar to men, concerning the soiled purity of woman, the lost innocence; the brand of shame upon her, which are commonly the foul sentimentalism of such as can be too eager in the chase of corruption when occasion suits, and are another side of pruriency, not absolutely foreign to the best of us in our youth—all passed away from him in Dahlia's presence.

The young man who can look on them we call fallen women with a noble eye, is to my mind he that is most nobly begotten of the race, and likeliest to be the sire of a noble line. Robert was less than he; but Dahlia's aspect helped him to his rightful manliness. He saw that her worth survived.

The creature's soul had put no gloss upon her sin. She had sinned, and her suffering was manifest.

She had chosen to stand up and take the scourge of God; after which the stones cast by men are not painful.

By this I mean that she had voluntarily stripped her spirit bare of evasion, and seen herself for what she was; pleading no excuse. His scourge is the Truth, and she had faced it.

Innumerable fanciful thoughts, few of them definite, beset the mind at interviews such as these; but Robert was distinctly impressed by her look. It was as that of one upon the yonder shore. Though they stood close together, he had the thought of their being separate—a gulf between.

The colourlessness of her features helped to it, and the odd little close-fitting white linen cap which she wore to conceal the stubborn-twisting clipped curls of her shorn head, made her unlike women of our world. She was dressed in black up to the throat. Her eyes were still luminously blue, and she let them dwell on Robert one gentle instant, giving him her hand humbly.

"Dahlia!—my dear sister, I wish I could say; but the luck's against me," Robert began.

She sat, with her fingers locked together in her lap, gazing forward on the floor, her head a little sideways bent.

"I believe," he went on—"I haven't heard, but I believe Rhoda is well."

"She and father are well, I know," said Dahlia.

Robert started: "Are you in communication with them?"

She shook her head. "At the end of some days I shall see them."

"And then perhaps you'll plead my cause, and make me thankful to you for life, Dahlia?"

"Rhoda does not love you."

"That's the fact, if a young woman's to be trusted to know her own mind, in the first place, and to speak it, in the second."

Dahlia, closed her lips. The long-lined underlip was no more very red. Her heart knew that it was not to speak of himself that he had come; but she was poor-witted, through weakness of her blood, and out of her own immediate line of thought could think neither far nor deep. He entertained her with talk of his notions of Rhoda, finishing:

"But at the end of a week you will see her, and I dare say she'll give you her notions of me. Dahlia! how happy this'll make them. I do say thank God! from my soul, for this."

She pressed her hands in her lap, trembling. "If you will, please, not speak of it, Mr. Robert."

"Say only you do mean it, Dahlia. You mean to let them see you?"

She shivered out a "Yes."

"That's right. Because, a father and a sister—haven't they a claim? Think a while. They've had a terrible time. And it's true that you've consented to a husband, Dahlia? I'm glad, if it is; and he's good and kind. Right soul-glad I am."

While he was speaking, her eyelids lifted and her eyes became fixed on him in a stony light of terror, like a creature in anguish before her executioner. Then again her eyelids dropped. She had not moved from her still posture.

"You love him?" he asked, in some wonderment.

She gave no answer.

"Don't you care for him?"

There was no reply.

"Because, Dahlia, if you do not I know I have no right to fancy you do not. How is it? Tell me. Marriage is an awful thing, where there's no love. And this man, whoever he is—is he in good circumstances? I wouldn't speak of him; but, you see, I must, as your friend—and I'm that. Come: he loves you? Of course he does. He has said so. I believe it. And he's a man you can honour and esteem? You wouldn't consent without, I'm sure. What makes me anxious—I look on you as my sister, whether Rhoda will have it so or not; I'm anxious because—I'm anxious it should be over, for then Rhoda will be proud of the faith she had in you, and it will lighten the old man's heart."

Once more the inexplicable frozen look struck over him from her opened eyes, as if one of the minutes of Time had yawned to show him its deep, mute, tragic abyss, and was extinguished.

"When does it take place, Dahlia?"

Her long underlip, white almost as the row of teeth it revealed, hung loose.

"When?" he asked, leaning forward to hear, and the word was "Saturday," uttered with a feeble harshness, not like the gentle voice of Dahlia.

"This coming Saturday?"

"No."

"Saturday week?"

She fell into a visible trembling.

"You named the day?"

He pushed for an indication of cheerful consent to the act she was about to commit, or of reluctance.

Possibly she saw this, for now she answered, "I did." The sound was deep in her throat.

"Saturday week," said Robert. "I feel to the man as a brother, already. Do you live—you'll live in the country?"

"Abroad."

"Not in Old England? I'm sorry for that. But—well! Things must be as they're ordered. Heigho! I've got to learn it."

Dahlia smiled kindly.

"Rhoda will love you. She is firm when she loves."

"When she loves. Where's the consolation to me?"

"Do you think she loves me as much—as much"

"As much as ever? She loves her sister with all her heart—all, for I haven't a bit of it."

"It is because," said Dahlia slowly, "it is because she thinks I am—"

Here the poor creature's bosom heaved piteously.

"What has she said of me? I wish her to have blamed me—it is less pain."

"Listen," said Robert. "She does not, and couldn't blame you, for it's a sort of religion with her to believe no wrong of you. And the reason why she hates me is, that I, knowing something more of the world, suspected, and chose to let her know it—I said it, in fact—that you had been deceived by a—But this isn't the time to abuse others. She would have had me, if I had thought proper to think as she thinks, or play hypocrite, and pretend to. I'll tell you openly, Dahlia; your father thinks the worst. Ah! you look the ghost again. It's hard for you to hear, but you give me a notion of having got strength to hear it. It's your father's way to think the worst. Now, when you can show him your husband, my dear, he'll lift his head. He's old English. He won't dream of asking questions. He'll see a brave and honest young man who must love you, or—he does love you, that's settled. Your father'll shake his hand, and as for Rhoda, she'll triumph. The only person to speak out to, is the man who marries you, and that you've done."

Robert looked the interrogation he did not utter.

"I have," said Dahlia.

"Good: if I may call him brother, some day, all the better for me. Now, you won't leave England the day you're married."

"Soon. I pray that it may be soon."

"Yes; well, on that morning, I'll have your father and Rhoda at my lodgings, not wide from here: if I'd only known it earlier!—and you and your husband shall come there and join us. It'll be a happy meeting at last."

Dahlia stopped her breathing.

"Will you see Rhoda?"

"I'll go to her to-morrow, if you like."

"If I might see her, just as I am leaving England! not before."

"That's not generous," said Robert.

"Isn't it?" she asked like a child.

"Fancy!—to see you she's been longing for, and the ship that takes you off, perhaps everlastingly, as far as this world's concerned!"

"Mr. Robert, I do not wish to deceive my sister. Father need not be distressed. Rhoda shall know. I will not be guilty of falsehoods any more—no more! Will you go to her? Tell her—tell Rhoda what I am. Say I have been ill. It will save her from a great shock."

She covered her eyes.

"I said in all my letters that my husband was a gentleman."

It was her first openly penitential utterance in his presence, and her cheeks were faintly reddened. It may have been this motion of her blood which aroused the sunken humanity within her; her heart leaped, and she cried "I can see her as I am, I can. I thought it impossible. Oh! I can. Will she come to me? My sister is a Christian and forgives. Oh! let me see her. And go to her, dear Mr. Robert, and ask her—tell her all, and ask her if I may be spared, and may work at something—anything, for my livelihood near my sister. It is difficult for women to earn money, but I think I can. I have done so since my illness. I have been in the hospital with brain fever. He was lodging in the house with me before. He found me at the hospital. When I came out, he walked with me to support me: I was very weak. He read to me, and then asked me to marry him. He asked again. I lay in bed one night, and with my eyes open, I saw the dangers of women, and the trouble of my father and sister; and pits of wickedness. I saw like places full of snakes. I had such a yearning for protection. I gave him my word I would be his wife, if he was not ashamed of a wife like me. I wished to look once in father's face. I had fancied that Rhoda would spurn me, when she discovered my falsehood. She—sweet dear! would she ever? Go to her. Say, I do not love any man. I am heart-dead. I have no heart except for her. I cannot love a husband. He is good, and it is kind: but, oh! let me be spared. His face!—"

She pressed her hands tight into the hollow of her eyes.

"No; it can't be meant. Am I very ungrateful? This does not seem to be what God orders. Only if this must be! only if it must be! If my sister cannot look on me without! He is good, and it is unselfish to take a moneyless, disgraced creature: but, my misery!—If my sister will see me, without my doing this!—Go to her, Mr. Robert. Say, Dahlia was false, and repents, and has worked with her needle to subsist, and can, and will, for her soul strives to be clean. Try to make her understand. If Rhoda could love you, she would know. She is locked up—she is only ideas. My sweet is so proud. I love her for her pride, if she will only let me creep to her feet, kiss her feet. Dear Mr. Robert, help me! help me! I will do anything she says. If she says I am to marry him, I will. Don't mind my tears—they mean nothing now. Tell my dear, I will obey her. I will not be false any more to her. I wish to be quite stripped. And Rhoda may know me, and forgive me, if she can. And—Oh! if she thinks, for father's sake, I ought, I will submit and speak the words; I will; I am ready. I pray for mercy."

Robert sat with his fist at his temples, in a frowning meditation.

Had she declared her reluctance to take the step, in the first moments of their interview, he might have been ready to support her: but a project fairly launched becomes a reality in the brain—a thing once spoken of attracts like a living creature, and does not die voluntarily. Robert now beheld all that was in its favour, and saw nothing but flighty flimsy objections to it. He was hardly moved by her unexpected outburst.

Besides, there was his own position in the case. Rhoda would smile on him, if he brought Dahlia to her, and brought her happy in the world's eye. It will act as a sort of signal for general happiness. But if he had to go and explain matters base and mournful to her, there would be no smile on her face, and not much gratitude in her breast. There would be none for a time, certainly. Proximity to her faded sister made him conceive her attainable, and thrice precious by contrast.

He fixed his gaze on Dahlia, and the perfect refinement of her simplicity caused him to think that she might be aware of an inappropriateness in the contemplated union.

"Is he a clumsy fellow? I mean, do you read straight off that he has no pretension to any manners of a gentleman—nothing near it?"

To this question, put with hesitation by Robert, Dahlia made answer, "I respect him."

She would not strengthen her prayer by drawing the man's portrait. Speedily she forgot how the doing so would in any way have strengthened her prayer. The excitement had left her brain dull. She did little more than stare mildly, and absently bend her head, while Robert said that he would go to Rhoda on the morrow, and speak seriously with her.

"But I think I can reckon her ideas will side with mine, that it is to your interest, my dear, to make your feelings come round warm to a man you can respect, and who offers you a clear path," he said.

Whereat Dahlia quietly blinked her eyes.

When he stood up, she rose likewise.

"Am I to take a kiss to Rhoda?" he said, and seeing her answer, bent his forehead, to which she put her lips.

"And now I must think all night long about the method of transferring it. Good-bye, Dahlia. You shall hear from your sister the morning after to-morrow. Good-bye!"

He pressed her hand, and went to the door.

"There's nothing I can do for you, Dahlia?"

"Not anything."

"God bless you, my dear!"

Robert breathed with the pleasant sense of breathing, when he was again in the street. Amazement, that what he had dreaded so much should be so easily over, set him thinking, in his fashion, on the marvels of life, and the naturalness in the aspect of all earthly things when you look at them with your eyes.

But in the depths of his heart there was disquiet.

"It's the best she can do; she can do no better," he said; and said it more frequently than it needed by a mind established in the conviction. Gradually he began to feel that certain things seen with the eyes, natural as they may then appear and little terrible, leave distinct, solid, and grave impressions. Something of what our human tragedy may show before high heaven possessed him. He saw it bare of any sentiment, in the person of the girl Dahlia. He could neither put a halo of imagination about her, nor could he conceive one degraded thought of the creature. She stood a naked sorrow, haunting his brain.

And still he continued saying, "It's the best she can do: it's best for all. She can do nothing better."

He said it, unaware that he said it in self-defence.

The pale nun-like ghostly face hung before him, stronger in outline the farther time widened between him and that suffering flesh.

CHAPTER XXXI

THE MELTING OF THE THOUSAND

The thousand pounds were in Algernon's hands at last. He had made his escape from Boyne's Bank early in the afternoon, that he might obtain the cheque and feel the money in his pocket before that day's sun was extinguished. There was a note for five hundred; four notes for a hundred severally; and two fifties. And all had come to him through the mere writing down of his name as a recipient of the sum!

It was enough to make one in love with civilization. Money, when it is once in your pocket, seems to have come there easily, even if you have worked for it; but if you have done no labour whatever, and still find it there, your sensations (supposing you to be a butterfly youth—the typical child of a wealthy country) exult marvellously, and soar above the conditions of earth.

He knew the very features of the notes. That gallant old Five Hundred, who might have been a Thousand, but that he had nobly split himself into centurions and skirmishers, stood in his imaginative contemplation like a grand white-headed warrior, clean from the slaughter and in court-ruffles—say, Blucher at the court of the Waterloo Regent. The Hundreds were his Generals; the Fifties his captains; and each one was possessed of unlimited power of splitting himself into serviceable regiments, at the call of his lord, Algernon.

He scarcely liked to make the secret confession that it was the largest sum he had ever as yet carried about; but, as it heightened his pleasure, he did confess it for half an instant. Five Hundred in the bulk he had never attained to. He felt it as a fortification against every mishap in life.

To a young man commonly in difficulties with regard to the paying of his cabman, and latterly the getting of his dinner, the sense of elevation imparted by the sum was intoxicating. But, thinking too much of the Five Hundred waxed dangerous for the fifties; it dwarfed them to such insignificance that it made them lose their self-respect. So, Algernon, pursuing excellent tactics, set his mind upon some stray shillings that he had a remainder of five pounds borrowed from old Anthony, when he endeavoured to obtain repayment of the one pound and interest dating from the night at the theatre. Algernon had stopped his mouth on that point, as well as concerning his acquaintance with Dahlia, by immediately attempting to borrow further, whenever Anthony led the way for a word in private. A one-pound creditor had no particular terrors for him, and he manoeuvred the old man neatly, saying, as previously, "Really, I don't know the young person you allude to: I happened to meet her, or some one like her, casually," and dropping his voice, "I'm rather short—what do you think? Could you?—a trifling accommodation?" from which Anthony fled.

But on the day closing the Epsom week he beckoned Anthony secretly to follow him out of the office, and volunteered to give news that he had just heard of Dahlia.

"Oh," said Anthony, "I've seen her."

"I haven't," said Algernon, "upon my honour."

"Yes, I've seen her, sir, and sorry to hear her husband's fallen a bit low." Anthony touched his pocket. "What they calls 'nip' tides, ain't it?"

Algernon sprang a compliment under him, which sent the vain old fellow up, whether he would or not, to the effect that Anthony's tides were not subject to lunar influence.

"Now, Mr. Blancove, you must change them notions o' me. I don't say I shouldn't be richer if I'd got what's owing to me."

"You'd have to be protected; you'd be Bullion on two legs," said Algernon, always shrewd in detecting a weakness. "You'd have to go about with sentries on each side, and sleep in an iron safe!"

The end of the interview was a visit to the public-house, and the transferring of another legal instrument from Algernon to Anthony. The latter departed moaning over his five pounds ten shillings in paper; the former rejoicing at his five pounds in gold. That day was Saturday. On Monday, only a few shillings of the five pounds remained; but they were sufficient to command a cab, and, if modesty in dining was among the prescriptions for the day, a dinner. Algernon was driven to the West.

He remembered when he had plunged in the midst of the fashionable whirlpool, having felt reckless there formerly, but he had become remarkably sedate when he stepped along the walks. A certain equipage, or horse, was to his taste, and once he would have said: "That's the thing for me;" being penniless. Now, on the contrary, he reckoned the possible cost, grudgingly, saying "Eh?" to himself, and responding "No," faintly, and then more positively, "Won't do."

He was by no means acting as one on a footing of equality with the people he beholds. A man who is ready to wager a thousand pounds that no other man present has that amount in his pocket, can hardly feel unequal to his company.

Charming ladies on horseback cantered past. "Let them go," he thought. Yesterday, the sight of one would have set him dreaming on grand alliances. When you can afford to be a bachelor, the case is otherwise. Presently, who should ride by but Mrs. Lovell! She was talking more earnestly than was becoming, to that easy-mannered dark-eyed fellow; the man who had made him savage by entering the opera-box.

"Poor old Ned!" said Algernon; "I must put him on his guard." But, even the lifting of a finger—a hint on paper—would bring Edward over from Paris, as he knew; and that was not in his scheme; so he only determined to write to his cousin.

A flood of evening gold lay over the Western park.

"The glory of this place," Algernon said to himself, "is, that you're sure of meeting none but gentlemen here;" and he contrasted it with Epsom Downs.

A superstitious horror seized him when, casting his eyes ahead, he perceived Sedgett among the tasteful groups—as discordant a figure as could well be seen, and clumsily aware of it, for he could neither step nor look like a man at ease. Algernon swung round and retraced his way; but Sedgett had long sight.

"I'd heard of London"—Algernon soon had the hated voice in his ears,—"and I've bin up to London b'fore; I came here to have a wink at the fash'nables—hang me, if ever I see such a scrumptious lot. It's worth a walk up and down for a hour or more. D' you come heer often, sir?"

"Eh? Who are you? Oh!" said Algernon, half mad with rage. "Excuse me;" and he walked faster.

"Fifty times over," Sedgett responded cheerfully. "I'd pace you for a match up and down this place if you liked. Ain't the horses a spectacle? I'd rather be heer than there at they Races. As for the ladies, I'll tell you what: ladies or no ladies, give my young woman time for her hair to grow; and her colour to come, by George! if she wouldn't shine against e'er a one—smite me stone blind, if she wouldn't! So she shall! Australia'll see. I owe you my thanks for interdoocin' me, and never fear my not remembering."

Where there was a crowd, Algernon could elude his persecutor by threading his way rapidly; but the open spaces condemned him to merciless exposure, and he flew before eyes that his imagination exaggerated to a stretch of supernatural astonishment. The tips of his fingers, the roots of his hair, pricked with vexation, and still, manoeuvre as he might, Sedgett followed him.

"Call at my chambers," he said sternly.

"You're never at home, sir."

"Call to-morrow morning, at ten."

"And see a great big black door, and kick at it till my toe comes through my boot. Thank ye."

"I tell you, I won't have you annoying me in public; once for all."

"Why, sir; I thought we parted friends, last time. Didn't you shake my hand, now, didn't you shake my hand, sir? I ask you, whether you shook my hand, or whether you didn't? A plain answer. We had a bit of a scrimmage, coming home. I admit we had; but shaking hands, means 'friends again we are.' I know you're a gentleman, and a man like me shouldn't be so bold as fur to strike his betters. Only, don't you see, sir, Full-o'-Beer's a hasty chap, and up in a minute; and he's sorry for it after."

Algernon conceived a brilliant notion. Drawing five shillings from his pocket, he held them over to Sedgett, and told him to drive down to his chambers, and await his coming. Sedgett took the money; but it was five shillings lost. He made no exhibition of receiving orders, and it was impossible to address him imperiously without provoking observations of an animated kind from the elegant groups parading and sitting.

Young Harry Latters caught Algernon's eye; never was youth more joyfully greeted. Harry spoke of the Friday's race, and the defection of the horse Tenpenny Nail. A man passed with a nod and "How d' ye do?" for which he received in reply a cool stare.

"Who's that?" Algernon asked.

"The son of a high dignitary," said Harry.

"You cut him."

"I can do the thing, you see, when it's a public duty."

"What's the matter with him?"

"Merely a black-leg, a grec, a cheat, swindler, or whatever name you like," said Harry. "We none of us nod to the professionals in this line; and I won't exchange salutes with an amateur. I'm peculiar. He chose to be absent on the right day last year; so from that date; I consider him absent in toto; 'none of your rrrrr—m reckonings, let's have the rrrrr—m toto;'—you remember Suckling's story of the Yankee fellow? Bye-bye; shall see you the day after to-morrow. You dine with me and Suckling at the club."

Latters was hailed by other friends. Algernon was forced to let him go. He dipped under the iron rail, and crossed the row at a run; an indecorous proceeding; he could not help it. The hope was that Sedgett would not have the like audacity, or might be stopped, and Algernon's reward for so just a calculation was, that on looking round, he found himself free. He slipped with all haste out of the Park. Sedgett's presence had the deadening power of the torpedo on the thousand pounds.

For the last quarter of an hour, Algernon had not felt a motion of it. A cab, to make his escape certain, was suggested to his mind; and he would have called a cab, had not the novel apparition of economy, which now haunted him, suggested that he had recently tossed five shillings into the gutter. A man might dine on four shillings and sixpence, enjoying a modest half-pint of wine, and he possessed that sum. To pinch himself and deserve well of Providence, he resolved not to drink wine, but beer, that day. He named the beverage; a pint-bottle of ale; and laughed, as a royal economist may, who punishes himself to please himself.

"Mighty jolly, ain't it, sir?" said Sedgett, at his elbow.

Algernon faced about, and swore an oath from his boots upward; so vehement was his disgust, and all-pervading his amazement.

"I'll wallop you at that game," said Sedgett.

"You infernal scoundrel!"

"If you begin swearing," Sedgett warned him.

"What do you want with me?"

"I'll tell you, sir. I don't want to go to ne'er a cock-fight, nor betting hole."

"Here, come up this street," said Algernon, leading the way into a dusky defile from a main parade of fashion. "Now, what's your business, confound you!"

"Well, sir, I ain't goin' to be confounded: that, I'll—I'll swear to. The long and the short is, I must have some money 'fore the week's out."

"You won't have a penny from me."

"That's blunt, though it ain't in my pocket," said Sedgett, grinning. "I say, sir, respectful as you like, I must. I've got to pay for passengerin' over the sea, self and wife; and quick it must be. There's things to buy on both sides. A small advance and you won't be bothered. Say, fifty. Fifty, and you don't see me till Saturday, when, accordin' to agreement, you hand to me the cash, outside the church door; and then we parts to meet no more. Oh! let us be joyful—I'll sing."

Algernon's loathing of the coarseness and profanity of villany increased almost to the depth of a sentiment as he listened to Sedgett.

"I do nothing of the sort," he said. "You shall not have a farthing. Be off. If you follow me, I give you into custody of a policeman."

"You durst n't." Sedgett eyed him warily.

He could spy a physical weakness, by affinity of cowardice, as quickly as Algernon a moral weakness, by the same sort of relationship to it.

"You don't dare," Sedgett pursued. "And why should you, sir? there's ne'er a reason why. I'm civil. I asks for my own: no more 'n my own, it ain't. I call the bargain good: why sh'd I want fur to break it? I want the money bad. I'm sick o' this country. I'd like to be off in the first ship that sails. Can't you let me have ten till to-morrow? then t' other forty. I've got a mortal need for it, that I have. Come, it's no use your walking at that rate; my legs are's good as yours."

Algernon had turned back to the great thoroughfare. He was afraid that ten pounds must be forfeited to this worrying demon in the flesh, and sought the countenance of his well-dressed fellows to encourage him in resisting. He could think of no subterfuge; menace was clearly useless: and yet the idea of changeing one of the notes and for so infamous a creature, caused pangs that helped him further to endure his dogging feet and filthy tongue. This continued until he saw a woman's hand waving from a cab. Presuming that such a signal, objectionable as it was, must be addressed to himself, he considered whether he should lift his hat, or simply smile as a favoured, but not too deeply flattered, man. The cab drew up, and the woman said, "Sedgett." She was a well-looking woman, strongly coloured, brown-eyed, and hearty in appearance.

"What a brute you are, Sedgett, not to be at home when you brought me up to London with all the boxes and bedding—my goodness! It's a Providence I caught you in my eye, or I should have been driving down to the docks, and seeing about the ship. You are a brute. Come in, at once."

"If you're up to calling names, I've got one or two for you," Sedgett growled.

Algernon had heard enough. Sure that he had left Sedgett in hands not likely to relinquish him, he passed on with elastic step. Wine was greatly desired, after his torments. Where was credit to be had? True, he looked contemptuously on the blooming land of credit now, but an entry to it by one of the back doors would have been convenient, so that he might be nourished and restored by a benevolent dinner, while he kept his Thousand intact. However, he dismissed the contemplation of credit and its transient charms. "I won't dine at all," he said.

A beggar woman stretched out her hand—he dropped a shilling in it.

"Hang me, if I shall be able to," was his next reflection; and with the remaining three and sixpence, he crossed the threshold of a tobacconist's shop and bought cigars, to save himself from excesses in charity. After gravely reproaching the tobacconist for the growing costliness of cigars, he came into the air, feeling extraordinarily empty. Of this he soon understood the cause, and it amused him. Accustomed to the smell of tobacco always when he came from his dinner, it seemed, as the fumes of the shop took his nostril, that demands were being made within him by an inquisitive spirit, and dissatisfaction expressed at the vacancy there.

"What's the use? I can't dine," he uttered argumentatively. "I'm not going to change a note, and I won't dine. I've no Club. There's not a fellow I can see who'll ask me to dine. I'll lounge along home. There is some Sherry there."

But Algernon bore vividly in mind that he did not approve of that Sherry.

"I've heard of fellows frying sausages at home, and living on something like two shillings a day," he remarked in meditation; and then it struck him that Mrs. Lovell's parcel of returned jewels lay in one of his drawers at home—that is, if the laundress had left the parcel untouched.

In an agony of alarm, he called a cab, and drove hotly to the Temple. Finding the packet safe, he put a couple of rings and the necklace with the opal in his waistcoat pocket. The cabman must be paid, of course; so a jewel must be pawned. Which shall it be? diamond or opal? Change a dozen times and let it be the trinket in the right hand—the opal; let it be the opal. How much would the opal fetch? The pawnbroker can best inform us upon that point. So he drove to the pawnbroker; one whom he knew. The pawnbroker offered him five-and-twenty pounds on the security of the opal.

"What on earth is it that people think disgraceful in your entering a pawnbroker's shop?" Algernon asked himself when, taking his ticket and the five-and-twenty pounds, he repelled the stare of a man behind a neighbouring partition.

"There are not many of that sort in the kingdom," he said to the pawnbroker, who was loftily fondling the unlucky opal.

"Well—h'm; perhaps there's not;" the pawnbroker was ready to admit it, now that the arrangement had been settled.

"I shan't be able to let you keep it long."

"As quick back as you like, sir."

Algernon noticed as he turned away that the man behind the partition, who had more the look of a dapper young shopman than of a needy petitioner for loans or securities, stretched over the counter to look at the opal; and he certainly heard his name pronounced. It enraged him; but policy counselled a quiet behaviour in this place, and no quarrelling with his pawnbroker. Besides, his whole nature cried out for dinner. He dined and had his wine; as good, he ventured to assert, as any man could get for the money; for he knew the hotels with the venerable cellars.

"I should have made a first-rate courier to a millionaire," he said, with scornful candour, but without abusing the disposition of things which had ordered his being a gentleman. Subsequently, from his having sat so long over his wine without moving a leg, he indulged in the belief that he had reflected profoundly; out of which depths he started, very much like a man who has dozed, and felt a discomfort in his limbs and head.

"I must forget myself," he said. Nor was any grave mentor by, to assure him that his tragic state was the issue of an evil digestion of his dinner and wine. "I must forget myself. I'm under some doom. I see it now. Nobody cares for me. I don't know what happiness is. I was born under a bad star. My fate's written." Following his youthful wisdom, this wounded hart dragged his slow limbs toward the halls of brandy and song.

One learns to have compassion for fools, by studying them: and the fool, though Nature is wise, is next door to Nature. He is naked in his simplicity; he can tell us much, and suggest more. My excuse for dwelling upon him is, that he holds the link of my story. Where fools are numerous, one of them must be prominent now and then in a veracious narration. There comes an hour when the veil drops on him, he not being always clean to the discreeter touch.

Algernon was late at the Bank next day, and not cheerful, though he received his customary reprimand with submission. This day was after the pattern of the day preceding, except that he did not visit the Park; the night likewise.

On Wednesday morning, he arose with the conviction that England was no place for him to dwell in. What if Rhoda were to accompany him to one of the colonies? The idea had been gradually taking shape in his mind from the moment that he had possessed the Thousand. Could she not make butter and cheeses capitally, while he rode on horseback through space? She was a strong girl, a loyal girl, and would be a grateful wife.

"I'll marry her," he said; and hesitated. "Yes, I'll marry her." But it must be done immediately.

He resolved to run down to Wrexby, rejoice her with a declaration of love, astound her with a proposal of marriage, bewilder her little brain with hurrying adjectives, whisk her up to London, and in little more than a week be sailing on the high seas, new born; nothing of civilization about him, save a few last very first-rate cigars which he projected to smoke on the poop of the vessel, and so dream of the world he left behind.

He went down to the Bank in better spirits, and there wrote off a straightforward demand of an interview, to Rhoda, hinting at the purpose of it. While at his work, he thought of Harry Latters and Lord Suckling, and the folly of his dining with men in his present position. Settling-day, it or yesterday might be, but a colonist is not supposed to know anything of those arrangements. One of his fellow-clerks reminded him of a loan he had contracted, and showed him his name written under obligatory initials. He paid it, ostentatiously drawing out one of his fifties. Up came another, with a similar strip of paper. "You don't want me to change this, do you?" said Algernon; and heard a tale of domestic needs—and a grappling landlady. He groaned inwardly: "Odd that I must pay for his landlady being a vixen!" The note was changed; the debt liquidated. On the door-step, as he was going to lunch, old Anthony waylaid him, and was almost noisily persistent in demanding his one pound three and his five pound ten. Algernon paid the sums, ready to believe that there was a suspicion abroad of his intention to become a colonist.

He employed the luncheon hour in a visit to a colonial shipping office, and nearly ran straight upon Sedgett at the office-door. The woman who had hailed him from the cab, was in Sedgett's company, but Sedgett saw no one. His head hung and his sullen brows were drawn moodily. Algernon escaped from observation. His first inquiry at the office was as to the business of the preceding couple, and he was satisfied by hearing that Sedgett wanted berths for himself and wife.

"Who's the woman, I wonder!" Algernon thought, and forgot her.

He obtained some particular information, and returning to the Bank, was called before his uncle, who curtly reckoned up his merits in a contemptuous rebuke, and confirmed him in his resolution to incur this sort of thing no longer. In consequence, he promised Sir William that he would amend his ways, and these were the first hopeful words that Sir William had ever heard from him.

Algernon's design was to dress, that evening, in the uniform of society, so that, in the event of his meeting Harry Latters, he might assure him he was coming to his Club, and had been compelled to dine elsewhere with his uncle, or anybody. When he reached the door of his chambers, a man was standing there, who said,—

"Mr. Algernon Blancove?"

"Yes," Algernon prolonged an affirmative, to diminish the confidence it might inspire, if possible.

"May I speak with you, sir?"

Algernon told him to follow in. The man was tall and large-featured, with an immense blank expression of face.

"I've come from Mr. Samuels, sir," he said, deferentially.

Mr. Samuels was Algernon's chief jeweller.

"Oh," Algernon remarked. "Well, I don't want anything; and let me say, I don't approve of this touting for custom. I thought Mr. Samuels was above it."

The man bowed. "My business is not that, sir. Ahem! I dare say you remember an opal you had from our house. It was set in a necklace."

"All right; I remember it, perfectly," said Algernon; cool, but not of the collected colour.

"The cost of it was fifty-five pounds, sir."

"Was it? Well, I've forgotten."

"We find that it has been pawned for five-and-twenty."

"A little less than half," said Algernon. "Pawnbrokers are simply cheats."

"They mayn't be worse than others," the man observed.

Algernon was exactly in the position where righteous anger is the proper weapon, if not the sole resource. He flushed, but was not sure of his opportunity for the explosion. The man read the flush.

"May I ask you, did you pawn it, sir? I'm obliged to ask the question."

"I?—I really don't—I don't choose to answer impudent questions. What do you mean by coming here?"

"I may as well be open with you, sir, to prevent misunderstandings. One of the young men was present when you pawned it. He saw the thing done."

"Suppose he did?"

"He would be a witness."

"Against me? I've dealt with Samuels for three-four years."

"Yes, sir; but you have never yet paid any account; and I believe I am right in saying that this opal is not the first thing coming from our house that has been pledged—I can't say you did it on the other occasions."

"You had better not," rejoined Algernon.

He broke an unpleasant silence by asking, "What further?"

"My master has sent you his bill."

Algernon glanced at the prodigious figures.

"Five hun—!" he gasped, recoiling; and added, "Well, I can't pay it on the spot."

"Let me tell you, you're liable to proceedings you'd better avoid, sir, for the sake of your relations."

"You dare to threaten to expose me to my relatives?" Algernon said haughtily, and immediately perceived that indignation at this point was a clever stroke; for the man, while deprecating the idea of doing so, showed his more established belief in the possible virtue of such a threat.

"Not at all, sir; but you know that pledging things not paid for is illegal, and subject to penalties. No tradesman likes it; they can't allow it. I may as well let you know that Mr. Samuels—"

"There, stop!" cried Algernon, laughing, as he thought, heartily. "Mr. Samuels is a very tolerable Jew; but he doesn't seem to understand dealing with gentlemen. Pressure comes;" he waved his hand swimmingly; "one wants money, and gets it how one can. Mr. Samuels shall not go to bed thinking he has been defrauded. I will teach Mr. Samuels to think better of us Gentiles. Write me a receipt."

"For what amount, sir?" said the man, briskly.

"For the value of the opal—that is to say, for the value put upon it by Mr. Samuels. Con! hang! never mind. Write the receipt."

He cast a fluttering fifty and a fluttering five on the table, and pushed paper to the man for a receipt.

The man reflected, and refused to take them.

"I don't think, sir," he said, "that less than two-thirds of the bill will make Mr. Samuels easy. You see, this opal was in a necklace. It wasn't like a ring you might have taken off your finger. It's a lady's ornament; and soon after you obtain it from us; you make use of it by turning it into cash. It's a case for a criminal prosecution, which, for the sake of your relations, Mr. Samuels wouldn't willingly bring on. The criminal box is no place for you, sir; but Mr. Samuels must have his own. His mind is not easy. I shouldn't like, sir, to call a policeman."

"Hey!" shouted Algernon; "you'd have to get a warrant."

"It's out, sir."

Though inclined toward small villanies, he had not studied law, and judging from his own affrighted sensations, and the man's impassive face, Algernon supposed that warrants were as lightly granted as writs of summons.

He tightened his muscles. In his time he had talked glibly of Perdition; but this was hot experience. He and the man measured the force of their eyes. Algernon let his chest fall.

"Do you mean?" he murmured.

"Why, sir, it's no use doing things by halves. When a tradesman says he must have his money, he takes his precautions."

"Are you in Mr. Samuels' shop?"

"Not exactly, sir."

"You're a detective?"

"I have been in the service, sir."

"Ah! now I understand." Algernon raised his head with a strain at haughtiness. "If Mr. Samuels had accompanied you, I would have discharged the debt: It's only fair that I should insist upon having a receipt from him personally, and for the whole amount."

With this, he drew forth his purse and displayed the notable Five hundred.

His glow of victory was short. The impassive man likewise had something to exhibit.

"I assure you, sir," he said, "Mr. Samuels does know how to deal with gentlemen. If you will do me the honour, sir, to run up with me to Mr. Samuels' shop? Or, very well, sir; to save you that annoyance here is his receipt to the bill."

Algernon mechanically crumpled up his note.

"Samuels?" ejaculated the unhappy fellow. "Why, my mother dealt with Samuels. My aunt dealt with Samuels. All my family have dealt with him for years; and he talks of proceeding against me, because— upon my soul, it's too absurd! Sending a policeman, too! I'll tell you what—the exposure would damage Mister Samuels most materially. Of course, my father would have to settle the matter; but Mister— Mister Samuels would not recover so easily. He'd be glad to refund the five hundred—what is it?—and twenty-five—why not, 'and sixpence three farthings?' I tell you, I shall let my father pay. Mr. Samuels had better serve me with a common writ. I tell you, I'm not going to denude myself of money altogether. I haven't examined the bill. Leave it here. You can tear off the receipt. Leave it here."

The man indulged in a slight demonstration of dissent.

"No, sir, that won't do."

"Half the bill," roared Algernon; "half the bill, I wouldn't mind paying."

"About two-thirds, sir, is what Mr. Samuels asked for, and he'll stop, and go on as before."

"He'll stop and he'll go on, will he? Mr. Samuels is amazingly like one of his own watches," Algernon sneered vehemently. "Well," he pursued, in fancied security, "I'll pay two-thirds."

"Three hundred, sir."

"Ay, three hundred. Tell him to send a receipt for the three hundred, and he shall have it. As to my entering his shop again, that I shall have to think over."

"That's what gentlemen in Mr. Samuels' position have to run risk of, sir," said the man.

Algernon, more in astonishment than trepidation, observed him feeling at his breast-pocket. The action resulted in an exhibition of a second bill, with a legal receipt attached to it, for three hundred pounds.

"Mr. Samuels is anxious to accommodate you in every way, sir. It isn't the full sum he wants; it's a portion. He thought you might prefer to discharge a portion."

After this exhibition of foresight on the part of the jeweller, there was no more fight in Algernon beyond a strenuous "Faugh!" of uttermost disgust.

He examined the bill and receipt in the man's hand with great apparent scrupulousness; not, in reality, seeing a clear syllable.

"Take it and change it," he threw his Five hundred down, but recovered it from the enemy's grasp; and with a "one, two, three," banged his hundreds on the table: for which he had the loathsome receipt handed to him.

"How," he asked, chokingly, "did Mr. Samuels know I could—I had money?"

"Why, sir, you see," the man, as one who throws off a mask, smiled cordially, after buttoning up the notes; "credit 'd soon give up the ghost, if it hadn't its own dodges,' as I may say. This is only a feeler on Mr. Samuels' part. He heard of his things going to pledge. Halloa! he sings out. And tradesmen are human, sir. Between us, I side with gentlemen, in most cases. Hows'-ever, I'm, so to speak, in Mr. Samuels' pay. A young gentleman in debt, give him a good fright, out comes his money, if he's got any. Sending of a bill receipted's a good trying touch. It's a compliment to him to suppose he can pay. Mr. Samuels, sir, wouldn't go issuing a warrant: if he could, he wouldn't. You named a warrant; that set me up to it. I shouldn't have dreamed of a gentleman supposing it otherwise. Didn't you notice me show a wall of a face? I shouldn't ha' dared to have tried that on an old hand—begging your pardon; I mean a real—a scoundrel. The regular ones must see features: we mustn't be too cunning with them, else they grow suspicious: they're keen as animals; they are. Good afternoon to you, sir."

Algernon heard the door shut. He reeled into a chair, and muffling his head in his two arms on the table, sobbed desperately; seeing himself very distinctly reflected in one of the many facets of folly. Daylight became undesireable to him. He went to bed.

A man who can, in such extremities of despair, go premeditatingly to his pillow, obeys an animal instinct in pursuit of oblivion, that will befriend his nerves. Algernon awoke in deep darkness, with a delicious sensation of hunger. He jumped up. Six hundred and fifty pounds of the money remained intact; and he was joyful. He struck a light to look at his watch: the watch had stopped;—that was a bad sign. He could not forget it. Why had his watch stopped? A chilling thought as to whether predestination did not govern the world, allayed all tumult in his mind. He dressed carefully, and soon heard a great City bell, with horrid gulfs between the strokes, tell him that the hour was eleven toward midnight. "Not late," he said.

"Who'd have thought it?" cried a voice on the landing of the stairs, as he went forth.

It was Sedgett.

Algernon had one inclination to strangle, and another to mollify the wretch.

"Why, sir, I've been lurking heer for your return from your larks. Never guessed you was in."

"It's no use," Algernon began.

"Ay; but it is, though," said Sedgett, and forced his way into the room. "Now, just listen. I've got a young woman I want to pack out o' the country. I must do it, while I'm a—a bachelor boy. She must go, or we shall be having shindies. You saw how she caught me out of a cab. She's sure to be in the place where she ain't wanted. She goes to America. I've got to pay her passage, and mine too. Here's the truth: she thinks I'm off with her. She knows I'm bankrup' at home. So I am. All the more reason for her thinking me her companion. I get her away by train to the vessel, and on board, and there I give her the slip.

"Ship's steaming away by this time t'morrow night. I've paid for her—and myself too, she thinks. Leave it to me. I'll manage all that neatly enough. But heer's the truth: I'm stumped. I must, and I will have fifty; I don't want to utter ne'er a threat. I want the money, and if you don't give it, I break off; and you mind this, Mr. Blancove: you don't come off s' easy, if I do break off, mind. I know all about your relations, and by—! I'll let 'em know all about you. Why, you're as quiet heer, sir, as if you was miles away, in a wood cottage, and ne'er a dog near."

So Algernon was thinking; and without a light, save the gas lamp in the square, moreover.

They wrangled for an hour. When Algernon went forth a second time, he was by fifty pounds poorer. He consoled himself by thinking that the money had only anticipated its destination as arranged, and it became a partial gratification to him to reflect that he had, at any rate, paid so much of the sum, according to his bond in assuming possession of it.

And what were to be his proceedings? They were so manifestly in the hands of fate, that he declined to be troubled on that head.

Next morning came the usual short impatient scrawl on thin blue paper from Edward, scarce worthy of a passing thought. In a postscript, he asked: "Are there, on your oath, no letters for me? If there are, send them immediately—every one, bills as well. Don't fail. I must have them."

Algernon was at last persuaded to pack up Dahlia's letters, saying: "I suppose they can't do any harm now." The expense of the postage afflicted him; but "women always cost a dozen to our one," he remarked. On his way to the City, he had to decide whether he would go to the Bank, or take the train leading to Wrexby. He chose the latter course, until, feeling that he was about to embark in a serious undertaking, he said to himself, "No! duty first;" and postponed the expedition for the day following.

CHAPTER XXXII

LA QUESTION D'ARGENT

Squire Blancove, having business in town, called on his brother at the Bank, asking whether Sir William was at home, with sarcastic emphasis on the title, which smelt to him of commerce. Sir William invited him to dine and sleep at his house that night.

"You will meet Mrs. Lovell, and a Major Waring, a friend of hers, who knew her and her husband in India," said the baronet.

"The deuce I shall," said the squire, and accepted maliciously.

Where the squire dined, he drank, defying ladies and the new-fangled subserviency to those flustering teabodies. This was understood; so, when the Claret and Port had made a few rounds, Major Waring was permitted to follow Mrs. Lovell, and the squire and his brother settled to conversation; beginning upon gout. Sir William had recently had a touch of the family complaint, and spoke of it in terms which gave the squire some fraternal sentiment. From that, they fell to talking politics, and differed. The breach was healed by a divergence to their sons. The squire knew his own to be a scamp.

"You'll never do anything with him," he said.

"I don't think I shall," Sir William admitted.

"Didn't I tell you so?"

"You did. But, the point is, what will you do with him?"

"Send him to Jericho to ride wild jackasses. That's all he's fit for."

The superior complacency of Sir William's smile caught the squire's attention.

"What do you mean to do with Ned?" he asked.

"I hope," was the answer, "to have him married before the year is out."

"To the widow?"

"The widow?" Sir William raised his eyebrows.

"Mrs. Lovell, I mean."

"What gives you that idea?"

"Why, Ned has made her an offer. Don't you know that?"

"I know nothing of the sort."

"And don't believe it? He has. He's only waiting now, over there in Paris, to get comfortably out of a scrape—you remember what I told you at Fairly—and then Mrs. Lovell's going to have him—as he thinks; but, by George, it strikes me this major you've got here, knows how to follow petticoats and get in his harvest in the enemy's absence."

"I think you're quite under a delusion, in both respects," observed Sir William.

"What makes you think that?"

"I have Edward's word."

"He lies as naturally as an infant sucks."

"Pardon me; this is my son you are speaking of."

"And this is your Port I'm drinking; so I'll say no more."

The squire emptied his glass, and Sir William thrummed on the table.

"Now, my dog has got his name," the squire resumed. "I'm not ambitious about him. You are, about yours; and you ought to know him. He spends or he don't spend. It's not the question whether he gets into debt, but whether he does mischief with what he spends. If Algy's a bad fish, Ned's a bit of a serpent; damned clever, no doubt. I suppose, you wouldn't let him marry old Fleming's daughter, now, if he wanted to?"

"Who is Fleming?" Sir William thundered out.

"Fleming's the father of the girl. I'm sorry for him. He sells his farm-land which I've been looking at for years; so I profit by it; but I don't like to see a man like that broken up. Algy, I said before, 's a bad fish. Hang me, if I think he'd have behaved like Ned. If he had, I'd have compelled him to marry her, and shipped them both off, clean out of the country, to try their luck elsewhere.

"You're proud; I'm practical. I don't expect you to do the same. I'm up in London now to raise money to buy the farm—Queen's Anne's Farm; it's advertized for sale, I see. Fleeting won't sell it to me privately, because my name's Blancove, and I'm the father of my son, and he fancies Algy's the man. Why? he saw Algy at the theatre in London with this girl of his;—we were all young fellows once!—and the rascal took

Ned's burden on his shoulders. So, I shall have to compete with other buyers, and pay, I dare say, a couple of hundred extra for the property. Do you believe what I tell you now?"

"Not a word of it," said Sir William blandly.

The squire seized the decanter and drank in a fury.

"I had it from Algy."

"That would all the less induce me to believe it."

"H'm!" the squire frowned. "Let me tell you—he's a dog—but it's a damned hard thing to hear one's own flesh and blood abused. Look here: there's a couple. One of them has made a fool of a girl. It can't be my rascal—stop a minute—he isn't the man, because she'd have been sure to have made a fool of him, that's certain. He's a soft-hearted dog. He'd aim at a cock-sparrow, and be glad if he missed. There you have him. He was one of your good boys. I used to tell his poor mother, 'When you leave off thinking for him, he'll go to the first handy villain—and that's the devil.' And he's done it. But, here's the difference. He goes himself; he don't send another. I'll tell you what: if you don't know about Mr. Ned's tricks, you ought. And you ought to make him marry the girl, and be off to New Zealand, or any of the upside-down places, where he might begin by farming, and soon, with his abilities, be cock o' the walk. He would, perhaps, be sending us a letter to say that he preferred to break away from the mother country and establish a republic. He's got the same political opinions as you. Oh! he'll do well enough over here; of course he will. He's the very fellow to do well. Knock at him, he's hard as nails, and 'll stick anywhere. You wouldn't listen to me, when I told you about this at Fairly, where some old sweetheart of the girl mistook that poor devil of a scapegoat, Algy, for him, and went pegging at him like a madman."

"No," said Sir William; "No, I would not. Nor do I now. At least," he struck out his right hand deprecatingly, "I listen."

"Can you tell me what he was doing when he went to Italy?"

"He went partly at my suggestion."

"Turns you round his little finger! He went off with this girl: wanted to educate her, or some nonsense of the sort. That was Mr. Ned's business. Upon my soul, I'm sorry for old Fleming. I'm told he takes it to heart. It's done him up. Now, if it should turn out to be Ned, would you let him right the girl by marrying her? You wouldn't!"

"The principle of examining your hypothesis before you proceed to decide by it, is probably unknown to you," Sir William observed, after bestowing a considerate smile on his brother, who muffled himself up from the chilling sententiousness, and drank.

Sir William, in the pride of superior intellect, had heard as good as nothing of the charge against his son.

"Well," said the squire, "think as you like, act as you like; all's one to me. You're satisfied; that's clear; and I'm some hundred of pounds out of pocket. This major's paying court to the widow, is he?"

"I can't say that he is."

"It would be a good thing for her to get married."

"I should be glad."

"A good thing for her, I say."

"A good thing for him, let us hope."

"If he can pay her debts."

Sir William was silent, and sipped his wine.

"And if he can keep a tight hand on the reins. That's wanted," said the squire.

The gentleman whose road to happiness was thus prescribed stood by Mrs. Lovell's chair, in the drawing-room. He held a letter in his hand, for which her own was pleadingly extended.

"I know you to be the soul of truth, Percy," she was saying.

"The question is not that; but whether you can bear the truth."

"Can I not? Who would live without it?"

"Pardon me; there's more. You say, you admire this friend of mine; no doubt you do. Mind, I am going to give you the letter. I wish you simply to ask yourself now, whether you are satisfied at my making a confidant of a man in Robert Eccles's position, and think it natural and just—you do?"

"Quite just," said Mrs. Lovell; "and natural? Yes, natural; though not common. Eccentric; which only means, hors du commun; and can be natural. It is natural. I was convinced he was a noble fellow, before I knew that you had made a friend of him. I am sure of it now. And did he not save your life, Percy?"

"I have warned you that you are partly the subject of the letter."

"Do you forget that I am a woman, and want it all the more impatiently?"

Major Waring suffered the letter to be snatched from his hand, and stood like one who is submitting to a test, or watching the effect of a potent drug.

"It is his second letter to you," Mrs. Lovell murmured. "I see; it is a reply to yours."

She read a few lines, and glanced up, blushing. "Am I not made to bear more than I deserve?"

"If you can do such mischief, without meaning any, to a man who is in love with another woman—," said Percy.

"Yes," she nodded, "I perceive the deduction; but inferences are like shadows on the wall—they are thrown from an object, and are monstrous distortions of it. That is why you misjudge women. You infer one thing from another, and are ruled by the inference."

He simply bowed. Edward would have answered her in a bright strain, and led her on to say brilliant things, and then have shown her, as by a sudden light, that she had lost herself, and reduced her to feel the strength and safety of his hard intellect. That was the idea in her brain. The next moment her heart ejected it.

"Petty, when I asked permission to look at this letter, I was not aware how great a compliment it would be to me if I was permitted to see it. It betrays your friend."

"It betrays something more," said he.

Mrs. Lovell cast down her eyes and read, without further comment.

These were the contents:—

"My Dear Percy,—Now that I see her every day again, I am worse than ever; and I remember thinking once or twice that Mrs. L. had cured me. I am a sort of man who would jump to reach the top of a mountain. I understand how superior Mrs. L. is to every woman in the world I have seen; but Rhoda cures me on that head. Mrs. Lovell makes men mad and happy, and Rhoda makes them sensible and miserable. I have had the talk with Rhoda. It is all over. I have felt like being in a big room with one candle alight ever since. She has not looked at me, and does nothing but get by her father whenever she can, and takes his hand and holds it. I see where the blow has struck her: it has killed her pride; and Rhoda is almost all pride. I suppose she thinks our plan is the best. She has not said she does, and does not mention her sister. She is going to die, or she turns nun, or marries a gentleman. I shall never get her. She will not forgive me for bringing this news to her. I told you how she coloured, the first day I came; which has all gone now. She just opens her lips to me. You remember Corporal Thwaites—you caught his horse, when he had his foot near wrenched off, going through the gate—and his way of breathing through the under-row of his teeth—the poor creature was in such pain—that's just how she takes her breath. It makes her look sometimes like that woman's head with the snakes for her hair. This bothers me—how is it you and Mrs. Lovell manage to talk together of such things? Why, two men rather hang their heads a bit. My notion is, that women— ladies, in especial, ought never to hear of sad things of this sort. Of course, I mean, if they do, it cannot harm them. It only upsets me. Why are ladies less particular than girls in Rhoda's place?"

("Shame being a virtue," was Mrs. Lovell's running comment.)

"She comes up to town with her father to-morrow. The farm is ruined. The poor old man had to ask me for a loan to pay the journey. Luckily, Rhoda has saved enough with her pennies and two-pences. Ever since I left the farm, it has been in the hands of an old donkey here, who has worked it his own way. What is in the ground will stop there, and may as well.

"I leave off writing, I write such stuff; and if I go on writing to you, I shall be putting these things '—!— !—!' The way you write about Mrs. Lovell, convinces me you are not in my scrape, or else gentlemen are just as different from their inferiors as ladies are from theirs. That's the question. What is the meaning of your 'not being able to leave her for a day, for fear she should fall under other influences'? Then, I copy your words, you say, 'She is all things to everybody, and cannot help it.' In that case, I would seize my opportunity and her waist, and tell her she was locked up from anybody else. Friendship with men— but I cannot understand friendship with women, and watching them to keep them right, which must mean that you do not think much of them."

Mrs. Lovell, at this point, raised her eyes abruptly from the letter and returned it.

"You discuss me very freely with your friend," she said.

Percy drooped to her. "I warned you when you wished to read it."

"But, you see, you have bewildered him. It was scarcely wise to write other than plain facts. Men of that class." She stopped.

"Of that class?" said he.

"Men of any class, then: you yourself: if any one wrote to you such things, what would you think? It is very unfair. I have the honour of seeing you daily, because you cannot trust me out of your sight? What is there inexplicable about me? Do you wonder that I talk openly of women who are betrayed, and do my best to help them?".

"On the contrary; you command my esteem," said Percy.

"But you think me a puppet?"

"Fond of them, perhaps?" his tone of voice queried in a manner that made her smile.

"I hate them," she said, and her face expressed it.

"But you make them."

"How? You torment me."

"How can I explain the magic? Are you not making one of me now, where I stand?"

"Then, sit."

"Or kneel?"

"Oh, Percy! do nothing ridiculous."

Inveterate insight was a characteristic of Major Waring; but he was not the less in Mrs. Lovell's net. He knew it to be a charm that she exercised almost unknowingly. She was simply a sweet instrument for those who could play on it, and therein lay her mighty fascination. Robert's blunt advice that he should seize the chance, take her and make her his own, was powerful with him. He checked the particular appropriating action suggested by Robert.

"I owe you an explanation," he said. "Margaret, my friend."

"You can think of me as a friend, Percy?"

"If I can call you my friend, what would I not call you besides? I did you a great and shameful wrong when you were younger. Hush! you did not deserve that. Judge of yourself as you will; but I know now what my feelings were then. The sublime executioner was no more than a spiteful man. You give me your pardon, do you not? Your hand?"

She had reached her hand to him, but withdrew it quickly.

"Not your hand, Margaret? But, you must give it to some one. You will be ruined, if you do not."

She looked at him with full eyes. "You know it then?" she said slowly; but the gaze diminished as he went on.

"I know, by what I know of you, that you of all women should owe a direct allegiance. Come; I will assume privileges. Are you free?"

"Would you talk to me so, if you thought otherwise?" she asked.

"I think I would," said Percy. "A little depends upon the person. Are you pledged at all to Mr. Edward Blancove?"

"Do you suppose me one to pledge myself?"

"He is doing a base thing."

"Then, Percy, let an assurance of my knowledge of that be my answer."

"You do not love the man?"

"Despise him, say!"

"Is he aware of it?"

"If clear writing can make him."

"You have told him as much?"

"To his apprehension, certainly."

"Further, Margaret, I must speak:—did he act with your concurrence, or knowledge of it at all, in acting as he has done?"

"Heavens! Percy, you question me like a husband."

"It is what I mean to be, if I may."

The frame of the fair lady quivered as from a blow, and then her eyes rose tenderly.

"I thought you knew me. This is not possible."

"You will not be mine? Why is it not possible?"

"I think I could say, because I respect you too much."

"Because you find you have not the courage?"

"For what?"

"To confess that you were under bad influence, and were not the Margaret I can make of you. Put that aside. If you remain as you are, think of the snares. If you marry one you despise, look at the pit. Yes; you will be mine! Half my love of my country and my profession is love of you. Margaret is fire in my blood. I used to pray for opportunities, that Margaret might hear of me. I knew that gallant actions touched her; I would have fallen gladly; I was sure her heart would leap when she heard of me. Let it beat against mine. Speak!"

"I will," said Mrs. Lovell, and she suppressed the throbs of her bosom. Her voice was harsh and her face bloodless. "How much money have you, Percy?"

This sudden sluicing of cold water on his heat of passion petrified him.

"Money," he said, with a strange frigid scrutiny of her features. As in the flash of a mirror, he beheld her bony, worn, sordid, unacceptable. But he was fain to admit it to be an eminently proper demand for enlightenment.

He said deliberately, "I possess an income of five hundred a year, extraneous, and in addition to my pay as major in Her Majesty's service."

Then he paused, and the silence was like a growing chasm between them.

She broke it by saying, "Have you any expectations?"

This was crueller still, though no longer astonishing. He complained in his heart merely that her voice had become so unpleasant.

With emotionless precision, he replied, "At my mother's death—"

She interposed a soft exclamation.

"At my mother's death there will come to me by reversion, five or six thousand pounds. When my father dies, he may possibly bequeath his property to me. On that I cannot count."

Veritable tears were in her eyes. Was she affecting to weep sympathetically in view of these remote contingencies?

"You will not pretend that you know me now, Percy," she said, trying to smile; and she had recovered the natural feminine key of her voice. "I am mercenary, you see; not a mercenary friend. So, keep me as a friend—say you will be my friend."

"Nay, you had a right to know," he protested.

"It was disgraceful—horrible; but it was necessary for me to know."

"And now that you do know?"

"Now that I know, I have only to say—be as merciful in your idea of me as you can."

She dropped her hand in his, and it was with a thrill of dismay that he felt the rush of passion reanimating his frozen veins.

"Be mercenary, but be mine! I will give you something better to live for than this absurd life of fashion. You reckon on what our expenditure will be by that standard. It's comparative poverty; but—but you can have some luxuries. You can have a carriage, a horse to ride. Active service may come: I may rise. Give yourself to me, and you must love me, and regret nothing."

"Nothing! I should regret nothing. I don't want carriages, or horses, or luxuries. I could live with you on a subaltern's pay. I can't marry you, Percy, and for the very reason which would make me wish to marry you."

"Charade?" said he; and the contempt of the utterance brought her head close under his.

"Dearest friend, you have not to learn how to punish me."

The little reproach, added to the wound to his pride, required a healing medicament; she put her lips to his fingers.

Assuredly the comedy would not have ended there, but it was stopped by an intrusion of the squire, followed by Sir William, who, while the squire—full of wine and vindictive humours—went on humming, "Ah! h'm—m—m! Soh!" said in the doorway to some one behind him: "And if you have lost your key, and Algernon is away, of what use is it to drive down to the Temple for a bed? I make it an especial request that you sleep here tonight. I wish it. I have to speak with you."

Mrs. Lovell was informed that the baronet had been addressing his son, who was fresh from Paris, and not, in his own modest opinion, presentable before a lady.

CHAPTER XXXIII

EDWARD'S RETURN

Once more Farmer Fleming and Rhoda prepared for their melancholy journey up to London. A light cart was at the gateway, near which Robert stood with the farmer, who, in his stiff brown overcoat, that reached to his ankles, and broad country-hat, kept his posture of dumb expectation like a stalled ox, and nodded to Robert's remarks on the care which the garden had been receiving latterly, the many roses clean in bud, and the trim blue and white and red garden beds. Every word was a blow to him; but he took it, as well as Rhoda's apparent dilatoriness, among the things to be submitted to by a man cut away by the roots from the home of his labour and old associations. Above his bowed head there was a board proclaiming that Queen Anne's Farm, and all belonging thereunto, was for sale. His prospect in the vague wilderness of the future, was to seek for acceptance as a common labourer on some kind gentleman's property. The phrase "kind gentleman" was adopted by his deliberate irony of the fate which cast him out. Robert was stamping fretfully for Rhoda to come. At times, Mrs. Sumfit showed her head from the window of her bed-room, crying, "D'rectly!" and disappearing.

The still aspect of the house on the shining May afternoon was otherwise undisturbed. Besides Rhoda, Master Gammon was being waited for; on whom would devolve the driving of the cart back from the station. Robert heaped his vexed exclamations upon this old man. The farmer restrained his voice in Master Gammon's defence, thinking of the comparison he could make between him and Robert: for Master Gammon had never run away from the farm and kept absent, leaving it to take care of itself. Gammon, slow as he might be, was faithful, and it was not he who had made it necessary for the farm to be sold. Gammon was obstinate, but it was not he who, after taking a lead, and making the farm dependent on his lead, had absconded with the brains and energy of the establishment. Such reflections passed through the farmer's mind.

Rhoda and Mrs. Sumfit came together down the trim pathway; and Robert now had a clear charge against Master Gammon. He recommended an immediate departure.

"The horse 'll bring himself home quite as well and as fast as Gammon will," he said.

"But for the shakin' and the joltin', which tells o' sovereigns and silver," Mrs. Sumfit was observing to Rhoda, "you might carry the box—and who would have guessed how stout it was, and me to hit it with a poker and not break it, I couldn't, nor get a single one through the slit;—the sight I was, with a poker in my hand! I do declare I felt azactly like a housebreaker;—and no soul to notice what you carries. Where you hear the gold, my dear, go so"—Mrs. Sumfit performed a methodical "Ahem!" and noised the sole of her shoe on the gravel "so, and folks 'll think it's a mistake they made."

"What's that?"—the farmer pointed at a projection under Rhoda's shawl.

"It is a present, father, for my sister," said Rhoda.

"What is it?" the farmer questioned again.

Mrs. Sumfit fawned before him penitently—"Ah! William, she's poor, and she do want a little to spend, or she will be so nipped and like a frost-bitten body, she will. And, perhaps, dear, haven't money in her sight for next day's dinner, which is—oh, such a panic for a young wife! for it ain't her hunger, dear William—her husband, she thinks of. And her cookery at a stand-still! Thinks she, 'he will charge it on the kitchen;' so unreasonable's men. Yes," she added, in answer to the rigid dejection of his look, "I said true to you. I know I said, 'Not a penny can I get, William,' when you asked me for loans; and how could I get it? I can't get it now. See here, dear!"

She took the box from under Rhoda's shawl, and rattled it with a down turn and an up turn.

"You didn't ask me, dear William, whether I had a money-box. I'd ha' told you so at once, had ye but asked me. And had you said, 'Gi' me your money-box,' it was yours, only for your asking. You do see, you can't get any of it out. So, when you asked for money I was right to say, I'd got none."

The farmer bore with her dreary rattling of the box in demonstration of its retentive capacities. The mere force of the show stopped him from retorting; but when, to excuse Master Gammon for his tardiness, she related that he also had a money-box, and was in search of it, the farmer threw up his head with the vigour of a young man, and thundered for Master Gammon, by name, vehemently wrathful at the combined hypocrisy of the pair. He called twice, and his face was purple and red as he turned toward the cart, saying,—

"We'll go without the old man."

Mrs. Sumfit then intertwisted her fingers, and related how that she and Master Gammon had one day, six years distant, talked on a lonely evening over the mischances which befel poor people when they grew infirm, or met with accident, and what "useless clays" they were; and yet they had their feelings. It was a long and confidential talk on a summer evening; and, at the end of it, Master Gammon walked into Wrexby, and paid a visit to Mr. Hammond, the carpenter, who produced two strong saving-boxes excellently manufactured by his own hand, without a lid to them, or lock and key: so that there would be no getting at the contents until the boxes were full, or a pressing occasion counselled the destruction of the boxes. A constant subject of jest between Mrs. Sumfit and Master Gammon was, as to which first of them would be overpowered by curiosity to know the amount of their respective savings; and their confessions of mutual weakness and futile endeavours to extract one piece of gold from the hoard.

"And now, think it or not," said Mrs. Sumfit, "I got that power over him, from doctorin' him, and cookin' for him, I persuaded him to help my poor Dahly in my blessed's need. I'd like him to do it by halves, but he can't."

Master Gammon appeared round a corner of the house, his box, draped by his handkerchief, under his arm. The farmer and Robert knew, when he was in sight, that gestures and shouts expressing extremities of the need for haste, would fail to accelerate his steps, so they allowed him to come on at his own equal pace, steady as Time, with the peculiar lopping bend of knees which jerked the moveless trunk regularly upward, and the ancient round eyes fixed contemplatively forward. There was an affectingness in this view of the mechanical old man bearing his poor hoard to bestow it.

Robert said out, unawares, "He mustn't be let to part with h'old pennies."

"No;" the farmer took him up; "nor I won't let him."

"Yes, father!" Rhoda intercepted his address to Master Gammon. "Yes, father!" she hardened her accent. "It is for my sister. He does a good thing. Let him do it."

"Mas' Gammon, what ha' ye got there?" the farmer sung out.

But Master Gammon knew that he was about his own business. He was a difficult old man when he served the farmer; he was quite unmanageable in his private affairs.

Without replying, he said to Mrs. Sumfit,—

"I'd gummed it."

The side of the box showed that it had been made adhesive, for the sake of security, to another substance.

"That's what's caused ye to be so long, Mas' Gammon?"

The veteran of the fields responded with a grin, designed to show a lively cunning.

"Deary me, Mas' Gammon, I'd give a fortnight's work to know how much you'm saved, now, I would. And, there! Your comfort's in your heart. And it shall be paid to you. I do pray heaven in mercy to forgive me," she whimpered, "if ever knowin'ly I hasted you at a meal, or did deceive you when you looked for the pickings of fresh-killed pig. But if you only knew how—to cookit spoils the temper of a woman! I'd a aunt was cook in a gentleman's fam'ly, and daily he dirtied his thirteen plates—never more nor never less; and one day—was ever a woman punished so! her best black silk dress she greased from the top to the bottom, and he sent down nine clean plates, and no word vouchsafed of explanation. For gentlefolks, they won't teach themselves how it do hang together with cooks in a kitchen—"

"Jump up, Mas' Gammon," cried the farmer, wrathful at having been deceived by two members of his household, who had sworn to him, both, that they had no money, and had disregarded his necessity. Such being human nature!

Mrs. Sumfit confided the termination of her story to Rhoda; or suggested rather, at what distant point it might end; and then, giving Master Gammon's box to her custody, with directions for Dahlia to take the boxes to a carpenter's shop—not attempting the power of pokers upon them—and count and make a mental note of the amount of the rival hoards, she sent Dahlia all her messages of smirking reproof, and delighted love, and hoped that they would soon meet and know happiness.

Rhoda, as usual, had no emotion to spare. She took possession of the second box, and thus laden, suffered Robert to lift her into the cart. They drove across the green, past the mill and its flashing waters, and into the road, where the waving of Mrs. Sumfit's desolate handkerchief was latest seen.

A horseman rode by, whom Rhoda recognized, and she blushed and had a boding shiver. Robert marked him, and the blush as well.

It was Algernon, upon a livery-stable hack. His countenance expressed a mighty disappointment.

The farmer saw no one. The ingratitude and treachery of Robert, and of Mrs. Sumfit and Master Gammon, kept him brooding in sombre disgust of life. He remarked that the cart jolted a good deal.

"If you goes in a cart, wi' company o' four, you expects to be jolted," said Master Gammon.

"You seem to like it," Robert observed to the latter.

"It don't disturb my in'ards," quoth the serenest of mankind.

"Gammon," the farmer addressed him from the front seat, without turning his head: "you'll take and look about for a new place."

Master Gammon digested the recommendation in silence. On its being repeated, with, "D' ye hear?" he replied that he heard well enough.

"Well, then, look about ye sharp, or maybe, you'll be out in the cold," said the farmer.

"Na," returned Master Gammon, "ah never frets till I'm pinched."

"I've given ye notice," said the farmer.

"No, you ha'n't," said Master Gammon.

"I give ye notice now."

"No, you don't."

"How d' ye mean?"

"Cause I don't take ne'er a notice."

"Then you'll be kicked out, old man."

"Hey! there y' have me," said Master Gammon. "I growed at the farm, and you don't go and tell ne'er a tree t' walk."

Rhoda laid her fingers in the veteran's palm.

"You're a long-lived family, aren't you, Master Gammon?" said Robert, eyeing Rhoda's action enviously.

Master Gammon bade him go to a certain churchyard in Sussex, and inspect a particular tombstone, upon which the ages of his ancestry were written. They were more like the ages of oaks than of men.

"It's the heart kills," said Robert.

"It's damned misfortune," murmured the farmer.

"It is the wickedness in the world," thought Rhoda.

"It's a poor stomach, I reckon," Master Gammon ruminated.

They took leave of him at the station, from which eminence it was a notable thing to see him in the road beneath, making preparations for his return, like a conqueror of the hours. Others might run, and stew, if they liked: Master Gammon had chosen his pace, and was not of a mind to change it for anybody or anything. It was his boast that he had never ridden by railway: "nor ever means to, if I can help it," he would say. He was very much in harmony with universal nature, if to be that is the secret of human life.

Meantime, Algernon retraced his way to the station in profound chagrin: arriving there just as the train was visible. He caught sight of the cart with Master Gammon in it, and asked him whether all his people were going up to London; but the reply was evidently a mile distant, and had not started; so putting a sovereign in Master Gammon's hand, together with the reins of his horse, Algernon bade the old man conduct the animal to the White Bear Inn, and thus violently pushing him off the tramways of his intelligence, left him stranded.

He had taken a first-class return-ticket, of course, being a gentleman. In the desperate hope that he might jump into a carriage with Rhoda, he entered one of the second-class compartments; a fact not only foreign to his tastes and his habits, but somewhat disgraceful, as he thought. His trust was, that the ignoble of this earth alone had beheld him: at any rate, his ticket was first class, as the guard would instantly and respectfully perceive, and if he had the discomforts, he had also some of the consolations of virtue.

Once on his way, the hard seat and the contemptible society surrounding him, assured his reflective spirit that he loved: otherwise, was it in reason that he should endure these hardships? "I really love the girl," he said, fidgeting for cushions.

He was hot, and wanted the window up, to which his fellow-travellers assented. Then, the atmosphere becoming loaded with offence to his morbid sense of smell, he wanted the windows down; and again they assented. "By Jove! I must love the girl," ejaculated Algernon inwardly, as cramp, cold, and afflicted nostrils combined to astonish his physical sensations. Nor was it displeasing to him to evince that he was unaccustomed to bare boards.

"We're a rich country," said a man to his neighbour; "but, if you don't pay for it, you must take your luck, and they'll make you as uncomfortable as they can."

"Ay," said the other. "I've travelled on the Continent. The second-class carriages there are fit for anybody to travel in. This is what comes of the worship of money—the individual is not respected. Pounds alone!"

"These," thought Algernon, "are beastly democrats."

Their remarks had been sympathetic with his manifestations, which had probably suggested them. He glowered out of the window in an exceedingly foreign manner. A plainly dressed woman requested that the window should be closed. One of the men immediately proceeded to close it. Algernon stopped him.

"Pardon me, sir," said the man; "it's a lady wants it done;" and he did it.

A lady! Algernon determined that these were the sort of people he should hate for life. "Go among them and then see what they are," he addressed an imaginary assembly of anti-democrats, as from a senatorial chair set in the after days. Cramp, cold, ill-ordered smells, and eternal hatred of his fellow-passengers, convinced him, in their aggregation, that he surmounted not a little for love of Rhoda.

The train arrived in London at dusk. Algernon saw Rhoda step from a carriage near the engine, assisted by Robert; and old Anthony was on the platform to welcome her; and Anthony seized her bag, and the troop of passengers moved away. It may be supposed that Algernon had angry sensations at sight of Robert; and to a certain extent this was the case; but he was a mercurial youth, and one who had satisfactorily proved superior strength enjoyed a portion of his respect. Besides, if Robert perchance should be courting Rhoda, he and Robert would enter into another field of controversy; and Robert might be taught a lesson.

He followed the party on foot until they reached Anthony's dwelling-place, noted the house, and sped to the Temple. There, he found a telegraphic message from Edward, that had been awaiting him since the morning.

"Stop It," were the sole words of the communication brief, and if one preferred to think so, enigmatic.

"What on earth does he mean?" cried Algernon, and affected again and again to see what Edward meant, without success. "Stop it?—stop what?—Stop the train? Stop my watch? Stop the universe? Oh! this is rank humbug." He flung the paper down, and fell to counting the money in his possession. The more it dwindled, the more imperative it became that he should depart from his country.

Behind the figures, he calculated that, in all probability, Rhoda would visit her sister this night. "I can't stop that," he said: and hearing a clock strike, "nor that" a knock sounded on the door; "nor that." The reflection inspired him with fatalistic views.

Sedgett appeared, and was welcome. Algernon had to check the impulse of his hand to stretch out to the fellow, so welcome was he: Sedgett stated that everything stood ready for the morrow. He had accomplished all that had to be done.

"And it's more than many'd reckon," he said, and rubbed his hands, and laughed. "I was aboard ship in Liverpool this morning, that I was. That ere young woman's woke up from her dream", (he lengthened the word inexpressibly) "by this time, that she is. I had to pay for my passage, though;" at which recollection he swore. "That's money gone. Never mind: there's worse gone with it. Ain't it nasty—don't you think, sir—to get tired of a young woman you've been keepin' company with, and have to be her companion, whether you will, or whether you won't? She's sick enough now. We travelled all night. I got her on board; got her to go to her bed; and, says I, I'll arrange about the luggage. I packs myself down into a boat, and saw the ship steam away a good'n. Hanged if I didn't catch myself singin'. And haven't touched a drop o' drink, nor will, till tomorrow's over. Don't you think 'Daehli's' a very pretty name, sir? I run back to her as hard as rail 'd carry me. She's had a letter from her sister, recommending o' her to marry me: 'a noble man,' she calls me—ha, ha! that's good. 'And what do you think, my dear?' says I; and, bother me, if I can screw either a compliment or a kiss out of her. She's got fine lady airs of her own. But I'm fond of her, that I am. Well, sir, at the church door, after the ceremony, you settle our business, honour bright—that's it, en't it?"

Algernon nodded. Sedgett's talk always produced discomfort in his ingenuous bosom.

"By the way, what politics are you?" he asked.

Sedgett replied, staring, that he was a Tory, and Algernon nodded again, but with brows perturbed at the thought of this ruffian being of the same political persuasion as himself.

"Eh?" cried Sedgett; "I don't want any of your hustings pledges, though. You'll be at the door tomorrow, or I'll have a row—mind that. A bargain's a bargain. I like the young woman, but I must have the money. Why not hand it over now?"

"Not till the deed's done," said Algernon, very reasonably.

Sedgett studied his features, and as a result remarked: "You put me up to this: I'll do it, and trust you so far, but if I'm played on, I throw the young woman over and expose you out and out. But you mean honourable?"

"I do," Algernon said of his meaning.

Another knock sounded on the door. It proved to be a footman in Sir William's livery, bearing a letter from Edward; an amplification of the telegram:

"Dear Algy, Stop it. I'm back, and have to see my father. I may be down about two, or three, or four, in the morning. No key; so, keep in. I want to see you. My whole life is changed. I must see her. Did you get my telegram? Answer, by messenger; I shall come to you the moment my father has finished his lecture.

"Yours,
"E.B."

Algernon told Sedgett to wait while he dressed in evening uniform, and gave him a cigar to smoke.

He wrote:—

"Dear Ned, Stop what? Of course, I suppose there's only one thing, and how can I stop it? What for? You ridiculous old boy! What a changeable old fellow you are!—Off, to see what I can do. After eleven o'clock to-morrow, you'll feel comfortable.—If the Governor is sweet, speak a word for the Old Brown; and bring two dozen in a cab, if you can. There's no encouragement to keep at home in this place. Put that to him. I, in your place, could do it. Tell him it's a matter of markets. If I get better wine at hotels, I go to hotels, and I spend twice—ten times the money. And say, we intend to make the laundress cook our dinners in chambers, as a rule. Old B. an inducement.

"Yours aff.
"A.B."

This epistle he dispatched by the footman, and groaned to think that if, perchance, the Old Brown Sherry should come, he would, in all probability, barely drink more than half-a-dozen bottles of that prime vintage. He and Sedgett, soon after, were driving down to Dahlia's poor lodgings in the West. On the way, an idea struck him:

Would not Sedgett be a noisier claimant for the thousand than Edward? If he obeyed Edward's direction and stopped the marriage, he could hand back a goodly number of hundreds, and leave it to be supposed that he had advanced the remainder to Sedgett. How to do it? Sedgett happened to say: "If you won't hand the money now, I must have it when I've married her. Swear you'll be in the vestry when we're signing. I know all about marriages. You swear, or I tell you, if I find I'm cheated, I will throw the young woman over slap."

Algernon nodded: "I shall be there," he said, and thought that he certainly would not. The thought cleared an oppression in his head, though it obscured the pretty prospect of a colonial but and horse, with Rhoda cooking for him, far from cares. He did his best to resolve that he would stop the business, if he could. But, if it is permitted to the fool to create entanglements and set calamity in motion, to arrest its course is the last thing the Gods allow of his doing.

CHAPTER XXXIV

FATHER AND SON

In the shadowy library light, when there was dawn out of doors, Edward sat with his father, and both were silent, for Edward had opened his heart, and his father had breathed some of the dry stock of wisdom on it. Many times Edward rose to go; and Sir William signalled with his finger that he should stay: an impassive motion, not succeeded by speech. And, in truth, the baronet was revolving such a problem as a long career of profitable banking refreshed by classical exercitations does not help us to solve. There sat the son of his trust and his pride, whose sound and equal temperament, whose precocious worldly wit, whose precise and broad intelligence, had been the visionary comfort of his paternal days to come; and his son had told him, reiterating it in language special and exact as that of a Chancery barrister unfolding his case to the presiding judge, that he had deceived and wronged an under-bred girl of the humbler classes; and that, after a term of absence from her, he had discovered her to be a part of his existence, and designed "You would marry her?" Sir William asked, though less forcibly than if he could have put on a moral amazement.

"That is my intention, sir, with your permission," Edward replied firmly, and his father understood that he had never known this young man, and dealt virtually with a stranger in his son—as shrewd a blow as the vanity which is in paternal nature may have to endure.

He could not fashion the words, "Cerritus fuit," though he thought the thing in both tenses: Edward's wits had always been too clearly in order: and of what avail was it to repeat great and honoured prudential maxims to a hard-headed fellow, whose choice was to steer upon the rocks? He did remark, in an undertone,—

"The 'misce stultitiam' seems to be a piece of advice you have adopted too literally. I quote what you have observed of some one else."

"It is possible, sir," said Edward. "I was not particularly sparing when I sat in the high seat. 'Non eadem est aetas, non mens.' I now think differently."

"I must take your present conduct as the fruit of your premature sagacity, I suppose. By the same rule, your cousin Algernon may prove to be some comfort to his father, in the end."

"Let us hope he will, sir. His father will not have deserved it so well as mine."

"The time is morning," said Sir William, looking at his watch, and bestowing, in the bitterness of his reflections, a hue of triumph on the sleep of his brother upstairs. "You are your own master, Edward. I will detain you no more."

Edward shook his limbs, rejoicing.

"You prepare for a life of hard work," Sir William resumed, not without some instigation to sternness from this display of alacrity. "I counsel you to try the Colonial Bar."

Edward read in the first sentence, that his income would be restricted; and in the second, that his father's social sphere was no longer to be his.

"Exactly, sir; I have entertained that notion myself," he said; and his breast narrowed and his features grew sharp.

"And, if I may suggest such matters to you, I would advise you to see very little company for some years to come."

"There, sir, you only anticipate my previously formed resolution. With a knavery on my conscience, and a giddy-pated girl on my hands, and the doors of the London world open to me, I should scarcely have been capable of serious work. The precious metal, which is Knowledge, sir, is only to be obtained by mining for it; and that excellent occupation necessarily sends a man out of sight for a number of years. In the meantime, 'mea virtute me involvo.'"

"You need not stop short," said his father, with a sardonic look for the concluding lines.

"The continuation is becoming in the mouth of a hero; but humbler persons must content themselves not to boast the patent fact, I think." Edward warmed as he spoke. "I am ready to bear it. I dislike poverty; but, as I say, I am ready to bear it. Come, sir; you did me the honour once to let me talk to you as a friend, with the limits which I have never consciously overstepped; let me explain myself plainly and simply."

Sir William signified, "Pray speak," from the arms of his chair! and Edward, standing, went on: "After all, a woman's devotion is worth having, when one is not asked for the small change every ten minutes. I am aware of the philosophic truth, that we get nothing in life for which we don't pay. The point is, to appreciate what we desire; and so we reach a level that makes the payment less—" He laughed. Sir William could hardly keep back the lines of an ironical smile from his lips.

"This," pursued the orator, "is not the language for the Colonial Bar. I wish to show you that I shall understand the character of my vocation there. No, sir; my deeper wish is that you may accept my view of the sole course left to a man whose sense of honour is of accord with the inclination of his heart, and not in hostility to his clearer judgement."

"Extremely forensic," said Sir William, not displeased by the promise of the periods.

"Well, sir, I need not remark to you that rhetoric, though it should fail to convey, does not extinguish, or imply the absence of emotion in the speaker; but rather that his imagination is excited by his theme, and that he addresses more presences than such as are visible. It is, like the Roman mask, fashioned for large assemblages."

"By a parity of reasoning, then,"—Sir William was seduced into colloquy,—"an eternal broad grin is not, in the instance of a dualogue, good comedy."

"It may hide profound grief." Edward made his eyes flash. "I find I can laugh; it would be difficult for me to smile. Sir, I pray that you will listen to me seriously, though my language is not of a kind to make you think me absolutely earnest in what I say, unless you know me."

"Which, I must protest, I certainly do not," interposed Sir William.

"I will do my best to instruct you, sir. Until recently, I have not known myself. I met this girl. She trusted herself to me. You are aware that I know a little of men and of women; and when I tell you that I respect her now even more than I did at first—much more—so thoroughly, that I would now put my honour in her hands, by the counsel of my experience, as she, prompted by her instinct and her faith in me, confided hers to mine,—perhaps, even if you persist in accusing me of rashness, you will allow that she must be in the possession of singularly feminine and estimable qualities. I deceived her. My object in doing so was to spare you. Those consequences followed which can hardly fail to ensue, when, of two living together, the woman is at a disadvantage, and eats her heart without complaining. I could have borne a shrewish tongue better, possibly because I could have answered it better. It is worse to see a pale sad face with a smile of unalterable tenderness. The very sweetness becomes repugnant."

"As little boys requiring much medicine have anticipated you by noting in this world," observed Sir William.

"I thank you for the illustration." Edward bowed, but he smarted. "A man so situated lives with the ghost of his conscience."

"A doubtful figure of speech," Sir William broke in. "I think you should establish the personality before you attempt to give a feature to the essence. But, continue."

Edward saw that by forfeiting simplicity, in order to catch his father's peculiar cast of mind, he had left him cold and in doubt as to the existence of the powerful impulse by which he was animated. It is a prime error in the orator not to seize the emotions and subdue the humanity of his hearers first. Edward perceived his mistake. He had, however, done well in making a show of the unabated vigour of his wits. Contempt did not dwell in the baronet's tone. On the contrary, they talked and fenced, and tripped one another as of old; and, considering the breach he had been compelled to explode between his father and himself, Edward understood that this was a real gain.

He resumed: "All figures of speech must be inadequate—"

"Ah, pardon me," said Sir William, pertinaciously; "the figure I alluded to was not inadequate. A soap-bubble is not inadequate."

"Plainly, sir, in God's name, hear me out," cried Edward. "She—what shall I call her? my mistress, my sweetheart, if you like—let the name be anything 'wife' it should have been, and shall be—I left her, and have left her and have not looked on her for many months. I thought I was tired of her—I was under odd influences—witchcraft, it seems. I could believe in witchcraft now. Brutal selfishness is the phrase for my conduct. I have found out my villany. I have not done a day's sensible work, or had a single clear thought, since I parted from her. She has had brain-fever. She has been in the hospital. She is now prostrate with misery. While she suffered, I—I can't look back on myself. If I had to plead before you for more than manly consideration, I could touch you. I am my own master, and am ready to subsist by my own efforts; there is no necessity for me to do more than say I abide by the choice I make, and my own actions. In deciding to marry her, I do a good thing—I do a just thing. I will prove to you that I have done a wise thing.

"Let me call to your recollection what you did me the honour to remark of my letters from Italy. Those were written with her by my side. Every other woman vexed me. This one alone gives me peace, and nerve to work. If I did not desire to work, should I venture to run the chances of an offence to you? Your girls of society are tasteless to me. And they don't makes wives to working barristers. No, nor to working Members.

"They are very ornamental and excellent, and, as I think you would call them, accomplished. All England would leap to arms to defend their incontestible superiority to their mothers and their duties. I have not the wish to stand opposed to my countrymen on any question, although I go to other shores, and may be called upon to make capital out of opposition. They are admirable young persons, no doubt. I do not offer you a drab for your daughter-in-law, sir. If I rise, she will be equal to my station. She has the manners of a lady; a lady, I say; not of the modern young lady; with whom, I am happy to think, she does not come into competition. She has not been sedulously trained to pull her way, when she is to go into harness with a yokefellow.

"But I am laying myself open to the charge of feeling my position weak, seeing that I abuse the contrary one. Think what you will of me, sir, you will know that I have obeyed my best instinct and my soundest judgement in this matter; I need not be taught, that if it is my destiny to leave England I lose the association with him who must ever be my dearest friend. And few young men can say as much of one standing in the relation of father."

With this, Edward finished; not entirely to his satisfaction; for he had spoken with too distinct a sincerity to please his own critical taste, which had been educated to delight in acute antithesis and culminating sentences—the grand Biscayan billows of rhetorical utterance, in comparison wherewith his talk was like the little chopping waves of a wind-blown lake. But he had, as he could see, produced an impression. His father stood up.

"We shall be always friends; I hope," Sir William said. "As regards a provision for you, suitable to your estate, that will be arranged. You must have what comforts you have been taught to look to. At the same time, I claim a personal freedom for my own actions."

"Certainly, sir," said Edward, not conceiving any new development in these.

"You have an esteem for Mrs. Lovell, have you not?"

Edward flushed. "I should have a very perfect esteem for her, if—" he laughed slightly—"you will think I want everybody to be married and in the traces now; she will never be manageable till she is married."

"I am also of that opinion," said Sir William. "I will detain you no longer. It is a quarter to five in the morning. You will sleep here, of course."

"No, I must go to the Temple. By the way, Algy prefers a petition for Sherry. He is beginning to discern good wine from bad, which may be a hopeful augury."

"I will order Holmes to send some down to him when he has done a week's real duty at the Bank."

"Sooner or later, then. Good morning, sir."

"Good morning." Sir William shook his son's hand.

A minute after, Edward had quitted the house. "That's over!" he said, sniffing the morning air gratefully, and eyeing certain tinted wisps of cloud that were in a line of the fresh blue sky.

CHAPTER XXXV

THE NIGHT BEFORE

A shy and humble entreaty had been sent by Dahlia through Robert to Rhoda, saying that she wished not to be seen until the ceremony was at an end; but Rhoda had become mentally stern toward her sister, and as much to uphold her in the cleansing step she was about to take, as in the desire to have the dear lost head upon her bosom, she disregarded Dahlia's foolish prayer, and found it was well that she had done so; for, to her great amazement, Dahlia, worn, shorn, sickened, and reduced to be a mark for the scorn of the cowardice which is in the world, through the selfishness of a lying man, loved the man still, and wavered, or rather shrank with a pitiful fleshly terror from the noble husband who would wipe the spot of shame from her forehead.

When, after their long separation, the sisters met, Dahlia was mistress of herself, and pronounced Rhoda's name softly, as she moved up to kiss her. Rhoda could not speak. Oppressed by the strangeness of the white face which had passed through fire, she gave a mute kiss and a single groan, while Dahlia gently caressed her on the shoulder. The frail touch of her hand was harder to bear than the dreary vision had been, and seemed not so real as many a dream of it. Rhoda sat by her, overcome by the awfulness of an actual sorrow, never imagined closely, though she had conjured up vague pictures of Dahlia's face. She had imagined agony, tears, despair, but not the spectral change, the burnt-out look. It was a face like a crystal lamp in which the flame has died. The ghastly little skull-cap showed forth its wanness rigidly. Rhoda wondered to hear her talk simply of home and the old life. At each question, the then and the now struck her spirit with a lightning flash of opposing scenes. But the talk deepened. Dahlia's martyrdom was near, and their tongues were hurried into plain converse of the hour, and then Dahlia faltered and huddled herself up like a creature swept by the torrent; Rhoda learnt that, instead of hate or loathing of the devilish man who had deceived her, love survived. Upon Dahlia's lips it was compassion and forgiveness; but Rhoda, in her contempt for the word, called it love. Dahlia submitted gladly to the torture of interrogation; "Do you, can you care for him still?" and sighed in shame and fear of her sister, not daring to say she thought her harsh, not daring to plead for escape, as she had done with Robert.

"Why is there no place for the unhappy, who do not wish to live, and cannot die?" she moaned.

And Rhoda cruelly fixed her to the marriage, making it seem irrevocable, and barring all the faint lights to the free outer world, by praise of her—passionate praise of her—when she confessed, that half inanimate after her recovery from the fever, and in the hope that she might thereby show herself to her father, she had consented to devote her life to the only creature who was then near her to be kind to her. Rhoda made her relate how this man had seen her first, and how, by untiring diligence, he had followed her up and found her. "He—he must love you," said Rhoda; and in proportion as she grew more conscious of her sister's weakness, and with every access of tenderness toward her, she felt that Dahlia must be thought for very much as if she were a child.

Dahlia tried to float out some fretting words for mercy, on one or other of her heavy breathings; but her brain was under lead. She had a thirst for Rhoda's praise in her desolation; it was sweet, though the price of it was her doing an abhorred thing. Abhorred? She did not realize the consequences of the act, or strength would have come to her to wrestle with the coil: a stir of her blood would have endued her with womanly counsel and womanly frenzy; nor could Rhoda have opposed any real vehemence of distaste to the union on Dahlia's part. But Dahlia's blood was frozen, her brain was under lead. She clung to the poor delight in her sister's praise, and shuddered and thirsted. She caught at the minutes, and saw them slip from her. All the health of her thoughts went to establish a sort of blind belief that God; having punished her enough, would not permit a second great misery to befall her. She expected a sudden intervention, even though at the altar. She argued to herself that misery, which follows sin, cannot surely afflict us further when we are penitent, and seek to do right: her thought being, that perchance if she refrained from striving against the current, and if she suffered her body to be borne along, God would be the more merciful. With the small cunning of an enfeebled spirit, she put on a mute submissiveness, and deceived herself by it sufficiently to let the minutes pass with a lessened horror and alarm.

This was in the first quarter of the night. The dawn was wearing near. Sedgett had been seen by Rhoda; a quiet interview; a few words on either side, attention paid to them by neither. But the girl doated on his ugliness; she took it for plain proof of his worthiness; proof too that her sister must needs have seen the latter very distinctly, or else she could not have submitted.

Dahlia looked at the window-blinds and at the candlelight. The little which had been spoken between her and her sister in such a chasm of time, gave a terrible swiftness to the hours. Half shrieking, she dropped her head in Rhoda's lap. Rhoda, thinking that with this demonstration she renounced the project finally, prepared to say what she had to say, and to yield. But, as was natural after a paroxysm of weakness, Dahlia's frenzy left no courage behind it.

Dahlia said, as she swept her brows, "I am still subject to nervous attacks."

"They will soon leave you," said Rhoda, nursing her hand.

Dahlia contracted her lips. "Is father very unforgiving to women?"

"Poor father!" Rhoda interjected for answer, and Dahlia's frame was taken with a convulsion.

"Where shall I see him to-morrow?" she asked; and, glancing from the beamless candle to the window-blinds "Oh! it's day. Why didn't I sleep! It's day! where am I to see him?"

"At Robert's lodgings. We all go there."

"We all go?—he goes?"

"Your husband will lead you there."

"My heaven! my heaven! I wish you had known what this is, a little—just a little."

"I do know that it is a good and precious thing to do right," said Rhoda.

"If you had only had an affection, dear! Oh I how ungrateful I am to you."

"It is only, darling, that I seem unkind to you," said Rhoda.

"You think I must do this? Must? Why?"

"Why?" Rhoda pressed her fingers. "Why, when you were ill, did you not write to me, that I might have come to you?"

"I was ashamed," said Dahlia.

"You shall not be ashamed any more, my sister."

Dahlia seized the window-blind with her trembling finger-tips, and looked out on the day. As if it had smitten her eyeballs, she covered her face, giving dry sobs.

"Oh! I wish—I wish you had known what this is. Must I do it? His face! Dear, I am very sorry to distress you. Must I do it? The doctor says I am so strong that nothing will break in me, and that I must live, if I am not killed. But, if I might only be a servant in father's house—I would give all my love to a little bed of flowers."

"Father has no home now," said Rhoda.

"I know—I know. I am ready. I will submit, and then father will not be ashamed to remain at the Farm. I am ready. Dear, I am ready. Rhoda, I am ready. It is not much." She blew the candle out. "See. No one will do that for me. We are not to live for ourselves. I have done wrong, and I am going to be humble; yes, I am. I never was when I was happy, and that proves I had no right to be happy. All I ask is for another night with you. Why did we not lie down together and sleep? We can't sleep now—it's day."

"Come and lie down with me for a few hours, my darling," said Rhoda.

While she was speaking, Dahlia drew the window-blind aside, to look out once more upon the vacant, inexplicable daylight, and looked, and then her head bent like the first thrust forward of a hawk's sighting quarry; she spun round, her raised arms making a cramped, clapping motion.

"He is there."

CHAPTER XXXVI

EDWARD MEETS HIS MATCH

At once Rhoda perceived that it was time for her to act. The name of him who stood in the street below was written on her sister's face. She started to her side, got possession of her hands, murmuring,—

"Come with me. You are to come with me. Don't speak. I know. I will go down. Yes; you are to obey, and do what I tell you."

Dahlia's mouth opened, but like a child when it is warned not to cry, she uttered a faint inward wailing, lost her ideas, and was passive in a shuddering fit.

"What am I to do?" she said supplicatingly, as Rhoda led her to her bedroom.

"Rest here. Be perfectly quiet. Trust everything to me. I am your sister."

Leaving her under the spell of coldly-spoken words, Rhoda locked the door on her. She was herself in great agitation, but nerved by deeper anger there was no faltering in her movements. She went to the glass a minute, as she tied her bonnet-strings under her chin, and pinned her shawl. A night's vigil had not chased the bloom from her cheek, or the swimming lustre from her dark eyes. Content that her aspect should be seemly, she ran down the stairs, unfastened the bolts, and without hesitation closed the door behind her. At the same instant, a gentleman crossed the road. He asked whether Mrs. Ayrton lived in that house? Rhoda's vision danced across his features, but she knew him unerringly to be the cruel enemy.

"My sister, Dahlia Fleming, lives there," she said.

"Then, you are Rhoda?"

"My name is Rhoda."

"Mine—I fear it will not give you pleasure to hear it—is Edward Blancove. I returned late last night from abroad."

She walked to a distance, out of hearing and out of sight of the house, and he silently followed. The streets were empty, save for the solitary footing of an early workman going to his labour.

She stopped, and he said, "I hope your sister is well."

"She is quite well."

"Thank heaven for that! I heard of some illness."

"She has quite recovered."

"Did she—tell me the truth—did she get a letter that I sent two days ago, to her? It was addressed to 'Miss Fleming, Wrexby, Kent, England.' Did it reach her?"

"I have not seen it."

"I wrote," said Edward.

His scrutiny of her features was not reassuring to him. But he had a side-thought, prompted by admiration of her perfect build of figure, her succinct expression of countenance, and her equable manner of speech: to the effect, that the true English yeomanry can breed consummate women. Perhaps—who knows? even resolute human nature is the stronger for an added knot—it approved the resolution he had formed, or stamped with a justification the series of wild impulses, the remorse, and the returned tenderness and manliness which had brought him to that spot.

"You know me, do you not?" he said.

"Yes," she answered shortly.

"I wish to see Dahlia."

"You cannot."

"Not immediately, of course. But when she has risen later in the morning. If she has received my letter, she will, she must see me."

"No, not later; not at all," said Rhoda.

"Not at all? Why not?"

Rhoda controlled the surging of her blood for a vehement reply; saying simply, "You will not see her."

"My child, I must."

"I am not a child, and I say what I mean."

"But why am I not to see her? Do you pretend that it is her wish not to see me? You can't. I know her perfectly. She is gentleness itself."

"Yes; you know that," said Rhoda, with a level flash of her eyes, and confronting him in a way so rarely distinguishing girls of her class, that he began to wonder and to ache with an apprehension.

"She has not changed? Rhoda—for we used to talk of you so often! You will think better of me, by-and-by."

"Naturally enough, you detest me at present. I have been a brute. I can't explain it, and I don't excuse myself. I state the fact to you—her sister. My desire is to make up for the past. Will you take a message to her from me?"

"I will not."

"You are particularly positive."

Remarks touching herself Rhoda passed by.

"Why are you so decided?" he said more urgently. "I know I have deeply offended and hurt you. I wish, and intend to repair the wrong to the utmost of my power. Surely it's mere silly vindictiveness on your part to seek to thwart me. Go to her; say I am here. At all events, let it be her choice not to see me, if I am to be rejected at the door. She can't have had my letter. Will you do that much?"

"She knows that you are here; she has seen you."

"Has seen me?" Edward drew in his breath sharply. "Well? and she sends you out to me?"

Rhoda did not answer. She was strongly tempted to belie Dahlia's frame of mind.

"She does send you to speak to me," Edward insisted.

"She knows that I have come."

"And you will not take one message in?"

"I will take no message from you."

"You hate me, do you not?"

Again she controlled the violent shock of her heart to give him hard speech. He went on:—

"Whether you hate me or not is beside the matter. It lies between Dahlia and me. I will see her. When I determine, I allow of no obstacles, not even of wrong-headed girls. First, let me ask, is your father in London?"

Rhoda threw a masculine meaning into her eyes.

"Do not come before him, I advise you."

"If," said Edward, with almost womanly softness, "you could know what I have passed through in the last eight-and-forty hours, you would understand that I am equal to any meeting; though, to speak truth, I would rather not see him until I have done what I mean to do. Will you be persuaded? Do you suppose that I have ceased to love your sister?"

This, her execrated word, coming from his mouth, vanquished her self-possession.

"Are you cold?" he said, seeing the ripple of a trembling run over her.

"I am not cold. I cannot remain here." Rhoda tightened her intertwisting fingers across under her bosom. "Don't try to kill my sister outright. She's the ghost of what she was. Be so good as to go. She will soon be out of your reach. You will have to kill me first, if you get near her. Never! you never shall. You have lied to her—brought disgrace on her poor head. We poor people read our Bibles, and find nothing that excuses you. You are not punished, because there is no young man in our family. Go."

Edward gazed at her for some time. "Well, I've deserved worse," he said, not sorry, now that he saw an opponent in her, that she should waste her concentrated antagonism in this fashion, and rejoiced by the testimony it gave him that he was certainly not too late.

"You know, Rhoda, she loves me."

"If she does, let her pray to God on her knees."

"My good creature, be reasonable. Why am I here? To harm her? You take me for a kind of monster. You look at me very much, let me say, like a bristling cat. Here are the streets getting full of people, and you ought not to be seen. Go to Dahlia. Tell her I am here. Tell her I am come to claim her for good, and that her troubles are over. This is a moment to use your reason. Will you do what I ask?"

"I would cut my tongue out, if it did you a service," said Rhoda.

"Citoyenne Corday," thought Edward, and observed: "Then I will dispense with your assistance."

He moved in the direction of the house. Rhoda swiftly outstripped him. They reached the gates together. She threw herself in the gateway. He attempted to parley, but she was dumb to it.

"I allow nothing to stand between her and me," he said, and seized her arm. She glanced hurriedly to right and left. At that moment Robert appeared round a corner of the street. He made his voice heard, and, coming up at double quick, caught Edward Blancove by the collar, swinging him off. Rhoda, with a sign, tempered him to muteness, and the three eyed one another.

"It's you," said Robert, and, understanding immediately the tactics desired by Rhoda, requested Edward to move a step or two away in his company.

Edward settled the disposition of his coat-collar, as a formula wherewith to regain composure of mind, and passed along beside Robert, Rhoda following.

"What does this mean?" said Robert sternly.

Edward's darker nature struggled for ascendancy within him. It was this man's violence at Fairly which had sickened him, and irritated him against Dahlia, and instigated him, as he remembered well, more than Mrs. Lovell's witcheries, to the abhorrent scheme to be quit of her, and rid of all botheration, at any cost.

"You're in some conspiracy to do her mischief, all of you," he cried.

"If you mean Dahlia Fleming," said Robert, "it'd be a base creature that would think of doing harm to her now."

He had a man's perception that Edward would hardly have been found in Dahlia's neighbourhood with evil intentions at this moment, though it was a thing impossible to guess. Generous himself, he leaned to the more generous view.

"I think your name is Eccles," said Edward. "Mr. Eccles, my position here is a very sad one. But first, let me acknowledge that I have done you personally a wrong. I am ready to bear the burden of your reproaches, or what you will. All that I beg is, that you will do me the favour to grant me five minutes in private. It is imperative."

Rhoda burst in—"No, Robert!" But Robert said, "It is a reasonable request;" and, in spite of her angry eyes, he waved her back, and walked apart with Edward.

She stood watching them, striving to divine their speech by their gestures, and letting her savage mood interpret the possible utterances. It went ill with Robert in her heart that he did not suddenly grapple and trample the man, and so break away from him. She was outraged to see Robert's listening posture. "Lies! lies!" she said to herself, "and he doesn't know them to be lies." The window-blinds in Dahlia's sitting-room continued undisturbed; but she feared the agency of the servant of the house in helping to release her sister. Time was flowing to dangerous strands. At last Robert turned back singly. Rhoda fortified her soul to resist.

"He has fooled you," she murmured, inaudibly, before he spoke.

"Perhaps, Rhoda, we ought not to stand in his way. He wishes to do what a man can do in his case. So he tells me, and I'm bound not to disbelieve him. He says he repents—says the word; and gentlemen seem to mean it when they use it. I respect the word, and them when they're up to that word. He wrote to her that he could not marry her, and it did the mischief, and may well be repented of; but he wishes to be forgiven and make amends—well, such as he can. He's been abroad, and only received Dahlia's letters within the last two or three days. He seems to love her, and to be heartily wretched. Just hear me out; you'll decide; but pray, pray don't be rash. He wishes to marry her; says he has spoken to his father this very night; came straight over from France, after he had read her letters. He says—and it seems fair—he only asks to see Dahlia for two minutes. If she bids him go, he goes. He's not a friend of mine, as I could prove to you; but I do think he ought to see her. He says he looks on her as his wife; always meant her to be his wife, but things were against him when he wrote that letter. Well, he says so; and it's true that gentlemen are situated—they can't always, or think they can't, behave quite like honest men. They've got a hundred things to consider for our one. That's my experience, and I know something of the best among 'em. The question is about this poor young fellow who's to marry her to-day. Mr. Blancove talks of giving him a handsome sum—a thousand pounds—and making him comfortable—"

"There!" Rhoda exclaimed, with a lightning face. "You don't see what he is, after that? Oh!—" She paused, revolted.

"Will you let me run off to the young man, wherever he's to be found, and put the case to him—that is, from Dahlia? And you know she doesn't like the marriage overmuch, Rhoda. Perhaps he may think differently when he comes to hear of things. As to Mr. Blancove, men change and change when they're young. I mean, gentlemen. We must learn to forgive. Either he's as clever as the devil, or he's a man in earnest, and deserves pity. If you'd heard him!"

"My poor sister!" sighed Rhoda. The mentioning of money to be paid had sickened and weakened her, as with the very physical taste of degradation.

Hearing the sigh, Robert thought she had become subdued. Then Rhoda said: "We are bound to this young man who loves my sister—bound to him in honour: and Dahlia must esteem him, to have consented. As for the other..." She waved the thought of his claim on her sister aside with a quick shake of her head. "I rely on you to do this:—I will speak to Mr. Blancove myself. He shall not see her there." She indicated the house. "Go to my sister; and lose no time in taking her to your lodgings. Father will not arrive till twelve. Wait and comfort her till I come, and answer no questions. Robert," she gave him her hand gently, and, looking sweetly, "if you will do this!"

"If I will!" cried Robert, transported by the hopeful tenderness. The servant girl of the house had just opened the front door, intent on scrubbing, and he passed in. Rhoda walked on to Edward.

CHAPTER XXXVII

EDWARD TRIES HIS ELOQUENCE

A profound belief in the efficacy of his eloquence, when he chose to expend it, was one of the principal supports of Edward's sense of mastery; a secret sense belonging to certain men in every station of life, and which is the staff of many an otherwise impressible and fluctuating intellect. With this gift, if he trifled, or slid downward in any direction, he could right himself easily, as he satisfactorily conceived. It is a gift that may now and then be the ruin of promising youths, though as a rule they find it helpful enough. Edward had exerted it upon his father, and upon Robert. Seeing Rhoda's approach, he thought of it as a victorious swordsman thinks of his weapon, and aimed his observation over her possible weak and strong points, studying her curiously even when she was close up to him. With Robert, the representative of force, to aid her, she could no longer be regarded in the light of a despicable hindrance to his wishes. Though inclined strongly to detest, he respected her. She had decision, and a worthy bearing, and a marvellously blooming aspect, and a brain that worked withal. When she spoke, desiring him to walk on by her side, he was pleased by her voice, and recognition of the laws of propriety, and thought it a thousand pities that she likewise should not become the wife of a gentleman. By degrees, after tentative beginnings, he put his spell upon her ears, for she was attentive, and walked with a demure forward look upon the pavement; in reality taking small note of what things he said, until he quoted, as against himself, sentences from Dahlia's letters; and then she fixed her eyes on him, astonished that he should thus heap condemnation on his own head. They were most pathetic scraps quoted by him, showing the wrestle of love with a petrifying conviction of its hopelessness, and with the stealing on of a malady of the blood. They gave such a picture of Dahlia's reverent love for this man, her long torture, her chastity of soul and simple innocence, and her gathering delirium of anguish, as Rhoda had never taken at all distinctly to her mind. She tried to look out on him from a mist of tears.

"How could you bear to read the letters?" she sobbed.

"Could any human being read them and not break his heart for her?" said he.

"How could you bear to read them and leave her to perish!"

His voice deepened to an impressive hollow: "I read them for the first time yesterday morning, in France, and I am here!"

It was undeniably, in its effect on Rhoda, a fine piece of pleading artifice. It partially excused or accounted for his behaviour, while it filled her with emotions which she felt to be his likewise, and therefore she could not remain as an unsympathetic stranger by his side.

With this, he flung all artifice away. He told her the whole story, saving the one black episode of it—the one incomprehensible act of a desperate baseness that, blindly to get free, he had deliberately permitted, blinked at, and had so been guilty of. He made a mental pause as he was speaking, to consider in amazement how and by what agency he had been reduced to shame his manhood, and he left it a marvel. Otherwise, he in no degree exonerated himself. He dwelt sharply on his vice of ambition, and scorned it as a misleading light. "Yet I have done little since I have been without her!" And then, with a persuasive sincerity, he assured her that he could neither study nor live apart from Dahlia. "She is the dearest soul to me on earth; she is the purest woman. I have lived with her, I have lived apart from her, and I cannot live without her. I love her with a husband's love. Now, do you suppose I will consent to be separated from her? I know that while her heart beats, it's mine. Try to keep her from me—you kill her."

"She did not die," said Rhoda. It confounded his menaces.

"This time she might," he could not refrain from murmuring.

"Ah!" Rhoda drew off from him.

"But I say," cried he, "that I will see her."

"We say, that she shall do what is for her good."

"You have a project? Let me hear it. You are mad, if you have."

"It is not our doing, Mr. Blancove. It was—it was by her own choice. She will not always be ashamed to look her father in the face. She dare not see him before she is made worthy to see him. I believe her to have been directed right."

"And what is her choice?"

"She has chosen for herself to marry a good and worthy man."

Edward called out, "Have you seen him—the man?"

Rhoda, thinking he wished to have the certainty of the stated fact established, replied, "I have."

"A good and worthy man," muttered Edward. "Illness, weakness, misery, have bewildered her senses. She thinks him a good and worthy man?"

"I think him so."

"And you have seen him?"

"I have."

"Why, what monstrous delusion is this? It can't be! My good creature, you're oddly deceived, I imagine. What is the man's name? I can understand that she has lost her will and distinct sight; but you are clear-sighted, and can estimate. What is the man's name?"

"I can tell you," said Rhoda; "his name is Mr. Sedgett."

"Mister—!" Edward gave one hollow stave of laughter. "And you have seen him, and think him—"

"I know he is not a gentleman," said Rhoda. "He has been deeply good to my sister, and I thank him, and do respect him."

"Deeply!" Edward echoed. He was prompted to betray and confess himself: courage failed.

They looked around simultaneously on hearing an advancing footstep.

The very man appeared—in holiday attire, flushed, smiling, and with a nosegay of roses in his hand. He studied the art of pleasing women. His eye struck on Edward, and his smile vanished. Rhoda gave him no word of recognition. As he passed on, he was led to speculate from his having seen Mr. Edward instead of Mr. Algernon, and from the look of the former, that changes were in the air, possibly chicanery, and the proclaiming of himself as neatly diddled by the pair whom, with another, he heartily hoped to dupe.

After he had gone by, Edward and Rhoda changed looks. Both knew the destination of that lovely nosegay. The common knowledge almost kindled an illuminating spark in her brain; but she was left in the dark, and thought him strangely divining, or only strange. For him, a horror cramped his limbs. He felt that he had raised a devil in that abominable smirking ruffian. It may not, perhaps, be said that he had distinctly known Sedgett to be the man. He had certainly suspected the possibility of his being the man. It is out of the power of most wilful and selfish natures to imagine, so as to see accurately, the deeds they prompt or permit to be done. They do not comprehend them until these black realities stand up before their eyes.

Ejaculating "Great heaven!" Edward strode some steps away, and returned.

"It's folly, Rhoda!—the uttermost madness ever conceived! I do not believe—I know that Dahlia would never consent—first, to marry any man but myself; secondly, to marry a man who is not a perfect gentleman. Her delicacy distinguishes her among women."

"Mr. Blancove, my sister is nearly dead, only that she is so strong. The disgrace has overwhelmed her, it has. When she is married, she will thank and honour him, and see nothing but his love and kindness. I will leave you now."

"I am going to her," said Edward.

"Do not."

"There's an end of talking. I trust no one will come in my path. Where am I?"

He looked up at the name of the street, and shot away from her. Rhoda departed in another direction, firm, since she had seen Sedgett pass, that his nobleness should not meet with an ill reward. She endowed him with fair moral qualities, which she contrasted against Edward Blancove's evil ones; and it was with a democratic fervour of contempt that she dismissed the superior outward attractions of the gentleman.

CHAPTER XXXVIII

TOO LATE

This neighbourhood was unknown to Edward, and, after plunging about in one direction and another, he found that he had missed his way. Down innumerable dusky streets of dwarfed houses, showing soiled silent window-blinds, he hurried and chafed; at one moment in sharp joy that he had got a resolution, and the next dismayed by the singular petty impediments which were tripping him. "My dearest!" his heart cried to Dahlia, "did I wrong you so? I will make all well. It was the work of a fiend." Now he turned to right, now to left, and the minutes flew. They flew; and in the gathering heat of his brain he magnified things until the sacrifice of herself Dahlia was preparing for smote his imagination as with a blaze of the upper light, and stood sublime before him in the grandeur of old tragedy. "She has blinded her eyes, stifled her senses, eaten her heart. Oh! my beloved! my wife! my poor girl! and all to be free from shame in her father's sight!" Who could have believed that a girl of Dahlia's class would at once have felt the shame so keenly, and risen to such pure heights of heroism? The sacrifice flouted conception; it mocked the steady morning. He refused to believe in it, but the short throbs of his blood were wiser.

A whistling urchin became his guide. The little lad was carelessly giving note to a popular opera tune, with happy disregard of concord. It chanced that the tune was one which had taken Dahlia's ear, and, remembering it and her pretty humming of it in the old days, Edward's wrestling unbelief with the fatality of the hour sank, so entirely was he under the sovereignty of his sensations. He gave the boy a big fee, desiring superstitiously to feel that one human creature could bless the hour. The house was in view. He knocked, and there came a strange murmur of some denial. "She is here," he said, menacingly.

"She was taken away, sir, ten minutes gone, by a gentleman," the servant tied to assure him.

The landlady of the house, coming up the kitchen stairs, confirmed the statement. In pity for his torpid incredulity she begged him to examine her house from top to bottom, and herself conducted him to Dahlia's room.

"That bed has not been slept in," said the lawyer, pointing his finger to it.

"No, sir; poor thing! she didn't sleep last night. She's been wearying for weeks; and last night her sister came, and they hadn't met for very long. Two whole candles they burnt out, or near upon it."

"Where?—" Edward's articulation choked.

"Where they're gone to, sir? That I do not know. Of course she will come back."

The landlady begged him to wait; but to sit and see the minutes—the black emissaries of perdition—fly upon their business, was torture as big as to endure the tearing off of his flesh till the skeleton stood out. Up to this point he had blamed himself; now he accused the just heavens. Yea! is not a sinner their lawful quarry? and do they not slip the hounds with savage glee, and hunt him down from wrong to evil, from evil to infamy, from infamy to death, from death to woe everlasting? And is this their righteousness?—He caught at the rusty garden rails to steady his feet.

Algernon was employed in the comfortable degustation of his breakfast, meditating whether he should transfer a further slice of ham or of Yorkshire pie to his plate, or else have done with feeding and light a cigar, when Edward appeared before him.

"Do you know where that man lives?"

Algernon had a prompting to respond, "Now, really! what man?" But passion stops the breath of fools. He answered, "Yes."

"Have you the thousand in your pocket?"

Algernon nodded with a sickly grin.

"Jump up! Go to him. Give it up to him! Say, that if he leaves London on the instant, and lets you see him off—say, it shall be doubled. Stay, I'll write the promise, and put my signature. Tell him he shall, on my word of honour, have another—another thousand pounds—as soon as I can possibly obtain it, if he holds his tongue, and goes with you; and see that he goes. Don't talk to me on any other subject, or lose one minute."

Algernon got his limbs slackly together, trying to think of the particular pocket in which he had left his cigar-case. Edward wrote a line on a slip of note-paper, and signed his name beneath. With this and an unsatisfied longing for tobacco Algernon departed, agreeing to meet his cousin in the street where Dahlia dwelt.

"By Jove! two thousand! It's an expensive thing not to know your own mind," he thought.

"How am I to get out of this scrape? That girl Rhoda doesn't care a button for me. No colonies for me. I should feel like a convict if I went alone. What on earth am I to do?"

It seemed preposterous to him that he should take a cab, when he had not settled upon a scheme. The sight of a tobacconist's shop charmed one of his more immediate difficulties to sleep. He was soon enabled to puff consoling smoke.

"Ned's mad," he pursued his soliloquy. "He's a weather-cock. Do I ever act as he does? And I'm the dog that gets the bad name. The idea of giving this fellow two thousand—two thousand pounds! Why, he might live like a gentleman."

And that when your friend proves himself to be distraught, the proper friendly thing to do is to think for him, became eminently clear in Algernon's mind.

"Of course, it's Ned's money. I'd give it if I had it, but I haven't; and the fellow won't take a farthing less; I know him. However, it's my duty to try."

He summoned a vehicle. It was a boast of his proud youth that never in his life had he ridden in a close cab. Flinging his shoulders back, he surveyed the world on foot. "Odd faces one sees," he meditated. "I suppose they've got feelings, like the rest; but a fellow can't help asking—what's the use of them? If I inherit all right, as I ought to—why shouldn't I?—I'll squat down at old Wrexby, garden and farm, and drink my Port. I hate London. The squire's not so far wrong, I fancy."

It struck him that his chance of inheriting was not so very obscure, after all. Why had he ever considered it obscure? It was decidedly next to certain, he being an only son. And the squire's health was bad!

While speculating in this wise he saw advancing, arm-in-arm, Lord Suckling and Harry Latters. They looked at him, and evidently spoke together, but gave neither nod, nor smile, nor a word, in answer to his flying wave of the hand. Furious, and aghast at this signal of exclusion from the world, just at the moment when he was returning to it almost cheerfully in spirit, he stopped the cab, jumped out, and ran after the pair.

"I suppose I must say Mr. Latters," Algernon commenced.

Harry deliberated a quiet second or two. "Well, according to our laws of primogeniture, I don't come first, and therefore miss a better title," he said.

"How are you?" Algernon nodded to Lord Suckling, who replied, "Very well, I thank you."

Their legs were swinging forward concordantly. Algernon plucked out his purse. "I have to beg you to excuse me," he said, hurriedly; "my cousin Ned's in a mess, and I've been helping him as well as I can—bothered—not an hour my own. Fifty, I think?" That amount he tendered to Harry Latters, who took it most coolly.

"A thousand?" he queried of Lord Suckling.

"Divided by two," replied the young nobleman, and the Blucher of bank-notes was proffered to him. He smiled queerly, hesitating to take it.

"I was looking for you at all the Clubs last night," said Algernon.

Lord Suckling and Latters had been at theirs, playing whist till past midnight; yet is money, even when paid over in this egregious public manner by a nervous hand, such testimony to the sincerity of a man, that they shouted a simultaneous invitation for him to breakfast with them, in an hour, at the Club, or dine with them there that evening. Algernon affected the nod of haste and acquiescence, and ran, lest they should hear him groan. He told the cabman to drive Northward, instead of to the South-west. The question of the thousand pounds had been decided for him—"by fate," he chose to affirm. The consideration that one is pursued by fate, will not fail to impart a sense of dignity even to the meanest. "After all, if I stop in England," said he, "I can't afford to lose my position in society; anything's better than that an unmitigated low scoundrel like Sedgett should bag the game." Besides, is it not somewhat sceptical to suppose that when Fate decides, she has not weighed the scales, and decided for the best? Meantime, the whole energy of his intellect was set reflecting on the sort of lie which Edward would, by nature and the occasion, be disposed to swallow. He quitted the cab, and walked in the Park, and au diable to him there! the fool has done his work.

It was now half-past ten. Robert, with a most heavy heart, had accomplished Rhoda's commands upon him. He had taken Dahlia to his lodgings, whither, when free from Edward, Rhoda proceeded in a mood of extreme sternness. She neither thanked Robert, nor smiled upon her sister. Dahlia sent one quivering look up at her, and cowered lower in her chair near the window.

"Father comes at twelve?" Rhoda said.

Robert replied: "He does."

After which a silence too irritating for masculine nerves filled the room.

"You will find, I hope, everything here that you may want," said Robert. "My landlady will attend to the bell. She is very civil."

"Thank you; we shall not want anything," said Rhoda. "There is my sister's Bible at her lodgings."

Robert gladly offered to fetch it, and left them with a sense of relief that was almost joy. He waited a minute in the doorway, to hear whether Dahlia addressed him. He waited on the threshold of the house, that he might be sure Dahlia did not call for his assistance. Her cry of appeal would have fortified him to stand against Rhoda; but no cry was heard. He kept expecting it, pausing for it, hoping it would come to solve his intense perplexity. The prolonged stillness terrified him; for, away from the sisters, he had power to read the anguish of Dahlia's heart, her frozen incapacity, and the great and remorseless mastery which lay in Rhoda's inexorable will.

A few doors down the street he met Major blaring, on his way to him. "Here's five minutes' work going to be done, which we may all of us regret till the day of our deaths," Robert said, and related what had passed during the morning hours.

Percy approved Rhoda, saying, "She must rescue her sister at all hazards. The case is too serious for her to listen to feelings, and regrets, and objections. The world against one poor woman is unfair odds, Robert. I come to tell you I leave England in a day or two. Will you join me?"

"How do I know what I shall or can do?" said Robert, mournfully: and they parted.

Rhoda's unflickering determination to carry out, and to an end, this tragic struggle of duty against inclination; on her own sole responsibility forcing it on; acting like a Fate, in contempt of mere emotions,—seemed barely real to his mind: each moment that he conceived it vividly, he became more certain that she must break down. Was it in her power to drag Dahlia to the steps of the altar? And would not her heart melt when at last Dahlia did get her voice? "This marriage can never take place!" he said, and was convinced of its being impossible. He forgot that while he was wasting energy at Fairly, Rhoda had sat hiving bitter strength in the loneliness of the Farm; with one vile epithet clapping on her ears, and nothing but unavailing wounded love for her absent unhappy sister to make music of her pulses.

He found his way to Dahlia's room; he put her Bible under his arm, and looked about him sadly. Time stood at a few minutes past eleven. Flinging himself into a chair, he thought of waiting in that place; but a crowd of undefinable sensations immediately beset him. Seeing Edward Blancove in the street below, he threw up the window compassionately, and Edward, casting a glance to right and left, crossed the road. Robert went down to him.

"I am waiting for my cousin." Edward had his watch in his hand. "I think I am fast. Can you tell me the time exactly?"

"Why, I'm rather slow," said Robert, comparing time with his own watch. "I make it four minutes past the hour."

"I am at fourteen," said Edward. "I fancy I must be fast."

"About ten minutes past, is the time, I think."

"So much as that!"

"It may be a minute or so less."

"I should like," said Edward, "to ascertain positively."

"There's a clock down in the kitchen here, I suppose," said Robert. "Safer, there's a clock at the church, just in sight from here."

"Thank you; I will go and look at that."

Robert bethought himself suddenly that Edward had better not. "I can tell you the time to a second," he said. "It's now twelve minutes past eleven."

Edward held his watch balancing. "Twelve," he repeated; and, behind this mask of common-place dialogue, they watched one another—warily, and still with pity, on Robert's side.

"You can't place any reliance on watches," said Edward.

"None, I believe," Robert remarked.

"If you could see the sun every day in this climate!" Edward looked up.

"Ah, the sun's the best timepiece, when visible," Robert acquiesced. "Backwoodsmen in America don't need watches."

"Unless it is to astonish the Indians with them."

"Ah! yes!" hummed Robert.

"Twelve—fifteen—it must be a quarter past. Or, a three quarters to the next hour, as the Germans say."

"Odd!" Robert ejaculated. "Foreigners have the queerest ways in the world. They mean no harm, but they make you laugh."

"They think the same of us, and perhaps do the laughing more loudly."

"Ah! let them," said Robert, not without contemptuous indignation, though his mind was far from the talk.

The sweat was on Edward's forehead. "In a few minutes it will be half-past—half-past eleven! I expect a friend; that makes me impatient. Mr. Eccles"—Edward showed his singular, smallish, hard-cut and flashing features, clear as if he had blown off a mist—"you are too much of a man to bear malice. Where is Dahlia? Tell me at once. Some one seems to be cruelly driving her. Has she lost her senses? She has:— or else she is coerced in an inexplicable and shameful manner."

"Mr. Blancove," said Robert, "I bear you not a bit of malice—couldn't if I would. I'm not sure I could have said guilty to the same sort of things, in order to tell an enemy of mine I was sorry for what I had done, and I respect you for your courage. Dahlia was taken from here by me."

Edward nodded, as if briefly assenting, while his features sharpened.

"Why?" he asked.

"It was her sister's wish."

"Has she no will of her own?"

"Very little, I'm afraid, just now, sir."

"A remarkable sister! Are they of Puritan origin?"

"Not that I am aware of."

"And this father?"

"Mr. Blancove, he is one of those sort—he can't lift up his head if he so much as suspects a reproach to his children."

Edward brooded. "I desire—as I told you, as I told her sister, as I told my father last night—I desire to make her my wife. What can I do more? Are they mad with some absurd country pride? Half-past eleven!—it will be murder if they force her to it! Where is she? To such a man as that! Poor soul! I can hardly fear it, for I can't imagine it. Here—the time is going. You know the man yourself."

"I know the man?" said Robert. "I've never set eyes on him—I've never set eyes on him, and never liked to ask much about him. I had a sort of feeling. Her sister says he is a good, and kind, honourable young fellow, and he must be."

"Before it's too late," Edward muttered hurriedly—"you know him—his name is Sedgett."

Robert hung swaying over him with a big voiceless chest.

"That Sedgett?" he breathed huskily, and his look was hard to meet.

Edward frowned, unable to raise his head.

"Lord in heaven! some one has something to answer for!" cried Robert. "Come on; come to the church. That foul dog?—Or you, stay where you are. I'll go. He to be Dahlia's husband! They've seen him, and can't see what he is!—cunning with women as that? How did they meet? Do you know?—can't you guess?"

He flung a lightning at Edward and ran off. Bursting into the aisle, he saw the minister closing the Book at the altar, and three persons moving toward the vestry, of whom the last, and the one he discerned, was Rhoda.

BOOK V

CHAPTER XXXIX

DAHLIA GOES HOME

Late into the afternoon, Farmer Fleming was occupying a chair in Robert's lodgings, where he had sat since the hour of twelve, without a movement of his limbs or of his mind, and alone. He showed no sign that he expected the approach of any one. As mute and unremonstrant as a fallen tree, nearly as insensible, his eyes half closed, and his hands lying open, the great figure of the old man kept this attitude as of stiff decay through long sunny hours, and the noise of the London suburb. Although the wedding people were strangely late, it was unnoticed by him. When the door opened and Rhoda stepped into the room, he was unaware that he had been waiting, and only knew that the hours had somehow accumulated to a heavy burden upon him.

"She is coming, father; Robert is bringing her up," Rhoda said.

"Let her come," he answered.

Robert's hold was tight under Dahlia's arm as they passed the doorway, and then the farmer stood. Robert closed the door.

For some few painful moments the farmer could not speak, and his hand was raised rejectingly. The return of human animation to his heart made him look more sternly than he felt; but he had to rid himself of one terrible question before he satisfied his gradual desire to take his daughter to his breast. It came at last like a short roll of drums, the words were heard,—

"Is she an honest woman?"

"She is," said Rhoda.

The farmer was looking on Robert.

Robert said it likewise in a murmur, but with steadfast look.

Bending his eyes now upon Dahlia, a mist of affection grew in them. He threw up his head, and with a choking, infantine cry, uttered, "Come."

Robert placed her against her father's bosom.

He moved to the window beside Rhoda, and whispered, and she answered, and they knew not what they said. The joint moans of father and daughter—the unutterable communion of such a meeting—filled their ears. Grief held aloof as much as joy. Neither joy nor grief were in those two hearts of parent and child; but the senseless contentment of hard, of infinite hard human craving.

The old man released her, and Rhoda undid her hands from him, and led the pale Sacrifice to another room.

"Where's...?" Mr. Fleming asked.

Robert understood him.

"Her husband will not come."

It was interpreted by the farmer as her husband's pride. Or, may be, the man who was her husband now had righted her at last, and then flung her off in spite for what he had been made to do.

"I'm not being deceived, Robert?"

"No, sir; upon my soul!"

"I've got that here," the farmer struck his ribs.

Rhoda came back. "Sister is tired," she said. "Dahlia is going down home with you, for...I hope, for a long stay."

"All the better, while home we've got. We mayn't lose time, my girl. Gammon's on 's way to the station now. He'll wait. He'll wait till midnight. You may always reckon on a slow man like Gammon for waitin'. Robert comes too?"

"Father, we have business to do. Robert gives me his rooms here for a little time; his landlady is a kind woman, and will take care of me. You will trust me to Robert."

"I'll bring Rhoda down on Monday evening," Robert said to the farmer. "You may trust me, Mr. Fleming."

"That I know. That I'm sure of. That's a certainty," said the farmer. "I'd do it for good, if for good was in the girl's heart, Robert. There seems," he hesitated; "eh, Robert, there seems a something upon us all. There's a something to be done, is there? But if I've got my flesh and blood, and none can spit on her, why should I be asking 'whats' and 'whys'? I bow my head; and God forgive me, if ever I complained. And you will bring Rhoda to us on Monday?"

"Yes; and try and help to make the farm look up again, if Gammon'll do the ordering about."

"Poor old Mas' Gammon! He's a rare old man. Is he changed by adversity, Robert? Though he's awful secret, that old man! Do you consider a bit Gammon's faithfulness, Robert!"

"Ay, he's above most men in that," Robert agreed.

"On with Dahlia's bonnet—sharp!" the farmer gave command. He felt, now that he was growing accustomed to the common observation of things, that the faces and voices around him were different from such as the day brings in its usual course. "We're all as slow as Mas' Gammon, I reckon."

"Father," said Rhoda, "she is weak. She has been very unwell. Do not trouble her with any questions. Do not let any questions be asked of her at hone. Any talking fatigues; it may be dangerous to her."

The farmer stared. "Ay, and about her hair....I'm beginning to remember. She wears a cap, and her hair's cut off like an oakum-picker's. That's more gossip for neighbours!"

"Mad people! will they listen to truth?" Rhoda flamed out in her dark fashion. "We speak truth, nothing but truth. She has had a brain fever. That makes her very weak, and every one must be silent at home. Father, stop the sale of the farm, for Robert will work it into order. He has promised to be our friend, and Dahlia will get her health there, and be near mother's grave."

The farmer replied, as from a far thought, "There's money in my pocket to take down two."

He continued: "But there's not money there to feed our family a week on; I leave it to the Lord. I sow; I dig, and I sow, and when bread fails to us the land must go; and let it go, and no crying about it. I'm astonishing easy at heart, though if I must sell, and do sell, I shan't help thinking of my father, and his father, and the father before him—mayhap, and in most likelihood, artfuller men 'n me—for what they was born to they made to flourish. They'll cry in their graves. A man's heart sticks to land, Robert; that you'll find, some day. I thought I cared none but about land till that poor, weak, white thing put her arms on my neck."

Rhoda had slipped away from them again.

The farmer stooped to Robert's ear. "Had a bit of a disagreement with her husband, is it?"

Robert cleared his throat. "Ay, that's it," he said.

"Serious, at all?"

"One can't tell, you know."

"And not her fault—not my girl's fault, Robert?"

"No; I can swear to that."

"She's come to the right home, then. She'll be near her mother and me. Let her pray at night, and she'll know she's always near her blessed mother. Perhaps the women 'll want to take refreshment, if we may so far make free with your hospitality; but it must be quick, Robert—or will they? They can't eat, and I can't eat."

Soon afterward Mr. Fleming took his daughter Dahlia from the house and out of London. The deeply-afflicted creature was, as the doctors had said of her, too strong for the ordinary modes of killing. She could walk and still support herself, though the ordeal she had gone through this day was such as few women could have traversed. The terror to follow the deed she had done was yet unseen by her; and for the hour she tasted, if not peace, the pause to suffering which is given by an act accomplished.

Robert and Rhoda sat in different rooms till it was dusk. When she appeared before him in the half light, the ravage of a past storm was visible on her face. She sat down to make tea, and talked with singular self command.

"Mr. Fleming mentioned the gossips down at Wrexby," said Robert: "are they very bad down there?"

"Not worse than in other villages," said Rhoda. "They have not been unkind. They have spoken about us, but not unkindly—I mean, not spitefully."

"And you forgive them?"

"I do: they cannot hurt us now."

Robert was but striving to master some comprehension of her character.

"What are we to resolve, Rhoda?"

"I must get the money promised to this man."

"When he has flung off his wife at the church door?"

"He married my sister for the money. He said it. Oh! he said it. He shall not say that we have deceived him. I told him he should have it. He married her for money!"

"You should not have told him so, Rhoda."

"I did, and I will not let my word be broken."

"Pardon me if I ask you where you will get the money? It's a large sum."

"I will get it," Rhoda said firmly.

"By the sale of the farm?"

"No, not to hurt father."

"But this man's a scoundrel. I know him. I've known him for years. My fear is that he will be coming to claim his wife. How was it I never insisted on seeing the man before—! I did think of asking, but fancied—a lot of things; that you didn't wish it and he was shy. Ah, Lord! what miseries happen from our not looking straight at facts! We can't deny she's his wife now."

"Not if we give him the money."

Rhoda spoke of "the money" as if she had taken heated metal into her mouth.

"All the more likely," said Robert. "Let him rest. Had you your eyes on him when he saw me in the vestry? For years that man has considered me his deadly enemy, because I punished him once. What a scene! I'd have given a limb, I'd have given my life, to have saved you from that scene, Rhoda."

She replied: "If my sister could have been spared! I ought to know what wickedness there is in the world. It's ignorance that leads to the unhappiness of girls."

"Do you know that I'm a drunkard?"

"No."

"He called me something like it; and he said something like the truth. There's the sting. Set me adrift, and I drink hard. He spoke a fact, and I couldn't answer him."

"Yes, it's the truth that gives such pain," said Rhoda, shivering. "How can girls know what men are? I could not guess that you had any fault. This man was so respectful; he sat modestly in the room when I saw him last night—last night, was it? I thought, 'he has been brought up with sisters and a mother.' And he has been kind to my dear—and all we thought love for her, was—shameful! shameful!"

She pressed her eyelids, continuing: "He shall have the money—he shall have it. We will not be in debt to such a man. He has saved my sister from one as bad—who offered it to be rid of her. Oh, men!—you heard that?—and now pretends to love her. I think I dream. How could she ever have looked happily on that hateful face?"

"He would be thought handsome," said Robert, marvelling how it was that Rhoda could have looked on Sedgett for an instant without reading his villanous nature. "I don't wish you to regret anything you have done or you may do, Rhoda. But this is what made me cry out when I looked on that man, and knew it was he who had come to be Dahlia's husband. He'll be torture to her. The man's temper, his habits—but you may well say you are ignorant of us men. Keep so. What I do with all my soul entreat of you is—to get a hiding-place for your sister. Never let him take her off. There's such a thing as hell upon earth. If she goes away with him she'll know it. His black temper won't last. He will come for her, and claim her."

"He shall have money." Rhoda said no more.

On a side-table in the room stood a remarkable pile, under cover of a shawl. Robert lifted the shawl, and beheld the wooden boxes, one upon the other, containing Master Gammon's and Mrs. Sumfit's rival savings, which they had presented to Dahlia, in the belief that her husband was under a cloud of monetary misfortune that had kept her proud heart from her old friends. The farmer had brought the boxes and left them there, forgetting them.

"I fancy," said Robert, "we might open these."

"It may be a little help," said Rhoda.

"A very little," Robert thought; but, to relieve the oppression of the subject they had been discussing, he forthwith set about procuring tools, with which he split first the box which proved to be Mrs. Sumfit's, for it contained, amid six gold sovereigns and much silver and pence, a slip of paper, whereon was inscribed, in a handwriting identified by Rhoda as peculiar to the loving woman,—

"And sweetest love to her ever dear."

Altogether the sum amounted to nine pounds, three shillings, and a farthing.

"Now for Master Gammon—he's heavy," said Robert; and he made the savings of that unpretentious veteran bare. Master Gammon had likewise written his word. It was discovered on the blank space of a bit of newspaper, and looked much as if a fat lobworm had plunged himself into a bowl of ink, and in his literary delirium had twisted uneasily to the verge of the paper. With difficulty they deciphered,—

"Complemens."

Robert sang, "Bravo, Gammon!" and counted the hoard. All was in copper coinage, Lycurgan and severe, and reached the sum of one pound, seventeen shillings. There were a number of farthings of Queen Anne's reign, and Robert supposed them to be of value. "So that, as yet, we can't say who's the winner," he observed.

Rhoda was in tears.

"Be kind to him, please, when you see him," she whispered. The smaller gift had touched her heart more tenderly.

"Kind to the old man!" Robert laughed gently, and tied the two hoards in separate papers, which he stowed into one box, and fixed under string. "This amount, put all in one, doesn't go far, Rhoda."

"No," said she: "I hope we may not need it." She broke out: "Dear, good, humble friends! The poor are God's own people. Christ has said so. This is good, this is blessed money!" Rhoda's cheeks flushed to their orange-rounded swarthy red, and her dark eyes had the fervour of an exalted earnestness. "They are my friends for ever. They save me from impiety. They help me, as if God had answered my prayer. Poor pennies! and the old man not knowing where his days may end! He gives all—he must have true faith in Providence. May it come back to him multiplied a thousand fold! While I have strength to work, the bread I earn shall be shared with him. Old man, old man, I love you—how I love you! You drag me out of deep ditches. Oh, good and dear old man, if God takes me first, may I have some power to intercede for you, if you have ever sinned! Everybody in the world is not wicked. There are some who go the ways directed by the Bible. I owe you more than I can ever pay."

She sobbed, but told Robert it was not for sorrow. He, longing to catch her in his arms, and punctilious not to overstep the duties of his post of guardian, could merely sit by listening, and reflecting on her as a strange Biblical girl, with Hebrew hardness of resolution, and Hebrew exaltation of soul; beautiful, too, as the dark women of the East. He admitted to himself that he never could have taken it on his conscience to subdue a human creature's struggling will, as Rhoda had not hesitated to do with Dahlia, and to command her actions, and accept all imminent responsibilities; not quailing with any outcry, or abandonment of strength, when the shock of that revelation in the vestry came violently on her. Rhoda, seeing there that it was a brute, and not a man, into whose hand she had perilously forced her sister's, stood steadying her nerves to act promptly with advantage; less like a woman, Robert thought, than a creature born for battle. And she appeared to be still undaunted, full of her scheme, and could cry without fear of floods. Something of the chivalrous restraint he put upon the motions of his heart, sprang from the shadowy awe which overhung that impressible organ. This feeling likewise led him to place a blind reliance on her sagacity and sense of what was just, and what should be performed.

"You promised this money to him," he said, half thinking it incredible.

"On Monday," said Rhoda.

"You must get a promise from him in return."

She answered: "Why? when he could break it the instant he cared to, and a promise would tempt him to it. He does not love her."

"No; he does not love her," said Robert, meditating whether he could possibly convey an idea of the character of men to her innocent mind.

"He flung her off. Thank heaven for it! I should have been punished too much—too much. He has saved her from the perils of temptation. He shall be paid for it. To see her taken away by such a man! Ah!" She shuddered as at sight of a hideous pit.

But Robert said: "I know him, Rhoda. That was his temper. It'll last just four-and-twenty hours, and then we shall need all our strength and cunning. My dear, it would be the death of Dahlia. You've seen the man as he is. Take it for a warning. She belongs to him. That's the law, human and divine."

"Not when he has flung her off, Robert?" Rhoda cried piteously.

"Let us take advantage of that. He did fling her off, spat at us all, and showed the blackest hellish plot I ever in my life heard of. He's not the worst sinner, scoundrel as he is. Poor girl! poor soul! a hard lot for women in this world! Rhoda, I suppose I may breakfast with you in the morning? I hear Major Waring's knock below. I want a man to talk to."

"Do come, Robert," Rhoda said, and gave him her hand. He strove to comprehend why it was that her hand was merely a hand, and no more to him just then; squeezed the cold fingers, and left her.

CHAPTER XL

A FREAK OF THE MONEY-DEMON, THAT MAY HAVE BEEN ANTICIPATED

So long as we do not know that we are performing any remarkable feat, we may walk upon the narrowest of planks between precipices with perfect security; but when we suffer our minds to eye the chasm underneath, we begin to be in danger, and we are in very great fear of losing our equal balance the moment we admit the insidious reflection that other men, placed as we are, would probably topple headlong over. Anthony Hackbut, of Boyne's Bank, had been giving himself up latterly to this fatal comparison. The hour when gold was entrusted to his charge found him feverish and irritable. He asked himself whether he was a mere machine to transfer money from spot to spot, and he spurned at the pittance bestowed upon honesty in this life. Where could Boyne's Bank discover again such an honest man as he? And because he was honest he was poor! The consideration that we alone are capable of doing the unparalleled thing may sometimes inspire us with fortitude; but this will depend largely upon the antecedent moral trials of a man. It is a temptation when we look on what we accomplish at all in that light. The temptation being inbred, is commonly a proof of internal corruption. "If I take a step, suppose now, to the right, or to the left," Anthony had got into the habit of saying, while he made his course, and after he had deposited his charge he would wipe his moist forehead, in a state of wretched exultation over his renowned trustworthiness.

He had done the thing for years. And what did the people in the streets know about him? Formerly, he had used to regard the people in the streets, and their opinions, with a voluptuous contempt; but he was no longer wrapped in sweet calculations of his savings, and his chances, and his connection with a mighty Bank. The virtue had gone out of him. Yet he had not the slightest appetite for other men's money; no hunger, nor any definite notion of enjoyment to be derived from money not his own. Imagination misled the old man. There have been spotless reputations gained in the service of virtue before now; and chaste and beautiful persons have walked the narrow plank, envied and admired; and they have ultimately tottered and all but fallen; or they have quite fallen, from no worse an incitement than curiosity. Cold curiosity, as the directors of our human constitution tell us, is, in the colder condition of our blood, a betraying vice, leading to sin at a period when the fruits of sin afford the smallest satisfaction. It is, in fact, our last probation, and one of our latest delusions. If that is passed successfully, we may really be pronounced as of some worth. Anthony wished to give a light indulgence to his curiosity; say, by running away and over London Bridge on one side, and back on the other, hugging the money. For two weeks, he thought of this absurd performance as a comical and agreeable diversion. How would he feel when going in the direction of the Surrey hills? And how, when returning, and when there was a prospect of the Bank, where the money was to be paid in, being shut? Supposing that he was a minute behind his time, would the Bank-doors remain open, in expectation of him? And if the money was not paid in, what would be thought? What would be thought at Boyne's, if, the next day, he was late in making his appearance?

"Holloa! Hackbut, how's this?"—"I'm a bit late, sir, morning."—"Late! you were late yesterday evening, weren't you?"—"Why, sir, the way the clerks at that Bank of Mortimer and Pennycuick's rush away from business and close the doors after 'em, as if their day began at four p.m., and business was botheration: it's a disgrace to the City o' London. And I beg pardon for being late, but never sleeping a wink all night for fear about this money, I am late this morning, I humbly confess. When I got to the Bank, the doors were shut. Our clock's correct; that I know. My belief, sir, is, the clerks at Mortimer and Pennycuick's put on the time."—"Oh! we must have this inquired into."

Anthony dramatized the farcical scene which he imagined between himself and Mr. Sequin, the head clerk at Boyne's, with immense relish; and terminated it by establishing his reputation for honesty higher than ever at the Bank, after which violent exercise of his fancy, the old man sank into a dulness during several days. The farmer slept at his lodgings for one night, and talked of money, and of selling his farm; and half hinted that it would be a brotherly proceeding on Anthony's part to buy it, and hold it, so as to keep it in the family. The farmer's deep belief in the existence of his hoards always did Anthony peculiar mischief. Anthony grew conscious of a giddiness, and all the next day he was scarcely fit for his work. But the day following that he was calm and attentive. Two bags of gold were placed in his hands, and he walked with caution down the steps of the Bank, turned the corner, and went straight on to the West, never once hesitating, or casting a thought behind upon Mortimer and Pennycuick's. He had not, in truth, one that was loose to be cast. All his thoughts were boiling in his head, obfuscating him with a prodigious steam, through which he beheld the city surging, and the streets curving like lines in water, and the people mixing and passing into and out of one another in an astonishing manner—no face distinguishable; the whole thick multitude appearing to be stirred like glue in a gallipot. The only distinct thought which he had sprang from a fear that the dishonest ruffians would try to steal his gold, and he hugged it, and groaned to see that villany was abroad. Marvellous, too, that the clocks on the churches, all the way along the Westward thoroughfare, stuck at the hour when Banks are closed to business! It was some time, or a pretence at some time, before the minute-hands surmounted that difficulty. Having done so, they rushed ahead to the ensuing hour with the mad precipitation of pantomimic machinery. The sight of them presently standing on the hour, like a sentinel presenting arms, was startling—laughable. Anthony could not have flipped with his fingers fifty times in the interval; he was sure of it, "or not much more," he said. So the City was shut to him behind iron bars.

Up in the West there is not so much to be dreaded from the rapacity of men. You do not hear of such alarming burglaries there every day; every hand is not at another's throat there, or in another's pocket; at least, not until after nightfall; and when the dark should come on, Anthony had determined to make for his own quarter with all speed. Darkness is horrible in foreign places, but foreign places are not so accusing to you by daylight.

The Park was vastly pleasant to the old man.

"Ah!" he sniffed, "country air," and betook himself to a seat. "Extraordinary," he thought, "what little people they look on their horses and in their carriages! That's the aristocracy, is it!" The aristocracy appeared oddly diminutive to him. He sneered at the aristocracy, but, beholding a policeman, became stolid of aspect. The policeman was a connecting link with his City life, the true lord of his fearful soul. Though the moneybags were under his arm, beneath his buttoned coat, it required a deep pause before he understood what he had done; and then the Park began to dance and curve like the streets, and there was a singular curtseying between the heavens and the earth. He had to hold his money-bags tight, to keep them from plunging into monstrous gulfs. "I don't remember that I've taken a drink of any sort," he said, "since I and the old farmer took our turn down in the Docks. How's this?" He seemed to rock. He was near upon indulging in a fit of terror; but the impolicy of it withheld him from any demonstration, save an involuntary spasmodic ague. When this had passed, his eyesight and sensations grew clearer, and he sat in a mental doze, looking at things with quiet animal observation. His recollection of the state, after a lapse of minutes, was pleasurable. The necessity for motion, however, set him on his feet, and off he went, still Westward, out of the Park, and into streets. He trotted at a good pace. Suddenly came a call of his name in his ear, and he threw up one arm in self-defence.

"Uncle Anthony, don't you know me?"

"Eh? I do; to be sure I do," he answered, peering dimly upon Rhoda: "I'm always meeting one of you."

"I've been down in the City, trying to find you all day, uncle. I meet you—I might have missed! It is direction from heaven, for I prayed."

Anthony muttered, "I'm out for a holiday."

"This"—Rhoda pointed to a house—"is where I am lodging."

"Oh!" said Anthony; "and how's your family?"

Rhoda perceived that he was rather distraught. After great persuasion, she got him to go upstairs with her.

"Only for two seconds," he stipulated. "I can't sit."

"You will have a cup of tea with me, uncle?"

"No; I don't think I'm equal to tea."

"Not with Rhoda?"

"It's a name in Scripture," said Anthony, and he drew nearer to her. "You're comfortable and dark here, my dear. How did you come here? What's happened? You won't surprise me."

"I'm only stopping for a day or two in London, uncle."

"Ah! a wicked place; that it is. No wickeder than other places, I'll be bound. Well; I must be trotting. I can't sit, I tell you. You're as dark here as a gaol."

"Let me ring for candles, uncle."

"No; I'm going."

She tried to touch him, to draw him to a chair. The agile old man bounded away from her, and she had to pacify him submissively before he would consent to be seated. The tea-service was brought, and Rhoda made tea, and filled a cup for him. Anthony began to enjoy the repose of the room. But it made the money-bags' alien to him, and serpents in his bosom. Fretting—on his chair, he cried: "Well! well! what's to talk about? We can't drink tea and not talk!"

Rhoda deliberated, and then said: "Uncle, I think you have always loved me."

It seemed to him a merit that he should have loved her. He caught at the idea.

"So I have, Rhoda, my dear; I have. I do."

"You do love me, dear uncle!"

"Now I come to think of it, Rhoda—my Dody, I don't think ever I've loved anybody else. Never loved e'er a young woman in my life. As a young man."

"Tell me, uncle; are you not very rich?"

"No, I ain't; not 'very'; not at all."

"You must not tell untruths, uncle."

"I don't," said Anthony; only, too doggedly to instil conviction.

"I have always felt, uncle, that you love money too much. What is the value of money, except to give comfort, and help you to be a blessing to others in their trouble? Does not God lend it you for that purpose? It is most true! And if you make a store of it, it will only be unhappiness to yourself. Uncle, you love me. I am in great trouble for money."

Anthony made a long arm over the projection of his coat, and clasped it securely; sullenly refusing to answer. "Dear uncle; hear me out. I come to you, because I know you are rich. I was on my way to your lodgings when we met; we were thrown together. You have more money than you know what to do with. I am a beggar to you for money. I have never asked before; I never shall ask again. Now I pray for your help. My life, and the life dearer to me than any other, depend on you. Will you help me, Uncle Anthony? Yes!"

"No!" Anthony shouted.

"Yes! yes!"

"Yes, if I can. No, if I can't. And 'can't' it is. So, it's 'No.'"

Rhoda's bosom sank, but only as a wave in the sea-like energy of her spirit.

"Uncle, you must."

Anthony was restrained from jumping up and running away forthwith by the peace which was in the room, and the dread of being solitary after he had tasted of companionship.

"You have money, uncle. You are rich. You must help me. Don't you ever think what it is to be an old man, and no one to love you and be grateful to you? Why do you cross your arms so close?"

Anthony denied that he crossed his arms closely.

Rhoda pointed to his arms in evidence; and he snarled out: "There, now; 'cause I'm supposed to have saved a trifle, I ain't to sit as I like. It's downright too bad! It's shocking!"

But, seeing that he did not uncross his arms, and remained bunched up defiantly, Rhoda silently observed him. She felt that money was in the room.

"Don't let it be a curse to you," she said. And her voice was hoarse with agitation.

"What?" Anthony asked. "What's a curse?"

"That."

Did she know? Had she guessed? Her finger was laid in a line at the bags. Had she smelt the gold?

"It will be a curse to you, uncle. Death is coming. What's money then? Uncle, uncross your arms. You are afraid; you dare not. You carry it about; you have no confidence anywhere. It eats your heart. Look at me. I have nothing to conceal. Can you imitate me, and throw your hands out—so? Why, uncle, will you let me be ashamed of you? You have the money there.

"You cannot deny it. Me crying to you for help! What have we talked together?—that we would sit in a country house, and I was to look to the flower-beds, and always have dishes of green peas for you-plenty, in June; and you were to let the village boys know what a tongue you have, if they made a clatter of their sticks along the garden-rails; and you were to drink your tea, looking on a green and the sunset. Uncle! Poor old, good old soul! You mean kindly. You must be kind. A day will make it too late. You have the money there. You get older and older every minute with trying to refuse me. You know that I can make you happy. I have the power, and I have the will. Help me, I say, in my great trouble. That money is a burden. You are forced to carry it about, for fear. You look guilty as you go running in the streets, because you fear everybody. Do good with it. Let it be money with a blessing on it! It will save us from horrid misery! from death! from torture and death! Think, uncle! look, uncle! You with the money—me wanting it. I pray to heaven, and I meet you, and you have it. Will you say that you refuse to give it, when I see—when I show you, you are led to meet me and help me? Open;—put down that arm."

Against this storm of mingled supplication and shadowy menace, Anthony held out with all outward firmness until, when bidding him to put down his arm, she touched the arm commandingly, and it fell paralyzed.

Rhoda's eyes were not beautiful as they fixed on the object of her quest. In this they were of the character of her mission. She was dealing with an evil thing, and had chosen to act according to her light, and by the counsel of her combative and forceful temper. At each step new difficulties had to be encountered by fresh contrivances; and money now—money alone had become the specific for present use. There was a limitation of her spiritual vision to aught save to money; and the money being bared to her eyes, a frightful gleam of eagerness shot from them. Her hands met Anthony's in a common grasp of the money-bags.

"It's not mine!" Anthony cried, in desperation.

"Whose money is it?" said Rhoda, and caught up her hands as from fire.

"My Lord!" Anthony moaned, "if you don't speak like a Court o' Justice. Hear yourself!"

"Is the money yours, uncle?"

"It—is," and "isn't" hung in the balance.

"It is not?" Rhoda dressed the question for him in the terror of contemptuous horror.

"It is. I—of course it is; how could it help being mine? My money? Yes. What sort o' thing's that to ask— whether what I've got's mine or yours, or somebody else's? Ha!"

"And you say you are not rich, uncle?"

A charming congratulatory smile was addressed to him, and a shake of the head of tender reproach irresistible to his vanity.

"Rich! with a lot o' calls on me; everybody wantin' to borrow—I'm rich! And now you coming to me! You women can't bring a guess to bear upon the right nature o' money."

"Uncle, you will decide to help me, I know."

She said it with a staggering assurance of manner.

"How do you know?" cried Anthony.

"Why do you carry so much money about with you in bags, uncle?"

"Hear it, my dear." He simulated miser's joy.

"Ain't that music? Talk of operas! Hear that; don't it talk? don't it chink? don't it sing?" He groaned "Oh, Lord!" and fell back.

This transition from a state of intensest rapture to the depths of pain alarmed her.

"Nothing; it's nothing." Anthony anticipated her inquiries. "They bags is so heavy."

"Then why do you carry them about?"

"Perhaps it's heart disease," said Anthony, and grinned, for he knew the soundness of his health.

"You are very pale, uncle."

"Eh? you don't say that?"

"You are awfully white, dear uncle."

"I'll look in the glass," said Anthony. "No, I won't." He sank back in his chair. "Rhoda, we're all sinners, ain't we? All—every man and woman of us, and baby, too. That's a comfort; yes, it is a comfort. It's a tremendous comfort—shuts mouths. I know what you're going to say—some bigger sinners than others. If they're sorry for it, though, what then? They can repent, can't they?"

"They must undo any harm they may have done. Sinners are not to repent only in words, uncle."

"I've been feeling lately," he murmured.

Rhoda expected a miser's confession.

"I've been feeling, the last two or three days," he resumed.

"What, uncle?"

"Sort of taste of a tremendous nice lemon in my mouth, my dear, and liked it, till all of a sudden I swallowed it whole—such a gulp! I felt it just now. I'm all right."

"No, uncle," said Rhoda: "you are not all right: this money makes you miserable. It does; I can see that it does. Now, put those bags in my hands. For a minute, try; it will do you good. Attend to me; it will. Or, let me have them. They are poison to you. You don't want them."

"I don't," cried Anthony. "Upon my soul, I don't. I don't want 'em. I'd give—it is true, my dear, I don't want 'em. They're poison."

"They're poison to you," said Rhoda; "they're health, they're life to me. I said, 'My uncle Anthony will help me. He is not—I know his heart—he is not a miser.' Are you a miser, uncle?"

Her hand was on one of his bags. It was strenuously withheld: but while she continued speaking, reiterating the word "miser," the hold relaxed. She caught the heavy bag away, startled by its weight.

He perceived the effect produced on her, and cried; "Aha! and I've been carrying two of 'em—two!"

Rhoda panted in her excitement.

"Now, give it up," said he. She returned it. He got it against his breast joylessly, and then bade her to try the weight of the two. She did try them, and Anthony doated on the wonder of her face.

"Uncle, see what riches do! You fear everybody—you think there is no secure place—you have more? Do you carry about all your money?"

"No," he chuckled at her astonishment. "I've...Yes. I've got more of my own." Her widened eyes intoxicated him. "More. I've saved. I've put by. Say, I'm an old sinner. What'd th' old farmer say now? Do you love your uncle Tony? 'Old Ant,' they call me down at—" "The Bank," he was on the point of uttering; but the vision of the Bank lay terrific in his recollection, and, summoned at last, would not be wiped away. The unbearable picture swam blinking through accumulating clouds; remote and minute as the chief scene of our infancy, but commanding him with the present touch of a mighty arm thrown out. "I'm honest," he cried. "I always have been honest. I'm known to be honest. I want no man's money. I've got money of my own. I hate sin. I hate sinners. I'm an honest man. Ask them, down at—Rhoda, my dear! I say, don't you hear me? Rhoda, you think I've a turn for misering. It's a beastly mistake: poor savings, and such a trouble to keep honest when you're poor; and I've done it for years, spite o' temptation 't 'd send lots o' men to the hulks. Safe into my hand, safe out o' my hands! Slip once, and there ain't mercy in men. And you say, 'I had a whirl of my head, and went round, and didn't know where I was for a minute, and forgot the place I'd to go to, and come away to think in a quiet part.'..." He stopped abruptly in his ravings. "You give me the money, Rhoda!"

She handed him the money-bags.

He seized them, and dashed them to the ground with the force of madness. Kneeling, he drew out his penknife, and slit the sides of the bags, and held them aloft, and let the gold pour out in torrents, insufferable to the sight; and uttering laughter that clamoured fierily in her ears for long minutes afterwards, the old man brandished the empty bags, and sprang out of the room.

She sat dismayed in the centre of a heap of gold.

CHAPTER XLI

DAHLIA'S FRENZY

On the Monday evening, Master Gammon was at the station with the cart. Robert and Rhoda were a train later, but the old man seemed to be unaware of any delay, and mildly staring, received their apologies, and nodded. They asked him more than once whether all was well at the Farm; to which he replied that all was quite well, and that he was never otherwise. About half-an-hour after, on the road, a gradual dumb chuckle overcame his lower features. He flicked the horse dubitatively, and turned his head, first to Robert, next to Rhoda; and then he chuckled aloud:

"The last o' they mel'ns rotted yest'day afternoon!"

"Did they?" said Robert. "You'll have to get fresh seed, that's all."

Master Gammon merely showed his spirit to be negative.

"You've been playing the fool with the sheep," Robert accused him.

It hit the old man in a very tender part.

"I play the fool wi' ne'er a sheep alive, Mr. Robert. Animals likes their 'customed food, and don't like no other. I never changes my food, nor'd e'er a sheep, nor'd a cow, nor'd a bullock, if animals was masters. I'd as lief give a sheep beer, as offer him, free-handed—of my own will, that's to say—a mel'n. They rots."

Robert smiled, though he was angry. The delicious unvexed country-talk soothed Rhoda, and she looked fondly on the old man, believing that he could not talk on in his sedate way, if all were not well at home.

The hills of the beacon-ridge beyond her home, and the line of stunted firs, which she had named "the old bent beggarmen," were visible in the twilight. Her eyes flew thoughtfully far over them, with the feeling that they had long known what would come to her and to those dear to her, and the intense hope that they knew no more, inasmuch as they bounded her sight.

"If the sheep thrive," she ventured to remark, so that the comforting old themes might be kept up.

"That's the particular 'if!'" said Robert, signifying something that had to be leaped over.

Master Gammon performed the feat with agility.

"Sheep never was heartier," he pronounced emphatically.

"Lots of applications for melon-seed, Gammon?"

To this the veteran's tardy answer was: "More fools 'n one about, I reckon"; and Robert allowed him the victory implied by silence.

"And there's no news in Wrexby? none at all?" said Rhoda.

A direct question inevitably plunged Master Gammon so deep amid the soundings of his reflectiveness, that it was the surest way of precluding a response from him; but on this occasion his honest deliberation bore fruit.

"Squire Blancove, he's dead."

The name caused Rhoda to shudder.

"Found dead in 's bed, Sat'day morning," Master Gammon added, and, warmed upon the subject, went on: "He's that stiff, folks say, that stiff he is, he'll have to get into a rounded coffin: he's just like half a hoop. He was all of a heap, like. Had a fight with 's bolster, and got th' wust of it. But, be 't the seizure, or be 't gout in 's belly, he's gone clean dead. And he wunt buy th' Farm, nether. Shutters is all shut up at the Hall. He'll go burying about Wednesday. Men that drinks don't keep."

Rhoda struck at her brain to think in what way this death could work and show like a punishment of the heavens upon that one wrong-doer; but it was not manifest as a flame of wrath, and she laid herself open to the peace of the fields and the hedgeways stepping by. The farm-house came in sight, and friendly old Adam and Eve turning from the moon. She heard the sound of water. Every sign of peace was around the farm. The cows had been milked long since; the geese were quiet. There was nothing but the white board above the garden-gate to speak of the history lying in her heart.

They found the farmer sitting alone, shading his forehead. Rhoda kissed his cheeks and whispered for tidings of Dahlia.

"Go up to her," the farmer said.

Rhoda grew very chill. She went upstairs with apprehensive feet, and recognizing Mrs. Sumfit outside the door of Dahlia's room, embraced her, and heard her say that Dahlia had turned the key, and had been crying from mornings to nights. "It can't last," Mrs. Sumfit sobbed: "lonesome hysterics, they's death to come. She's falling into the trance. I'll go, for the sight o' me shocks her."

Rhoda knocked, waited patiently till her persistent repetition of her name gained her admission. She beheld her sister indeed, but not the broken Dahlia from whom she had parted. Dahlia was hard to her caress, and crying, "Has he come?" stood at bay, white-eyed, and looking like a thing strung with wires.

"No, dearest; he will not trouble you. Have no fear."

"Are you full of deceit?" said Dahlia, stamping her foot.

"I hope not, my sister."

Dahlia let fall a long quivering breath. She went to her bed, upon which her mother's Bible was lying, and taking it in her two hands, held it under Rhoda's lips.

"Swear upon that?"

"What am I to swear to, dearest?"

"Swear that he is not in the house."

"He is not, my own sister; believe me. It is no deceit. He is not. He will not trouble you. See; I kiss the Book, and swear to you, my beloved! I speak truth. Come to me, dear." Rhoda put her arms up entreatingly, but Dahlia stepped back.

"You are not deceitful? You are not cold? You are not inhuman? Inhuman! You are not? You are not? Oh, my God! Look at her!"

The toneless voice was as bitter for Rhoda to hear as the accusations. She replied, with a poor smile: "I am only not deceitful. Come, and see. You will not be disturbed."

"What am I tied to?" Dahlia struggled feebly as against a weight of chains. "Oh! what am I tied to? It's on me, tight like teeth. I can't escape. I can't breathe for it. I was like a stone when he asked me—marry him!—loved me! Some one preached—my duty! I am lost, I am lost! Why? you girl!—why?—What did you do? Why did you take my hand when I was asleep and hurry me so fast? What have I done to you? Why did you push me along?—I couldn't see where. I heard the Church babble. For you—inhuman! inhuman! What have I done to you? What have you to do with punishing sin? It's not sin. Let me be sinful, then. I am. I am sinful. Hear me. I love him; I love my lover, and," she screamed out, "he loves me!"

Rhoda now thought her mad.

She looked once at the rigid figure of her transformed sister, and sitting down, covered her eyes and wept.

To Dahlia, the tears were at first an acrid joy; but being weak, she fell to the bed, and leaned against it, forgetting her frenzy for a time.

"You deceived me," she murmured; and again, "You deceived me." Rhoda did not answer. In trying to understand why her sister should imagine it, she began to know that she had in truth deceived Dahlia. The temptation to drive a frail human creature to do the thing which was right, had led her to speak falsely for a good purpose. Was it not righteously executed? Away from the tragic figure in the room, she might have thought so, but the horror in the eyes and voice of this awakened Sacrifice, struck away the support of theoretic justification. Great pity for the poor enmeshed life, helpless there, and in a woman's worst peril,—looking either to madness, or to death, for an escape—drowned her reason in a heavy cloud of tears. Long on toward the stroke of the hour, Dahlia heard her weep, and she murmured on, "You deceived me;" but it was no more to reproach; rather, it was an exculpation of her reproaches.

"You did deceive me, Rhoda." Rhoda half lifted her head; the slight tone of a change to tenderness swelled the gulfs of pity, and she wept aloud. Dahlia untwisted her feet, and staggered up to her, fell upon her shoulder, and called her, "My love!—good sister!" For a great mute space they clung together. Their lips met and they kissed convulsively. But when Dahlia had close view of Rhoda's face, she drew back, saying in an under-breath,—

"Don't cry. I see my misery when you cry."

Rhoda promised that she would check her tears, and they sat quietly, side by side, hand in hand. Mrs. Sumfit, outside, had to be dismissed twice with her fresh brews of supplicating tea and toast, and the cakes which, when eaten warm with good country butter and a sprinkle of salt, reanimate (as she did her utmost to assure the sisters through the closed door) humanity's distressed spirit. At times their hands interchanged a fervent pressure, their eyes were drawn to an equal gaze.

In the middle of the night Dahlia said: "I found a letter from Edward when I came here."

"Written—Oh, base man that he is!" Rhoda could not control the impulse to cry it out.

"Written before," said Dahlia, divining her at once. "I read it; did not cry. I have no tears. Will you see it? It is very short-enough; it said enough, and written before—" She crumpled her fingers in Rhoda's; Rhoda, to please her, saying "Yes," she went to the pillow of the bed, and drew the letter from underneath.

"I know every word," she said; "I should die if I repeated it. 'My wife before heaven,' it begins. So, I was his wife. I must have broken his heart—broken my husband's." Dahlia cast a fearful eye about her; her eyelids fluttered as from a savage sudden blow. Hardening her mouth to utter defiant spite: "My lover's," she cried. "He is. If he loves me and I love him, he is my lover, my lover, my lover! Nothing shall stop me from saying it—lover! and there is none to claim me but he. Oh, loathsome! What a serpent it is I've got round me! And you tell me God put it. Do you? Answer that; for I want to know, and I don't know where I am. I am lost! I am lost! I want to get to my lover. Tell me, Rhoda, you would curse me if I did. And listen to me. Let him open his arms to me, I go; I follow him as far as my feet will bear me. I would go if it lightened from heaven. If I saw up there the warning, 'You shall not!' I would go. But, look on me!" she smote contempt upon her bosom. "He would not call to such a thing as me. Me, now? My skin is like a toad's to him. I've become like something in the dust. I could hiss like adders. I am quite impenitent. I pray by my bedside, my head on my Bible, but I only say, 'Yes, yes; that's done; that's deserved, if there's no mercy.' Oh, if there is no mercy, that's deserved! I say so now. But this is what I say, Rhoda (I see nothing but blackness when I pray), and I say, 'Permit no worse!' I say, 'Permit no worse, or take the consequences.' He calls me his wife. I am his wife. And if—" Dahlia fell to speechless panting; her mouth was open; she made motion with her hands; horror, as of a blasphemy struggling to her lips, kept her dumb, but the prompting passion was indomitable.... "Read it," said her struggling voice; and Rhoda bent over the letter, reading and losing thought of each sentence as it passed. To Dahlia, the vital words were visible like evanescent blue gravelights. She saw them rolling through her sister's mind; and just upon the conclusion, she gave out, as in a chaunt: "And I who have sinned against my innocent darling, will ask her to pray with me that our future may be one, so that may make good to her what she has suffered, and to the God whom we worship, the offence I have committed."

Rhoda looked up at the pale penetrating eyes.

"Read. Have you read to the last?" said Dahlia. "Speak it. Let me hear you. He writes it.... Yes? you will not? 'Husband,' he says," and then she took up the sentences of the letter backwards to the beginning, pausing upon each one with a short moan, and smiting her bosom. "I found it here, Rhoda. I found his letter here when I came.. I came a dead thing, and it made me spring up alive. Oh, what bliss to be dead! I've felt nothing...nothing, for months." She flung herself on the bed, thrusting her handkerchief to her mouth to deaden the outcry. "I'm punished. I'm punished, because I did not trust to my darling. No, not for one year! Is it that since we parted? I am an impatient creature, and he does not reproach me. I tormented my own, my love, my dear, and he thought I—I was tired of our life together. No; he does not accuse me," Dahlia replied to her sister's unspoken feeling, with the shrewd divination which is passion's breathing space. "He accuses himself. He says it—utters it—speaks it 'I sold my beloved.' There is no guile in him. Oh, be just to us, Rhoda! Dearest," she came to Rhoda's side, "you did deceive me, did you not? You are a deceiver, my love?"

Rhoda trembled, and raising her eyelids, answered, "Yes."

"You saw him in the street that morning?"

Dahlia smiled a glittering tenderness too evidently deceitful in part, but quite subduing.

"You saw him, my Rhoda, and he said he was true to me, and sorrowful; and you told him, dear one, that I had no heart for him, and wished to go to hell—did you not, good Rhoda? Forgive me; I mean 'good;' my true, good Rhoda. Yes, you hate sin; it is dreadful; but you should never speak falsely to sinners, for that does not teach them to repent. Mind you never lie again. Look at me. I am chained, and I have no repentance in me. See me. I am nearer it...the other—sin, I mean. If that man comes...will he?"

"No—no!" Rhoda cried.

"If that man comes—"

"He will not come!"

"He cast me off at the church door, and said he had been cheated. Money! Oh, Edward!"

Dahlia drooped her head.

"He will keep away. You are safe," said Rhoda.

"Because, if no help comes, I am lost—I am lost for ever!"

"But help will come. I mean peace will come. We will read; we will work in the garden. You have lifted poor father up, my dear."

"Ah! that old man!" Dahlia sighed.

"He is our father."

"Yes, poor old man!" and Dahlia whispered: "I have no pity for him. If I am dragged away, I'm afraid I shall curse him. He seems a stony old man. I don't understand fathers. He would make me go away. He talks the Scriptures when he is excited. I'm afraid he would shut my Bible for me. Those old men know nothing of the hearts of women. Now, darling, go to your room."

Rhoda begged earnestly for permission to stay with her, but Dahlia said: "My nights are fevers. I can't have arms about me."

They shook hands when they separated, not kissing.

CHAPTER XLII

ANTHONY IN A COLLAPSE

Three days passed quietly at the Farm, and each morning Dahlia came down to breakfast, and sat with the family at their meals; pale, with the mournful rim about her eyelids, but a patient figure. No questions were asked. The house was guarded from visitors, and on the surface the home was peaceful. On the Wednesday Squire Blancove was buried, when Master Gammon, who seldom claimed a holiday or specified an enjoyment of which he would desire to partake, asked leave to be spared for a couple of hours, that he might attend the ceremonious interment of one to whom a sort of vagrant human sentiment of clanship had made him look up, as to the chief gentleman of the district, and therefore one having claims on his respect. A burial had great interest for the old man.

"I'll be home for dinner; it'll gi'e me an appetite," Master Gammon said solemnly, and he marched away in his serious Sunday hat and careful coat, blither than usual.

After his departure, Mrs. Sumfit sat and discoursed on deaths and burials, the certain end of all: at least, she corrected herself, the deaths were. The burials were not so certain. Consequently, we might take the burials, as they were a favour, to be a blessing, except in the event of persons being buried alive. She tried to make her hearers understand that the idea of this calamity had always seemed intolerable to her, and told of numerous cases which, the coffin having been opened, showed by the convulsed aspect of the corpse, or by spots of blood upon the shroud, that the poor creature had wakened up forlorn, "and not a kick allowed to him, my dears."

"It happens to women, too, does it not, mother?" said Dahlia.

"They're most subject to trances, my sweet. From always imitatin' they imitates their deaths at last; and, oh!" Mrs. Sumfit was taken with nervous chokings of alarm at the thought. "Alone—all dark! and hard wood upon your chest, your elbows, your nose, your toes, and you under heaps o' gravel! Not a breath for you, though you snap and catch for one—worse than a fish on land."

"It's over very soon, mother," said Dahlia.

"The coldness of you young women! Yes; but it's the time—you feeling, trying for air; it's the horrid 'Oh, dear me!' You set your mind on it!"

"I do," said Dahlia. "You see coffin-nails instead of stars. You'd give the world to turn upon one side. You can't think. You can only hate those who put you there. You see them taking tea, saying prayers, sleeping in bed, putting on bonnets, walking to church, kneading dough, eating—all at once, like the firing of a gun. They're in one world; you're in another."

"Why, my goodness, one'd say she'd gone through it herself," ejaculated Mrs. Sumfit, terrified.

Dahlia sent her eyes at Rhoda.

"I must go and see that poor man covered." Mrs. Sumfit succumbed to a fit of resolution much under the pretence that it had long been forming.

"Well, and mother," said Dahlia, checking her, "promise me. Put a feather on my mouth; put a glass to my face, before you let them carry me out. Will you? Rhoda promises. I have asked her."

"Oh! the ideas of this girl!" Mrs. Sumfit burst out. "And looking so, as she says it. My love, you didn't mean to die?"

Dahlia soothed her, and sent her off.

"I am buried alive!" she said. "I feel it all—the stifling! the hopeless cramp! Let us go and garden. Rhoda, have you got laudanum in the house?"

Rhoda shook her head, too sick at heart to speak. They went into the garden, which was Dahlia's healthfullest place. It seemed to her that her dead mother talked to her there. That was not a figure of speech, when she said she felt buried alive. She was in the state of sensational delusion. There were times when she watched her own power of motion curiously: curiously stretched out her hands, and touched things, and moved them. The sight was convincing, but the shudder came again. In a frame less robust the brain would have given way. It was the very soundness of the brain which, when her blood was a simple tide of life in her veins, and no vital force, had condemned her to see the wisdom and the righteousness of the act of sacrifice committed by her, and had urged her even up to the altar. Then the sudden throwing off of the mask by that man to whom she had bound herself, and the reading of Edward's letter of penitence and love, thwarted reason, but without blinding or unsettling it. Passion grew dominant; yet against such deadly matters on all sides had passion to strive, that, under a darkened sky, visibly chained, bound down, and hopeless, she felt between-whiles veritably that she was a living body buried. Her senses had become semi-lunatic.

She talked reasonably; and Rhoda, hearing her question and answer at meal-times like a sane woman, was in doubt whether her sister wilfully simulated a partial insanity when they were alone together. Now, in the garden, Dahlia said: "All those flowers, my dear, have roots in mother and me. She can't feel them, for her soul's in heaven. But mine is down there. The pain is the trying to get your soul loose. It's the edge of a knife that won't cut through. Do you know that?"

Rhoda said, as acquiescingly as she could, "Yes."

"Do you?" Dahlia whispered. "It's what they call the 'agony.' Only, to go through it in the dark, when you are all alone! boarded round! you will never know that. And there's an angel brings me one of mother's roses, and I smell it. I see fields of snow; and it's warm there, and no labour for breath. I see great beds of flowers; I pass them like a breeze. I'm shot, and knock on the ground, and they bury me for dead again. Indeed, dearest, it's true."

She meant, true as regarded her sensations. Rhoda could barely give a smile for response; and Dahlia's intelligence being supernaturally active, she read her sister's doubt, and cried out,—

"Then let me talk of him!"

It was the fiery sequence to her foregone speech, signifying that if her passion had liberty to express itself, she could clear understandings. But even a moment's free wing to passion renewed the blinding terror within her. Rhoda steadied her along the walks, praying for the time to come when her friends, the rector and his wife, might help in the task of comforting this poor sister. Detestation of the idea of love made her sympathy almost deficient, and when there was no active work to do in aid, she was nearly valueless, knowing that she also stood guilty of a wrong.

The day was very soft and still. The flowers gave light for light. They heard through the noise of the mill-water the funeral bell sound. It sank in Rhoda like the preaching of an end that was promise of a beginning, and girdled a distancing land of trouble. The breeze that blew seemed mercy. To live here in forgetfulness with Dahlia was the limit of her desires. Perhaps, if Robert worked among them, she would gratefully give him her hand. That is, if he said not a word of love.

Master Gammon and Mrs. Sumfit were punctual in their return near the dinner-hour; and the business of releasing the dumplings and potatoes, and spreading out the cold meat and lettuces, restrained for some period the narrative of proceedings at the funeral. Chief among the incidents was, that Mrs. Sumfit had really seen, and only wanted, by corroboration of Master Gammon, to be sure she had positively seen, Anthony Hackbut on the skirts of the funeral procession. Master Gammon, however, was no supporter of conjecture. What he had thought he had thought; but that was neither here nor there. He would swear to nothing that he had not touched;—eyes deceived;—he was never a guesser. He left Mrs. Sumfit to pledge herself in perturbation of spirit to an oath that her eyes had seen Anthony Hackbut; and more, which was, that after the close of the funeral service, the young squire had caught sight of Anthony crouching in a corner of the churchyard, and had sent a man to him, and they had disappeared together. Mrs. Sumfit was heartily laughed at and rallied both by Robert and the farmer. "Tony at a funeral! and train expenses!" the farmer interjected. "D'ye think, mother, Tony'd come to Wrexby churchyard 'fore he come Queen Anne's Farm? And where's he now, mayhap?"

Mrs. Sumfit appealed in despair to Master Gammon, with entreaties, and a ready dumpling.

"There, Mas' Gammon; and why you sh'd play at 'do believe' and at 'don't believe,' after that awesome scene, the solem'est of life's, when you did declare to me, sayin', it was a stride for boots out o' London this morning. Your words, Mas' Gammon! and 'boots'-=it's true, if by that alone! For, 'boots,' I says to myself—he thinks by 'boots,' there being a cord'er in his family on the mother's side; which you yourself told to me, as you did, Mas' Gammon, and now holds back, you did, like a bad horse."

"Hey! does Gammon jib?" said the farmer, with the ghost of old laughter twinkling in his eyes.

"He told me this tale," Mrs. Sumfit continued, daring her irresponsive enemy to contradict her, with a threatening gaze. "He told me this tale, he did; and my belief's, his game 's, he gets me into a corner—there to be laughed at! Mas' Gammon, if you're not a sly old man, you said, you did, he was drownded; your mother's brother's wife's brother; and he had a brother, and what he was to you—that brother—" Mrs. Sumfit smote her hands—"Oh, my goodness, my poor head! but you shan't slip away, Mas'

Gammon; no, try you ever so much. Drownded he was, and eight days in the sea, which you told me over a warm mug of ale by the fire years back. And I do believe them dumplings makes ye obstinate; for worse you get, and that fond of 'em, I sh'll soon not have enough in our biggest pot. Yes, you said he was eight days in the sea, and as for face, you said, poor thing! he was like a rag of towel dipped in starch, was your own words, and all his likeness wiped out; and Joe, the other brother, a cord'er—bootmaker, you call 'em—looked down him, as he was stretched out on the shore of the sea, all along, and didn't know him till he come to the boots, and he says, 'It's Abner;' for there was his boots to know him by. Now, will you deny, Mas' Gammon, you said, Mr. Hackbut's boots, and a long stride it was for 'em from London? And I won't be laughed at through arts of any sly old man!"

The circumstantial charge made no impression on Master Gammon, who was heard to mumble, as from the inmost recesses of tight-packed dumpling; but he left the vindication of his case to the farmer's laughter. The mention of her uncle had started a growing agitation in Rhoda, to whom the indication of his eccentric behaviour was a stronger confirmation of his visit to the neighbourhood. And wherefore had he journeyed down? Had he come to haunt her on account of the money he had poured into her lap? Rhoda knew in a moment that she was near a great trial of her strength and truth. She had more than once, I cannot tell you how distantly, conceived that the money had been money upon which the mildest word for "stolen" should be put to express the feeling she had got about it, after she had parted with the bulk of it to the man Sedgett. Not "stolen," not "appropriated," but money that had perhaps been entrusted, and of which Anthony had forgotten the rightful ownership. This idea of hers had burned with no intolerable fire; but, under a weight of all discountenancing appearances, feeble though it was, it had distressed her. The dealing with money, and the necessity for it, had given Rhoda a better comprehension of its nature and value. She had taught herself to think that her suspicion sprang from her uncle's wild demeanour, and the scene of the gold pieces scattered on the floor, as if a heart had burst at her feet.

No sooner did she hear that Anthony had been, by supposition, seen, than the little light of secret dread flamed a panic through her veins. She left the table before Master Gammon had finished, and went out of the house to look about for her uncle. He was nowhere in the fields, nor in the graveyard. She walked over the neighbourhood desolately, until her quickened apprehension was extinguished, and she returned home relieved, thinking it folly to have imagined her uncle was other than a man of hoarded wealth, and that he was here. But, in the interval, she had experienced emotions which warned her of a struggle to come. Who would be friendly to her, and an arm of might? The thought of the storm she had sown upon all sides made her tremble foolishly. When she placed her hand in Robert's, she gave his fingers a confiding pressure, and all but dropped her head upon his bosom, so sick she was with weakness. It would have been a deceit toward him, and that restrained her; perhaps, yet more, she was restrained by the gloomy prospect of having to reply to any words of love, without an idea of what to say, and with a loathing of caresses. She saw herself condemned to stand alone, and at a season when she was not strengthened by pure self-support.

Rhoda had not surrendered the stern belief that she had done well by forcing Dahlia's hand to the marriage, though it had resulted evilly. In reflecting on it, she had still a feeling of the harsh joy peculiar to those who have exercised command with a conscious righteousness upon wilful, sinful, and erring spirits, and have thwarted the wrongdoer. She could only admit that there was sadness in the issue; hitherto, at least, nothing worse than sad disappointment. The man who was her sister's husband could no longer complain that he had been the victim of an imposition. She had bought his promise that he would leave the country, and she had rescued the honour of the family by paying him. At what cost? She asked herself that now, and then her self-support became uneven. Could her uncle have parted with the great sum—have shed it upon her, merely beneficently, and because he loved her? Was it possible that he had the habit of carrying his own riches through the streets of London? She had to silence all questions imperiously, recalling exactly her ideas of him, and the value of money in the moment when money was an object of hunger—when she had seized it like a wolf, and its value was quite unknown, unguessed at.

Rhoda threw up her window before she slept, that she might breathe the cool night air; and, as she leaned out, she heard steps moving away, and knew them to be Robert's, in whom that pressure of her hand had cruelly resuscitated his longing for her. She drew back, wondering at the idleness of men—slaves while they want a woman's love, savages when they have won it. She tried to pity him, but she had not an emotion to spare, save perhaps one of dull exultation, that she, alone of women, was free from that wretched mess called love; and upon it she slept.

It was between the breakfast and dinner hours, at the farm, next day, when the young squire, accompanied by Anthony Hackbut, met farmer Fleming in the lane bordering one of the outermost fields of wheat. Anthony gave little more than a blunt nod to his relative, and slouched on, leaving the farmer in amazement, while the young squire stopped him to speak with him. Anthony made his way on to the house. Shortly after, he was seen passing through the gates of the garden, accompanied by Rhoda. At the dinner-hour, Robert was taken aside by the farmer. Neither Rhoda nor Anthony presented themselves. They did not appear till nightfall. When Anthony came into the room, he took no greetings and gave none. He sat down on the first chair by the door, shaking his head, with vacant eyes. Rhoda took off her bonnet, and sat as strangely silent. In vain Mrs. Sumfit asked her; "Shall it be tea, dear, and a little cold meat?" The two dumb figures were separately interrogated, but they had no answer.

"Come! brother Tony?" the farmer tried to rally him.

Dahlia was knitting some article of feminine gear. Robert stood by the musk-pots at the window, looking at Rhoda fixedly. Of this gaze she became conscious, and glanced from him to the clock.

"It's late," she said, rising.

"But you're empty, my dear. And to think o' going to bed without a dinner, or your tea, and no supper! You'll never say prayers, if you do," said Mrs. Sumfit.

The remark engendered a notion in the farmer's head, that Anthony promised to be particularly prayerless.

"You've been and spent a night at the young squire's, I hear, brother Tony. All right and well. No complaints on my part, I do assure ye. If you're mixed up with that family, I won't bring it in you're anyways mixed up with this family; not so as to clash, do you see. Only, man, now you are here, a word'd be civil, if you don't want a doctor."

"I was right," murmured Mrs. Sumfit. "At the funeral, he was; and Lord be thanked! I thought my eyes was failin'. Mas' Gammon, you'd ha' lost no character by sidin' wi' me."

"Here's Dahlia, too," said the farmer. "Brother Tony, don't you see her? She's beginning to be recognizable, if her hair'd grow a bit faster. She's...well, there she is."

A quavering, tiny voice, that came from Anthony, said: "How d' ye do—how d' ye do;" sounding like the first effort of a fife. But Anthony did not cast eye on Dahlia.

"Will you eat, man?—will you smoke a pipe?—won't you talk a word?—will you go to bed?"

These several questions, coming between pauses, elicited nothing from the staring oldman.

"Is there a matter wrong at the Bank?" the farmer called out, and Anthony jumped in a heap.

"Eh?" persisted the farmer.

Rhoda interposed: "Uncle is tired; he is unwell. Tomorrow he will talk to you."

"No, but is there anything wrong up there, though?" the farmer asked with eager curiosity, and a fresh smile at the thought that those Banks and city folk were mortal, and could upset, notwithstanding their crashing wheels. "Brother Tony, you speak out; has anybody been and broke? Never mind a blow, so long, o' course, as they haven't swallowed your money. How is it? Why, I never saw such a sight as you. You come down from London; you play hide and seek about your relation's house; and here, when you do condescend to step in—eh? how is it? You ain't, I hope, ruined, Tony, are ye?"

Rhoda stood over her uncle to conceal him.

"He shall not speak till he has had some rest. And yes, mother, he shall have some warm tea upstairs in bed. Boil some water. Now, uncle, come with me."

"Anybody broke?" Anthony rolled the words over, as Rhoda raised his arm. "I'm asked such a lot, my dear, I ain't equal to it. You said here 'd be a quiet place. I don't know about money. Try my pockets. Yes, mum, if you was forty policemen, I'm empty; you'd find it. And no objection to nod to prayers; but never was taught one of my own. Where am I going, my dear?"

"Upstairs with me, uncle."

Rhoda had succeeded in getting him on his feet.

The farmer tapped at his forehead, as a signification to the others that Anthony had gone wrong in the head, which reminded him that he had prophesied as much. He stiffened out his legs, and gave a manful spring, crying, "Hulloa, brother Tony! why, man, eh? Look here. What, goin' to bed? What, you, Tony? I say—I say—dear me!" And during these exclamations intricate visions of tripping by means of gold wires danced before him.

Rhoda hurried Anthony out.

After the door had shut, the farmer said: "That comes of it; sooner or later, there it is! You give your heart to money—you insure in a ship, and as much as say, here's a ship, and, blow and lighten, I defy you. Whereas we day-by-day people, if it do blow and if it do lighten, and the waves are avilanches, we've nothing to lose. Poor old Tony—a smash, to a certainty. There's been a smash, and he's gone under the harrow. Any o' you here might ha' heard me say, things can't last for ever. Ha'n't you, now?"

The persons present meekly acquiesced in his prophetic spirit to this extent. Mrs. Sumfit dolorously said, "Often, William dear," and accepted the incontestable truth in deep humiliation of mind.

"Save," the farmer continued, "save and store, only don't put your heart in the box."

"It's true, William;" Mrs. Sumfit acted clerk to the sermon.

Dahlia took her softly by the neck, and kissed her.

"Is it love for the old woman?" Mrs. Sumfit murmured fondly; and Dahlia kissed her again.

The farmer had by this time rounded to the thought of how he personally might be affected by Anthony's ill-luck, supposing; perchance, that Anthony was suffering from something more than a sentimental attachment to the Bank of his predilection: and such a reflection instantly diverted his tendency to moralize.

"We shall hear to-morrow," he observed in conclusion; which, as it caused a desire for the morrow to spring within his bosom, sent his eyes at Master Gammon, who was half an hour behind his time for bed, and had dropped asleep in his chair. This unusual display of public somnolence on Master Gammon's part, together with the veteran's reputation for slowness, made the farmer fret at him as being in some way an obstruction to the lively progress of the hours.

"Hoy, Gammon!" he sang out, awakeningly to ordinary ears; but Master Gammon was not one who took the ordinary plunge into the gulf of sleep, and it was required to shake him and to bellow at him—to administer at once earthquake and thunder—before his lizard eyelids would lift over the great, old-world eyes; upon which, like a clayey monster refusing to be informed with heavenly fire, he rolled to the right of his chair and to the left, and pitched forward, and insisted upon being inanimate. Brought at last to a condition of stale consciousness, he looked at his master long, and uttered surprisingly "Farmer, there's queer things going on in this house," and then relapsed to a combat with Mrs. Sumfit, regarding the candle; she saying that it was not to be entrusted to him, and he sullenly contending that it was.

"Here, we'll all go to bed," said the farmer. "What with one person queer, and another person queer, I shall be in for a headache, if I take to thinking. Gammon's a man sees in 's sleep what he misses awake. Did you ever know," he addressed anybody, "such a thing as Tony Hackbut coming into a relation's house, and sitting there, and not a word for any of us? It's, I call it, dumbfoundering. And that's me: why didn't I go up and shake his hand, you ask. Well, why not? If he don't know he's welcome, without ceremony, he's no good. Why, I've got matters t' occupy my mind, too, haven't I? Every man has, and some more'n others, let alone crosses. There's something wrong with my brother-in-law, Tony, that's settled. Odd that we country people, who bide, and take the Lord's gifts—" The farmer did not follow out this reflection, but raising his arms, shepherd-wise, he puffed as if blowing the two women before him to their beds, and then gave a shy look at Robert, and nodded good-night to him. Robert nodded in reply. He knew the cause of the farmer's uncommon blitheness. Algernon Blancove, the young squire, had proposed for Rhoda's hand.

CHAPTER XLIII

Anthony had robbed the Bank. The young squire was aware of the fact, and had offered to interpose for him, and to make good the money to the Bank, upon one condition. So much, Rhoda had gathered from her uncle's babbling interjections throughout the day. The farmer knew only of the young squire's proposal, which had been made direct to him; and he had left it to Robert to state the case to Rhoda, and plead for himself. She believed fully, when she came downstairs into the room where Robert was awaiting her, that she had but to speak and a mine would be sprung; and shrinking from it, hoping for it, she entered, and tried to fasten her eyes upon Robert distinctly, telling him the tale. Robert listened with a calculating seriousness of manner that quieted her physical dread of his passion. She finished; and he said "It will, perhaps, save your uncle: I'm sure it will please your father."

She sat down, feeling that a warmth had gone, and that she was very bare.

"Must I consent, then?"

"If you can, I suppose."

Both being spirits formed for action, a perplexity found them weak as babes. He, moreover, was stung to see her debating at all upon such a question; and he was in despair before complicated events which gave nothing for his hands and heart to do. Stiff endurance seemed to him to be his lesson; and he made a show of having learnt it.

"Were you going out, Robert?"

"I usually make the rounds of the house, to be sure all's safe."

His walking about the garden at night was not, then, for the purpose of looking at her window. Rhoda coloured in all her dark crimson with shame for thinking that it had been so.

"I must decide to-morrow morning."

"They say, the pillow's the best counsellor."

A reply that presumed she would sleep appeared to her as bitterly unfriendly.

"Did father wish it?"

"Not by what he spoke."

"You suppose he does wish it?"

"Where's the father who wouldn't? Of course, he wishes it. He's kind enough, but you may be certain he wishes it."

"Oh! Dahlia, Dahlia!" Rhoda moaned, under a rush of new sensations, unfilial, akin to those which her sister had distressed her by speaking shamelessly out.

"Ah! poor soul!" added Robert.

"My darling must be brave: she must have great courage. Dahlia cannot be a coward. I begin to see."

Rhoda threw up her face, and sat awhile as one who was reading old matters by a fresh light.

"I can't think," she said, with a start. "Have I been dreadfully cruel? Was I unsisterly? I have such a horror of some things—disgrace. And men are so hard on women; and father—I felt for him. And I hated that base man. It's his cousin and his name! I could almost fancy this trial is brought round to me for punishment."

An ironic devil prompted Robert to say, "You can't let harm come to your uncle."

The thing implied was the farthest in his idea of any woman's possible duty.

"Are you of that opinion?" Rhoda questioned with her eyes, but uttered nothing.

Now, he had spoken almost in the ironical tone. She should have noted that. And how could a true-hearted girl suppose him capable of giving such counsel to her whom he loved? It smote him with horror and anger; but he was much too manly to betray these actual sentiments, and continued to dissemble. You see, he had not forgiven her for her indifference to him.

"You are no longer your own mistress," he said, meaning exactly the reverse.

This—that she was bound in generosity to sacrifice herself—was what Rhoda feared. There was no forceful passion in her bosom to burst through the crowd of weak reasonings and vanities, to bid her be a woman, not a puppet; and the passion in him, for which she craved, that she might be taken up by it and whirled into forgetfulness, with a seal of betrothal upon her lips, was absent so that she thought herself loved no more by Robert. She was weary of thinking and acting on her own responsibility, and would gladly have abandoned her will; yet her judgement, if she was still to exercise it, told her that the step she was bidden to take was one, the direct consequence and the fruit of her other resolute steps. Pride whispered, "You could compel your sister to do that which she abhorred;" and Pity pleaded for her poor old uncle Anthony. She looked back in imagination at that scene with him in London, amazed at her frenzy of power, and again, from that contemplation, amazed at her present nervelessness.

"I am not fit to be my own mistress," she said.

"Then, the sooner you decide the better," observed Robert, and the room became hot and narrow to him.

"Very little time is given me," she murmured. The sound was like a whimper; exasperating to one who had witnessed her remorseless energy.

"I dare say you won't find the hardship so great," said he.

"Because," she looked up quickly, "I went out one day to meet him? Do you mean that, Robert? I went to hear news of my sister. I had received no letters from her. And he wrote to say that he could tell me about her. My uncle took me once to the Bank. I saw him there first. He spoke of Wrexby, and of my sister. It is pleasant to inexperienced girls to hear themselves praised. Since the day when you told me to turn back I have always respected you."

Her eyelids lowered softly.

Could she have humbled herself more? But she had, at the same time, touched his old wound: and his rival then was the wooer now, rich, and a gentleman. And this room, Robert thought as he looked about it, was the room in which she had refused him, when he first asked her to be his.

"I think," he said, "I've never begged your pardon for the last occasion of our being alone here together. I've had my arm round you. Don't be frightened. That's my marriage, and there was my wife. And there's an end of my likings and my misconduct. Forgive me for calling it to mind."

"No, no, Robert," Rhoda lifted her hands, and, startled by the impulse, dropped them, saying: "What forgiveness? Was I ever angry with you?"

A look of tenderness accompanied the words, and grew into a dusky crimson rose under his eyes.

"When you went into the wood, I saw you going: I knew it was for some good object," he said, and flushed equally.

But, by the recurrence to that scene, he had checked her sensitive developing emotion. She hung a moment in languor, and that oriental warmth of colour ebbed away from her cheeks.

"You are very kind," said she.

Then he perceived in dimmest fashion that possibly a chance had come to ripeness, withered, and fallen, within the late scoffing seconds of time. Enraged at his blindness, and careful, lest he had wrongly guessed, not to expose his regret (the man was a lover), he remarked, both truthfully and hypocritically: "I've always thought you were born to be a lady." (You had that ambition, young madam.)

She answered: "That's what I don't understand." (Your saying it, O my friend!)

"You will soon take to your new duties." (You have small objection to them even now.)

"Yes, or my life won't be worth much." (Know, that you are driving me to it.)

"And I wish you happiness, Rhoda." (You are madly imperilling the prospect thereof.)

To each of them the second meaning stood shadowy behind the utterances. And further,—

"Thank you, Robert." (I shall have to thank you for the issue.)

"Now it's time to part." (Do you not see that there's a danger for me in remaining?)

"Good night." (Behold, I am submissive.)

"Good night, Rhoda." (You were the first to give the signal of parting.)

"Good night." (I am simply submissive.)

"Why not my name? Are you hurt with me?"

Rhoda choked. The indirectness of speech had been a shelter to her, permitting her to hint at more than she dared clothe in words.

Again the delicious dusky rose glowed beneath his eyes.

But he had put his hand out to her, and she had not taken it.

"What have I done to offend you? I really don't know, Rhoda."

"Nothing." The flower had closed.

He determined to believe that she was gladdened at heart by the prospect of a fine marriage, and now began to discourse of Anthony's delinquency, saying,—

"It was not money taken for money's sake: any one can see that. It was half clear to me, when you told me about it, that the money was not his to give, but I've got the habit of trusting you to be always correct."

"And I never am," said Rhoda, vexed at him and at herself.

"Women can't judge so well about money matters. Has your uncle no account of his own at the Bank? He was thought to be a bit of a miser."

"What he is, or what he was, I can't guess. He has not been near the Bank since that day; nor to his home. He has wandered down on his way here, sleeping in cottages. His heart seems broken. I have still a great deal of the money. I kept it, thinking it might be a protection for Dahlia. Oh! my thoughts and what I have done! Of course, I imagined him to be rich. A thousand pounds seemed a great deal to me, and very little for one who was rich. If I had reflected at all, I must have seen that Uncle Anthony would never have carried so much through the streets. I was like a fiend for money. I must have been acting wrongly. Such a craving as that is a sign of evil."

"What evil there is, you're going to mend, Rhoda."

"I sell myself, then."

"Hardly so bad as that. The money will come from you instead of from your uncle."

Rhoda bent forward in her chair, with her elbows on her knees, like a man brooding. Perhaps, it was right that the money should come from her. And how could she have hoped to get the money by any other means? Here at least was a positive escape from perplexity. It came at the right moment; was it a help divine? What cowardice had been prompting her to evade it? After all, could it be a dreadful step that she was required to take?

Her eyes met Robert's, and he said startlingly: "Just like a woman!"

"Why?" but she had caught the significance, and blushed with spite.

"He was the first to praise you."

"You are brutal to me, Robert."

"My name at last! You accused me of that sort of thing before, in this room."

Rhoda stood up. "I will wish you good night."

"And now you take my hand."

"Good night," they uttered simultaneously; but Robert did not give up the hand he had got in his own. His eyes grew sharp, and he squeezed the fingers.

"I'm bound," she cried.

"Once!" Robert drew her nearer to him.

"Let me go."

"Once!" he reiterated. "Rhoda, as I've never kissed you—once!"

"No: don't anger me."

"No one has ever kissed you?"

"Never."

"Then, I—" His force was compelling the straightened figure.

Had he said, "Be mine!" she might have softened to his embrace; but there was no fire of divining love in her bosom to perceive her lover's meaning. She read all his words as a placard on a board, and revolted from the outrage of submitting her lips to one who was not to be her husband. His jealousy demanded that gratification foremost. The "Be mine!" was ready enough to follow.

"Let me go, Robert."

She was released. The cause for it was the opening of the door. Anthony stood there.

A more astounding resemblance to the phantasm of a dream was never presented. He was clad in a manner to show forth the condition of his wits, in partial night and day attire: one of the farmer's nightcaps was on his head, surmounted by his hat. A confused recollection of the necessity for trousers, had made him draw on those garments sufficiently to permit of the movement of his short legs, at which point their subserviency to the uses ended. Wrinkled with incongruous clothing from head to foot, and dazed by the light, he peered on them, like a mouse magnified and petrified.

"Dearest uncle!" Rhoda went to him.

Anthony nodded, pointing to the door leading out of the house.

"I just want to go off—go off. Never you mind me. I'm only going off."

"You must go to your bed, uncle."

"Oh, Lord! no. I'm going off, my dear. I've had sleep enough for forty. I—" he turned his mouth to Rhoda's ear, "I don't want t' see th' old farmer." And, as if he had given a conclusive reason for his departure, he bored towards the door, repeating it, and bawling additionally, "in the morning."

"You have seen him, uncle. You have seen him. It's over," said Rhoda.

Anthony whispered: "I don't want t' see th' old farmer."

"But, you have seen him, uncle."

"In the morning, my dear. Not in the morning. He'll be looking and asking, 'Where away, brother Tony?' 'Where's your banker's book, brother Tony?' 'How's money-market, brother Tony?' I can't see th' old farmer."

It was impossible to avoid smiling: his imitation of the farmer's country style was exact.

She took his hands, and used every persuasion she could think of to induce him to return to his bed; nor was he insensible to argument, or superior to explanation.

"Th' old farmer thinks I've got millions, my dear. You can't satisfy him. He... I don't want t' see him in the morning. He thinks I've got millions. His mouth'll go down. I don't want... You don't want him to look... And I can't count now; I can't count a bit. And every post I see 's a policeman. I ain't hiding. Let 'em take the old man. And he was a faithful servant, till one day he got up on a regular whirly-go-round, and ever since...such a little boy! I'm frightened o' you, Rhoda."

"I will do everything for you," said Rhoda, crying wretchedly.

"Because, the young squire says," Anthony made his voice mysterious.

"Yes, yes," Rhoda stopped him; "and I consent:" she gave a hurried half-glance behind her. "Come, uncle. Oh! pity! don't let me think your reason's gone. I can get you the money, but if you go foolish, I cannot help you."

Her energy had returned to her with the sense of sacrifice. Anthony eyed her tears. "We've sat on a bank and cried together, haven't we?" he said. "And counted ants, we have. Shall we sit in the sun together to-morrow? Say, we shall. Shall we? A good long day in the sun and nobody looking at me 's my pleasure."

Rhoda gave him the assurance, and he turned and went upstairs with her, docile at the prospect of hours to be passed in the sunlight.

Yet, when morning came, he had disappeared. Robert also was absent from the breakfast-table. The farmer made no remarks, save that he reckoned Master Gammon was right—in allusion to the veteran's somnolent observation overnight; and strange things were acted before his eyes.

There came by the morning delivery of letters one addressed to "Miss Fleming." He beheld his daughters rise, put their hands out, and claim it, in a breath; and they gazed upon one another like the two women demanding the babe from the justice of the Wise King. The letter was placed in Rhoda's hand; Dahlia laid hers on it. Their mouths were shut; any one not looking at them would have been unaware that a supreme conflict was going on in the room. It was a strenuous wrestle of their eyeballs, like the "give way" of athletes pausing. But the delirious beat down the constitutional strength. A hard bright smile ridged the hollow of Dahlia's cheeks. Rhoda's dark eyes shut; she let go her hold, and Dahlia thrust the letter in against her bosom, snatched it out again, and dipped her face to roses in a jug, and kissing Mrs. Sumfit, ran from the room for a single minute; after which she came back smiling with gravely joyful eyes and showing a sedate readiness to eat and conclude the morning meal.

What did this mean? The farmer could have made allowance for Rhoda's behaving so, seeing that she notoriously possessed intellect; and he had the habit of charging all freaks and vagaries of manner upon intellect.

But Dahlia was a soft creature, without this apology for extravagance, and what right had she to letters addressed to "Miss Fleming?" The farmer prepared to ask a question, and was further instigated to it by seeing Mrs. Sumfit's eyes roll sympathetic under a burden of overpowering curiosity and bewilderment. On the point of speaking, he remembered that he had pledged his word to ask no questions; he feared to—that was the secret; he had put his trust in Rhoda's assurance, and shrank from a spoken suspicion. So, checking himself, he broke out upon Mrs. Sumfit: "Now, then, mother!" which caused her to fluster guiltily, she having likewise given her oath to be totally unquestioning, even as was Master Gammon, whom she watched with a deep envy. Mrs. Sumfit excused the anxious expression of her face by saying that she was thinking of her dairy, whither, followed by the veteran, she retired.

Rhoda stood eyeing Dahlia, nerved to battle against the contents of that letter, though in the first conflict she had been beaten. "Oh, this curse of love!" she thought in her heart; and as Dahlia left the room, flushed, stupefied, and conscienceless, Rhoda the more readily told her father the determination which was the result of her interview with Robert.

No sooner had she done so, than a strange fluttering desire to look on Robert awoke within her bosom. She left the house, believing that she went abroad to seek her uncle, and walked up a small grass-knoll, a little beyond the farm-yard, from which she could see green corn-tracts and the pastures by the river, the river flowing oily under summer light, and the slow-footed cows, with their heads bent to the herbage; far-away sheep, and white hawthorn bushes, and deep hedge-ways bursting out of the trimness of the earlier season; and a nightingale sang among the hazels near by.

This scene of unthrobbing peacefulness was beheld by Rhoda with her first conscious delight in it. She gazed round on the farm, under a quick new impulse of affection for her old home. And whose hand was it that could alone sustain the working of the farm, and had done so, without reward? Her eyes travelled up to Wrexby Hall, perfectly barren of any feeling that she was to enter the place, aware only that it was full of pain for her. She accused herself, but could not accept the charge of her having ever hoped for transforming events that should twist and throw the dear old farm-life long back into the fields of memory. Nor could she understand the reason of her continued coolness to Robert. Enough of accurate reflection was given her to perceive that discontent with her station was the original cause of her discontent now. What she had sown she was reaping:—and wretchedly colourless are these harvests of our dream! The sun has not shone on them. They may have a tragic blood-hue, as with Dahlia's; but they will never have any warm, and fresh, and nourishing sweetness—the juice which is in a single blade of grass.

A longing came upon Rhoda to go and handle butter. She wished to smell it as Mrs. Sumfit drubbed and patted and flattened and rounded it in the dairy; and she ran down the slope, meeting her father at the gate. He was dressed in his brushed suit, going she knew whither, and when he asked if she had seen her uncle, she gave for answer a plain negative, and longed more keenly to be at work with her hands, and to smell the homely creamy air under the dairy-shed.

CHAPTER XLIV

THE ENEMY APPEARS

She watched her father as he went across the field and into the lane. Her breathing was suppressed till he appeared in view at different points, more and more distant, and then she sighed heavily, stopped her breathing, and hoped her unshaped hope again. The last time he was in sight, she found herself calling to him with a voice like that of a burdened sleeper: her thought being, "How can you act so cruelly to Robert!" He passed up Wrexby Heath, and over the black burnt patch where the fire had caught the furzes on a dry Maynight, and sank on the side of the Hall.

When we have looked upon a picture of still green life with a troubled soul, and the blow falls on us, we accuse Nature of our own treachery to her. Rhoda hurried from the dairy-door to shut herself up in her room and darken the light surrounding her. She had turned the lock, and was about systematically to pull down the blind, when the marvel of beholding Dahlia stepping out of the garden made her for a moment less the creature of her sickened senses. Dahlia was dressed for a walk, and she went very fast. The same paralysis of motion afflicted Rhoda as when she was gazing after her father; but her hand stretched out instinctively for her bonnet when Dahlia had crossed the green and the mill-bridge, and was no more visible. Rhoda drew her bonnet on, and caught her black silk mantle in her hand, and without strength to throw it across her shoulders, dropped before her bed, and uttered a strange prayer. "Let her die rather than go back to disgrace, my God! my God!"

She tried to rise, and failed in the effort, and superstitiously renewed her prayer. "Send death to her rather!"—and Rhoda's vision under her shut eyes conjured up clouds and lightnings, and spheres in conflagration.

There is nothing so indicative of fevered or of bad blood as the tendency to counsel the Almighty how he shall deal with his creatures. The strain of a long uncertainty, and the late feverish weeks had distempered the fine blood of the girl, and her acts and words were becoming remoter exponents of her character.

She bent her head in a blind doze that gave her strength to rise. As swiftly as she could she went in the track of her sister.

That morning, Robert had likewise received a letter. It was from Major Waring, and contained a bank-note, and a summons to London, as also an enclosure from Mrs. Boulby of Warbeach; the nature of which was an advertisement cut out of the county paper, notifying to one Robert Eccles that his aunt Anne had died, and that there was a legacy for him, to be paid over upon application. Robert crossed the fields, laughing madly at the ironical fate which favoured him a little and a little, and never enough, save just to keep him swimming.

The letter from Major Waring said:—

"I must see you immediately. Be quick and come. I begin to be of your opinion—there are some things which we must take into our own hands and deal summarily with."

"Ay!—ay!" Robert gave tongue in the clear morning air, scenting excitement and eager for it as a hound.

More was written, which he read subsequently

"I wrong," Percy's letter continued, "the best of women. She was driven to my door. There is, it seems, some hope that Dahlia will find herself free. At any rate, keep guard over her, and don't leave her. Mrs. Lovell has herself been moving to make discoveries down at Warbeach. Mr. Blancove has nearly quitted this sphere. She nursed him—I was jealous!—the word's out. Truth, courage, and suffering touch Margaret's heart.

"Yours,

"Percy."

Jumping over a bank, Robert came upon Anthony, who was unsteadily gazing at a donkey that cropped the grass by a gate.

"Here you are," said Robert, and took his arm.

Anthony struggled, though he knew the grasp was friendly; but he was led along: nor did Robert stop until they reached Greatham, five miles beyond Wrexby, where he entered the principal inn and called for wine.

"You want spirit: you want life," said Robert.

Anthony knew that he wanted no wine, whatever his needs might be. Yet the tender ecstacy of being paid for was irresistible, and he drank, saying, "Just one glass, then."

Robert pledged him. They were in a private room, of which, having ordered up three bottles of sherry, Robert locked the door. The devil was in him. He compelled Anthony to drink an equal portion with himself, alternately frightening and cajoling the old man.

"Drink, I tell you. You've robbed me, and you shall drink!"

"I haven't, I haven't," Anthony whined.

"Drink, and be silent. You've robbed me, and you shall drink! and by heaven! if you resist, I'll hand you over to bluer imps than you've ever dreamed of, old gentleman! You've robbed me, Mr. Hackbut. Drink! I tell you."

Anthony wept into his glass.

"That's a trick I could never do," said Robert, eyeing the drip of the trembling old tear pitilessly. "Your health, Mr. Hackbut. You've robbed me of my sweetheart. Never mind. Life's but the pop of a gun. Some of us flash in the pan, and they're the only ones that do no mischief. You're not one of them, sir; so you must drink, and let me see you cheerful."

By degrees, the wine stirred Anthony's blood, and he chirped feebly, as one who half remembered that he ought to be miserable. Robert listened to his maundering account of his adventure with the Bank money, sternly replenishing his glass. His attention was taken by the sight of Dahlia stepping forth from a chemist's shop in the street nearly opposite to the inn. "This is my medicine," said Robert; "and yours too," he addressed Anthony.

The sun had passed its meridian when they went into the streets again. Robert's head was high as a cock's, and Anthony leaned on his arm; performing short half-circles headlong to the front, until the mighty arm checked and uplifted him. They were soon in the fields leading to Wrexby. Robert saw two female figures far ahead. A man was hastening to join them. The women started and turned suddenly: one threw up her hands, and darkened her face. It was in the pathway of a broad meadow, deep with grass, wherein the red sorrel topped the yellow buttercup, like rust upon the season's gold. Robert hastened on. He scarce at the moment knew the man whose shoulder he seized, but he had recognised Dahlia and Rhoda, and he found himself face to face with Sedgett.

"It's you!"

"Perhaps you'll keep your hands off; before you make sure, another time."

Robert said: "I really beg your pardon. Step aside with me."

"Not while I've a ha'p'orth o' brains in my noddle," replied Sedgett, drawling an imitation of his enemy's courteous tone. "I've come for my wife. I'm just down by train, and a bit out of my way, I reckon. I'm come, and I'm in a hurry. She shall get home, and have on her things—boxes packed, and we go."

Robert waved Dahlia and Rhoda to speed homeward. Anthony had fallen against the roots of a banking elm, and surveyed the scene with philosophic abstractedness. Rhoda moved, taking Dahlia's hand.

"Stop," cried Sedgett. "Do you people here think me a fool? Eccles, you know me better 'n that. That young woman's my wife. I've come for her, I tell ye."

"You've no claim on her," Rhoda burst forth weakly, and quivered, and turned her eyes supplicatingly on Robert. Dahlia was a statue of icy fright.

"You've thrown her off, man, and sold what rights you had," said Robert, spying for the point of his person where he might grasp the wretch and keep him off.

"That don't hold in law," Sedgett nodded. "A man may get in a passion, when he finds he's been cheated, mayn't he?"

"I have your word of honour," said Rhoda; muttering, "Oh! devil come to wrong us!"

"Then, you shouldn't ha' run ferreting down in my part o' the country. You, or Eccles—I don't care who 'tis—you've been at my servants to get at my secrets. Some of you have. You've declared war. You've been trying to undermine me. That's a breach, I call it. Anyhow, I've come for my wife. I'll have her."

"None of us, none of us; no one has been to your house," said Rhoda, vehemently. "You live in Hampshire, sir, I think; I don't know any more. I don't know where. I have not asked my sister. Oh! spare us, and go."

"No one has been down into your part of the country," said Robert, with perfect mildness.

To which Sedgett answered bluffly, "There ye lie, Bob Eccles;" and he was immediately felled by a tremendous blow. Robert strode over him, and taking Dahlia by the elbow, walked three paces on, as to set her in motion. "Off!" he cried to Rhoda, whose eyelids cowered under the blaze of his face.

It was best that her sister should be away, and she turned and walked swiftly, hurrying Dahlia, and touching her. "Oh! don't touch my arm," Dahlia said, quailing in the fall of her breath. They footed together, speechless; taking the woman's quickest gliding step. At the last stile of the fields, Rhoda saw that they were not followed. She stopped, panting: her heart and eyes were so full of that flaming creature who was her lover. Dahlia took from her bosom the letter she had won in the morning, and held it open in both hands to read it. The pause was short. Dahlia struck the letter into her bosom again, and her starved features had some of the bloom of life. She kept her right hand in her pocket, and Rhoda presently asked,—

"What have you there?"

"You are my enemy, dear, in some things," Dahlia replied, a muscular shiver passing over her.

"I think," said Rhoda, "I could get a little money to send you away. Will you go? I am full of grief for what I have done. God forgive me."

"Pray, don't speak so; don't let us talk," said Dahlia.

Scorched as she felt both in soul and body, a touch or a word was a wound to her. Yet she was the first to resume: "I think I shall be saved. I can't quite feel I am lost. I have not been so wicked as that."

Rhoda gave a loving answer, and again Dahlia shrank from the miserable comfort of words.

As they came upon the green fronting the iron gateway, Rhoda perceived that the board proclaiming the sale of Queen Anne's Farm had been removed, and now she understood her father's readiness to go up to Wrexby Hall. "He would sell me to save the farm." She reproached herself for the thought, but she could not be just; she had the image of her father plodding relentlessly over the burnt heath to the Hall, as conceived by her agonized sensations in the morning, too vividly to be just, though still she knew that her own indecision was to blame.

Master Gammon met them in the garden.

Pointing aloft, over the gateway, "That's down," he remarked, and the three green front teeth of his quiet grin were stamped on the impressionable vision of the girls in such a way that they looked at one another with a bare bitter smile. Once it would have been mirth.

"Tell father," Dahlia said, when they were at the back doorway, and her eyes sparkled piteously, and she bit on her underlip. Rhoda tried to detain her; but Dahlia repeated, "Tell father," and in strength and in will had become more than a match for her sister.

CHAPTER XLV

THE FARMER IS AWAKENED

Rhoda spoke to her father from the doorway, with her hand upon the lock of the door.

At first he paid little attention to her, and, when he did so, began by saying that he hoped she knew that she was bound to have the young squire, and did not intend to be prankish and wilful; because the young squire was eager to settle affairs, that he might be settled himself. "I don't deny it's honour to us, and it's a comfort," said the farmer. "This is the first morning I've thought easily in my chair for years. I'm sorry about Robert, who's a twice unlucky 'un; but you aimed at something higher, I suppose."

Rhoda was prompted to say a word in self-defence, but refrained, and again she told Dahlia's story, wondering that her father showed no excitement of any kind. On the contrary, there was the dimple of one of his voiceless chuckles moving about the hollow of one cheek, indicating some slow contemplative action that was not unpleasant within. He said: "Ah! well, it's very sad;—that is, if 'tis so," and no more, for a time.

She discovered that he was referring to her uncle Anthony, concerning whose fortunate position in the world, he was beginning to entertain some doubts. "Or else," said the farmer, with a tap on his forehead, "he's going here. It 'd be odd after all, if commercially, as he 'd call it, his despised brother-in-law—and I say it in all kindness—should turn out worth, not exactly millions, but worth a trifle."

The farmer nodded with an air of deprecating satisfaction.

Rhoda did not gain his ear until, as by an instinct, she perceived what interest the story of her uncle and the money-bags would have for him. She related it, and he was roused. Then, for the third time, she told him of Dahlia.

Rhoda saw her father's chest grow large, while his eyes quickened with light. He looked on her with quite a strange face. Wrath, and a revived apprehension, and a fixed will were expressed in it, and as he catechized her for each particular of the truth which had been concealed from him, she felt a respectfulness that was new in her personal sensations toward her father, but it was at the expense of her love.

When he had heard and comprehended all, he said, "Send the girl down to me."

But Rhoda pleaded, "She is too worn, she is tottering. She cannot endure a word on this; not even of kindness and help."

"Then, you," said the farmer, "you tell her she's got a duty's her first duty now. Obedience to her husband! Do you hear? Then, let her hear it. Obedience to her husband! And welcome's the man when he calls on me. He's welcome. My doors are open to him. I thank him. I honour him. I bless his name. It's to him I owe—You go up to her and say, her father owes it to the young man who's married her that he can lift up his head. Go aloft. Ay! for years I've been suspecting something of this. I tell ye, girl, I don't understand about church doors and castin' of her off—he's come for her, hasn't he? Then, he shall have her. I tell ye, I don't understand about money: he's married her. Well, then, she's his wife; and how can he bargain not to see her?"

"The base wretch!" cried Rhoda.

"Hasn't he married her?" the farmer retorted. "Hasn't he given the poor creature a name? I'm not for abusing her, but him I do thank, and I say, when he calls, here's my hand for him. Here, it's out and waiting for him."

"Father, if you let me see it—" Rhoda checked the intemperate outburst. "Father, this is a bad—a bad man. He is a very wicked man. We were all deceived by him. Robert knows him. He has known him for years, and knows that he is very wicked. This man married our Dahlia to get—" Rhoda gasped, and could not speak it. "He flung her off with horrible words at the church door. After this, how can he claim her? I paid him all he had to expect with uncle's money, for his promise by his sacred oath never, never to disturb or come near my sister. After that he can't, can't claim her. If he does—"

"He's her husband," interrupted the farmer; "when he comes here, he's welcome. I say he's welcome. My hand's out to him:—If it's alone that he's saved the name of Fleming from disgrace! I thank him, and my daughter belongs to him. Where is he now? You talk of a scuffle with Robert. I do hope Robert will not forget his proper behaviour. Go you up to your sister, and say from me—All's forgotten and forgiven; say, It's all underfoot; but she must learn to be a good girl from this day. And, if she's at the gate to welcome her husband, so much the better 'll her father be pleased;—say that. I want to see the man. It'll gratify me to feel her husband's flesh and blood. His being out of sight so long's been a sore at my heart; and when I see him I'll welcome him, and so must all in my house."

This was how William Fleming received the confession of his daughter's unhappy plight.

Rhoda might have pleaded Dahlia's case better, but that she was too shocked and outraged by the selfishness she saw in her father, and the partial desire to scourge which she was too intuitively keen at the moment not to perceive in the paternal forgiveness, and in the stipulation of the forgiveness.

She went upstairs to Dahlia, simply stating that their father was aware of all the circumstances.

Dahlia looked at her, but dared ask nothing.

So the day passed. Neither Robert nor Anthony appeared. The night came: all doors were locked. The sisters that night slept together, feeling the very pulses of the hours; yet neither of them absolutely hopelessly, although in a great anguish.

Rhoda was dressed by daylight. The old familiar country about the house lay still as if it knew no expectation. She observed Master Gammon tramping forth afield, and presently heard her father's voice below. All the machinery of the daily life got into motion; but it was evident that Robert and Anthony continued to be absent. A thought struck her that Robert had killed the man. It came with a flash of joy that was speedily terror, and she fell to praying vehemently and vaguely. Dahlia lay exhausted on the bed, but nigh the hour when letters were delivered, she sat up, saying, "There is one for me; get it."

There was in truth a letter for her below, and it was in her father's hand and open.

"Come out," said the farmer, as Rhoda entered to him. When they were in the garden, he commanded her to read and tell him the meaning of it. The letter was addressed to Dahlia Fleming.

"It's for my sister," Rhoda murmured, in anger, but more in fear.

She was sternly bidden to read, and she read,—

Dahlia,—There is mercy for us. You are not lost to me.

"Edward."

After this, was appended in a feminine hand:—

"There is really hope. A few hours will tell us. But keep firm. If he comes near you, keep from him. You are not his. Run, hide, go anywhere, if you have reason to think he is near. I dare not write what it is we expect. Yesterday I told you to hope; to-day I can say, believe that you will be saved. You are not lost. Everything depends on your firmness.

"Margaret L."

Rhoda lifted up her eyes.

The farmer seized the letter, and laid his finger on the first signature.

"Is that the christian name of my girl's seducer?"

He did not wait for an answer, but turned and went into the breakfast-table, when he ordered a tray with breakfast for Dahlia to betaken up to her bed-room; and that done, he himself turned the key of the door, and secured her. Mute woe was on Mrs. Sumfit's face at all these strange doings, but none heeded her, and she smothered her lamentations. The farmer spoke nothing either of Robert or of Anthony. He sat in his chair till the dinner hour, without book or pipe, without occupation for eyes or hands; silent, but acute in his hearing.

The afternoon brought relief to Rhoda's apprehensions. A messenger ran up to the farm bearing a pencilled note to her from Robert, which said that he, in company with her uncle, was holding Sedgett at a distance by force of arm, and that there was no fear. Rhoda kissed the words, hurrying away to the fields for a few minutes to thank and bless and dream of him who had said that there was no fear. She knew that Dahlia was unconscious of her imprisonment, and had less compunction in counting the minutes of her absence. The sun spread in yellow and fell in red before she thought of returning, so sweet it had become to her to let her mind dwell with Robert; and she was half a stranger to the mournfulness of the house when she set her steps homeward. But when she lifted the latch of the gate, a sensation, prompted by some unwitting self-accusal, struck her with alarm. She passed into the room, and beheld her father, and Mrs. Sumfit, who was sitting rolling, with her apron over her head.

The man Sedgett was between them.

CHAPTER XLVI

WHEN THE NIGHT IS DARKEST

No sooner had Rhoda appeared than her father held up the key of Dahlia's bed-room, and said, "Unlock your sister, and fetch her down to her husband."

Mechanically Rhoda took the key.

"And leave our door open," he added.

She went up to Dahlia, sick with a sudden fright lest evil had come to Robert, seeing that his enemy was here; but that was swept from her by Dahlia's aspect.

"He is in the house," Dahlia said; and asked, "Was there no letter—no letter; none, this morning?"

Rhoda clasped her in her arms, seeking to check the convulsions of her trembling.

"No letter! no letter! none? not any? Oh! no letter for me!"

The strange varying tones of musical interjection and interrogation were pitiful to hear.

"Did you look for a letter?" said Rhoda, despising herself for so speaking.

"He is in the house! Where is my letter?"

"What was it you hoped? what was it you expected, darling?"

Dahlia moaned: "I don't know. I'm blind. I was told to hope. Yesterday I had my letter, and it told me to hope. He is in the house!"

"Oh, my dear, my love!" cried Rhoda; "come down a minute. See him. It is father's wish. Come only for a minute. Come, to gain time, if there is hope."

"But there was no letter for me this morning, Rhoda. I can't hope. I am lost. He is in the house!"

"Dearest, there was a letter," said Rhoda, doubting that she did well in revealing it.

Dahlia put out her hands dumb for the letter.

"Father opened it, and read it, and keeps it," said Rhoda, clinging tight to the stricken form.

"Then, he is against me? Oh, my letter!" Dahlia wrung her hands.

While they were speaking, their father's voice was heard below calling for Dahlia to descend. He came thrice to the foot of the stairs, and shouted for her.

The third time he uttered a threat that sprang an answer from her bosom in shrieks.

Rhoda went out on the landing and said softly, "Come up to her, father."

After a little hesitation, he ascended the stairs.

"Why, girl, I only ask you to come down and see your husband," he remarked with an attempt at kindliness of tone. "What's the harm, then? Come and see him; that's all; come and see him."

Dahlia was shrinking out of her father's sight as he stood in the doorway. "Say," she communicated to Rhoda, "say, I want my letter."

"Come!" William Fleming grew impatient.

"Let her have her letter, father," said Rhoda. "You have no right to withhold it."

"That letter, my girl" (he touched Rhoda's shoulder as to satisfy her that he was not angry), "that letter's where it ought to be. I've puzzled out the meaning of it. That letter's in her husband's possession."

Dahlia, with her ears stretching for all that might be uttered, heard this. Passing round the door, she fronted her father.

"My letter gone to him!" she cried. "Shameful old man! Can you look on me? Father, could you give it? I'm a dead woman."

She smote her bosom, stumbling backward upon Rhoda's arm.

"You have been a wicked girl," the ordinarily unmoved old man retorted. "Your husband has come for you, and you go with him. Know that, and let me hear no threats. He's a modest-minded, quiet young man, and a farmer like myself, and needn't be better than he is. Come you down to him at once. I'll tell you: he comes to take you away, and his cart's at the gate. To the gate you go with him. When next I see you—you visiting me or I visiting you—I shall see a respected creature, and not what you have been and want to be. You have racked the household with fear and shame for years. Now come, and carry out what you've begun in the contrary direction. You've got my word o' command, dead woman or live woman. Rhoda, take one elbow of your sister. Your aunt's coming up to pack her box. I say I'm determined, and no one stops me when I say that. Come out, Dahlia, and let our parting be like between parent and child. Here's the dark falling, and your husband's anxious to be away. He has business, and 'll hardly get you to the station for the last train to town. Hark at him below! He's naturally astonished, he is, and you're trying his temper, as you'd try any man's. He wants to be off. Come, and when next we meet I shall see you a happy wife."

He might as well have spoken to a corpse.

"Speak to her still, father," said Rhoda, as she drew a chair upon which she leaned her sister's body, and ran down full of the power of hate and loathing to confront Sedgett; but great as was that power within her, it was overmatched by his brutal resolution to take his wife away. No argument, no irony, no appeals, can long withstand the iteration of a dogged phrase. "I've come for my wife," Sedgett said to all her instances. His voice was waxing loud and insolent, and, as it sounded, Mrs. Sumfit moaned and flapped her apron.

"Then, how could you have married him?"

They heard the farmer's roar of this unanswerable thing, aloft.

"Yes—how! how!" cried Rhoda below, utterly forgetting the part she had played in the marriage.

"It's too late to hate a man when you've married him, my girl."

Sedgett went out to the foot of the stairs.

"Mr. Fleming—she's my wife. I'll teach her about hating and loving. I'll behave well to her, I swear. I'm in the midst of enemies; but I say I do love my wife, and I've come for her, and have her I will. Now, in two minutes' time. Mr. Fleming, my cart's at the gate, and I've got business, and she's my wife."

The farmer called for Mrs. Sumfit to come up and pack Dahlia's box, and the forlorn woman made her way to the bedroom. All the house was silent. Rhoda closed her sight, and she thought: "Does God totally abandon us?"

She let her father hear: "Father, you know that you are killing your child."

"I hear ye, my lass," said he.

"She will die, father."

"I hear ye, I hear ye."

"She will die, father."

He stamped furiously, exclaiming: "Who's got the law of her better and above a husband? Hear reason, and come and help and fetch down your sister. She goes!"

"Father!" Rhoda cried, looking at her open hands, as if she marvelled to see them helpless.

There was for a time that silence which reigns in a sickchamber when the man of medicine takes the patient's wrist. And in the silence came a blessed sound—the lifting of a latch. Rhoda saw Robert's face.

"So," said Robert, as she neared him, "you needn't tell me what's happened. Here's the man, I see. He dodged me cleverly. The hound wants practice; the fox is born with his cunning."

Few words were required to make him understand the position of things in the house. Rhoda spoke out all without hesitation in Sedgett's hearing.

But the farmer respected Robert enough to come down to him and explain his views of his duty and his daughter's duty. By the kitchen firelight he and Robert and Sedgett read one another's countenances.

"He has a proper claim to take his wife, Robert," said the farmer. "He's righted her before the world, and I thank him; and if he asks for her of me he must have her, and he shall."

"All right, sir," replied Robert, "and I say too, shall, when I'm stiff as log-wood."

"Oh! Robert, Robert!" Rhoda cried in great joy.

"Do you mean that you step 'twixt me and my own?" said Mr. Fleming.

"I won't let you nod at downright murder—that's all," said Robert. "She—Dahlia, take the hand of that creature!"

"Why did she marry me?" thundered Sedgett.

"There's one o' the wonders!" Robert rejoined. "Except that you're an amazingly clever hypocrite with women; and she was just half dead and had no will of her own; and some one set you to hunt her down. I tell you, Mr. Fleming, you might as well send your daughter to the hangman as put her in this fellow's hands."

"She's his wife, man."

"May be," Robert assented.

"You, Robert Eccles!" said Sedgett hoarsely; "I've come for my wife—do you hear?"

"You have, I dare say," returned Robert. "You dodged me cleverly, that you did. I'd like to know how it was done. I see you've got a cart outside and a boy at the horse's head. The horse steps well, does he? I'm about three hours behind him, I reckon:—not too late, though!"

He let fall a great breath of weariness.

Rhoda went to the cupboard and drew forth a rarely touched bottle of spirits, with which she filled a small glass, and handing the glass to him, said, "Drink." He smiled kindly and drank it off.

"The man's in your house, Mr. Fleming," he said.

"And he's my guest, and my daughter's husband, remember that," said the farmer.

"And mean to wait not half a minute longer till I've taken her off—mark that," Sedgett struck in. "Now, Mr. Fleming, you see you keep good your word to me."

"I'll do no less," said the farmer. He went into the passage shouting for Mrs. Sumfit to bring down the box.

"She begs," Mrs. Sumfit answered to him—"She begs, William, on'y a short five minutes to pray by herself, which you will grant unto her, dear, you will. Lord! what's come upon us?"

"Quick, and down with the box, then, mother," he rejoined.

The box was dragged out, and Dahlia's door was shut, that she might have her last minutes alone.

Rhoda kissed her sister before leaving her alone: and so cold were Dahlia's lips, so tight the clutch of her hands, that she said: "Dearest, think of God:" and Dahlia replied: "I do."

"He will not forsake you," Rhoda said.

Dahlia nodded, with shut eyes, and Rhoda went forth.

"And now, Robert, you and I'll see who's master on these premises," said the farmer. "Hear, all! I'm bounders under a sacred obligation to the husband of my child, and the Lord's wrath on him who interferes and lifts his hand against me when I perform my sacred duty as a father. Place there! I'm going to open the door. Rhoda, see to your sister's bonnet and things. Robert, stand out of my way. There's no refreshment of any sort you'll accept of before starting, Mr. Sedgett? None at all! That's no fault of my hospitality. Stand out of my way, Robert."

He was obeyed. Robert looked at Rhoda, but had no reply for her gaze of despair.

The farmer threw the door wide open.

There were people in the garden—strangers. His name was inquired for out of the dusk. Then whisperings were heard passing among the ill-discerned forms, and the farmer went out to them. Robert listened keenly, but the touch of Rhoda's hand upon his own distracted his hearing. "Yet it must be!" he said. "Why does she come here?"

Both he and Rhoda followed the farmer's steps, drawn forth by the ever-credulous eagerness which arises from an interruption to excited wretchedness. Near and nearer to the group, they heard a quaint old woman exclaim: "Come here to you for a wife, when he has one of his own at home; a poor thing he shipped off to America, thinking himself more cunning than devils or angels: and she got put out at a port, owing to stress of weather, to defeat the man's wickedness! Can't I prove it to you, sir, he's a married man, which none of us in our village knew till the poor tricked thing crawled back penniless to find him;—and there she is now with such a story of his cunning to tell to anybody as will listen; and why he kept it secret to get her pension paid him still on. It's all such a tale for you to hear by-and-by."

Robert burst into a glorious laugh.

"Why, mother! Mrs. Boulby! haven't you got a word for me?"

"My blessedest Robert!" the good woman cried, as she rushed up to kiss him. "Though it wasn't to see you I came exactly." She whispered: "The Major and the good gentleman—they're behind. I travelled down with them. Dear,—you'd like to know:—Mrs. Lovell sent her little cunning groom down to Warbeach just two weeks back to make inquiries about that villain; and the groom left me her address, in case, my dear, when the poor creature—his true wife—crawled home, and we knew of her at Three-Tree Farm and knew her story. I wrote word at once, I did, to Mrs. Lovell, and the sweet good lady sent down her groom to fetch me to you to make things clear here. You shall understand them soon. It's Providence at work. I do believe that now there's a chance o' punishing the wicked ones."

The figure of Rhoda with two lights in her hand was seen in the porch, and by the shadowy rays she beheld old Anthony leaning against the house, and Major Waring with a gentleman beside him close upon the gate.

At the same time a sound of wheels was heard.

Robert rushed back into the great parlour-kitchen, and finding it empty, stamped with vexation. His prey had escaped.

But there was no relapse to give spare thoughts to that pollution of the house. It had passed. Major Waring was talking earnestly to Mr. Fleming, who held his head low, stupefied, and aware only of the fact that it was a gentleman imparting to him strange matters. By degrees all were beneath the farmer's roof—all, save one, who stood with bowed head by the threshold.

There is a sort of hero, and a sort of villain, to this story: they are but instruments. Hero and villain are combined in the person of Edward, who was now here to abase himself before the old man and the family he had injured, and to kneel penitently at the feet of the woman who had just reason to spurn him. He had sold her as a slave is sold; he had seen her plunged into the blackest pit; yet was she miraculously kept pure for him, and if she could give him her pardon, might still be his. The grief for which he could ask no compassion had at least purified him to meet her embrace. The great agony he had passed through of late had killed his meaner pride. He stood there ready to come forward and ask forgiveness from unfriendly faces, and beg that he might be in Dahlia's eyes once—that he might see her once.

He had grown to love her with the fullest force of a selfish, though not a common, nature. Or rather he had always loved her, and much of the selfishness had fallen away from his love. It was not the highest form of love, but the love was his highest development. He had heard that Dahlia, lost to him, was free. Something like the mortal yearning to look upon the dead risen to life, made it impossible for him to remain absent and in doubt. He was ready to submit to every humiliation that he might see the rescued features; he was willing to pay all his penalties. Believing, too, that he was forgiven, he knew that Dahlia's heart would throb for him to be near her, and he had come.

The miraculous agencies which had brought him and Major Waring and Mrs. Boulby to the farm, that exalted woman was relating to Mrs. Sumfit in another part of the house.

The farmer, and Percy, and Robert were in the family sitting-room, when, after an interval, William Fleming said aloud, "Come in, sir," and Edward stepped in among them.

Rhoda was above, seeking admittance to her sisters door, and she heard her father utter that welcome. It froze her limbs, for still she hated the evil-doer. Her hatred of him was a passion. She crouched over the stairs, listening to a low and long-toned voice monotonously telling what seemed to be one sole thing over and over, without variation, in the room where the men were. Words were indistinguishable. Thrice, after calling to Dahlia and getting no response, she listened again, and awe took her soul at last, for, abhorred as he was by her, his power was felt: she comprehended something of that earnestness which made the offender speak of his wrongful deeds, and his shame, and his remorse, before his fellow-men, straight out and calmly, like one who has been plunged up to the middle in the fires of the abyss, and is thereafter insensible to meaner pains. The voice ended. She was then aware that it had put a charm upon her ears. The other voices following it sounded dull.

"Has he—can he have confessed in words all his wicked baseness?" she thought, and in her soul the magnitude of his crime threw a gleam of splendour on his courage, even at the bare thought that he might have done this. Feeling that Dahlia was saved, and thenceforth at liberty to despise him and torture him, Rhoda the more readily acknowledged that it might be a true love for her sister animating him. From the height of a possible vengeance it was perceptible.

She turned to her sister's door and knocked at it, calling to her, "Safe, safe!" but there came no answer; and she was half glad, for she had a fear that in the quick revulsion of her sister's feelings, mere earthly love would act like heavenly charity, and Edward would find himself forgiven only too instantly and heartily.

In the small musk-scented guest's parlour, Mrs. Boulby was giving Mrs. Sumfit and poor old sleepy Anthony the account of the miraculous discovery of Sedgett's wickedness, which had vindicated all one hoped for from Above; as also the narration of the stabbing of her boy, and the heroism and great-heartedness of Robert. Rhoda listened to her for a space, and went to her sister's door again; but when she stood outside the kitchen she found all voices silent within.

It was, in truth, not only very difficult for William Fleming to change his view of the complexion of circumstances as rapidly as circumstances themselves changed, but it was very bitter for him to look upon Edward, and to see him in the place of Sedgett.

He had been struck dumb by the sudden revolution of affairs in his house; and he had been deferentially convinced by Major Waring's tone that he ought rightly to give his hearing to an unknown young gentleman against whom anger was due. He had listened to Edward without one particle of comprehension, except of the fact that his behaviour was extraordinary. He understood that every admission made by Edward with such grave and strange directness, would justly have condemned him to punishment which the culprit's odd, and upright, and even-toned self-denunciation rendered it impossible to think of inflicting. He knew likewise that a whole history was being narrated to him, and that, although the other two listeners manifestly did not approve it, they expected him to show some tolerance to the speaker.

He said once, "Robert, do me the favour to look about outside for t' other." Robert answered him, that the man was far away by this time.

The farmer suggested that he might be waiting to say his word presently.

"Don't you know you've been dealing with a villain, sir?" cried Robert. "Throw ever so little light upon one of that breed, and they skulk in a hurry. Mr. Fleming, for the sake of your honour, don't mention him again. What you're asked to do now, is to bury the thoughts of him."

"He righted my daughter when there was shame on her," the farmer replied.

That was the idea printed simply on his understanding.

For Edward to hear it was worse than a scourging with rods. He bore it, telling the last vitality of his pride to sleep, and comforting himself with the drowsy sensuous expectation that he was soon to press the hand of his lost one, his beloved, who was in the house, breathing the same air with him; was perhaps in the room above, perhaps sitting impatiently with clasped fingers, waiting for the signal to unlock them and fling them open. He could imagine the damp touch of very expectant fingers; the dying look of life-drinking eyes; and, oh! the helplessness of her limbs as she sat buoying a heart drowned in bliss.

It was unknown to him that the peril of her uttermost misery had been so imminent, and the picture conjured of her in his mind was that of a gentle but troubled face—a soul afflicted, yet hoping because it had been told to hope, and half conscious that a rescue, almost divine in its suddenness and unexpectedness, and its perfect clearing away of all shadows, approached.

Manifestly, by the pallid cast of his visage, he had tasted shrewd and wasting grief of late. Robert's heart melted as he beheld the change in Edward.

"I believe, Mr. Blancove, I'm a little to blame," he said. "Perhaps when I behaved so badly down at Fairly, you may have thought she sent me, and it set your heart against her for a time. I can just understand how it might."

Edward thought for a moment, and conscientiously accepted the suggestion; for, standing under that roof, with her whom he loved near him, it was absolutely out of his power for him to comprehend that his wish to break from Dahlia, and the measures he had taken or consented to, had sprung from his own unassisted temporary baseness.

Then Robert spoke to the farmer.

Rhoda could hear Robert's words. Her fear was that Dahlia might hear them too, his pleading for Edward was so hearty. "Yet why should I always think differently from Robert?" she asked herself, and with that excuse for changeing, partially thawed.

She was very anxious for her father's reply; and it was late in coming. She felt that he was unconvinced. But suddenly the door opened, and the farmer called into the darkness,—

"Dahlia down here!"

Previously emotionless, an emotion was started in Rhoda's bosom by the command, and it was gladness. She ran up and knocked, and found herself crying out: "He is here—Edward."

But there came no answer.

"Edward is here. Come, come and see him."

Still not one faint reply.

"Dahlia! Dahlia!"

The call of Dahlia's name seemed to travel endlessly on. Rhoda knelt, and putting her mouth to the door, said,—

"My darling, I know you will reply to me. I know you do not doubt me now. Listen. You are to come down to happiness."

The silence grew heavier; and now a doubt came shrieking through her soul.

"Father!" rang her outcry.

The father came; and then the lover came, and neither to father nor to lover was there any word from Dahlia's voice.

She was found by the side of the bed, inanimate, and pale as a sister of death.

But you who may have cared for her through her many tribulations, have no fear for this gentle heart. It was near the worst; yet not the worst.

CHAPTER XLVII

DAWN IS NEAR

Up to the black gates, but not beyond them. The dawn following such a night will seem more like a daughter of the night than promise of day. It is day that follows, notwithstanding: The sad fair girl survived, and her flickering life was the sole light of the household; at times burying its members in dusk, to shine on them again more like a prolonged farewell than a gladsome restoration.

She was saved by what we call chance; for it had not been in her design to save herself. The hand was firm to help her to the deadly draught. As far as could be conjectured, she had drunk it between hurried readings from her mother's Bible; the one true companion to which she had often clung, always half-availingly. The Bible was found by her side, as if it had fallen from the chair before which she knelt to read her last quickening verses, and had fallen with her. One arm was about it; one grasped the broken phial with its hideous label.

It was uncomplainingly registered among the few facts very distinctly legible in Master Gammon's memory, that for three entire weeks he had no dumplings for dinner at the farm; and although, upon a computation, articles of that description, amounting probably to sixty-three (if there is any need for our being precise), were due to him, and would necessarily be for evermore due to him, seeing that it is beyond all human and even spiritual agency to make good unto man the dinner he has lost, Master Gammon uttered no word to show that he was sensible of a slight, which was the only indication given by him of his knowledge of a calamity having changed the order of things at the farm. On the day when dumplings reappeared, he remarked, with a glance at the ceiling: "Goin' on better—eh, marm?"

"Oh! Mas' Gammon," Mrs. Sumfit burst out; "if I was only certain you said your prayers faithful every night!" The observation was apparently taken by Master Gammon to express one of the mere emotions within her bosom, for he did not reply to it.

She watched him feeding in his steady way, with the patient bent back, and slowly chopping old grey jaws, and struck by a pathos in the sight, exclaimed,—

"We've all been searched so, Mas' Gammon! I feel I know everything that's in me. I'd say, I couldn't ha' given you dumplin's and tears; but think of our wickedness, when I confess to you I did feel spiteful at you to think that you were wiltin' to eat the dumplin's while all of us mourned and rocked as in a quake, expecting the worst to befall; and that made me refuse them to you. It was cruel of me, and well may you shake your head. If I was only sure you said your prayers!"

The meaning in her aroused heart was, that if she could be sure Master Gammon said his prayers, so as to be searched all through by them, as she was herself, and to feel thereby, as she did, that he knew everything that was within him, she would then, in admiration of his profound equanimity, acknowledge him to be a superior Christian.

Naturally enough, Master Gammon allowed the interjection to pass, regarding it as simply a vagrant action of the engine of speech; while Mrs. Sumfit, with an interjector's consciousness of prodigious things implied which were not in any degree comprehended, left his presence in kindness, and with a shade less of the sense that he was a superior Christian.

Nevertheless, the sight of Master Gammon was like a comforting medicine to all who were in the house. He was Mrs. Sumfit's clock; he was balm and blessedness in Rhoda's eyes; Anthony was jealous of him; the farmer held to him as to a stake in the ground: even Robert, who rallied and tormented, and was vexed by him, admitted that he stood some way between an example and a warning, and was a study. The grand primaeval quality of unchangeableness, as exhibited by this old man, affected them singularly in their recovery from the storm and the wreck of the hours gone by; so much so that they could not divest themselves of the idea that it was a manifestation of power in Master Gammon to show forth undisturbed while they were feeling their life shaken in them to the depths. I have never had the opportunity of examining the idol-worshipping mind of a savage; but it seems possible that the immutability of aspect of his little wooden God may sometimes touch him with a similar astounded awe;—even when, and indeed especially after, he has thrashed it. Had the old man betrayed his mortality in a sign of curiosity to know why the hubbub of trouble had arisen, and who was to blame, and what was the story, the effect on them would have been diminished. He really seemed granite among the turbulent waves. "Give me Gammon's life!" was Farmer Fleming's prayerful interjection; seeing him come and go, sit at his meals, and sleep and wake in season, all through those tragic hours of suspense, without a question to anybody. Once or twice, when his eye fell upon the doctor, Master Gammon appeared to meditate. He observed that the doctor had never been called in to one of his family, and it was evident that he did not understand the complication of things which rendered the doctor's visit necessary.

"You'll never live so long as that old man," the farmer said to Robert.

"No; but when he goes, all of him's gone," Robert answered.

"But Gammon's got the wisdom to keep himself safe, Robert; there's no one to blame for his wrinkles."

"Gammon's a sheepskin old Time writes his nothings on," said Robert. "He's safe—safe enough. An old hulk doesn't very easily manage to founder in the mud, and Gammon's been lying on the mud all his life."

"Let that be how 't will," returned the farmer; "I've had days o' mortal envy of that old man."

"Well, it's whether you prefer being the fiddle or the fiddle-case," quoth Robert.

Of Anthony the farmer no longer had any envy. In him, though he was as passive as Master Gammon, the farmer beheld merely a stupefied old man, and not a steady machine. He knew that some queer misfortune had befallen Anthony.

"He'll find I'm brotherly," said Mr. Fleming; but Anthony had darkened his golden horizon for him, and was no longer an attractive object to his vision.

Upon an Autumn afternoon; Dahlia, looking like a pale Spring flower, came down among them. She told her sister that it was her wish to see Edward. Rhoda had lost all power of will, even if she had desired to keep them asunder. She mentioned Dahlia's wish to her father, who at once went for his hat, and said: "Dress yourself neat, my lass." She knew what was meant by that remark. Messages daily had been coming down from the Hall, but the rule of a discerning lady was then established there, and Rhoda had been spared a visit from either Edward or Algernon, though she knew them to be at hand. During Dahlia's convalescence, the farmer had not spoken to Rhoda of her engagement to the young squire. The great misery intervening, seemed in her mind to have cancelled all earthly engagements; and when he said that she must use care in her attire he suddenly revived a dread within her bosom, as if he had plucked her to the verge of a chasm.

But Mrs. Lovell's delicacy was still manifest: Edward came alone, and he and Dahlia were left apart.

There was no need to ask for pardon from those gentle eyes. They joined hands. She was wasted and very weak, but she did not tremble. Passion was extinguished. He refrained from speaking of their union, feeling sure that they were united. It required that he should see her to know fully the sinner he had been. Wasted though she was, he was ready to make her his own, if only for the sake of making amends to this dear fair soul, whose picture of Saint was impressed on him, first as a response to the world wondering at his sacrifice of himself, and next, by degrees, as an absolute visible fleshly fact. She had come out of her martyrdom stamped with the heavenly sign-mark.

"Those are the old trees I used to speak of," she said, pointing to the two pines in the miller's grounds. "They always look like Adam and Eve turning away."

"They do not make you unhappy to see them, Dahlia?"

"I hope to see them till I am gone."

Edward pressed her fingers. He thought that warmer hopes would soon flow into her.

"The neighbours are kind?" he asked.

"Very kind. They, inquire after me daily."

His cheeks reddened; he had spoken at random, and he wondered that Dahlia should feel it pleasurable to be inquired after, she who was so sensitive.

"The clergyman sits with me every day, and knows my heart," she added.

"The clergyman is a comfort to women," said Edward.

Dahlia looked at him gently. The round of her thin eyelids dwelt on him. She wished. She dared not speak her wish to one whose remembered mastery in words forbade her poor speechlessness. But God would hear her prayers for him.

Edward begged that he might come to her often, and she said,—

"Come."

He misinterpreted the readiness of the invitation.

When he had left her, he reflected on the absence of all endearing epithets in her speech, and missed them. Having himself suffered, he required them. For what had she wrestled so sharply with death, if not to fall upon his bosom and be his in a great outpouring of gladness? In fact he craved the immediate reward for his public acknowledgement of his misdeeds. He walked in this neighbourhood known by what he had done, and his desire was to take his wife away, never more to be seen there. Following so deep a darkness, he wanted at least a cheerful dawn: not one of a penitential grey—not a hooded dawn, as if the paths of life were to be under cloistral arches. And he wanted a rose of womanhood in his hand like that he had parted with, and to recover which he had endured every earthly mortification, even to absolute abasement. The frail bent lily seemed a stranger to him.

Can a man go farther than his nature? Never, when he takes passion on board. By other means his nature may be enlarged and nerved, but passion will find his weakness, and, while urging him on, will constantly betray him at that point. Edward had three interviews with Dahlia; he wrote to her as many times. There was but one answer for him; and when he ceased to charge her with unforgivingness, he came to the strange conclusion that beyond our calling of a woman a Saint for rhetorical purposes, and esteeming her as one for pictorial, it is indeed possible, as he had slightly discerned in this woman's presence, both to think her saintly and to have the sentiments inspired by the overearthly in her person. Her voice, her simple words of writing, her gentle resolve, all issuing of a capacity to suffer evil, and pardon it, conveyed that character to a mind not soft for receiving such impressions.

CHAPTER XLVIII

CONCLUSION

Major Waring came to Wrexby Hall at the close of the October month. He came to plead his own cause with Mrs. Lovell; but she stopped him by telling him that his friend Robert was in some danger of losing his love.

"She is a woman, Percy; I anticipate your observation. But, more than that, she believes she is obliged to give her hand to my cousin, the squire. It's an intricate story relating to money. She does not care for Algy a bit, which is not a matter that greatly influences him. He has served her in some mysterious way; by relieving an old uncle of hers. Algy has got him the office of village postman for this district, I believe; if it's that; but I think it should be more, to justify her. At all events, she seems to consider that her hand is pledged. You know the kind of girl your friend fancies. Besides, her father insists she is to marry 'the squire,' which is certainly the most natural thing of all. So, don't you think, dear Percy, you had better take your friend on the Continent for some weeks? I never, I confess, exactly understood the intimacy existing between you, but it must be sincere."

"Are you?" said Percy.

"Yes, perfectly; but always in a roundabout way. Why do you ask me in this instance?"

"Because you could stop this silly business in a day."

"I know I could."

"Then, why do you not?"

"Because of a wish to be sincere. Percy, I have been that throughout, if you could read me. I tried to deliver my cousin Edward from what I thought was a wretched entanglement. His selfish falseness offended me, and I let him know that I despised him. When I found that he was a man who had courage, and some heart, he gained my friendship once more, and I served him as far as I could—happily, as it chanced. I tell you all this, because I don't care to forfeit your esteem, and heaven knows, I may want it in the days to come. I believe I am the best friend in the world—and bad anything else. No one perfectly pleases me, not even you: you are too studious of character, and, like myself, exacting of perfection in one or two points. But now hear what I have done, and approve it if you think fit. I have flirted—abominable word!—I am compelled to use the language of the Misses—yes, I have flirted with my cousin Algy. I do it too well, I know—by nature! and I hate it. He has this morning sent a letter down to the farm saying, that, as he believes he has failed in securing Rhoda's affections, he renounces all pretensions, etc., subject to her wishes, etc. The courting, I imagine, can scarcely have been pleasant to him. My delightful manner with him during the last fortnight has been infinitely pleasanter. So, your friend Robert may be made happy by-and-by; that is to say, if his Rhoda is not too like her sex."

"You're an enchantress," exclaimed Percy.

"Stop," said she, and drifted into seriousness. "Before you praise me you must know more. Percy, that duel in India—"

He put out his hand to her.

"Yes, I forgive," she resumed. "You were cruel then. Remember that, and try to be just now. The poor boy would go to his doom. I could have arrested it. I partly caused it. I thought the honour of the army at stake. I was to blame on that day, and I am to blame again, but I feel that I am almost excuseable, if you are not too harsh a judge. No, I am not; I am execrable; but forgive me."

Percy's face lighted up in horrified amazement as Margaret Lovell unfastened the brooch at her neck and took out the dull-red handkerchief.

"It was the bond between us," she pursued, "that I was to return this to you when I no longer remained my own mistress. Count me a miserably heartless woman. I do my best. You brought this handkerchief to me dipped in the blood of the poor boy who was slain. I have worn it. It was a safeguard. Did you mean it to serve as such? Oh, Percy! I felt continually that blood was on my bosom. I felt it fighting with me. It has saved me from much. And now I return it to you."

He could barely articulate "Why?"

"Dear friend, by the reading of the bond you should know. I asked you when I was leaving India, how long I was to keep it by me. You said, 'Till you marry.' Do not be vehement, Percy. This is a thing that could not have been averted."

"Is it possible," Percy cried, "that you carried the play out so far as to promise him to marry him?"

"Your forehead is thunder, Percy. I know that look."

"Margaret, I think I could bear to see our army suffer another defeat rather than you should be contemptible."

"Your chastisement is not given in half measures, Percy."

"Speak on," said he; "there is more to come. You are engaged to marry him?"

"I engaged that I would take the name of Blancove."

"If he would cease to persecute Rhoda Fleming!"

"The stipulation was exactly in those words."

"You mean to carry it out?"

"To be sincere? I do, Percy!"

"You mean to marry Algernon Blancove?"

"I should be contemptible indeed if I did, Percy!

"You do not?"

"I do not."

"And you are sincere? By all the powers of earth and heaven, there's no madness like dealing with an animated enigma! What is it you do mean?"

"As I said—to be sincere. But I was also bound to be of service to your friend. It is easy to be sincere and passive."

Percy struck his brows. "Can you mean that Edward Blancove is the man?"

"Oh! no. Edward will never marry any one. I do him the justice to say that his vice is not that of unfaithfulness. He had but one love, and her heart is quite dead. There is no marriage for him—she refuses. You may not understand the why of that, but women will. She would marry him if she could bring herself to it;—the truth is, he killed her pride. Her taste for life has gone. She is bent on her sister's marrying your friend. She has no other thought of marriage, and never will have. I know the state. It is not much unlike mine."

Waring fixed her eyes. "There is a man?"

"Yes," she answered bluntly.

"It is somebody, then, whose banker's account is, I hope, satisfactory."

"Yes, Percy;" she looked eagerly forward, as thanking him for releasing her from a difficulty. "You still can use the whip, but I do not feel the sting. I marry a banker's account. Do you bear in mind the day I sent after you in the park? I had just heard that I was ruined. You know my mania for betting. I heard it, and knew when I let my heart warm to you that I could never marry you. That is one reason, perhaps, why I have been an enigma. I am sincere in telling Algy I shall take the name of Blancove. I marry the banker. Now take this old gift of yours."

Percy grasped the handkerchief, and quitted her presence forthwith, feeling that he had swallowed a dose of the sex to serve him for a lifetime. Yet he lived to reflect on her having decided practically, perhaps wisely for all parties. Her debts expunged, she became an old gentleman's demure young wife, a sweet hostess, and, as ever, a true friend: something of a miracle to one who had inclined to make a heroine of her while imagining himself to accurately estimate her deficiencies. Honourably by this marriage the lady paid for such wild oats as she had sown in youth.

There were joy-bells for Robert and Rhoda, but none for Dahlia and Edward.

Dahlia lived seven years her sister's housemate, nurse of the growing swarm. She had gone through fire, as few women have done in like manner, to leave their hearts among the ashes; but with that human heart she left regrets behind her. The soul of this young creature filled its place. It shone in her eyes and in her work, a lamp to her little neighbourhood; and not less a lamp of cheerful beams for one day being as another to her. In truth, she sat above the clouds. When she died she relinquished nothing. Others knew the loss. Between her and Robert there was deeper community on one subject than she let Rhoda share. Almost her last words to him, spoken calmly, but with the quaver of breath resembling sobs, were: "Help poor girls."

George Meredith – A Concise Bibliography

Novels
The Shaving of Shagpat (1856)
Farina (1857)
The Ordeal of Richard Feverel (1859)
Evan Harrington (1861)
Emilia in England (1864), republished as Sandra Belloni in 1887
Rhoda Fleming (1865)
Vittoria (1867)
The Adventures of Harry Richmond (1871)
Beauchamp's Career (1875)
The House on the Beach (1877)
The Case of General Ople and Lady Camper (1877)
The Tale of Chloe (1879)
The Egoist (1879)
The Tragic Comedians (1880)
Diana of the Crossways (1885)
One of our Conquerors (1891)
Lord Ormont and his Aminta (1894)
The Amazing Marriage (1895)
Celt and Saxon (1910)

Poetry
Poems (1851)
Modern Love (1862)
The Lark Ascending (1881)
Poems and Lyrics of the Joy of Earth (1883)
The Woods of Westermain (1883)
A Faith on Trial (1885)
Ballads and Poems of Tragic Life (1887)
A Reading of Earth (1888)
The Empty Purse (1892)
Odes in Contribution to the Song of French History (1898)
A Reading of Life (1901)
Selected Poems of George Meredith (1903, author's supervision)
Last Poems (1909)

Essays
Essay on Comedy (1877)

www.ingramcontent.com/pod-product-compliance
Lightning Source LLC
Chambersburg PA
CBHW070558260626
47161CB00002B/644